THE MAMMOTH BOOK OF
ROMAN
WHODUNNITS

THE MAMMOTH BOOK OF
ROMAN
WHODUNNITS

Edited by Mike Ashley

CARROLL & GRAF PUBLISHERS
New York

Carroll & Graf Publishers
An imprint of Avalon Publishing Group, Inc.
161 William Street
NY 10038–2607
www.carrollandgraf.com

First published in the UK by Robinson,
an imprint of Constable & Robinson Ltd 2003

First Carroll & Graf edition 2003

ISBN 0-7867-1241-4

Printed and bound in the EU

Contents

Copyright and Acknowledgments   vii

Introduction:
  The Long Reach of Rome, *Steven Saylor*   xi

Never Forget, *Tom Holt*   1

A Gladiator Dies Only Once, *Steven Saylor*   27

The Hostage to Fortune, *Michael Jecks*   74

De Crimine, *Miriam Allen deFord*   100

The Will, *John Maddox Roberts*   120

Honey Moon, *Marilyn Todd*   142

Damnum Fatale, *Philip Boast*   169

Heads You Lose, *Simon Scarrow*   198

Great Caesar's Ghost, *Michael Kurland*   222

The Cleopatra Game, *Jane Finnis*   260

Bread and Circuses, *Caroline Lawrence*   282

The Missing Centurion, *Anonymous*   321

Some Unpublished Correspondence of
the Younger Pliny, *Darrell Schweitzer*   341

A Golden Opportunity, *Jean Davidson*   363

Caveat Emptor, *Rosemary Rowe*   387

Sunshine and Shadow, *R. H. Stewart*   407

The Case of his Own Abduction, *Wallace Nichols*   431

The Malice of the Anicii, *Gillian Bradshaw*   447

The Finger of Aphrodite,
Mary Reed and Eric Mayer   473

The Lost Eagle, *Peter Tremayne*   501

Copyright and Acknowledgments

INTRODUCTION
The Long Reach of Rome

Steven Saylor

T owards the end of the last century (circa 1987), I took my
first trip to Rome, and like many a traveller I was
overwhelmed by the sensation of making visceral contact with
the past. In no other city do so many layers of history coexist so
palpably within such a small space. In a matter of hours one
can follow Caesar's footsteps through the Forum, take a short
rail excursion to the excavated ruins at Ostia, view the art of
Michelangelo and contemplate Papal intrigues at the Vatican,
gawk at the Fascist architecture at Mussolini's EUR, and even
take a tour of the film studios at Cinecittá with their echoes of
Fellini and *La Dolce Vita*.

Inspired by that visit, and having developed an insatiable
appetite for crime fiction, I found myself craving a murder
mystery set in ancient Rome.

It seems remarkable now that no such thing was to be
found on the bookshelves as recently as 1987, but such was
the case, and so I felt compelled to fill the gap myself. A
couple of years later I finished a novel called *Roman Blood*
featuring a sleuth called Gordianus the Finder. Only days

after sending the manuscript to an editor in New York, I came across a copy of Lindsey Davis's *The Silver Pigs* among the new titles at my local bookshop, and had an inkling that a whole subgenre combining murder mystery and Roman history was about to be born.

Indeed, so popular has this particular field of literary escapism become in the last dozen years that a volume like the one you hold in your hands seems as inevitable as it does intriguing.

The booming subgenre has grown to include its own well-established crime-solvers, and here readers will find new adventures for John Maddox Roberts's hero of the *SPQR* series, Decius Mettelus; for that randy vixen Claudia, the heroine of Marilyn Todd's novels; for Rosemary Rowe's Libertus, a freedman who solves crimes in Roman Britain; for John the Eunuch, the Byzantine sleuth of Mary Reed and Eric Mayer; for Peter Tremayne's Sister Fidelma, who dwells on the furthest edges and in the last feeble twilight of the Roman Empire's glow; and even for the young detectives of Caroline Lawrence, who takes the Roman mystery into the realm of children's fiction (grooming a new generation of readers for my own Gordianus books, I hope).

Here readers will find traditional forms of the mystery story, including a "locked-room" puzzler by Michael Kurland, in which the great pedagogue Quintilian plays sleuth for the emperor Vespasian; traditional forms of historical fiction, such as Darrell Schweitzer's epistolary "Some Unpublished Correspondence of the Young Pliny"; and even a story which purports to be actual history, Gillian Bradshaw's "The Malice of the Anicii", complete with footnotes.

Many of the stories are set in Rome itself, but the locales range from ancient Egypt ("The Missing Centurion") to the besieged city of Jerusalem (Simon Scarrow's "Heads You

Lose") to the Canterbury of Tremayne's Sister Fidelma – all the better to demonstrate the extraordinary reach of Rome across both seas and centuries. (Quite a few of the stories take place in Roman Britain, including those by R.H. Stewart and Jean Davidson.)

Inevitably, perhaps, the shadow of Julius Caesar falls across these pages (see Michael Jecks's "A Hostage to Fortune" and John Maddox Roberts's "The Will"), as does that of Cleopatra (whose demise haunts Roman high society in Jane Finnis's "The Cleopatra Game").

Given the imperial might of Rome, it's not surprising that a number of these stories are set in a military milieu. But Rome was also about the world of intellect and spiritual contemplation. Confronted by a bizarre death, it makes perfect sense that the mighty conqueror Scipio Africanus should seek a Greek philosopher's advice in Tom Holt's "Never Forget", and even the advent of that curious sect, the Christians, is occasioned by murder, as seen in Philip Boast's "Damnum Fatale".

For my own part, as a bit of homage to a movie that gave a considerable boost to our subgenre (and because I've never written at length on the subject before), I decided to spin a tale set in the world of gladiators. The most famous gladiator of all does not appear in my story, but his shadow is eventually cast over the proceedings, as it was cast, if only briefly, over the entire Roman world.

While it may have gained its greatest popularity in recent years, the crime story set in ancient Rome was not actually invented in the 1990s, but has numerous precursors. This volume includes a small but intriguing sampling of some earlier forays, including Miriam Allen deFord's "De Crimine" from 1952, featuring the famous advocate Cicero and based on actual events, as well as one of Wallace Nicholls's vintage tales of the Slave Detective. The anonymously authored "The Missing Centurion" dates from 1862, and so constitutes one of the earliest efforts to mingle historical and mystery fiction; kudos to editor Mike Ashley for rescuing it from utter obscurity.

Here then is the panoply of ancient Rome cast across continents and ages, viewed through the gimlet eyes of those who make it their business to write about the lowest human activity (murder) and the highest (the quest for truth). What better way to celebrate the virtues and the vices of a city that claims to be eternal?

Steven Saylor

Never Forget

Tom Holt

We start our investigations in ancient Rome at a time when Rome was establishing its pre-eminence in the Mediterranean world with Scipio's defeat of Hannibal in the Second Punic War in 202 BC. Tom Holt may be best known for his humorous fantasy novels such as Who's Afraid of Beowulf? *(1988),* Paint Your Dragon *(1996) and* Snow White and the Seven Samurai *(1999), but he is also the author of several fine historical novels set in the ancient world. These include* Goatsong *(1989),* The Walled Orchard *(1990),* Alexander at the World's End *(1999) and* Olympiad *(2000).*

"Fine," said Publius Cornelius Scipio, the World's Biggest Man, "but what does a philosopher actually do?"

Your typical Roman question; ignorant, offensive and unpleasantly awkward to deal with. "We think about things," I said.

"You think about things?"

"Yes."

"And that's it?"

Oh no you don't, I said to myself. You may be a military

genius and the man who beat Hannibal, but I'm a Greek lawyer. You don't stand a chance.

"That's it," I said. "Because, after all, thought's what separates men from animals. Thought's the part of us that makes us like the gods. So we think about things."

He shrugged. "What things?" he asked.

Outside the tent, soldiers were moving about; I could feel the tramp of their nailed sandals on the baked ground, coming up through the soles of my own feet. Where the tent-flap was slightly open, I couldn't see anything except the blinding African sun, occasionally eclipsed for a split second as people hurried past. The smell of Army was everywhere and overpowering, but I tried to ignore it.

"Everything," I said. "Everything separately, and everything together, in the context of everything else. That's what's so special about thought."

"Really." I could see I'd lost him, which wasn't good. I needed the job. "In other words, you sit on your bum in the shade with your mouth open, and for that you're worth more per day than a blacksmith makes in a year." He shook his head. "No disrespect," he said, "but you're full of it."

I smothered a grin. "Absolutely," I said. "I'm full of everything, because I'm full of thought. In thought, the whole universe exists in microcosm inside my head, perfect in every detail. More to the point, I can recreate the universe any time I like, just by thinking. You give me a feather, and I can think you the whole chicken. From first principles, as it were."

He turned his head ever so slightly, and I knew I'd got him. Using his own tactics against him, of course. In the great battle, a week ago, he'd provoked Hannibal into committing his elephants to a charge, and then opened his lines and let them pass harmlessly through. Scipio's mind was all elephants.

"You reckon," he said.

"Yes, I do," I replied. "Which is, of course, why you need me on your team. It's the perfect combination; Roman energy, vigour and muscle, Greek intellect. And please bear in mind, so far all you've done is the easy bit; fight Hannibal, win the war, that stuff. Now you've got to face the tricky part. Which is why you need me."

"Tricky part," he repeated. To do him credit, he spoke Greek like – well, not like a proper Greek, but he could've passed for a half-breed Sicilian, on a good day, with a bad cold to mask his accent. "Like?"

"Like going home," I said. "Surviving victory. Winning is easy. Staying won; that's hard."

He laughed; strange man, I thought. "Well," he said, "tell you what, here's the deal. I have a very nasty, inconvenient problem that needs to be cleared up fast; in two days, to be precise, and assuming the weather doesn't get even hotter. And the thing of it is, this is a thinking problem, not a doing one. It means going back into the past. Do you reckon you can manage that, just by thinking?"

"Of course," I said. "And if I succeed, I get the job. Agreed?"

He smiled. Good-looking man, for a Roman. "Agreed," he said.

"Excellent. So, what's the problem?"

Here's a rule of life for you; don't try being clever around Roman generals. They're all of them thick as valley oaks, but sly. There's not a lot that your finely honed lawyer-philosopher's brain can do about sly; it sneaks past your defences and bites your ankles.

Scipio grinned at me, then led me through the camp to the big open space in the middle, where the soldiers do drill and stuff. Just off this main square (Roman camps are like towns,

with a square and streets and everything) was a little canvas
and ox-hide alleyway, backing on to a high paling fence.
When we reached the end of it, I saw something that made
me realize I'd just been taken for a garlic-nibbler.

Dead body. Very dead. The glorious Plato, looking for the
perfect encapsulation of the essential nature of Dead,
would've jumped up and down and clapped his hands in glee.

I have this thing with dead bodies. I don't like them
terribly much.

"That's the problem," said Scipio, pointing at the red and
black thing slumped in the dust, attractively garnished with
flies. "Marcus Vitellius Acer, Roman senator, sort of a
second-cum-third cousin of mine. If you look closely, you'll
see he's had his head bashed in. It'd be a great help to me if
you could think about it, and tell me who did it."

Silly fool; last thing I wanted to do was look closely at that.
I've seen worse, I ought to point out. I've seen half a
stonemason sticking out from under a three-by-six granite
block, where a bit of second-hand rope couldn't take the
strain. I've seen kites stripping sun-dried meat off a ribcage,
where some old nuisance of a beggar dropped dead beside the
road and it was nobody's business to tidy him away. And I've
seen a battlefield, but I'd rather not remind myself by talking
about it. Marcus Vitellius Acer was bad, but he could've
been worse. I guess.

"Hence," Scipio was saying, "the need for urgency; because unless we get him burned in the next two days, he's
going to stink the place out so bad you won't be able to smell
the elephant dung. Also, the family are going to want to know
why I made poor dear Marcus hang about on the wrong side
of the River with all the riff-raff, and I have better things to
do with my time than explain myself to my second cousin
Vitellia."

I was thinking; investigate deaths, what do I know about

investigating deaths? Whereupon, I thought, elephants; he's tricked me into charging, then opened his ranks. And me a lawyer. I was ashamed.

"No problem," I said. When all else fails, act cocky. "Only, I've got to ask you this, what sort of investigation are you looking for?"

He looked at me. "I want the truth," he said.

"Oh," I replied. "That old thing. You sure? I mean, it's not for me to tell you your business, but wouldn't it be neater just to arrest someone you want to get shot of anyway, and make out it was him? It's how we handle these situations back home, and we find it works pretty well."

Romans do scorn very well; they've got the lips for it. "Kind thought," he said, "but the plain old truth will do me just fine. So; are you up for it or not?"

It occurs to me that when my mother taught me to speak, she entrusted a deadly weapon to my worst enemy. "Of course," I said.

"Now you've examined the body," Scipio said, as we sat opposite each other in his tent behind big cups of wine, "I expect you'll be wanting some background on Acer. Right?"

I nodded slowly. I was reluctant to open my mouth just then, for fear of what might come gushing out of it. It's embarrassing when strangers can see what you've been eating lately.

"Fine," he said. "The main thing about Acer was, he was a Senator. Big man in the Senate, all through the war; supported Fabius after Trasimene, stuck with him after the Metaurus, when everyone else was on my side about the invasion of Africa. I respected him for that, but nobody much else did. Probably that's why he was so keen to come out here, to show them all he was big enough to accept the Senate's decision even though he didn't agree with it. So he wrote to me asking for a command; and he'd been a good soldier when he was young, fought against Demetrius in Illyria, so I didn't mind accommodating him, and anyhow, he was family. Did well in the battle, too; I'd tucked him away at the back of the heavy infantry where he couldn't get hurt, but an elephant broke through the line and went crazy, caused a real mess. Acer was back there with the reserve; he charged out in front of the horrible creature, on foot, alone, and actually managed to keep it pinned down until the archers shot off its crew and our people were able to get ropes on it. Not quite sure how he managed it, because every time he told the story it was slightly different, but a man who was there said he stuck a spear right up through its lower lip, then danced about in front of it dodging and yelling, and somehow contrived not to get trampled or swatted. Not bad work for a man in his fifties."

I nodded. Vitellius Acer had been living on borrowed time after that, no question. It's a Roman knack, doing bloody stupid things that History later turns to gold, like the contents of Midas' chamber-pot.

"Anyway," Scipio went on, "that tells you he was brave, impetuous, not the sharpest needle in the case maybe, but he had nerve."

"Enemies," I said.

Scipio laughed. "Oh, he had enemies all right," he said. "In politics, the number of enemies you make is one of the most reliable ways of keeping score. I can give you three names straight off the top; Servius Gnatho, Publius Licinius – " he paused, and grinned. "And me, of course."

I hadn't been expecting that. "You," I said. "But I thought –"

"I liked him, actually," Scipio said. "And he was a sort of cousin, and he did well in the battle. Fact remains, he was a very effective supporter of Fabius Maximus, and therefore my sworn enemy, politically. Also," he added, with a shrug, "he hated me like poison, which made him a security risk, if you follow me. Oh, I didn't kill him, and I didn't tell anybody else to take care of it, either. Trouble with being the man in charge, though, you get a lot of people who're always trying to guess what you want well in advance, so they can suck up to you by doing it. Killing my acknowledged enemy is just the sort of thing some ambitious hothead'd do on the offchance there'd be a nice reward."

"In which case," I said quietly, "you wouldn't want him caught, right?"

"Wrong." He looked all Roman at me, down his nose. "Unauthorized murders aren't approved procedure in my army."

"Fine," I said. "And approved murders?"

He smiled. "War is approved murder," he said. "But Hannibal didn't kill this poor sucker."

Thing about being a lawyer, you get used to the other guy being the straight man. "You assume," I said. "But there's escaped prisoners, spies –"

"Or maybe he was hit by extremely solid lightning. But it's rather unlikely."

"Noted," I said. "Tell me about those other two people you just mentioned."

"Ah yes." Scipio nodded. "Gnatho. Nasty piece of work, though you wouldn't think so to look at him. You're a Greek, so I'm assuming you buy into this beauty-equals-virtue idea that my teachers tried to beat into me when I was a kid. Don't believe it. Gnatho's a good example. Rich man, young, handsome; Calabrian, if I remember correctly. The short version is, Acer stole his boyfriend, so he got back by seducing Acer's wife."

"Which means," I interrupted, "Acer had a good motive for killing Gnatho, not the other –"

"No, that was just the start of it. Since then, they've been at each other's throats like Spartan hounds. In fact, I think the feud led to the seductions, rather than the other way about. They just didn't like each other much, fundamentally."

"Well," I said, "that's a start. Who's the other man? Licinius?"

"Wealthy knight," Scipio said. "Made a fortune buying prisoners straight off the battlefield in the Gallic war, selling them quick and cheap to the big Senatorial estates. Quite the inspirational success story, because he came out of nowhere, father was a blacksmith in Apulia, and suddenly he appeared on the scene with a purseful of money, and nobody knew where he'd got it from. Turned out some time later he was fronting for Acer – as I'm sure I don't need to tell you, since a philosopher like yourself will undoubtedly have figured it out from first principles, Roman senators are forbidden by law to sully their paws with Trade, so what we all do is set up some likely character in a good line of business and quietly collect 60 per cent of the profits. As Acer did with Licinius; only he misjudged his man, because Licinius ran the business but quietly omitted to pay Acer his share; and of course Acer couldn't sue or do anything about it, because he wasn't supposed to be waddling about in the cesspit of commerce in the first place. So Acer had to use other methods to get his money."

"Such as?"

"Such as sending a couple of retired gladiators to kidnap Licinius' family, as a bargaining aid. But the boys he hired must've got clonked on the head once too often; they made a hash of it, Licinius' houseboys started a fight, and the result was that Licinius' father, brother and kid son all got killed. Well, Licinius paid up after that; but I'd call that a motive for murder, wouldn't you?"

"Sure," I said.

"And," he went on, "Licinius has been following this whole campaign, buying prisoners at the pit head, so to speak; he hadn't left last evening, waiting for half a dozen of his convoy escorts to turn up, and I'll send someone just to check he's still here in camp."

"Thanks," I said.

He shrugged.

"So, that's two strong leads for me to follow up," I said. "I'll go away and have a think about it, and catch up with you later today."

He grinned. "Don't pull a muscle in your head," he replied. "Like I told you, you've got till tomorrow evening."

"Thanks," I said, "but it shouldn't take me as long as that. Thought, you see; all I've got to do is sit down and think about it for an hour or so, and I'll have the answer for you, smooth and warm as a hen's egg."

I do say some stupid things, don't I?

But, like I said, I needed the job; so I waited till he was out of sight, then went straight to work. Solving mysteries is all about prepositions, the first being how? Acer had had his head bashed in, with spectacular thoroughness. First question therefore had to be, what with? No way a human fist could've scrunched bone like that; but there were no blood-spattered rocks, sticks, iron bars or heavy implements anywhere to be seen. Conclusion; the killer either took the weapon away with him, or hid it somewhere.

Well, I could search the whole camp for a brain-speckled rock; but I wasn't in the mood, so I looked for something that'd give me a clue. Shuffling round on my belly isn't my idea of a big time, but I did find something down there on the ground that set me thinking; a long row of little round dimples pressed into the dirt, next to a tent where they stored great big skeins of horsehair.

A couple of off-duty soldiers were lounging about nearby. I decided that Scipio would want me to make whatever use I felt necessary of all available facilities, and called them over. They didn't seem thrilled with the job I gave them, which basically consisted of a lot of scrabbling about in dirt and splintered wood. Their bad luck; they shouldn't have joined.

Anyhow; I had a hunch about the how, and no other leads whatsoever. Rather than waste time, I made up my mind to skip resolving how, and make a start on when.

Roman army camps; they're crowded, noisy and smelly, and there's always someone about. But all Scipio had said was that Acer's body "was found", by the first patrol of the day, just after reveille. Helpful.

Yes, really. When is a doddle in an army camp, because at night, when there's nobody about, they have sentries. A little bit of bluff with the duty officer got me a look at the previous day's duty roster, and I sent a runner to fetch me the decurion in charge of the night watch; he in turn gave me the names of the sentries who should've been guarding that sector of the camp, and I had them brought up to see me.

No, they assured me, they hadn't seen or heard anything. I told them I knew they were lying and why. They panicked and said they'd tell me the truth; they hadn't seen or heard anything, really.

I believed them; but it was awkward, because if they genuinely hadn't seen anybody alive or dead (and they'd have noticed a dead body, for sure) it meant that Acer arrived at the place where he died and was killed in the short period of time between the sentries' last stroll down the alley, and the end of the nightwatch, which was when the body was found, according to Scipio. I worked out how long that period was by walking the route myself with my hand on my wrist, counting heartbeats. Figuring that reveille must be the cut-off point – the whole camp seething with people getting up and rushing about – I ended up coming to the conclusion that Acer must've left his tent, which was where he'd last been seen, five thousand heartbeats before reveille, in order to have time to walk from his tent to the place where he was killed; furthermore, that he was killed pretty well as soon as he got there. Implication; the killer knew he'd be coming, and was waiting for him.

Which made it interesting; since the killer had to get there too, unless his assigned sleeping-place was in the alley itself – and nobody matched those criteria; I checked. The alleyway was formed by the stores on one side and the plunder-stash on the other, and it goes without saying that both of those were heavily guarded at night against the depredations of light-fingered squaddies, so no chance of anybody sneaking in during the day and hiding till Acer arrived.

Fine, I thought; so I went and talked to the guards. The quartermaster, in charge of the stores, swore by the River that he hadn't seen or heard, et cetera. More to the point, he had four Greek clerks who spread their bedrolls out in the four entrances to the stores compound, a simple and praiseworthy precaution. On the other side, the soldiers who'd guarded the plunder were equally adamant, which accounted for three points of the compass; "and you don't have to worry about anybody coming from the north," one of them added with a grin, while the other two sniggered.

"Don't I?" I said. "Why's that?"

The soldier smiled and pointed.

"All right," I said, "there's a palisade of high stakes. What about it?"

"That's the animal pen," the soldier said. "Where all the captured livestock's kept; horses, loads of mules, several dozen camels –"

"And the elephant," his mate reminded him.

"And the elephant. Bloody thing," the soldier added.

"Never goes to sleep, and a sneeze'll set it off crashing about. No way anybody could sneak in through there without a hell of a racket."

Well, that ruled out access from either side; which meant Acer, and Acer's killer, must've come up the alley, during the period (nine hundred heartbeats) between the last time the nightwatch passed the entrance to the alleyway, and reveille. I had when.

I was doing well. I'd got when, I had a gut feeling about how, and Scipio had presumably given me all I needed for a shortlist of candidates for why. Trouble was, all those together had to make up who, and they didn't.

Well; I supposed I could get rid of one suspect, one way or the other. I went and found Licinius, the slave dealer. His compound was just inside the camp (he was allowed inside as a special privilege by the camp prefect, who owed him money), and I found him perched on the rail like a small boy at a fair, flanked by two Syrian clerks, taking inventory.

"Bloody sun," he said. "You'd think they'd be used to it, since they live in this godsforsaken country. But apparently not; it boils their brains inside their heads, and they die. After I've paid for them," he added bitterly. "Six since the battle; that's a lot of money."

I sighed. "Some people have no consideration," I told him. Then I reached into my purse and pulled something out for him to see. "This belong to you?" I asked.

He took it and examined it; a longish iron nail with a ring passed through its head. "No," he said.

"You know what it is."

"Course I do, it's a tethering-peg. We use them to peg down the stock en route. But this isn't one of mine."

"You can tell?"

He nodded. "This is army issue," he said. "I don't use anything that's military specification. Saves bother, see;

otherwise, my stuff would have a bad habit of getting mixed in with government property, since I spend so much time around army camps, and I'd never see it again. That's why all my pegs are wood, with bronze rings."

"Ah," I said. "That's that, then. Sorry to have bothered you."

"No bother," he assured me. "So," he added, "where did you get this from?"

"Under the body of Vitellius Acer," I told him. "Look, you can see the blood on the spike, and this bit of frayed rope tied to the ring. At least, I'm assuming it's blood; could be brains, or –"

He gave me a very nasty look. "You implying I had something to do with that?"

I shrugged. "Well," I said, "I'd heard you weren't the best of friends."

"You could say that," he replied. "But it wasn't me stabbed him, so you're wasting your time. I spent the whole of last night playing knucklebones with Caius Laelius – you know, General Scipio's bestest friend in all the world? Ask him if you don't believe me."

Quite some alibi. "Who won?" I asked.

"He did. You seriously think I'm dumb enough to gamble with Laelius and win?"

Proving nothing, I reflected, as I walked back; a rich man like Licinius doesn't do his own murdering. Interesting that he'd said it wasn't me stabbed him. I'd shown him the tethering-pin with blood all over it, and he'd assumed it was the murder weapon; assumed that confronting him with it was meant to be my winning throw. But Acer hadn't been stabbed, of course.

Quick detour, to get a chicken. Next call after that, inevitably, was the camp blacksmith.

"One of mine," he confirmed. "I remember doing them;

drew down a load of busted spearheads we picked up off the field at Numantia. Can't waste good material."

"Quite," I said. All his hammers were neatly arranged in iron hoops stuck into the side of the log on which his anvil rested. Their heads were all dry and shiny with use, apart from one, which was spotted with rust, and the wooden stem was swollen and wet. Licinius' father had been a blacksmith in Apulia, and the camp smithy backed on to the stores. Only one door, of course, but a very wide smokehole in the roof. "You just do army work, or do you sometimes do civvy jobs as well?"

"Depends on how we're fixed," he said. "If there's nothing particular on, I can fit in a few bits and pieces now and again."

"Do anything for Licinius the slaver recently?"

He frowned. "Yes, as a matter of fact. Sort of. He sent one of his blokes over, said the tyre on one of his carts had sprung and could I weld it? I said no, too busy; he said that's all right, I used to be a smith myself. Fine, I said, you fetch it in here, you're welcome to use that anvil over there and anything you like. Did a good job, too, for a foreigner."

High praise from a smith. "That was good-natured of you," I said. "I'd heard your lot are pretty touchy about letting other people use their gear."

He grinned. "Some smiths are like that," he said. "Not me. Just as well," he went on, "because he broke the head off my two-pound crosspein hammer. Good as gold about it, though, he was. Said he'd get the wheelwright to put the head on again, and he did. A bloke brought it back this morning first thing, and there it is in the rack."

A bloke, I noted, not the ex-smith himself. "It's all wet," I said.

"Well, of course," he replied indulgently. "When you put a stem on a hammer you leave it in a tub of water overnight to soak. Swells the wood, see, to get a better grip."

I thanked him and left. Two-pound crosspein; doesn't mean anything to me, either. But the rusty hammer was a substantial piece of metal, I dreaded to think what it could do to a man's head.

Gnatho. Handsome and rich; not the sort to do his own dirty work, either. Scipio had as good as told me to suspect him, so I did.

If you want to know who's who in an army camp, ask the pay clerks.

"Oh, I know who he is all right," the chief clerk said. "And yes, there's a poor relation of his on the roll – Vipsanius Gnatho, junior tribune attached to the Spanish auxiliary. Good man, as far as I know; won the headless spear at Numantia, no less."

I whistled. Headless spears aren't given away free, like nuts at a bad play; they're only awarded for conspicuous valour and saving the life of a fellow soldier. "I didn't hear about that," I said.

"Pretty strange business," the clerk said, "considering who it was he saved."

"Go on."

He grinned; born showman. I hate those. "Vitellius Acer," said the clerk. "You know, him that was killed last night. Waste of time saving him, really," he added.

"I see what you mean," I said. "I thought Acer and Servius Gnatho hated each other."

"They do," the clerk said. "Or did; whatever. But this cousin, Vipsanius Gnatho; seems like Acer was riding round in his fancy chariot just when the enemy sent out a sortie. Sly about it, they were, first thing our boys knew was when their archers opened up on our sappers coming off shift. Anyhow, Acer's riding along like Zeus Almighty in his chariot, suddenly Vipsanius jumps up behind him, grabs hold of him by the shoulders and throws him off, then jumps down after him; broke a leg by all accounts. Anyhow a heartbeat later, two dozen Spanish mercenaries hop up from behind a low wall and start shooting. They reckon if Vipsanius hadn't got Acer down off that chariot, he'd have been more full of points than a hedgehog."

"Hold on," I said. "Spanish mercenaries? I thought they were on our side."

He laughed. "They're on anybody's side who pays," he said. "Best light infantry in the world, some people reckon, but personally I wouldn't give them the time of day."

Well, that showed me the direction I had to go. "Thanks for your help," I said. "I wonder, could you tell me where I'd find Caius Laelius?"

Now I'll tell you something I bet you don't know about the Romans; their ponderous, galumphing excuse for a language doesn't have a word for "Yes". Instead, when they want to express assent, they've got to say things like certainly or I agree or even by Hercules! Bizarre; but at least it explains, to my satisfaction at least, why Scipio and Laelius learned Greek. Not, as they'll try and persuade you in Rome, so that the dazzling young general and his trusty sidekick could enjoy the glories of our literature. As if. No; the only possible explanation is that, using Greek, Laelius would be able to express agreement with every damnfool thing Scipio said without having to overtax his dismally limited imagination.

Caius Laelius, Scipio's best buddy, was a chubby, curly man who could've been anywhere between fifteen and forty. As soon as I told him I was investigating Acer's death, he was so eager to help he was practically frothing at the mouth.

"Sure I know Licinius," he said, nodding eagerly. "I bought a whole bunch of field-hands off him just after the battle, and he's looking after getting them shipped back home for me. Made me a good price, too; but I can't say as I took to him much."

"Really?" I raised my eyebrows. "You can't dislike him too much, if you sat up all night playing knucklebones with the man."

He frowned. "Who told you that?" he said.

"He did," I replied.

Laelius shrugged. "How odd. Yes, he did drop round – uninvited, I might add – and it took me a hell of a long time to get rid of him, because you've got to be polite to these people. And yes, come to think of it, we did play knucklebones, but only a couple of hands, thank goodness. I'm not saying he cheated, but Lady Luck was definitely on his side. Reckon I lost more in a few hands than I paid for those slaves."

I managed to hide my smile. "Licinius reckons he sat up with you all night," I said, "which is why it was impossible for him to have killed Acer. I take it you're telling me that's not so."

"Absolutely." Laelius' enormous features arranged themselves into a study in puzzlement. "You know," he said, "that's disturbing, isn't it? Everyone knows Licinius and Acer weren't on good terms. You don't think –"

"On the contrary," I interrupted, "I do virtually nothing else. Thanks for your time."

One more visit to pay, and then I'd be done; just as well, since it was getting dark and I was worn out. I was going to have trouble convincing Scipio that I'd figured it all out while reclining in the shade if I was staggering all over the place from exhaustion. I went to the wheelwright's tent; he remembered a man bringing him a broken hammer to fix, even showed me a pail of water where, he assured me, the hammer had been dunked afterwards; "though," he said sorrowfully, "I could've told him, you got to leave it in there overnight. Just dipping it in and taking it out again's no good at all."

That chore out of the way, I sent a runner to Scipio, asking him to spare me a little time at his earliest convenience, as I'd solved his puzzle for him. I'd barely had time to take the weight off my feet and scrub my face with sand when back the messenger came; Scipio's compliments, and he could see me right away. Fine.

"First," I said, after we'd done all the hospitality and offering and refusing cups of wine and so forth, "I want to ask you one more time. What do you want from me, as far as this business is concerned?"

He sighed. "I already told you, the truth."

I smiled. "I'm delighted to hear it," I said. "And I have to say, my view of the courage and integrity of the Roman nobility's just gone up a whole lot."

"What's that supposed to mean?"

"What I said," I replied. "You see, a lot of my people, Greeks in general, have a very poor attitude towards you Romans. We make out that you're – well, you make a lot of noise about the basic simple virtues of bravery, honesty, loyalty and what have you, but in fact you're the exact opposite. Not true, goes without saying."

Scipio was looking at me. "Get to the point," he said.

"If you like," I replied; and I proceeded to tell him about my day, and the various things I'd seen or been told about. "Now then," I went on, "the way I see it, everything turns on one thing, this simple iron peg." I took it out, displayed it on the flat of my hand. "Like I said, I found this under Acer's body, all covered in his blood. I also found the hole in the ground it came out of; I can show it to you if you like."

"No need."

"As you wish. Now, you'll see that the peg is sharp at this

end, and there's dry caked blood on the sharp tip, going all round it. But Acer wasn't stabbed. If he just fell on top of the peg, which just happened to be lying there, you'd expect to see blood on one side only. Agreed?"

"I guess so," said Scipio.

"Fine," I said. "In which case, here's a hypothesis for you to consider. Acer is attacked; having no sword or dagger to defend himself with, he grabs for the nearest excuse for a weapon he can find – he grabs the rope that was tied to this ring, to pull the peg up out of the ground. The rope is frayed and breaks, but he's got the peg out. He uses it as a dagger, though it doesn't do him a lot of good, he dies anyhow. But my guess is, the blood on this peg isn't Acer's. It's the blood of the man who killed him."

Scipio leaned forward a little. "Good," he said. "A man with a wound like that'll be easy to find. If you're right about Acer stabbing him – well, you can see how deep the stab was by the tidemark of dried blood."

I nodded gravely. "Precisely," I said. "Just think about that. It must've gone in a good finger's depth. The murderer was lucky to be able to walk away, with a hole in him like that."

"So?" Scipio said. "Have you found him?"

I shook my head. "I haven't been through the whole camp looking for wounded men or corpses, but the duty officer tells me everyone was present and correct on parade this morning. And you know how places like this are for gossip and rumours; if any of the non-combatants or camp-followers had wound up dead, we'd all know about it. Unless, of course," I added, "it was a slave who died."

Scipio conceded that with a minor shrug.

"Bearing that in mind," I said, "here's two alternative theories. We're taking motive as read, since there's no point me telling you what you told me this morning."

He smiled.

"Theory one," I went on. "Acer was killed on the orders of Servius Gnatho. Now there's one thing about this theory that puzzles me; namely, not so very long ago, Acer's life was saved by Servius Gnatho's poor relation and hanger-on, Vipsanius Gnatho; Vipsanius rescued Acer from an ambush by Spanish irregulars, for which he received the headless spear. Strikes me as odd that Servius' dependent cousin should put himself out to save the man his rich patron later has assassinated. Wasted effort, yes?"

"Fine," Scipio said. "We'll forget about Gnatho, then."

"All right," I told him, "now let's think about the slave-dealer, Licinius. Acer was killed by a massive bash on the head. No weapon was to be found in the vicinity. Earlier that day, according to the blacksmith, one of Licinius' slaves dropped by the smithy and left with a hammerhead and a broken handle. He went to the wheelwright's. The hammer gets taken back to the smithy by a different man. The hammer shows signs of having been in water – which might mean it was used to pulp Acer's brains, and needed washing; but dunking in water overnight is what you do when you mend hammer handles, according to the smith, and the wheelwright. But," I continued, "the wheelwright says that after the hammer was fixed, it was just dunked briefly, which is useless."

"Interesting," Scipio said.

"Ah," I replied, "but not nearly as interesting as the other stuff the wheelwright told me. But we'll leave that for now. About the murderer; we believe he was stabbed, so deep it could've been fatal. But nobody seems to be dead except Acer, or even seriously injured."

"So it must've been a slave," Scipio said.

"That'd explain it," I said. "And when I went to see Licinius, practically the first thing he told me was that he'd had another item of stock just die on him. Who knows, or cares, what happens to dead slaves' bodies? Buried in a lime-pit or left out for the birds or burned on a bonfire with the trash; no body left to examine for major stab wounds. Theory; either the slave died of the wound or was knocked on the head to keep things quiet, but his body was disposed of and nobody thought twice about it. Neat?"

"Very," Scipio said.

"Well, quite," I said. "Neat enough to earn Licinius a view from the top of a cross, unless he apes his betters and opens a vein first." I paused. "Except," I said, "that's not what happened."

Scipio didn't say anything.

"Because," I carried on, "when I went to the wheel-wright's, I asked him if he knew the man who'd collected the hammer. He said yes. He identified the man as the property of Caius Laelius."

Absolute silence for a moment. Then Scipio looked up at me.

"Meaning?" he said.

"Meaning," I answered, "we now have to stop and think. Would you like to hazard a guess as to what thoughts've been crossing my mind lately?"

Scipio lifted his head; "Why don't you just tell me?" he said.

"All right, I will." I settled back a little in my chair. "And something that's been snagging my attention all along is, what an easy job this has been. No, I don't mean it in the look-how-clever-I-am sense. It was easy, simple as that. You listed the prime suspects for me; I looked at the scene and found the tethering-peg, which led me to the smith, and from there on it was like Theseus' golden thread in the Labyrinth. Even better, in fact; because just in case I didn't fancy the Licinius theory, there's a perfectly good Gnatho theory to fall back on. Because, of course, it's really easy to explain away Vipsanius saving Acer's life. For instance, it could be that Vipsanius was trying to kill Acer when he pulled him off the chariot; he failed, but there you go, bad luck happens. And Vipsanius was a commander of Spanish auxiliaries, and the ambushers were Spanish, because there's Spanish mercenaries on both sides. Dead easy for Vipsanius to arrange for his Spaniards to pass the word to their friends and relations on the other side to stage the ambush. And then there's another nice selection of choice; either Vipsanius got cold feet, realized he'd be in the frame if Acer died, and saved him; or he screwed up killing him, as previously argued; or maybe even Vipsanius arranged the ambush and the rescue, possibly even contrived to break his own leg, just so he and his cousin wouldn't be suspected when Acer was subsequently killed by Gnatho's assassin – exactly the conclusion you and I jumped to, in fact."

Scipio scowled at me. "Where's this all leading?" he asked.

"Ah," I said, in my best trial-advocate manner. "Here's where thinking helps. Think about what we've got; we've got a neat set of clues and coincidences that point to Licinius; we've also got a whole quiverful of plausible arguments in favour of Gnatho being the guilty party. Also, as well as the positive evidence, there's the negative evidence – the other possible lines of enquiry sealed off so definitely, if you like. An army camp, with sentries everywhere, and nobody saw or heard a damn thing. That's evidence; without it, I'd never have reached the point I'm at now. The point I'm making is this; instead of having to scratch round, I'm awash with helpful facts, strong leads, corroborative circumstances, and negative facts that rule out other possibilities. Basically, this job is too easy."

Scipio drew his forefinger and thumb down the line of his jaw. "I think I see what you're saying," he said. "Go on."

"Right," I said. "Now, when you gave me that helpful briefing, you mentioned a third possibility; namely, that someone had killed Acer, your enemy, under the misguided impression he'd be doing you a favour. I really don't want to dwell on that, because I hate offending powerful men, especially generals who command the army surrounding me on all sides. I would just like to point out that the most damning point against Licinius is his statement that he spent the night gambling with Caius Laelius, which Laelius denies. Furthermore, the wheelwright says that the man who fetched the hammer was Laelius' slave. I don't need to tell you of all people that sentries are trained to stay awake and be observant, but they're also trained to obey orders from superior officers, even if it means telling lies to Greek civilians. What I'm not saying," I added, as Scipio shifted in his chair, "is that your personal friend Laelius decided to rid you of the pest Acer, and covered up the killing by framing not one but two widely disliked men who nobody'd ever miss – a slave dealer and a notorious seducer – because even though I now firmly believe in Roman integrity, courage and (above all) forbearance, a poxy little Greek clerk could come to harm that way, and I have this unfulfilled ambition to live to be forty." I paused, drew a breath and added; "And that's about it, really. Sorry I couldn't be more help to you."

I managed to keep my knees from buckling under me until I was out of Scipio's tent and halfway across the yard to the stables, where I devoutly hoped my horse was saddled and ready. My heart nearly stopped when a bunch of soldiers appeared at me out of the gloom; but it was all right, they were just the men I'd sent out earlier to check out my theory about the murder weapon, finally reporting back, when it didn't really matter any more.

"This what you were after?" one of them said, handing me something small, round and heavy, wrapped in a cloak.

I unwrapped it. "Yes," I said. "You found it where I said it'd be?"

"Yes."

I smiled. "Thanks."

"No bother," the soldier lied blatantly, and he walked away. What he'd brought me was a catapult ball; about the size of a cabbage heart, stone, and (as I confirmed by the light of the nearest lantern) stained brown with dried blood in one place. He'd found it on the practice range, among all the other catapult shot; I'd told him to find the one with blood on it. I guessed there'd be a bloodstained one when I saw those little dimples in the dust, the marks left behind by a neat stack of the things, just what you'd expect to find outside the stores, near where they store the horsehair they use to make spare catapult springs from.

I got rid of it on the way to the stables, where my horse was waiting.

Scipio didn't do anything overt about Laelius; they were friends and political allies, and besides, if he'd made any of it public he'd inevitably have been suspected of complicity. But from then on, the friendship waned, Laelius' influence grew less, his advice and policies were neglected, almost as if Scipio didn't trust him quite so much any more. A pity, from Rome's point of view, since Laelius, though hardly a military or political genius, was at least cleverer and more sensible than Scipio himself, and had been responsible for a great deal of Scipio's better and brighter actions in the past.

In case you were wondering, by the way, I did get the job I was so anxious about. The job was a position I'd been after for ages; chief spy for King Philip of Macedon, last and strongest of Rome's substantial enemies, and the only hope of the Greek world against the shadow rising in the West. He was so pleased at the way I'd contrived to discredit such a key player as Caius Laelius, framing him for something he hadn't even done, that I was promoted to controller in chief of Macedonian intelligence operations in the Roman empire. I'm proud that I've been able to do something for the Greek cause, and I'll never forget Acer and his killer, who made it all possible.

Ah yes, Acer's killer.

Vitellius Acer was, of course, killed by the captured elephant penned up in the stockyard adjoining the plunder store. As everybody knows, elephants have a prodigious memory for past injuries, and an uncanny ability to tell humans apart. As soon as it saw the man who'd wounded it during the battle by sticking a spear through its lip, it pulled up the tethering-pins that were holding it down, rushed across the enclosure, grabbed a stone in its trunk (lucky for it that there was a pile of stones just handy, in the form of the catapult balls) and smashed Acer's head in for him. Acer did his bit by falling on one of the tethering pegs and smearing blood on it (I wiped chicken's blood on the other side before I showed it to Scipio); and by knocking over the pile of catapult balls. Some tidy-minded squaddie replaced them at some point before I got there, thereby conveniently smuggling the real murder weapon away from the scene – it was taken along with the rest of the pile to the range and used for target practice. It also helped that Licinius, worried about being accused because his hatred of Acer was so well known, exaggerated how long he'd been with Laelius so as to provide himself with an alibi, though it's just the sort of thing a clown like that might be expected to do. As for the blacksmith's hammer, that was pure serendipity, or, as I prefer to believe, the gods helping out a righteous cause.

I was proud of how few outright lies I had to tell Scipio, and how well I blended them in. I am, after all, a trained lawyer.

Elephants are a bit like Greeks, I guess. They never forget who their enemies are.

A Gladiator Dies Only Once

Steven Saylor

*As Steven Saylor states in his introduction, the following
story is something of a homage to the film* Gladiator. *It's
the latest in Saylor's popular Roma Sub Rosa series
featuring Gordianus the Finder. The series began with*
Roman Blood *(1991) and now runs to nine volumes. This
story, set just before the famous revolt of the slaves led by
Spartacus, takes place before the events in the novel* Arms
of Nemesis *(1992). Gordianus finds himself trying to
solve, not a murder but, a resurrection!*

"A beautiful day for it," I said begrudgingly. Cicero
nodded and squinted up at the filtered red sunlight
that penetrated the awning above our seats. Below, in the
arena, the first pair of gladiators strode across the sand to
meet each other in combat.

The month was Junius, at the beginning of what promised
to be a long, hot summer. The blue sky and undulating green
hills were especially beautiful here in the Etrurian countryside outside the town of Saturnia, where Cicero and I,
travelling separately from Rome, had arrived the day before
to attend the funeral of a local magistrate. Sextus Thorius
had been struck down in the prime of life, thrown from his

horse while riding down the Clodian Way to check on the progress of a slave gang doing repair work on the road. The next day, word of his demise reached Rome, where quite a few important persons had felt obligated to attend the funeral.

Earlier that morning, not a few of the senators and bankers who gathered to watch the funeral procession had raised an eyebrow at the sight of Gordianus the Finder among them; feeling the beady gaze of a prune-faced matron on me, I distinctly overheard her whisper to her husband, "What's *he* doing here? Does someone suspect foul play at work in the death of Sextus Thorius?" But Cicero, when he caught sight of me, smiled grimly and moved to join me, and asked no questions. He knew why I had come. A few years ago, facing the prospect of a ruinous business scandal, Thorius had consulted Cicero for legal advice, and Cicero had sent Thorius to me to get to the bottom of the affair. In the end, both scandal and litigation were averted. Thorius had rewarded me generously, and had subsequently sent quite a bit of business my way. The least I could do on the occasion of his death was to pack my best toga, spend the night at a seedy inn in Saturnia, and show up at his funeral.

We had followed the procession of musicians, hired mourners and family members to the little necropolis outside Saturnia, where, after a few speeches of remembrance, Thorius's remains had been set alight atop a funeral pyre. At the soonest opportunity to do so without seeming impolite, I had turned to leave, eager to start back to Rome, when Cicero caught my arm.

"Surely you're not leaving yet, Gordianus. We must stay for the funeral games."

"Games?" I meant to load the word with irony, but Cicero took the question in my voice literally.

"There's to be a gladiator show, of course. It's not as if

Thorius was a nobody. His family wasn't rich, but they'll have spent whatever they can afford, I'm sure."

"I hate watching gladiators," I said bluntly.

"So do I. But they're a part of the funeral, no less than the procession and the eulogies. One has to stay."

"I'm not in the mood to see blood spilled."

"But if you leave now, people will notice," he said, lowering his voice. "You can't afford to have them think you're squeamish, Gordianus. Not in your line of work."

I glanced at the faces around us, lit by the funeral pyre. The prune-faced matron was among them, along with her husband and numerous others from the same social set back in Rome. Much as I might hate to admit it, I was dependent on the trust and good will of such people, the sort who had occasion to call on my services and means to pay for them. I ferreted out the truth, and in return they put bread on my table.

"But I have to get back to Rome," I protested. "I can't afford another night at that seedy inn."

"Then you'll stay with me," said Cicero. "I have accommodations with a local banker. Good food. Comfortable beds." He raised an eyebrow.

Why did Cicero want so badly for me to stay? It occurred to me that he was the squeamish one. To watch the gladiators, he wanted the company of someone who wouldn't needle him about his squeamishness, as so many of his social equals were likely to do.

Begrudgingly, I acquiesced, and so found myself, that fine afternoon in Junius, seated in a wooden amphitheatre constructed especially for the funeral games to honour the passing of Sextus Thorius of Saturnia. Since I was with Cicero, I had been admitted into the more exclusive section of seats beneath the shade of the blood-red awning, along with the bereaved family, various local dignitaries, and important visitors from Rome. The local villagers and farmers sat in the sun-drenched seats across from ours. They wore brimmed hats for shade and waved brightly coloured fans. For a brief moment, bemused by the fluttering fans, I had the illusion that the crowd had been covered by a swarm of huge butterflies flapping their wings.

There were to be three matches, all fought to the death. Any less than three would have seemed parsimonious on the part of the family. Any more would have begun to look ostentatious, and added to the cost. As Cicero had said, the family of Sextus Thorius, while eminently respectable, was not rich.

The three pairs of gladiators were paraded before us. Helmets hid their faces, but they were easy to tell apart by their different armour and their contrasting physiques. One stood out from all the rest because of his coloration, a Nubian whose muscular arms and legs shone beneath the hot sun like burnished ebony. As the fighters strode before us, each raised his weapon. The crowd responded with polite cheering, but I overheard two men behind us complaining:

"Pretty obscure outfit. Owned by some freedman from Ravenna, I'm told; fellow called Ahala. Never heard of him!"

"Me neither. How did the family settle on this crew? Probably came cheap. Still, I suppose the Nubian's something of a novelty . . ."

There followed the ritual inspection of weapons for sharpness and armour for soundness, performed by the local magistrate in charge of the games, then the gladiators departed from the arena. The magistrate invoked the gods and delivered yet another eulogy to Sextus Thorius. A few moments later, to a blare of trumpets, a pair of gladiators re-emerged and the first bout commenced. The shorter, stockier fighter was outfitted in the Thracian manner with a small round shield and a short sword. His tall, lumbering opponent wore heavier Samnite armour and carried an oblong shield.

"Samnite versus Thracian – a typical match," noted Cicero, who often fell to lecturing when he was uneasy or nervous. "Did you know that the very first gladiatorial matches took place right here in Etruria? Oh, yes; we Romans inherited the custom from the Etruscans. They began by sacrificing captive warriors before the funeral pyres of their leaders –" Cicero gave a start as the sword of the Samnite struck one of the iron bosses on the shield of the Thracian with a resounding clang, then he cleared his throat and continued. "Eventually, instead of simply strangling the captives, the Etruscans decided to have them fight each other, allowing the victors to live. We Romans took up the custom, and so developed the tradition of death-matches at the funerals of great men. Of course, nowadays, anyone who was anyone must be honoured with games at his funeral. I've even heard of gladiator matches at the funerals of prominent women! The result is a tremendous demand for fresh gladiators. You still see captive warriors among them, but more and more often they're simply slaves who've been trained to fight, or sometimes convicted criminals – murderers who'd otherwise be executed, or thieves who'd rather take a chance in the arena than have a hand chopped off."

Below us, the Thracian thrust past the Samnite's shield and scored a glancing cut across the man's sword-arm. Blood sprinkled the sand. Cicero shuddered.

"Ultimately, one should remember that it's a religious occasion," he noted primly, "and the people must have their religion. And quite candidly, I don't mind watching a death-match if both the combatants are convicted criminals. Then at least there's something instructive about the blood-letting. Or even if the fighters are captured warriors; that can be instructive as well, to take a good look at our enemies and to see how they fight, and to celebrate the favour of the gods, who've put us in the stands and them down there in the arena. But more and more the trend is to have trained slaves do the fighting –"

The tall Samnite, after a staggering retreat under the Thracian's relentless assault, suddenly rallied and managed to score a solid thrust at the other's flank. Blood spattered the sand. From behind his helmet the Thracian let out a cry and staggered back.

Behind us, the two men who had earlier complained now both roared with excitement.

"That's how to turn the tables! You've got him now, Samnite!"

"Make the little fellow squeal again!"

Cicero fidgeted in his seat and cast a a disapproving glance behind us, then looked sidelong at the young woman seated next to him. She was watching the bout with narrowed eyes, one hand touching her parted lips and the other patting her heaving bosom. Cicero looked at me and raised an eyebrow. "And then there's the unwholesome glamour which these gladiators exert on certain women – and on more than a few men, as well, I'm sad to say. The whole culture has gone gladiator-mad! Roman boys play at being gladiators instead of generals, Roman ladies swoon whenever they see one, and do you know, I've even heard of Roman citizens who've volunteered to fight as gladiators themselves. And not just for the money – although I understand even some slaves are paid handsomely if they can survive and make a name for themselves – but for some sort of perverse thrill. I can't begin to imagine –"

His objection was abruptly drowned out by the roar of the crowd. The stocky Thracian had rallied and was once again relentlessly pushing the taller Samnite back. Sword clanged against sword, until the Samnite, tripping, fell backwards.

The Thracian stepped onto the shield the Samnite had drawn over his chest, pinning the man down. He pressed the tip of his sword against the Samnite's wind-pipe. The Samnite released his sword and instinctively grasped the blade, then drew back his hand, flinging blood from the cuts across his fingers.

The Samnite had been worsted. From behind the visor of his helmet, the triumphant Thracian scanned the stands, looking to the crowd for judgment. Following the ancient custom, those who thought the Samnite should be spared would produce handkerchiefs and wave them, while those who wanted to see him put to death would raise their fists in the air. Here and there I saw a few fluttering handkerchiefs, all but submerged in a sea of clenched fists.

"I don't agree," said one of the men behind us. "I rather liked the Samnite. He put up a good fight."

"Bah!" said his friend, shaking his fist in the air. "They're both amateurs! The whole match was barely acceptable; I wouldn't give a fig to watch either of them fight again. Send the loser straight to Hades, I say! Anything less would dishonour the memory of Sextus Thorius."

"I suppose you're right," said the other, and from the corner of my eye I saw him put away his handkerchief and raise his fist.

The Thracian looked to the magistrate in charge of the games for the final judgment. The man raised his fist and nodded curtly, and the Thracian drove the sword into the Samnite's throat. A great fountain of blood spurted from the wound, gushing across the Samnite's helmet and chest and onto the sand all around. The man thrashed and convulsed, very nearly throwing the Thracian off-balance. But the Thracian steadied himself, shifting more weight onto the shield that confined the Samnite and bearing down on his sword until it penetrated the back of the

Samnite's neck and was driven firmly into the packed sand beneath.

With a roar of triumph, the Thracian stepped back and thrust his fists in the air. The Samnite bucked his hips and thrashed his limbs, pinned to the earth by the sword through his neck. The Thracian performed a victory strut in a circle around him.

"Disgusting!" muttered Cicero, pressing a clenched fist to his lips and looking queasy.

"Delightful!" uttered one of the men behind us. "Now that's more like it! What a finish!"

Then, as a single body – myself included – the crowd drew a gasp. With one of his thrashing hands the Samnite had managed to grab hold of the Thracian's ankle, and with his other hand he had somehow managed to regain his sword. He pounded the pommel against the sand, as if to still that arm from thrashing, so that the blade pointed rigidly upright. The Thracian lost his balance and, making circles in the air with his arms, began to tumble backwards.

For a long, breathless moment, it looked as if no power in the heavens or on the earth could stop the Thracian from falling backwards directly onto the upright blade of the Samnite's sword, impaling himself.

Even Cicero bolted forward, rigid with suspense. The woman next to him swooned. The men behind us bleated with excitement.

The Thracian swayed back – regained his balance – and swayed back again. The upright sword glinted in the sunlight.

Making a tremendous circle with his arms, the Thracian at last managed to propel himself forwards. Wrenching his ankle from the Samnite's grasp, he took a few staggering steps forwards, then wheeled about. The Samnite had stopped thrashing, but the sword in his fist still pointed skyward. Approaching cautiously, as one might a snake that seemed to have writhed its last but might yet strike, the Thracian squatted down and snatched the sword from the Samnite's grip – then jerked back in alarm as a bizarre noise emerged from the Samnite's throat, a gurgling death-rattle that froze my blood. Gripping the pommel in both hands, the Thracian pointed the sword downwards. As one might strike a last blow to make sure that a snake was finished, he drove the blade deep into the Samnite's groin.

Again, the crowd gasped in unison. Like Cicero beside me, I put my hand to my groin and flinched. But the Samnite was now truly dead. Fresh blood stained the loincloth around the wound, but he did not move.

His chest heaving, the Thracian stood and recommenced his victory strut. After a moment of stunned silence, the exhilarated crowd rewarded him with thunderous cheering. The magistrate strode into the arena and rewarded him with a palm frond to mark his victory. Waving it over his head, the gladiator departed to raucous applause.

"Well!" declared Cicero, clearly impressed despite his avowed distaste for the games. "That will be hard to top."

The body of the Samnite was dragged away, the pools of blood were raked over with fresh sand, and the next match commenced. It was a novelty bout between two *dimacheri*, so-called because each wielded not one but two daggers. To compensate for their lack of shields, they wore more pieces of armour than other types of fighters – greaves to protect their forearms and shins, plated pectorals to guard their throats and chests, and various bands about their limbs and bits of metal over their naked flesh that suggested adornment as much as armour. Instead of the nerve-wracking banging of swords against shields, the sound of their match was a constant, grating slither of blade against blade as they engaged in a dizzying dance of parries and thrusts. One was swarthy and the other pale, but otherwise their physiques were much alike; not as muscular as either of the previous fighters, they had the lithesome bodies of dancers. Speed and agility counted for more than brute strength in such a match, and they were so evenly matched, and their manoeuvres so elegant, that their contest seemed almost choreographed. Instead of grunts and cheers, they elicited "ahs" and "ohs" of appreciation from the crowd. Watching them whirl about, I felt the pleasure one feels from watching dancers rather than warriors, so that I almost forgot that for one of them, death waited at the end of the match.

Then, with a scraping noise that set my teeth on edge, a dagger slid over armour and successfully connected with unprotected flesh, and the first blood was spilled. The crowd exhaled an "Ah!" at a higher pitch than before, and I sensed the stirring of their collective blood-lust.

Both fighters seemed to be wearying, losing the unerring focus that had kept them from harming each other. More blood was spilled, though the wounds were minor, mere scratches that dabbed the blades with just enough blood to send red droplets flying through the air to mingle with the fine spray of sweat cast from the gladiators' glistening limbs.

Slowly but surely the pace of the parries and thrusts accelerated, even as their rhythm became more ragged and unpredictable. My heartbeat quickened. I glanced at Cicero and realized that he had not said a word throughout the match. He leaned forwards, his eyes glittering with fascination.

The swarthy fighter suddenly seized the advantage. His arms became a blur of movement, like the wings of a bee. And like a bee he stung, managing to prick first the right hand of his opponent, then the left hand, so that the pale gladiator released both of his daggers and stood defenceless. Pressing his daggers to the other's wrists, the swarthy fighter forced the disarmed man to spread his arms wide open, like a crucified slave.

It was a brazen gesture on the part of the swarthy gladiator to humiliate his foe, but it contained a miscalculation. At such close quarters, almost chest-to-chest, the pale gladiator was able to thrust one knee into his opponent's groin, and simultaneously to butt his helmet against the other's. The swarthy gladiator was sent staggering back. The hushed crowd erupted in shrieks of laughter.

The pale gladiator's advantage was short-lived. He made a dash to recover one of his daggers, but the distance was too great. The swarthy gladiator was upon him like a pouncing lion, hemming him in with his daggers, jabbing and pricking him, forcing him to perform a spastic, backward dance, controlling him at every step. To pay him back, the swarthy gladiator kneed him not once but twice in the groin. The pale gladiator folded forwards in agony, then abruptly performed the motion in reverse, straining upright onto his toes, for not one but two daggers were pressed against the soft, unarmoured flesh beneath his chin. The movement was so neatly performed that it seemed like the climax to a dance which the two had been performing from the moment their bout commenced. They stood like statues, one with daggers poised, the other on tiptoes, quivering, empty hands at his sides, helpless. The crowd roared its approval.

The victor looked towards the magistrate, who raised an eyebrow and turned his head from side to side to assess the will of the crowd. Spontaneously, the crowd produced a multitude of fluttering handkerchiefs. Voices cried, "Spare him! Spare him!" Even the men behind me took up the chant: "Spare him! Spare him!"

In my experience, the judgment of the mob is like quicksilver, hard to pin down and impossible to predict. If I had turned at that moment and asked the men behind me, "Why spare the pale gladiator?", no doubt they would have given the rote answer: "Because he fought well, and deserves to fight another day." But the Samnite had fought just as bravely, if not as beautifully, and they had been eager to see him die. I think it was the fact that the two *dimacheri* had fought so well together that swayed the crowd to spare the loser; they were like a matched set that no one wished to see broken. The pale gladiator owed his life as much to his opponent as to himself; had they not been so precisely matched and performed so well together, those two daggers would have been thrust into his gullet in the blink of an eye. Instead, one by one, the daggers withdrew. The pale gladiator dropped to his knees, his head bowed to show deference both to the spectators who had spared him and to the man who had bested him, as the victor received his palm frond from the presiding magistrate.

"Well!" said Cicero, breaking his silence. "So far it's been a better show than any of us expected, I dare say. I wonder what the final match will bring."

Sometimes, if the games are boring, spectators begin to vacate the stands after the first or second match, deciding they've adequately paid their respects to the dead and need stay no longer. On this day, for the final match, not a single spectator stirred from his seat. Instead, there was a new arrival. I was not the only one who noticed her; one of the men behind me released a wolf-whistle.

"Feast your eyes on that beauty!" he murmured.

"Where?" said his friend.

"Right across from us, looking for a place to sit."

"Oh, yes, I see. A beauty, you say? Too dark for my taste."

"You need to broaden your palate, then. Ha! I'll bet you've never had a Nubian."

"As if *you* had!"

"Of course I have. You forget that I spent a few years travelling around Libya and Egypt . . ."

I grew deaf to their prattling, fascinated by the newcomer. She was strikingly beautiful, with high cheekbones, full lips and flashing eyes. Her dense black hair was piled on her head in the latest style and tied with ribbons, and she wore a tunic of pale blue that contrasted with the ebony sheen of her naked arms and throat. Her burnished copper necklace and bracelets glinted in the bright sunlight. Her breast heaved slightly, as if she were excited or slightly out of breath. One seldom saw a Nubian in Italy who was not a slave, but from her dress and the fact that she appeared to be out and about on her own, I took her to be a free woman. While I watched, a row of male spectators, clearly as struck by her beauty as I was, nudged one another and obligingly made room for her, giving her an aisle seat.

The two gladiators who strode into the arena for the final bout could not have been more different. The first was stoutly built, his chest and legs covered by curly red hair. He was outfitted in the manner of the Gauls, with a short sword and a tall, rectangular shield, a loose loincloth and bands of metal-plated leather wrapped around his mid-section, leaving his legs and chest bare. His helmet covered not only his head but, tapering and flaring out again like an hourglass, extended down to cover his neck and breastbone as well.

Following him into the arena was a *retiarius*, to my mind the most fearsomely attired class of gladiators. *Retiarii* carry not a sword and shield, but a long trident and a net. This one was all the more striking because of his contrast to the red-haired Gaul, for he was the tall, smoothly muscled Nubian we had seen in the opening parade of gladiators, as ebon-hued as the woman who had just found a seat in the stands. I wondered briefly if there might be some connection between them – then drew in a breath as the Gaul made a rush at the *retiarius* and the combat commenced.

Sword clanged against trident. Already heated to fever-pitch by the previous matches, the crowd became raucously vocal at once, jumping from their seats and crying out for blood. The gladiators responded with a bout that exceeded anything we had previously seen that day. For two men so heavily muscled, they moved with surprising speed (although the *retiarius*, with his long legs, was considerably more graceful than his opponent). They seemed almost to read one another's thoughts, as blows were deflected or dodged at the last possible instant, and each attack was followed at once by a counter-attack of equal cunning and ferocity. Beside me, Cicero repeatedly flinched and gasped, but did not look away. Neither did I, swept up by the primal fascination of watching two men in a struggle for life and death.

As the match continued, the attributes of each fighter became clear. The Gaul was stronger, the Nubian quicker; he would need to be, if he were to succeed in casting the net over his prey. Several times, when the Gaul closed the distance between them in order to slash and thrust, the net almost captured him, but the Gaul eluded it by dropping to the sand, rolling out of harm's way, and springing back to his feet.

"At this rate, the Gaul's going to exhaust himself," said one of the men behind me. "Then watch the Nubian catch him in that net like a fish out of water and start poking holes in him!"

Irritated, Cicero turned to shush the man, but I was thinking exactly the same thought. And indeed, almost more quickly than my eyes could apprehend it, the very thing happened. The Gaul rushed in, slashing his sword. Wielding the trident with one hand, the Nubian parried the Gaul's thrust, and with his other hand he spun the net in the air and brought it down directly over the Gaul. The lead weights sewn at various points around the edge of the net caused it to collapse around the Gaul and swallow him, sword, shield and all.

If the Gaul had tripped, which seemed almost inevitable, that would have been the end of him. But somehow he managed to stay upright, and when the Nubian, wielding his trident with both hands now, rushed towards him, he managed to spin about so that the three sharp prongs landed squarely against his shield. The prongs, failing to penetrate flesh, instead became enmeshed in the fabric of the net. The Nubian yanked at his trident to free it, but the net held it fast, and the Gaul, though pulled forwards, managed to stand his ground.

Sensing more than seeing his advantage – for the net must have greatly blocked the view from his narrow visor – the Gaul rushed forwards. Holding fast to the trident, the Nubian was unable to stand his ground and was pushed back. Tripping, he fell onto his rump and released the shaft of the trident with one hand, still gripping it with the other. The Gaul, using his bull-like strength, twisted to one side. The Nubian, his wrist unnaturally bent, gave a cry and released the trident altogether.

The Gaul, slashing at the net with his sword and thrusting upwards with his shield, managed to push the net up and over his head, taking the trident with it. Stepping free, he kicked the net behind him, and with it the now hopelessly entangled trident. The Nubian, meanwhile, managed to scramble to his feet, but he was now without a weapon.

The Gaul might have made short work of his opponent but, eschewing his sword, he used his shield as a weapon instead. Rushing headlong at the Nubian, he struck him with his shield, so hard that the Nubian was knocked backwards against the wooden wall of the arena. The spectators directly above him, unable to see, rushed forwards from their seats and craned their necks, peering over the railing. Among them – not hard to pick out in that crowd – I saw the Nubian woman. Even greater than the contrast of her dark flesh next to the paleness of those around her was the marked contrast of her expression. Submerged in a sea of faces that leered, gaped and howled with bloodlust, she was silent and stricken, wearing a look of shock and dismay.

The Gaul played cat and mouse with his prey. He stepped back, allowing the Nubian to stagger forwards, gasping for breath, then stuck him full-force again with shield, knocking him against the wall. Over and over the Gaul struck the Nubian, knocking the breath out of him each time, until the man was barely able to stand. The Gaul delivered one last body-blow with his shield, and the Nubian, recoiling from the wall, fell forwards onto his face.

Casting aside his shield, the Gaul grabbed hold of the Nubian's ankle and dragged him towards the centre of the arena. The Nubian thrashed ineffectively, seemingly unable to catch a breath. To judge from the intermittent red trail he left in the sand, he was bleeding from some part of his body, perhaps from his mouth.

"Ha!" said one of the men behind me. "Who's the fish out of water now?"

The Gaul reached the centre of the ring. Releasing the Nubian's ankle, he held up his fists and performed a victory strut in a circle around him. The crowd gasped at the man's audacity. The Thracian had behaved with the same careless bravado, and had very nearly paid for it with his life.

But the Nubian was in no condition to take advantage of any miscalculation by his opponent. At one point he stirred and tried to raise himself on his arms, and the crowd let out a cry; but his arms failed him and he fell back again, flat on his chest. The Gaul stood over him and looked to the spectators for judgment.

The reaction from the stands was mixed. People rose to their feet. "Spare him!" cried some. "Send him to Hades!" cried others. The magistrate in charge turned his head this way and that, looking distinctly uncomfortable at the lack of consensus. Whichever course he chose, some in the crowd would be disappointed. At last he gave a sign to the waiting gladiator, and I was not surprised that he did the predictable thing. Mercy to a defeated fighter had already been granted once that day; mercy was the exception, not the rule. The crowd had come expecting to see bloodshed and death, and those who wanted to see the Nubian killed had more reason to see their expectation gratified than did those who preferred the novelty of allowing him to live. The magistrate raised his fist in the air.

There were cries of triumph in the stands, and groans of disappointment. Some cheered the magistrate, others booed. But to all this commotion I was largely deaf, for my eyes were on the Nubian woman directly across from me. Her body stiffened and her face froze in a grimace as the Gaul raised his sword for the death blow; I had the impression that she was struggling to contain herself, to exhibit dignity despite the despair that was overwhelming her. But as the sword descended, she lost all composure. She clutched her hair. She opened her mouth. The sound of her scream was drowned in the roar of the crowd as the Nubian convulsed on the sand, blood spurting like a fountain around the sword thrust between his shoulder blades.

For an instant, the Nubian woman's gaze met mine. I was drawn into the depths of her suffering as surely as if I tumbled into a well. Cicero gripped my arm. "Steady, Gordianus," he said. I turned towards him. His face was pale but his tone was smug; at last, it seemed to say, he had found someone more squeamish at the sight of death than himself.

When I looked back, the woman had vanished.

With their palm fronds held aloft, the victors paraded once more around the arena. The magistrate invoked the memory of Sextus Thorius and uttered a closing prayer to the gods. The spectators filed out of the amphitheatre.

"Did you notice her?" I asked Cicero.

"Who, that hyperventilating young woman next to me?"

"No, the Nubian across from us."

"A Nubian female?"

"I don't think she showed up until the final bout. I think she was alone."

"That seems unlikely."

"Perhaps she's related somehow to the Nubian gladiator."

He shrugged. "I didn't notice her. How observant you are, Gordianus! You and your endless curiosity. But what did you think of the games?" I started to answer, but Cicero gave me no chance. "Do you know," he said, "I actually rather enjoyed myself, far more than I expected to. A most instructive afternoon, and the audience seemed quite uplifted by the whole experience. But it seems to me a mistake on the part of the organizers, simply as a matter of presentation, not to show us the faces of the gladiators at some point, either at the beginning or the end. Their individual helmets project a certain personality, to be sure, like masks in the theatre. Or do you think that's the point, to keep them anonymous and abstract? If we could see into their eyes, we might make a more emotional connection – they'd become human beings first, and gladiators second, and that would interfere with the pure symbolism of their role in the funeral games. It would thwart the religious intent . . ." Safe once more from the very real bloodshed of the arena, Cicero nattered on, falling into his role of aloof lecturer.

We arrived at Cicero's lodgings, where he continued to pontificate to his host, a rich Etrurian yokel who seemed quite overwhelmed to have such a famous advocate from Rome sleeping under his roof. After a parsimonious meal, I excused myself as quickly as I could and went to bed. I could not help thinking that the lice at the inn had been more congenial, and the cook more generous.

I fell asleep thinking of the Nubian woman, haunted by my final image of her – her fists tearing at her hair, her mouth opened to scream.

The next day I made my way back to Rome. I proceeded to forget about the funeral of Sextus Thorius, the games, and the Nubian woman. The month of Junius passed into Quinctilis.

Then, one day, as Rome sweltered through the hottest summer I could remember, my mute son Eco came to me in my garden to announce a visitor.

"A woman?" I said, watching his hands shape curves in the air.

Eco nodded. *Rather young*, he went on to say, in the elaborate system of gestures we had devised between us, *with skin the colour of night*.

I raised an eyebrow. "A Nubian?"

Eco nodded.

"Show her in."

My memory did not do justice to her beauty. As before, her hair was done up with ribbons and she was attired in pale blue and burnished copper. Probably the outfit was the best she possessed. She had worn it to attend the funeral games; now she wore it for me. I was flattered.

She studied me for a long moment, a quizzical expression

on her face. "I've seen you somewhere before," she finally said.

"Yes. In Saturnia, at the funeral games for Sextus Thorius."

She sucked in a breath. "I remember now. You sat across from me. You weren't like the rest – laughing, joking, screaming for blood. When Zanziba was killed, you saw the suffering on my face, and I could tell that you . . ." Her voice trailed off. She lowered her eyes. "How strange, the paths upon which the gods lead us! When I asked around the Subura for a man who might be able to help me, yours was the name people gave me, but I never imagined that I'd seen you before – and in that place of all places, on that day of all accursed days!"

"You know who I am, then?"

"Gordianus. They call you the Finder."

"Yes. And you?"

"My name is Zuleika."

"Not a Roman name."

"I had a Roman name once. A man who was my master gave it to me. But Zuleika is the name I was born with, and Zuleika is the name I'll die with."

"I take it you shed your slave name when you shed your former master. You're a freedwoman, then?"

"Yes."

"Let's sit here in the garden. My son will bring us wine to drink."

We sat in the shade, and Zuleika told me her story.

She had been born in a city with an unpronounceable name, in a country unimaginably far away – beyond Nubia, she said, even beyond the fabled source of the Nile. Her father had been a wealthy trader in ivory, who often travelled and took his family with him. In a desert land, at a tender age, she had seen her father and mother murdered by bandits. Zuleika and her younger brother, Zanziba, were abducted and sold into slavery.

"Our fortunes varied, as did our masters," she said, "but at least we were kept together as a pair; because we were exotic, you see." *And beautiful*, I thought, assuming that her brother's beauty matched her own. "Eventually we found ourselves in Egypt. Our new owner was the master of a mime troupe. He trained us to be performers."

"You have a particular talent?"

"I dance and sing."

"And your brother?"

"Zanziba excelled at acrobatics – cartwheels, balancing acts, somersaults in mid-air. The master said that Zanziba must have a pair of wings hidden somewhere between those massive shoulders of his." She smiled, but only briefly. "Our master had once been a slave himself. He was a kind and generous man; he allowed his slaves to earn their own money, with the goal of eventually buying their freedom. When we had earned enough, Zanziba and I, we used the money to purchase Zanziba's freedom, with the intention of putting aside more money until we could do the same for me.

"But then the master fell on hard times. He was forced to disband the troupe and sell his performers piecemeal – a dancer here, a juggler there. I ended up with a new master, a Roman merchant living in Alexandria. He didn't want me for my dancing or my singing. He wanted me for my body." She lowered her eyes. "When Zanziba came to him and said he wanted to buy my freedom, the man named a very steep price. Zanziba vowed to earn it, but he could never hope to do so as an acrobat, performing for coins in the street. He disappeared from Alexandria. Time passed, and more time. For such a long time I heard no word from him that I began to despair, thinking that my brother was dead, or had forgotten about me.

"Then, finally, money arrived – a considerable sum, enough to buy my freedom and more. And with it came a letter – not in Zanziba's hand, because neither of us had ever learned to read or write, but written for him by the banker who transmitted the money."

"What did the letter say?"

"Can you read?"

"Yes."

"Then read it for yourself." Zuleika handed me a worn and tattered scrap of parchment.

Beloved Sister, I am in Italy, among the Romans. I have become a gladiator, a man who fights to the death to honour the Roman dead. It is a strange thing to be. The Romans profess to despise our kind, yet all the men want to buy us drinks in the taverns and all the women want to sleep with us. I despise this life, but it is the only way a freedman can earn the sort of money we need. It is a hard, cruel life, not fit for an animal, and it comes to a terrible end. Do not follow or try to find me. Forget me. Find your way back to our homeland, if you can. Live free, sister. I, too, shall live free, and though I may die young, I shall die a free man. Your loving brother, Zanziba.

I handed the scrap of parchment back to her. "Your brother told you not to come to Italy."

"How could I not come? Zanziba hadn't forgotten me, after all. I was not going to forget him. As soon as I was able, I booked passage on a ship to Rome."

"Travel is expensive."

"I paid for the fare from the money Zanziba sent me."

"Surely he meant for you to live off that money."

"Here in Rome I make my own living." She raised her

chin high. The haughty angle flattered her. She was beautiful; she was exotic; she was obviously clever. I could well imagine that Zuleika was able to demand a high fee for the pleasure of her company.

"You came to Rome. And then?"

"I looked for Zanziba, of course. I started with the banker who'd sent the money. He sent me to a gladiator camp near Neapolis. I talked to the man who owned the camp – the trainer, what you Romans call a *lanista*. He told me Zanziba had fought with his troupe of gladiators for a while, but had long since moved on. The *lanista* didn't know where. Most gladiators are captives or slaves, but Zanziba was a free agent; he went where the money was best. I followed his trail by rumour and hearsay. I came to one dead-end after another, and each time I had to start all over again. If you're as good as people say, Gordianus the Finder, I could have used the skills of a man like you to track him down." She raised an eyebrow. "Do you have any idea how many gladiator camps there are in Italy?"

"Scores, I should imagine."

"Hundreds, scattered all over the countryside! Over the last few months I've travelled the length and breadth of Italy, looking for Zanziba without luck, until . . . until a man who knew Zanziba told me that he was fighting for a *lanista* named Ahala who runs a camp in Ravenna. But the man said I needn't bother going all the way to Ravenna, because Ahala's gladiators would be fighting at funeral games the very next day up in Saturnia."

"At the funeral of Sextus Thorius," I said.

"Yes. I wasn't able to leave Rome until the next morning. I travelled all day. I arrived just when Zanziba's match was beginning – excited, fearful, out of breath. Just in time to see –"

"Are you sure it was him?"

"Of course."

"But he wore a helmet."

She shook her head. "With or without the helmet, I'd have known him. By his limbs and legs. By the way he *moved*. 'Zanziba must have wings hidden between those massive shoulders,' the master in Alexandria used to say . . ." Her voice trembled and her eyes glittered with tears. "After all my travels, all my searching, I arrived just in time to see my brother die!"

I lowered my eyes, remembering the scene: the Nubian flat on his chest, the Gaul with his sword poised to strike, the uncertain magistrate, the raucous crowd, the death-blow, the fountain of blood . . .

"I'm sorry you had to see such a thing, Zuleika. Did you attend to his body afterwards?"

"I wasn't even allowed to see him! I went to the quarters where the gladiators were kept, but the *lanista* wouldn't let me in."

"Did you tell him who you were?"

"If anything, that made him even more hostile. He told me it didn't matter whose sister I was, that I had no business being there. 'Clear off!' he shouted, and one of the gladiators shook a sword at me, and I ran away, crying. I should have stood up to him, I suppose, but I was so upset . . ."

Stood up to him?, I thought. That would have been impossible. A freedwoman Zuleika might be, but that hardly gave her the privileges of a Roman citizen, or the prerogatives of being male. No one in Saturnia that day would have taken her side against the *lanista*.

I sighed, wondering, now that her story was told, why she had come to see me. "Your brother did an honourable thing when he sent you money to buy your freedom. But perhaps he was right. You shouldn't have followed him here. You shouldn't have tried to find him. A gladiator's life is brutish and short. He chose that life, and he saw it through to the only possible end."

"No!" she whispered, shaking her head, fixing me with a fiery gaze. "It wasn't the end."

"What do you mean?"

"It wasn't the end of Zanziba!"

"I don't understand."

"Zanziba didn't die that day. I know, because . . . because I've seen him!"

"Where? When?"

"Yesterday, here in Rome, in the market place down by the river. I saw Zanziba!"

Was the glint in her eyes excitement, or madness? "Did you speak to him?"

"No. He was on the far side of the market. A cart blocked my way, and before I could reach him, he was gone."

"Perhaps you were mistaken," I said quietly. "It happens to me all the time. I see a face across a crowd, or from the corner of my eye, and I'm sure it's someone I know. But when I take a second look, I realize the familiarity was merely an illusion, a trick of the mind."

She shook her head. "How many men who look like Zanziba have you ever seen in the Roman market?"

"All the more reason why you might mistake such a fellow for your brother. Any tall, muscular man with ebony skin, glimpsed at a distance –"

"But it wasn't a glimpse! I saw him clearly –"

"You said a cart blocked the way."

"That was *after* I saw him, when I tried to move towards him. Before that, I saw him as clearly as I'm seeing you now. I saw his face! It was Zanziba I saw!"

I considered this for a long moment. "Perhaps, Zuleika, you saw his lemur. You wouldn't be the first person to see the restless spirit of a loved one wandering the streets of Rome in broad daylight."

She shook her head. "I saw a man, not a lemur."

"But how do you know?"

"He was buying a plum from a vendor. Tell me, Gordianus: do lemures eat plums?"

I tried to dissuade her from hiring me by naming the same fee I would have asked from Cicero, but she agreed to the figure at once, and paid me a first instalment on the spot. Zuleika seemed quite proud of her financial resources.

It was her idea that we should begin our search in Rome, and I agreed, duly making the rounds of the usual eyes and ears. I quickly discovered that a large Nubian of Zanziba's description had indeed been seen around the marketplace, but no one could identify the man and no one knew where he'd come from, or where he'd gone. Zuleika wanted to visit every hostel and tavern in the city, but I counselled patience; put out a reward for information, I told her, and the information would come to us. Sure enough, a few days later, a street-sweeper in the Subura arrived at my door with word that the Nubian I was seeking had spent a single night at a seedy little hostel off the Street of the Coppersmiths, but had given no name and had moved on the next day.

Again I counselled patience. But days passed with no new information, and Zuleika grew impatient to commence with the next obvious step: to pay a call on Ahala, Zanziba's *lanista*, the man who had turned her away when she tried to see her brother's corpse. I remained dubious, but made preparations for the journey. Ravenna is a long way from Rome, especially when the traveller suspects in his heart of hearts that at journey's end lies bitter disappointment.

Zuleika travelled with me and paid all expenses – sometimes with coins, but more often, I suspected, by exchanging favours with tavern keepers along the way, or by plying her trade with other guests. How she made her living was her business. I minded my own.

During the day, we rode on horseback. Zuleika was no stranger to horses. One of her brother's acrobatic tricks had been to stand upright on the back of a cantering horse, and she had learned to do so as well. She offered to show me, but I dissuaded her; if she fell and broke her neck, who would pay my way home?

She was a good conversationalist, a skill that no doubt contributed to her ability to make a decent living; men pay for pleasure, but come back for good company. To pass the hours, we talked a great deal about Alexandria, where I had lived for a while when I was young. I was amused to hear her impressions of the teeming city and its risible inhabitants. In return, I told her the tale of the Alexandrian cat, whose killer I had discovered, and the terrible revenge exacted by the cat-worshipping mob of the city.

I was also intrigued by her newcomer's impressions of Rome and Italy. Her search for Zanziba had taken her to many places and her livelihood had acquainted her with men from all levels of society. She knew both the city and the countryside, and due to the nature of her search she had inadvertently become something of an expert on the state of gladiators.

"Do you know the strongest impression I have of this land of yours?" she said one day, as we passed a gang of slaves working in a field along the Flaminian Way. "Too many slaves!"

I shrugged. "There are slaves in Alexandria, too. There are slaves in every city and every country."

"Perhaps, but it's different here. Maybe it's because the Romans have conquered so many other people, and become so wealthy, and brought in so many slaves from so many places. In Egypt, there are small farmers all along the Nile; they may own slaves, but they also till the earth themselves. Everyone pulls together; in years of a good inundation, everyone eats well, and in years when the Nile runs low, everyone eats less. Here, it seems to me the farmers are all rich men who live in the city, and slaves do every bit of the work, and the free men who should be farmers are all in Rome, crowded into tenements and living off the dole. It doesn't seem right."

"The farms are run well enough, I suppose."

"Are they? Then why does Rome import so much grain from Egypt? Look at how these field slaves are treated – how shabbily they're dressed, how skinny they are, how hard they're made to work, even under this blistering sun. An Egyptian farmer would be out in the fields alongside his slaves, pushing them to work harder, yes, but also seeing just how hard they do work, and making sure they're healthy and well-fed so they're fit to work the next day, too. To an Egyptian, slaves are a valuable investment, and you don't squander them. Here, there's a different attitude: work a slave as hard as you can, invest as little as possible in his upkeep, and when you've used him up, dispose of him and get another, because slaves are cheap and Rome's provinces provide an endless supply."

As if to illustrate her point, we passed a huddled figure in the gutter alongside the road, a creature so shrivelled and filthy that I could tell neither its age nor its sex – an abandoned slave, kicked out by its master, no doubt. As we passed by, the creature croaked a few unintelligible words and extended a claw-like hand. Zuleika reached into her travelling bag and threw the unfortunate a crust of bread left over from her breakfast.

"Too many slaves," she repeated. "And far too many gladiators! I can scarcely believe how many camps full of gladiators I had occasion to visit since I arrived here. So many captured warriors, from so many conquered lands, all flowing into Italy. What to do with them all? Put on gladiator games and make them fight each other to the death! Put on a show with six gladiators, and three will likely be dead by the end of the day. But ten more will arrive the next day, bought cheap at auction! Not all of them are good fighters, of course; the ones who turn out to be clumsy or cowardly or near-sighted can be sent off to a farm or a ship's galley or the mines. The ones who remain have to be outfitted and trained, and fed reasonably well to keep them strong.

"That's how the *best* camps are run. But those *lanistas* charge a lot of money to hire out their gladiators. Not everyone can afford the best, but every Roman wants to host games at his father's funeral, even if it's only a single pair of fighters spilling each other's blood in a sheep pen while the family sit on the fence and cheer. So there's a market for gladiators who can be hired cheaply. You can imagine how those gladiators are kept – fed slop and housed in pens, like animals. But their lives are more miserable than any animal's, because animals don't fall asleep at night wondering if the next day they'll die a horrible death for a stranger's amusement. Such gladiators are poorly trained and armed with the cheapest weapons. Can you imagine a fight to the death where both men are armed with nothing better than wooden swords? There's no way to make a clean, quick kill; the result is a cruel, bloody farce. I've seen such a death-match with my own eyes. I didn't know which man to pity more, the one who died, or the one who had to take the other's life using such a crude weapon."

She shook her head. "So many gladiators, scattered all over Italy, all trained to kill without mercy. So many weapons within easy reach. So much misery. I think, some day, there may be a reckoning."

When we reached the outskirts of Ravenna, I asked a man on the road for directions to the gladiator camp of the *lanista* Ahala.

The man eyed the two of us curiously for a moment, then saw the iron citizen's ring on my finger. "On the far side of town you'll come to a big oak tree where the road forks. Take the left branch for another mile. But unless you've come to hire some of his gladiators, I'd stay clear of the place. Unfriendly. Guard dogs. High fences."

"To keep the gladiators in?"

"To keep everybody else out! A while back, a neighbour's slave wandered onto the property. One of those dogs tore his leg off. Fellow bled to death. Ahala refused to make restitution. He doesn't like folks coming 'round."

Leaving Zuleika at a hostel near the town forum, I made my way alone to the oak tree on the far side of town and took the branch to the left. After a mile or so, just as the man had said, a rutted dirt road branched off the stone-paved highway. I followed the road around a bend and came to a gateway that appeared to mark the boundary of Ahala's property. The structure itself was probably enough to keep out most unwanted visitors. Nailed to the two upright posts were various bones bleached white by the sun, and adorning the beam above my head was a collection of human skulls.

I passed through the gate and rode on for another mile or so, through a landscape of thickets and wild brush. At last I arrived at a compound surrounded by a high palisade of sharpened stakes. From within I heard a man's voice shouting commands, and the clatter of wood striking wood – gladiators drilling with practice swords, I presumed. I heard other, more incongruous noises – the bleating of sheep and goats, a smith's hammer, and the sound of men laughing, not in a harsh or mean-spirited way, but quite boisterously. I approached a door in the palisade, but had no chance to knock; on the other side, so close and with such ferocity that I jerked back and my heart skipped a beat, dogs began to bark and jump against the gate, scraping their claws against the wood.

A shouting voice chastised the dogs, who stopped barking. A peep-hole opened in the gate, so high up that I assumed the man beyond was standing on a stool. Two blood-shot eyes peered down at me.

"Who are you and what do you want?"

"Is this the gladiator camp of Ahala?"

"Who wants to know?"

"Are you Ahala?"

"Who's asking?"

"My name is Gordianus. I've come all the way from Rome."

"Have you, indeed?"

"I saw some of your gladiators perform at Saturnia a while back."

"Did you, now?"

"I was most impressed."

"Were you?"

"More to the point," I said, improvising, "my good friend Marcus Tullius Cicero was impressed."

"Cicero, you say?"

"You've heard of him, I presume? Cicero's a man to be reckoned with, a rising politician and a very famous advocate who handles the legal affairs of some of the most powerful families in Rome."

The man lifted an eyebrow. "Don't think much of politicians and lawyers."

"No? Well, as a rule, Cicero doesn't think much of funeral games. But he thought your men put on quite a show." So far, everything I had said was true; when lying, I have found it best to begin with the truth and embellish only as necessary. "In his line of work, Cicero is frequently called upon to advise the bereaved. On legal matters such as wills, you

understand. But they often ask his advice about all sorts of
other things – such as who to call upon to produce a truly
memorable afternoon of funeral games."

"I see. So this Cicero thought my boys put on a memorable show?"

"He did indeed. And as I happened to be coming to
Ravenna on business of my own, and as you happen to have
your camp here, I promised my good friend Cicero that I
would call on you if I had a chance, to see what sort of
operation you run – how many gladiators you've got, how
long you've been in business, how much you charge, that sort
of thing."

The man nodded. The peep-hole banged shut. The barking resumed, but receded into the distance, as if someone
were dragging the dogs elsewhere. A bolt was thrown back.
The gate swung open.

"Ahala – *lanista* – at your service." I had assumed the
speaker was standing on something to reach the peephole,
but I was wrong. Towering over me was a grizzled, hulking
giant of a man. He looked like a gladiator himself, though few
gladiators live long enough to attain such a magnificent mane
of grey hair. Was Ahala the exception? It was not entirely
unheard of for a fighter to survive long enough to buy his
freedom and become a professional trainer; it was far less
common for such a survivor to become the owner of a cadre
of gladiators, as Ahala apparently was. Whatever his origins
and history, he was obviously smarter than his lumbering
physique and terse manner might suggest.

"Come in," he said. "Have a look around."

The compound within the palisade included several barn-
like buildings set close together, separated by garden plots
and pens for horses, goats and sheep.

"You raise livestock," I said.

"Gladiators eat a lot of meat."

"And you grow your own garlic, I see."

"Gives the fellows extra strength."

"So I've heard." Whole treatises had been written about the proper care and feeding of gladiators.

At a shouted command, the clatter of wooden weapons resumed. The noise seemed to come from beyond another palisade of sharpened stakes. "This is the outer compound," Ahala explained. "Gladiators are kept in the inner compound. Safer that way, especially for visitors like you. Wouldn't want you to end up with your skull decorating that gate out by the highway."

I smiled uncertainly, not entirely sure the man was joking. "Still, I'd like to have a look at the gladiators."

"In a bit. Show you the armoury first. Explain how I do business." He led me into a long, low shed festooned with chains, upon which were hung all manner of helmets, greaves, swords, shields and tridents. There were also a number of devices I didn't recognize, including some tubes made of metal and wood that looked as if they might fit into a man's mouth. Ahala saw me looking at them, but offered no explanation. Some of the weapons also looked a bit odd to me. I reached out to touch a hanging sword, but Ahala seized my wrist.

"You'll cut yourself," he grumbled, then ushered me to the far end of the shed, where a trio of smiths in leather aprons were hammering a red-hot piece of metal.

"You make your own weapons?" I asked.

"Sometimes. A customized fit can make the difference between a good fighter and a great one. Mostly I keep these fellows busy with repairs and alterations. I like to keep the armoury in tip-top shape."

He led me past the smiths, into another shed where carpenters were whittling wood into pegs. "Amphitheatre seeds, I call those," said Ahala with a laugh. "Some of the people who hire me want a temporary arena built especially for the games. Maybe they need to seat a hundred people, maybe a thousand. My carpenters can throw up a decent amphitheatre practically overnight, provided there's a good source of local timber. Client pays for the materials, of course. But I've found it saves time and considerable expense if I've got nails and pegs ready to go. All a part of a complete package."

I nodded. "I'd never thought of that – the added expense of erecting a place to put on the games."

Ahala shrugged. "Funeral games don't come cheap."

We passed through a small slaughterhouse where the carcass of a sheep had been hung for butchering. Certain parts of previously slaughtered animals that might normally have been discarded had been saved and hung to dry. I stepped towards the back corner of the room to have a closer look, but Ahala gripped my elbow.

"You wanted to see the fighters. Step this way."

He led me to a gate in the inner palisade, lifted the bar and opened the narrow door. "That way, to your right, are the barracks, where they eat and sleep. The training area is this way. Visitor coming!" he shouted. We walked through a covered passage and emerged on a sandy square open to the sky, where five pairs of men abruptly pulled apart and raised their wooden practice swords in a salute to their *lanista*.

"Carry on!" barked Ahala.

The men resumed their mock-battles, banging swords against shields.

"I thought . . ."

"You thought we'd be above them, looking down, like in an amphitheatre?" said Ahala.

"Yes."

He chuckled. "We don't stage exhibition bouts here. Only

way to see the training area is to walk right in. Stand closer if
you want. Smell the sweat. Look them eye-to-eye."

I felt acutely vulnerable. I was used to seeing gladiators at
a distance, in the arena. To stand among them, with nothing
between them and me, was like entering a cage full of wild
animals. Even the shortest man among them was a head taller
than me. All ten wore helmets, but were otherwise naked.
Apparently they were training to receive blows to the head,
because their rhythmic exercise consisted of exchanging
repeated blows to each other's helmets. The blows were
relatively gentle, but the racket was unnerving.

From his physique, I thought I recognized at least one of
the gladiators from the games at Saturnia, the bull-necked
Thracian who had triumphed in the opening bout. About the
others I was less sure.

"I wonder, do you have any Nubians among your men?"

Ahala raised an eyebrow. "Why do you ask?"

"There was a Nubian that day in Saturnia, a *retiarius*.
Cicero took particular note of him – 'just the sort of exotic
touch to ensure a memorable day,' he said."

Ahala nodded. "A *retiarius*? Ah, yes, I remember now.
That fellow's dead, of course. But it just so happens that I *do*
have another Nubian in the troupe. Tall, strapping fellow
like the one you saw."

"Also a *retiarius*?"

"He can fight with net and trident, certainly. All my
gladiators are trained to be versatile. They can fight in
whatever style you wish."

"Yes, it's all about giving the spectators what they want,
isn't it? Delivering a thrill and an eyeful." I watched the
practising pairs of gladiators advance and retreat, advance
and retreat with the rhythmic precision of acrobats. "Can I
see this Nubian?" I said.

"See him train, you mean?"

"Yes, why not?"

Ahala called to an assistant. "Bring the Nubian. This man wants to see him train with net and trident." He turned back to me. "While we wait, I'll explain how I calculate my prices, depending on the size of funeral games you need . . ."

For the next few moments I had to struggle to keep my face a blank; I'd never imagined that funeral games could be so costly. To be sure, a *lanista* faced considerable expenses, but I suspected that Ahala was making a considerable profit as well. Was that why Zanziba had come to him, because Ahala had the wherewithal to pay him handsomely?

"Are they all slaves?" I asked, interrupting Ahala as he was reciting a complicated formula for payment on instalment plans.

"What's that?"

"Your gladiators – are they all slaves? One hears occasionally of free men who hire themselves out as gladiators. They make good money, I'm told. Have their choice of women, too."

"Are you thinking of taking it up?" He looked me up and down and laughed, rather unkindly, I thought.

"No. I'm merely curious. That Nubian who fought in Saturnia, for example –"

"Who cares about him?" snapped Ahala. "Gone to Hades!" He scowled, then brightened. "Ah, here's his replacement."

Seen at such close quarters, the *retiarius* who entered the training area was a magnificent specimen of a man, tall and broad and elegantly proportioned. He immediately engaged in a mock combat with the gladiator who had accompanied him, putting on a lively demonstration for my benefit. Was it the same Nubian I had seen in Saturnia? I thought so – or was I doing what I had accused Zuleika of doing, seeing what I wanted or expected to see?

"Enough fighting!" I said. "I want to see his face."

"His face?" Ahala stared at me, perplexed.

"I've seen a Nubian fight – I've seen one die, at Saturnia – but I've never seen one this close, face-to-face. Indulge my curiosity, *lanista*. Show me the fellow's face."

"Very well." At Ahala's signal, the gladiators drew apart. Ahala beckoned the Nubian to come to us. "Take off your helmet," he said.

The Nubian put aside his weapons, removed his helmet and stood naked before me. I had never seen the face of the Nubian who fought in Saturnia. I had never seen Zanziba's face. But those two brown eyes which stared back at me – had I seen before? Were they Zuleika's soulful eyes, set in a man's face? Was this the face of her brother Zanziba? The high cheekbones were much the same, as were the broad nose and forehead. But I could not be sure.

"What is your name, gladiator?"

He hesitated, as slaves not used to being addressed by strangers often do. He glanced at Ahala, then looked straight ahead. "Chiron," he said.

"Like the centaur? A good name for a gladiator, I suppose. Were you born with that name?"

Again he hesitated and glanced at Ahala. "I don't know."

"Where do you come from?"

"I . . . don't know."

"How odd. And how long have you been at this camp, with Ahala as your *lanista*?"

"I . . ."

"Enough of this!" snapped Ahala. "Can't you see the fellow's simple-minded? But he's a damned good fighter, I guarantee. If you want the personal history of each and every gladiator, put some sesterces on my table first and hire them! Now the tour is over. I've other things to do. If your friend Cicero or some of his rich clients have need of funeral games, they'll know where to find me. You men, get back to your training. Gordianus, allow me to show you the way out."

As the gate to the compound slammed shut behind me, the dogs, silent throughout my visit, recommenced their barking.

"It's him!" insisted Zuleika. "It must be. Describe him again, Gordianus."

"Zuleika, I've described the man to you a dozen times. Neither of us can say if it was Zanziba I saw, or not."

"It *was* him. I know it was. But if he died in Saturnia, how can be alive now?"

"That's a very good question. But I have a suspicion . . ."

"You know something you're not telling me. You saw something, there in the compound!"

"Perhaps. I'll have to go back and have another look, to be sure."

"When?"

I sighed, looking around the little room we had been given to share at the hostel in Ravenna. It was a plain room with two hard beds, a small lamp and a single chamber pot, but to my weary eyes, as the long summer day faded to twilight, it looked very inviting. "Tonight, I suppose. Might as well get it over with."

"What if the *lanista* won't let you in?"

"I don't intend to ask him."

"You're going to sneak in? But how?"

"I do have *some* experience at this sort of thing, Zuleika. I noticed a particular spot in the palisade where the posts are a bit shorter than elsewhere. If I climb over at that point, and manage not to impale myself, I think I can drop right onto the roof of the slaughterhouse. From there I can easily climb down –"

"But the dogs! You heard dogs barking. The man on the road said a dog tore a slave's leg off."

I cleared my throat. "Yes, well, the dogs do pose a challenge. But I think I know, from the sound of their barking, where their kennel is located. That's why I bought those pieces of meat at the butcher shop near the forum this afternoon; and why I travel with that small pouch full of various powders and potions. In my line of work, you never know when you might have need of a powerful soporific. A few pieces of steak, generously dusted with pulverized harpy root and tossed over the palisade . . ."

"But even if you put the dogs to sleep, there are all those gladiators, men who've been trained to kill –"

"I shall carry a dagger for self-defence."

"A dagger! From the way you describe Ahala, the *lanista* himself could kill you with his bare hands." She shook her head. "You'll be taking a terrible risk, Gordianus."

"That's what you're paying me for, Zuleika."

"I should go with you."

"Absolutely not!

Some distance from the compound, I tethered my horse to a stunted tree and proceeded on foot. Hours past midnight, the half-moon was low in the sky. It shed just enough light for me to cautiously pick my way, while casting ample shadows to offer concealment.

The compound was quiet and dark; gladiators need their sleep. As I drew near the palisade, one of the dogs began to bark. I tossed bits of steak over the wall. The barking immediately ceased, followed by slavering sounds, followed by silence.

The climb over the palisade was easier than I expected. A running start, a quick scamper up the rough bark of the poles, a leap of faith over the sharp spikes, and I landed solidly atop the roof of the slaughterhouse, making only a faint, plunking noise. I paused for breath, listening intently.

From outside the compound I heard a quiet, scurrying noise – some nocturnal animal, I presumed – but within the compound there was only a deep silence.

I climbed off the roof and proceeded quickly to the gate that opened into the inner compound, where the gladiators were quartered. As I suspected, it was unbarred. At night, the men inside were free to come and go at will.

I returned to the slaughterhouse and stepped inside. As I had thought, the organs I had seen hanging to dry in the back corner were bladders harvested from slaughtered beasts. I took one down and examined it in the moonlight. Ahala was a frugal man; this bladder already had been used at least once, and was ready to be used again. The opening had been stitched shut but then carefully unstitched; a gash in the side had been repaired with some particularly fine stitch work. The inside of the bladder had been thoroughly cleaned, but by the moonlight I thought I could nonetheless discern bits of dried blood within.

I left the slaughterhouse and made my way to the armoury shed, by night a hanging forest of weird shapes. Navigating through the darkness amid dangling helmets and swords, I located one of the peculiar wood and metal tubes I had noticed earlier. I hefted the object in my hand, then put it in my mouth. I blew through it, cautiously, quietly – and even so, gave myself a fright, so uncanny was the gurgling death-rattle that emerged from the tube.

It frightened the other person in the shed, as well; for I was not alone. A silhouette behind me gave a start, whirled about and collided with a hanging helmet. The helmet knocked against a shield with a loud, clanging noise. The silhouette staggered back and collided with more pieces of hanging armour, knocking some from their hooks and sending them clattering across the floor.

The cacophony roused at least one of the drugged canines.

From the kennel I heard a blood-curdling howl. A moment later, a man began to shout an alarm.

"Gordianus! Where are you?" The stumbling, confused silhouette had a voice.

"Zuleika! I told you not to follow me!"

"All these hanging swords, like a bloody maze – Hades! I've cut myself . . ."

Perhaps it was her blood that attracted the beast. I saw its silhouette enter from the direction of the kennels and career towards us, like a missile shot from a sling. The snarling creature took a flying leap and knocked Zuleika to the ground. She screamed.

Suddenly there were others in the armoury – not dogs, but men. "Was that a woman?" one of them muttered.

The dog snarled. Zuleika screamed again.

"Zuleika!" I cried.

"Did he say . . . *Zuleika*?" One of the men – tall, broad, majestic in silhouette – broke away from the others and ran towards her. Seizing a hanging trident, he drove it into the snarling dog – then gave a cry of exasperation and cast the trident aside. "Numa's balls, I grabbed one of the fakes! Somebody hand me a *real* weapon!"

I was closest. I reached into my tunic, pulled out my dagger and thrust it into his hand. He swooped down. The dog gave a single plaintive yelp, then went limp. The man scooped up the lifeless dog and thrust it aside.

"Zuleika!" he cried.

"Zanziba?" she answered, her voice weak.

In blood, fear and darkness, the siblings were reunited.

The danger was not over, but just beginning; for having discovered the secret of Ahala's gladiator camp, how could I be allowed to live? Their success – indeed, their survival – depended on absolute secrecy.

If Zuleika had not followed me, I would have climbed over the palisade and ridden back to Ravenna, satisfied that I knew the truth and reasonably certain that the Nubian I had seen earlier that day was indeed Zanziba, still very much alive. For my suspicion had been confirmed: Ahala and his gladiators had learned to cheat death. The bouts they staged at funeral games looked real, but in fact were shams, not spontaneous but very carefully choreographed. When they appeared to bleed, the blood was animal blood that spurted from animal bladders concealed under their scanty armour or loincloths, or from the hollow, blood-filled tips of weapons with retractable points, cleverly devised by Ahala's smiths; when they appeared to expire, the death rattles that issued from their throats actually came from sound-makers like the one I had blown through. No doubt there were many other tricks of their trade which I had not discovered with my cursory inspection, or even conceived of; they were seasoned professionals, after all, an experienced troupe of acrobats, actors and mimes making a very handsome living by pretending to be a troupe of gladiators.

Any doubt was dispelled when I was dragged from the armoury into the open and surrounded by a ring of naked, rudely-awakened men. The torches in their hands turned night to day and lit up the face of Zuleika, who lay bleeding but alive on the sand, attended by an unflappable, grey-bearded physician; it made sense that Ahala's troupe would have a skilled doctor among them, to attend to accidents and injuries.

Among the assembled gladiators, I was quite sure I saw the tall, lumbering Samnite who had "died" in Saturnia, along with the shorter, stockier Thracian who had "killed" him – and who had put on such a convincing show of tottering off-balance and almost impaling himself on the Samnite's upright sword. I also saw the two *dimacheri* who had put on such a show with their flashing daggers that the spectators had spared them both. There was the red-headed Gaul who had delivered the "death-blow" to Zanziba – and there was Zanziba himself, hovering fretfully over his sister and the physician attending to her.

"I can't understand it," the physician finally announced. "The dog should have torn her limb from limb, but he seems hardly to have broken the skin. The beast must have been dazed – or drugged." He shot a suspicious glance at me. "At any rate, she's lost very little blood. The wounds are shallow, and I've cleaned them thoroughly. Unless an infection sets in, that should be the end of it. Your sister is a lucky woman."

The physician stepped back and Zanziba knelt over her. "Zuleika! How did you find me?"

"The gods led me to you," she whispered.

I cleared my throat.

"With some help from the Finder," she added. "It *was* you I saw at the funeral games in Saturnia that day?"

"Yes."

"And then again in Rome?"

He nodded. "I was there very briefly, some days ago, then came straight back to Ravenna."

"But Zanziba, why didn't you send for me?"

He sighed. "When I sent you the money, I was in great despair. I expected every day to be my last. I moved from place to place, plying my trade as a gladiator, expecting death but handing it out to others instead. Then I fell in with these fellows, and everything changed." He smiled and gestured to the men around him. "A company of free men, all experienced gladiators, who've realized that it simply isn't necessary to kill or be killed to put on a good show for the spectators. Ahala is our leader, but he's only first among equals. We all pull together. After I joined these fellows, I *did* send for you – I sent a letter to your old master in

Alexandria, but he had no idea where you'd gone. I had no way to find you. I thought we'd lost each other forever."

Regaining her strength, Zuleika rose onto her elbows. "Your fighting is all illusion, then?"

Her brother grinned. "The Romans have a saying: a gladiator dies only once. But I've died in the arena many, many times! And been paid quite handsomely for it."

I shook my head. "The game you're playing is incredibly dangerous."

"Not as dangerous as being a real gladiator," said Zanziba.

"You've pulled it off so far," I said. "But the more famous this troupe becomes, the more widely you travel and the more people who see you – some of them on more than one occasion – the harder it will become to maintain the deception. The risk of discovery will grow greater each time you perform. If you're found out, you'll be charged with sacrilege, at the very least. Romans save their cruellest punishments for that sort of crime."

"You're talking to men who've stared death in the face many times," growled Ahala. "We have nothing to lose. But you, Gordianus, on the other hand . . ."

"He'll have to die," said one of the men. "Like the others who've discovered our secret."

"The skulls decorating the gateway?" I said.

Ahala nodded grimly.

"But we can't kill him!" protested Zanziba.

"He lied about his purpose in coming here," said Ahala.

"But his purpose was to bring Zuleika to me . . ."

So began the debate over what to do with me, which lasted through the night. In the end, as was their custom, they decided by voting. I was locked away while the deliberations took place. What was said, I never knew; but at daybreak I was released, and after making me pledge never to betray them, Ahala showed me to the gate.

"Zuleika is staying?" I said.

He nodded.

"How did the voting go?"

"The motion to release you was decided by a bare majority of one."

"That close? How did you vote, Ahala?"

"Do you really want to know?"

The look on his face told me I didn't.

I untethered my horse and rode quickly away, never looking back.

On my first day back in Rome, I saw Cicero in the Forum. I tried to avoid him, but he made a bee-line for me, smiling broadly.

"Well-met, Gordianus! Except for this beastly weather. Not yet noon, and already a scorcher. Reminds me of the last time I saw you, at those funeral games in Saturnia. Do you remember?"

"Of course," I said.

"What fine games those were!"

"Yes," I agreed, a bit reluctantly.

"But do you know, since then I've seen some even more spectacular funeral games. It was down in Capua. Amazing fighters! The star of the show was a fellow with some barbaric Thracian name. What was it, now? Ah, yes: Spartacus, they called him. Like the city of warriors, Sparta. A good name for a gladiator, eh?"

I nodded, and quickly changed the subject. But for some reason, the name Cicero had spoken stuck in my mind. As Zuleika had said, how strange are the coincidences dropped in our paths by the gods; for in a matter of days, that name would be on the lips of everyone in Rome and all over Italy.

For that was the month that the great slave revolt began,

led by Spartacus and his rebel gladiators. It would last for many months, spreading conflagration and chaos all over Italy. It would take me to the Bay of Neapolis for my first fateful meeting with Rome's richest man, Marcus Licinius Crassus, and a household of ninety-nine slaves all marked for death; but that is another story.

What became of Zanziba and Zuleika? In the ensuing months of warfare and panic, I lost track of them, but thought of them often. I especially remembered Zuleika's comments on Roman slavery. Were her sympathies enflamed by the revolt? Did she manage to persuade her brother and his comrades, if indeed they needed persuading, to join the revolt and take up arms against Rome? If they did, then almost certainly things went badly for them; for eventually Spartacus and his followers were trapped and defeated, hunted and slaughtered like animals and crucified by the thousands.

After the revolt was over and the countryside gradually returned to normal, I eventually had occasion to travel to Ravenna again. I rode out to the site of Ahala's compound. The gate of bones was still there, but worn and weathered and tilted to one side, on the verge of collapsing. The palisade was intact, but the gate stood open. No weapons hung in the armoury. The animals' pens were empty. Spider webs filled the slaughterhouse. The gladiator quarters were abandoned.

And then, many months later, from across the sea I received a letter on papyrus, written by a hired Egyptian scribe:

To Gordianus, Finder and Friend: By the will of the gods, we find ourselves back in Alexandria. What a civilized place this seems, after Rome! The tale of our adventures in Italy would fill a book; suffice to say that we escaped by the skin of our teeth. Many of our comrades, including Ahala, were not so lucky.

We have saved enough money to buy passage back to our native land. In the country of our ancestors, we hope to find family and make new friends. What appalling tales we shall have to tell of the strange lands we visited; and of those lands, surely none was stranger or more barbaric than Rome! But to you it is home, Gordianus, and we wish you all happiness there. Farewell from your friends, Zuleika and her brother Zanziba.

For many years I have saved that scrap of papyrus. I shall never throw it away.

The Hostage to Fortune

Michael Jecks

We move forwards some eighteen years to Caesar's invasion of Britain, a troubling enough time without having a murder to investigate. This is Michael Jecks's first venture into the Roman world. He is best known for his series of mysteries set on Dartmoor in the fourteenth century featuring Bailiff Simon Puttock and the disgruntled Sir Baldwin Furnshill, which began with The Last Templar *(1995).*

There are days when you wake up and you know, you just *know*, that this one's going to be a bastard.

All right. As a soldier, you get used to bad days. There are days when you have to stand watch all night, days when you have to break camp and carry all your belongings miles to some other gods-forsaken spot, days when you're detailed to dig the new latrines, or clear the old ones . . . Yes, as a legionnaire, you get enough shitty days for the average lifetime. And every so often there are the other days, when you get to do what the citizens back home expect you're doing the whole time, and risk getting a blade in the guts or an arrow in the face as your glorious general orders you to shove some barbaric, painted scum from some boggy wasteland just so that the general can claim his glory. They're all bastards, believe me. Especially generals. They're no better than any other politicians.

Not that my low estimation of the intelligence and ability of the average general has anything to do with this particular bad day. No. This bad day was caused by my own mates. For my offences against the gods, which must be many, as soon as my comrades learned that I had some education, they elected me as their own private leader. Silly sods.

And now these same silly sods had let the King's son die.

King? He was a chieftain of the Britons; one of those with a tongue-breaking name that any sensible man would refuse to try to repeat. There never seemed much point. The bastards were never around for long. Either they'd submit to our authority, or they'd die. Either way, they wouldn't be with the army for long.

His son was taken to ensure his father's good behaviour, along with eight other close relatives: some other of the chieftain's family, including his own brother, and so on. We didn't piss about when it came to taking folks. And now, as I stared down at his bloody body, a great gash in his chest like a second sodding mouth, I knew that my mates and me were all in trouble. We'd been in charge of this pen of hostages, my mates had all been guarding them, and me? I'd bloody fallen asleep, hadn't I, with no chance of an excuse if our general got to hear of it.

Not that I was safe anyway. Not with the most important hostage, the second in line after the tribal chief, lying dead on the packed earth in front of me.

Of course, you'd think that he was killed by someone left in that stockade with him, wouldn't you? But I knew that the first thing a hostage learned was, no knives, no swords, nothing. They'd have been patted down before they were put in our stockade. And when the body was found, my boys would have searched the lot of them for a weapon. Since they had all been frisked and checked clear before they'd been allowed through the door, it wasn't much of a surprise to learn that they were all clean.

Yup. No weapons in there. Other than the good old Roman ones in my lads' hands.

I guess I should explain what we were doing there.

It was already late in the year when the army was sent on its recce of Britain. Two legions had been selected for this operation: mine, the VIIth, and another well-blooded legion, the Xth. I had only just joined. A free man, I had little cash, and couldn't join one of the greater cohorts. No, I was stuck in the mob called the *"velites"* of the VIIth legion. The cohorts weren't split into the four groups now, but the front line, the skirmishers, still got that nickname. *Velites* – men with little money and no standing. I suited them perfectly. And, my, wasn't I glad to learn that I was to be attached to the force going over the sea to attack a land filled with hordes of particularly vicious pagans. I had hardly learned how to use my *gladius* or *pilum* when I was told I was to go.

The men of my band were a shabby lot. We all had the same woollen tunic, leather coat reinforced with bands of steel, leather caps, greaves, a cloak and all the paraphernalia of a soldier, but somehow my companions managed to make all appear filthy and worn, no matter how new it might be.

Here in the hostages' pen at least they looked smarter because of the comparison with our prisoners.

They were an odd assortment. The king's relations had uniformly broad shoulders, but they weren't tall, and their rickety legs spoke of malnutrition. Two had lost a lot of teeth; I think it was the scurvy got them because of bad harvests. The way these natives tried to farm was laughable, and many starved even when the weather was kind. All were tattooed, with various black and green swirls adorning their cheeks, foreheads, arms and breasts. God knows why pagans do that. It must hurt like hell.

The dead boy's uncle (he had a very long name – I'll call him "Verc" because that's the nearest I can get to it) was at his side, tears of rage dropping from his sallow cheeks. He was heavily tattooed, with the drawn features of a man who has suffered hunger and the pain of loss. Deep-set eyes met mine unflinchingly. Behind him were the cousins of the dead man, as though ordered away, so that Verc could denounce us and demand compensation without risking their lives. I felt a fleeting respect for him at the sight.

One, a lad called "Trin" by us, stood back at the wall, his black eyes restless, going from one to another of us, like a man who was about to spring an attack, and I gripped my sword more tightly as I met his gaze. The stupid arse was actually thinking of making a break for it, and I motioned with my hand to the men behind me to block the entrance. There was a sturdy gate for the stockade, and my lads pulled it across quickly, the guards remaining outside sliding the bar across to lock it. Only then did the lad seem to realize he had no escape. Like a trapped dog, he glared and walked up and down, but made no attempt on us.

There were three in there who were my own personal comrades. Pugio, named after the dagger made from a cut-down *gladius*, was well named. Short, dark, wiry, with high cheekbones and narrow features, his eyes were suspicious and sharp in a face already scarred from a hundred fights; he was as unforgiving as a whore from Syracuse. Quick to anger, it took the three of us to calm him when he felt insulted. Once, I remember all of us dragging him to the ground when he thought a man cursing a dog had referred to his own ancestry. The man had been a legionnaire, but that wouldn't hold him back, not Pugio. If he thought he'd been maligned, he would strike. But for all that, Pugio was loyal and steadfast as I had learned during the landing from the sea. If you were standing in line waiting for the enemy, you didn't want a better man at your side.

Certainly he was better than the man we all called Consul. He was a languid, tall, well-bred man, with the ability to sneer at his superiors without their being able to respond, he was so careful in his language. His hair was a peculiar light shade, and some had said that his mother had been a slave from one of the northern tribes, which maybe explained his pale complexion too, but I don't know. He never spoke to me of his family. When we hunkered down around the fire at night, there were better things to discuss. Women, booze . . . you know the sort of stuff. I always reckoned he had a miserable time of it, because he seemed to have some breeding. Know what I mean? He was from a leading family, all right. That's what I thought.

And then there was As, named after the tiny coin. It takes sixteen copper "as" to make one *denarius*, so you can guess what he was like. Short, stunted, permanently sniffing as though he had a cold, always pot-bellied, with a pair of broken teeth in the front of his mouth when he smiled, breath reeking, he was the worst nightmare of a decent centurion, which was why our own averted his gaze whenever he caught sight of As. The little man was perpetually grinning. Oddly, he hardly looked a professional killing machine. Not many of us did. That meant keeping clean and weapons shining. None of us could manage that in a good summer, let alone at the grim beginning of a damp winter. At least with his clear grey eyes gazing out from his pox-scarred face he looked like a killer of sorts, especially when you saw the lunatic expression in his face. It wasn't his fault, but he was dim to the point of real stupidity, and that look can scare the bravest. He had the *look* of a man who enjoyed killing for killing's sake. It took a brave man to stand in front of him.

Yet for all his apparent murderousness, he wasn't really violent. The only fights he ever got into were the ones he was supposed to: protecting the legion's honour, or saving his mates when they were drunk and legionnaires from another cohort started ripping into us.

Mind you, then he was a demon.

The boy was lying on his back when I first saw him. He'd been on his face before, I saw, because nearby was the starting point of all the blood. It lay in a vast puddle, soaking into the ground, and the little shack reeked of it.

I never knew his name. All about him were the other hostages, and the one who squatted like an animal was Verc, eyeing me with unblinking rage. The others behind him were snivelling. As the gate shut, Verc rose to his feet, his tattooed face working with fury. He shouted at me, pointing at the boy, then shouted again, spittle flying. Even as I sighed and bellowed for a translator, I knew it was unnecessary. This big bastard with the mudstained shirt and britches was asking what value were my sureties now, since one of the lads had already started killing the hostages.

He was a good-looking boy, too, the dead one. The sort a man would have been proud of. Wide mouth, broad forehead, strong chin, exactly the sort that the matrons would go for in the gladiators' ring. His hair was a dusky brown, the still-open eyes dark and serious, but there was a bit of a smile at the corner of his mouth.

"Some reckon that when a man dies, you can see the face of the last person he saw in his eyes," As said.

"Bollocks," Consul said. "Do you see the slaughterman's face in the boar's head when it's carried to your table?"

"Never had a boar's head," As said glumly, but then shot a vicious glance at his elegant companion. "Not being a fucking patrician like you."

"Shut it, both of you," I snapped, but I studied the body. All I could see in his eyes was a certain calmness, as though he'd thought he was about to go to sleep. It meant nothing. Trouble was, I was depressed. The only men who could have done this were behind me. My own group. All the hostages were his family. I can remember thinking: *they* wouldn't kill the king's son, would they?

In theory there were eighty men in our century when it was up to complement, but how often does a century have the luxury of a full complement while it's on campaign? Never, in my experience. There are always men who dodge the selection, and once the legion marches, illness, cowardice, death in battle and desertion mean that the numbers are reduced steadily. Especially under a leader like ours. Our centurion was determined to make a name for himself in Gaul, and he'd risk any number of us to win it. He'd shown that when we landed.

Our cohort was formed of six centuries of maybe sixty men in each, after the ferocious battles in Gaul of the past year, and especially after the fighting to land here in Britain. The natives had thrown everything they had, rocks, bullets from slings, arrows, the lot. While I stood on the ship, two men beside me were struck down by the mad bastards. It made the lads anxious about making the jump down into the deep water. Well, not surprising. Our ship was made for deep waters, not for shelving sands. It stood high over the water, and the water itself was obviously deep. In the end it was the *aquilifer*, the man who held the standard of the Xth legion, who leaped in and exhorted his mates to get down there to protect him. He'll not do badly; there'll be a good reward for the mad arse. After all, any good general knows that his men only follow so long as there's good chances for money and slaves.

Still, after the fight there were only maybe three hundred and sixty in the cohort instead of the complement of four hundred and eighty, so you can see that the general was not going to be happy. What? You need to ask *why*?

Look, when you're over there, in some land you know sod-all about, apart from the bits and pieces of intelligence you've gleaned from dodgy spies (who are as likely to be working for the enemy as for you, spying out your strengths and weaknesses to sell to the best bidder); when you've already had one hard fight; when the lads are tired; when you don't know how many enemy hordes there are and you depend on the sea for your escape, with all the risks *that* entails; well, the most important thing is, to keep the locals subjugated. Keep them quiet. Make them feel that they're better off tolerating you than trying to kill you. Right?

Right. So you go in heavy, grab the most important leaders you can, and hold them hostage against the good behaviour of the tribe. It makes sense. Nine times out of ten, they'll do what we want. Some of the hostages get to like our life so much, it's hard to get rid of them later, but the tribes don't know that. They assume that their leaders are being held in foul conditions, because that's how they'd treat us; it's impossible to get them to realise the benefits of civilization. Well, how could they? They haven't the foggiest idea. Poor devils, living in their cold, draughty huts, sleeping on a pile of rags on packed earth floors, if they were lucky . . . that's why we have a *duty* to invade them. It's their destiny – and ours. We have to lead them, and in the end they will learn to appreciate the benefits of Roman culture.

But I'm getting away from the point. Point is: we're safe while we've got our hostages, but if it gets known that one of us killed one of them, especially a king's son, that doesn't leave us in a strong position. In fact, it leaves us in a shite position. So the general, he'd come down on us like a ton of lead. It could mean crucifixion for the daft bugger who killed that little sod. Or worse.

While we waited for the translator, I glanced at the three of them. Pugio, As and Consul. Strange that none of us ever used our given names. We all lived with our nicknames. Pugio: Dagger – it wasn't hard to see where the most believable murderer was.

Consul caught my eye. I jerked my head at him and he followed me to the corner of the stockade, leaving As and Pugio to guard the remaining men.

"What is it?" Consul asked laconically.

"What happened?"

He smiled. "We were all outside the enclosure so far as I know. I certainly was. I remained out at the gate itself. I was there all night."

"Did you fall asleep?"

"I remained standing," he said, eyeing me pityingly. "How about you?"

"Piss off! I was asleep, true, but at least I can't have killed anyone," I hissed. There had been certain rumours, and I stepped forwards, forcing him to retreat until his back was against the stockade's wall. "Did you see anyone?"

"No. No one. Not after the Centurion."

"What did that prick want?"

"He just went in to inspect our hostages." Consul gave a chuckle. "He looks on them as his own property, I think."

His words made my heart thrill. "Could he have killed the boy?"

"Not a chance!" Consul said scathingly. "I was there, I kept my eyes on them, and there was nothing amiss when the

Centurion left. He just walked in, stared at them, and walked out. I shut the gate and barred it after him."

"I see. What of your 'Little Flower'?"

"Well, you know," he said easily.

"No, I don't. Tell me!"

His teeth flashed. "She was busy early on, but yes, she tripped past later and waggled her arse at me. It was all I could do not to leap on her right there, but she wouldn't have been grateful, not in this climate. It's too cold."

"So you left your post at the gate?"

"Only for a short while," he protested. "Some of us were asleep! But yes, I did. And she'll confirm it."

"I'm sure she bloody will," I grunted, but it was easily believable. He'd been slotting this little tart ever since they met in port waiting to sail, and I'd never known him miss a night. No army can manage without women and, to be fair, this one was pleasing, with all the right curves and a tempting grin. "Did you hear anything while you were on duty? Did you hear Pugio or As making a racket? Shouting at the hostages or anything? If the hostages provoked them, maybe . . ."

"Nothing like that, no. There were snores from all over, especially in here, and unsettled sleepers, but I'd swear that the lot were asleep." He gave me a sympathetic shrug. "We both know what happened, don't we?"

"Yeah," I grunted.

It was while we were returning to this camp with the hostages. The king's boy had slowed and gazed about him as he was brought into our makeshift fort, staring about him with obvious awe, but with some calculation too, assessing the best means of attack. It was Pugio who was nearest, and he used the butt of his lance to urge the boy on. Instantly the boy whirled, eyes blazing at being mistreated, and seeing the tatty figure of Pugio, he hawked and spat at Pugio's feet.

Pugio glanced down at the gob of phlegm at his feet, and before he could thrust the *pilum* through the arrogant little sod's face, Consul and I jumped on him and calmed him.

But Pugio came from a hot-blooded people. Insults like that spit rankled. And a man like Pugio didn't like to leave the sun to go down on his revenge. He preferred his vengeance still nicely warm.

So Consul had left his post. He had gone with his waggle-tailed whore to while away a good portion of his watch, rather than standing at the gate. That meant anyone could have lifted the bar and entered, walked inside and stabbed the boy with a lance or knife.

Except . . .

Now I was new to this life of soldiering, but I'd seen enough corpses to know what a wound looked like. The boy's chest had been stabbed once, heavily, by a broad-bladed weapon. It had entered deeply, although not through to the back, and when pulled back, it had sucked or pulled the inner flesh with it. Perhaps a barbed blade, I wondered, looking at it more closely.

When I heard the translator arrive, it was a relief. Gazing at the body was merely a means of avoiding asking Pugio whether he had murdered the lad. I didn't want to ask, because I didn't want to hear him lie – and still less did I want to hear him confess. That would mean a short walk to the cross, or perhaps to the tribe whose prince he had killed. The thought of that was repellent, but Pugio had endangered the whole legion by killing this piece of carrion.

I motioned to the translator as soon as the gate opened. He was not one of those arrogant "Damn your mother" toadies who was here only to serve for a limited campaign before riding back home at the first opportunity, claiming to understand the fighting man and war before entering the Senate,

but a nervous-looking fellow of maybe some twenty sum-
mers.

"Oh, shit!" he muttered when he saw the body.

"I know. What do these fellows have to say?"

He gave me a wan look. "You want me to talk to them?"

"That's what you're here for," I snarled.

"Fuck! I was trained in Gallic, but this lot speak Belgic."

I grabbed his shoulder and shoved him forwards. "You're
getting a short lesson, then, friend! Maybe the old bastard
speaks Gallic as well. Why don't you try him?"

Smarting with anger, I left him muttering his incomprehen-
sible nonsense and went over to As. He wasn't the sharpest
lance in the box, As wasn't. Yes, I'd trust him entirely, with
my life if necessary, because he had strength and courage,
but still, if it was a test needing intelligence or quick thinking, I'd rather rely on a drunken Nubian.

"As, last night, did you hear Consul bugger off?"

"Oh yes. He came to me to tell me," As smiled.

"Wonderful!" So he hadn't tried to conceal vacating his
post to tup a wench. At least I'd been asleep because I'd had
a tough day, and I'd got three others to guard. A fourth
shouldn't have been necessary. But when one left his place,
leaving two, that was a problem. "What did he say?"

"That he was seeing his woman. The one with the big . . ."

I didn't need to be reminded. "And when he was gone –
did you hear anything in the stockade?"

"Oh no. I wasn't listening. There were bats flying from
the trees, and I was watching them."

I stared at him blankly, and he must have seen my weary
disbelief, because he pointed westwards. "The trees in those
woods. There are many bats. I heard one, over there, and
then I could hear them squeaking, high-pitched noises. Do
you think they talk to each other?"

"What of the hostages?" I rasped. My temper was not improved to learn that two-thirds of my guards had not been listening to the hostages, especially since it meant Pugio would have had an even easier kill. They hadn't protected him from himself.

"Them?" His face was blank for a moment, then brightened. "I heard them whispering. And then there was a scuffle. Yes, a scuffle."

"A fight?"

"I think someone started to climb the wall over near the gate."

Where Consul should have been, I told myself. Was Consul part of a conspiracy to break out from the stockade?

"But then he got down. Pugio told him to."

There was a cold weight in my gut. "Pugio told him to. Was Pugio in the stockade with the prisoners?"

"Of course not! Pugio was told to guard outside, like me!" As chuckled.

And that was that. The fool simply couldn't believe that someone would have disobeyed orders, because As himself wouldn't. No, As could not comprehend Pugio entering the stockade to murder a boy.

That was my trouble. I could.

The translator was waving at me, and I felt as though my feet were nailed to the ground, it was so hard to move towards him.

"Well?"

The translator shot a look at the uncle. "This man says that one of the guards came in here last night, rushed at his nephew and slew him. There was no reason. Most of the fellows in here were already asleep. Only he woke, and saw the Roman tugging his lance free from the boy's breast. He would have called the alarm, but was scared. He thought he might be killed as well."

I looked at the translator, then at the Briton. "Ask him whether the lad tried to escape by climbing the walls."

There was that gutteral row again, and then the translator turned to me again. "He thinks so, yes. It was that which woke him. Then the boy tried to scream for help, but the cry was cut off by the thrust."

It was possible. Even with my limited experience, I had seen men die that way in battle. Yet there was something that seemed oddly out of place. Those whom I had seen die had opened their mouths and then fallen as the blow fell – but all about them were other men screaming defiance, bellowing orders, shrieking their battle cries and drowning out any small cry of pain or terror as a spirit fled its body. Was it possible that a man should die so silently that As should not be able to hear it in the stillness of the night? It seemed odd, certainly.

"What of the others? Were there no others awake to witness the attack?" I asked.

"All the others were asleep," the translator said.

"I see."

I had my hand on my sword still, but my eyes had travelled beyond Verc to the boy Trin, who still glowered suspiciously towards me from the far side of the stockade. He was a cousin, I remembered, but not Verc's son. His father was another brother of the chieftain, long dead. Apparently the chieftain had had him executed for treachery or disloyalty.

Trin's look met mine for a moment, and suddenly I felt a quickening interest. In his eyes there was a killing rage, the rage that might allow him to murder even a cousin. Especially if that meant equalling the score with his uncle, the man who had executed his father.

Now that was a possibility. Perhaps Pugio had a defence after all.

*   *   *

Pugio was sullen as I approached him.

"I didn't do it."

"I didn't say you did," I countered.

"You are working up to it."

"I just want to know what happened last night."

He was standing taut as a ballista's rope, grasping his lance with whitened knuckles. I stared at his lance. There was no sign of blood on it, and anyway, I'd seen lance wounds often enough. They didn't suck the flesh from the wound in the way this weapon had. No, it had to be another weapon. Pugio's eyes met mine briefly, but then moved on over the men we were guarding, his eyes black. "You don't trust me, do you?"

"How often have we fought together, Pugio? Don't be fucking stupid," I hissed. "Look, I want to know that you're innocent here. If you aren't, I don't want to hear it. I just want to make sure that you're safe."

"You believe I did it, don't you?" he demanded.

I couldn't answer that. "It was the boy who spat at your feet."

"Yeah. You think I killed him."

"He could have tried to climb out of the stockade, over the walls, and you stabbed him as he rose over because he wouldn't go back when you told him," I hazarded. "That would be an easy mistake. Perhaps he didn't understand our language."

There was justice in that. Pugio's dialect was so strong that most Romans couldn't understand him at first – how much more difficult would it be for a Briton?

"I didn't see him climbing the wall. I didn't see anything."

"Did you hear him trying to climb?"

"Oh, there was a bit of a noise and I heard someone on the wall, but I shouted at them to quiet down, and soon they did."

"Were you here at your post all the night?"

"Of course I was. When have you known me desert?"

"Never. That hostage, the uncle, he says someone went into the stockade and stabbed the lad. A Roman."

"That's bullshit. He's a liar," Pugio spat.

"Why?"

"Look, if someone went in there, he'd have woken the whole lot! He went in there, he'd have to pull the bolt from the gate, wouldn't he? You know how loud the thing is. If anyone went in there, I'd have heard. And so would As," he said pointedly.

"Very well. So you won't accept that someone else went inside and you deny that you did yourself," I said.

"Of course I do."

"Yes." Well, of course he did. Anything else would mean that he was guilty. He had to deny it if he wanted to save his skin.

"You know what that means, don't you?" he grated, his lance still held at the ready, his eyes fixed on the other hostages.

"What?"

"Someone in there killed the boy."

Yes. I knew that was the only reasonable answer, the only way to protect us. It would be good to come to that conclusion – but it was not going to be easy to tell my centurion or the general that the hostage had been murdered by his own cousin. Even in Rome feuds among political rivals didn't often lead to murder. I had the beginning of a motive, I suppose, but this affair could threaten the legion or whole army. Unless I could have someone inside confess, the general might just get the feeling that he'd be better to apologize for a rogue legionary, and hand over someone anyway. Perhaps Pugio; or even me. I was asleep, after all.

There was one other minor problem: if it was a relative,

where had the weapon come from? All the men in the stockade were checked clear of all weapons. Where had the weapon come from – and where had it gone?

If I could find it, we still needed proof that someone inside had killed the boy. The question was, how in Hades we could get that proof.

"Open the gate."

"Who is . . ." I could hear the guard outside the stockade doing a mental double-take, and could almost hear the mental, "Oh, fuck!" as he sprang to obey.

There was a restrained tension inside the stockade, and we all stood slightly more stiffly, as soldiers should, even As trying to make his rusting armour look less shameful by passing a grubby hand over the worst of it. Personally, I found myself glancing over the faces of the other hostages.

I had no doubt, uncle Verc had an expression of rage, like a man who was determined not to be bullied by anyone, no matter how fierce the torture; behind him, the lad against the wall roved up and down like a caged lion, and in his eyes I was sure I could see fear, real, bowel-twisting fear.

Perhaps he was terrified that he was about to be exposed, I thought as I faced the gate.

"Oh God. I should have guessed it'd be you," grunted the Centurion as he entered.

Now I wouldn't want anyone to think that the man who came in now, his nose wrinkling gently at the odour of excrement, his long cloak gathered up and looped over his arm to prevent its sweeping over any ordure, his patrician face pulled into an expression of revulsion as he cast a look over the hostages, was a bastard just because I disliked him. I *did* dislike him, it's true, but it went further than simple dislike. It was more mutual detestation.

"I should have guessed it'd be you at the bottom of it all," he said with a grimace.

He was very tall, was Lucius Minucius Baculus. At least a half head taller than me, and that's saying something, but it wasn't the height that first grabbed your attention, it was his biceps and thighs. Even under his shirt and kilt, his immense muscles were as apparent as a bear's. His face was scarred in three places. One slash had nearly taken off his nose, another had exposed his cheekbone in a battle, and a third was like a big wrinkle across his brow. Each was badly healed, and each laid its own character on his features. If it wasn't for them, his face would have been quite regular and attractive, with his clear grey eyes which opened so wide he looked perpetually surprised, and the square jaw with the thin but wide mouth. His eyes were set far apart, and you really did get the feeling that the bastard could see through a wall when he fixed them on you.

"I will not remain in this midden. You! Gaius Antistius Fabius! Have the hostages brought out and . . ." his cold eyes moved about us all. "Perhaps this time you could prevent your men killing them?"

It was his arrogant rudeness which made me square my back and march out, throwing out orders as I went.

Lucius Minucius Baculus, the proud master of seventy-odd men, including me and my lads. Not a friend. Where some leaders would sit with their men and chew the fat, Lucius Minucius Baculus felt himself above such things. He was too superior for that; his destiny would take him higher and higher, if he had anything to do with it. A warrior to his fingers, his scars proved his courage and unshakeable belief in himself. Me, I thought he was mad.

It wasn't just our hatred of each other, it was the way he had stormed up the beach when we landed. Glory and laurels, that was what he wanted. Mad bastard was determined to work his way up the ranks, and he didn't give a shit about the men he ground down on his way.

When we landed, everyone held back, seeing how deep the sea was and how the Britons fought. Like I said, it was only when the Xth's standard-bearer leaped down that the rest of us all followed, shamefaced. Me too. On the beach everything was confused, with men flocking to any standard they could see, and there was a fair amount of panic, because the Britons attacked any weak group, throwing their javelins and rocks, anything that came to their hands. They even tried to throw back our own javelins, but they were designed to stop that. Each point had a soft, deforming, section of steel behind the hardened tip, which made them fly badly once they'd been used, and we were safe from their return.

Most were all for a defensive line, linking shields to protect our heads, until more could join us, but not our leader. No, with a loud bellow of defiance, he rushed at the enemy.

I can't deny that there were a few of us who were thoughtful to the extent of letting him go on alone. He'd get cut down and trampled, and then, I suppose, we could have gone and got his body. Saved it from dishonour. But you know, it's a strange thing about being a soldier. Sometimes your training takes over. Me, I couldn't believe that my legs were pounding away underneath me and taking me nearer the melée. I must have been mad. Luckily I wasn't alone, and other men were with me. Seven fell there on the beach, but the centurion was safe, the bastard! These death or glory merchants always seem to win the glory while their companions get the other.

That he was furious today, I could see in his flaring nostrils and the cold, unblinking stare which he fixed upon the hostages and my men as they filed into the open space of the market next to the general's tent. There was always a certain amount of business being conducted here, and I was aware of soldiers buying flour and hard tack and a few other things. I noticed the dark hair and voluptuous figure of Consul's tart. While the Centurion arranged for his seat to be positioned just so, I beckoned her, and she all but ran to me, seeking another client.

"Where is the body?"

The Centurion's harsh bass voice caused a short alarm, and then two men brought in the corpse and set it before him.

"Stabbed. So who did this?"

I stepped forwards. "We do not know. All we are sure of is that no one opened the gate, so the killer must be among the hostages."

"You think so?" he sneered. "It is good to hear from a man with such a wealth of experience of legal matters."

His tone made me stiffen, and hearing a chuckle from one of his guards, I felt the flush begin to rise from my collar. I had been forced to leave Rome because of an accusation of fraud made against me, and that was why I was penniless and in the army. My Centurion had quickly learned of the accusation, and enjoyed that knowledge at my expense. Now, though, there was a harsh edge to his tone. It wasn't simple ribbing of an underling. Yes, the gods must have had a good laugh when they saw fit to put me in his century.

He continued, "Perhaps you have a better understanding of the criminal mind? Or maybe you're protecting one of your own comrades? Like that fool there, or the one you call the dagger? Who was on guard duty last night?"

Reluctantly Pugio, As, Consul and I myself moved forwards. Briefly, he questioned us all. When I said that I was asleep, he gave me a hard stare.

Pointing, he called As and Pugio forwards, and had them give up their weapons before questioning them in his rough, cynical manner. While he did so, I spoke to the whore.

"Last night. Did Consul go to you?"

"Why?"

I realized he might have covered his tracks. "He has already told me he did, so you can tell me."

"I had a quiet night. I might have again tonight, too," she said, and suddenly I felt her hot little hand sliding down under my kilt, caressing my buttocks.

"Um, no, please," I said weakly. "I am trying to learn what happened, that's all."

"He came to see me later. Perhaps you should come to my tent tonight and question me again?"

"Look, he went to you, right?"

"You look worried." Her face was suddenly sharply concerned. "Is he in trouble?"

"Yes. If the Centurion learns . . ."

She chuckled. "He knows."

"Shit."

"No! It was the Centurion suggested I should go to him. He said that your men had all been fighting hard, and Consul deserved a little rest. He even paid me a little money to go to him. Soon after I got back to my tent, there was Consul."

She had given me plenty to think about, but it was a relief to see her swaggering backside rotating away along the roadway. Still, I was left with the question of why the Centurion would have paid to have Consul taken away. Perhaps he had taken a "liking" to Consul. I glanced at the Centurion. No. There were some things that stretched the imagination too much. Anyway, he'd hardly send a woman if he was after Consul himself.

Someone with a weapon had killed the lad. Someone who wanted him dead. Perhaps the Centurion wanted him dead. Yet he still couldn't have opened that gate without Pugio and As hearing it. No one could have got in. Which left the impossible position of the people inside the stockade having killed the lad. Except there was no weapon.

And then a snippet of conversation came back to me. As the Centurion lost interest in As and Pugio, I beckoned As to me and spoke to him quickly. I also sent Consul with him to make sure he didn't get confused. They were not long in returning, and As handed me the bloody weapon. It was a used Roman javelin tip without the shaft, the tip bent at the soft steel section.

"Centurion, I think that I can clear this up quickly," I announced.

"Certainly, step forwards and enlighten us," he said sarcastically.

Holding the javelin-point behind my back, I stepped forwards. "This murder must have been committed by someone inside the compound. If a Roman had entered, the noise of the bar must alert all those inside. They did not all wake. Thus the gate remained shut."

"Perhaps some of them did wake."

"Only one admitted to waking."

"So you are saying that your men didn't search them properly? The hostages were allowed to bring in a weapon?"

"No, sir. I think that while one of my men was away from the gate, someone threw in a weapon . . ." I paused as I brought the weapon into the open and suddenly, as I saw the Centurion's expression alter, I realized what had really happened. Suddenly I wasn't sure how to continue. All I could do was point at Trin and demand that the translator question him.

"Did you kill the prince to avenge your dead father?"

"No!" The emphatic nature of the denial was very convincing.

"You found this javelin point and stabbed him . . ."

"I didn't get it!"

"You don't deny you saw it?"

"I . . ."

"Perhaps we should use a little torture?" I enquired. The translator obliged me by telling the lad.

"No! I saw it after the Centurion visited us yesterday. Verc took it up. I saw him. Later, he killed my cousin. My cousin tried to escape the stockade when he saw Verc advancing towards him, he tried to climb the wall, but someone told him to stop. He was grabbed and killed before he could demand help."

"You say this, yet you kept away from the body like a man who felt his guilt."

"My uncle told me to keep away. I was scared of him. He could have killed me with his bare hands."

"Why should he kill your cousin?"

"He wants to have all power," Trin said, his eyes sliding over towards his uncle, who stood silent and calm.

I shot him a look. Any man usually who heard himself accused in this way would argue, would declare his innocence, or try to bolt. This man did nothing. He stood with a half smile on his face. The look he returned to me held only contempt, as though I was achieving nothing. And then he glanced at the Centurion.

Trin continued, "He killed my cousin so that he could take the leadership of the tribe when our chieftain dies."

"And he agreed to make sure that the chieftain will die," I heard the Centurion mutter.

Now, thinking back, I find it hard to imagine why I had not realized what had happened. All so clear, all so simple. The Centurion had spoken to all the hostages when they arrived, and no doubt sounded out Verc immediately. Last night he had gone through the gate with Consul specifically to drop the weapon, proof of his arrangement with Verc. Verc took it up as soon as Consul and the Centurion left; Consul hadn't seen the weapon dropped because he had been watching the hostages, like any sensible guard.

He hadn't expected the danger to come from his own leader.

The Centurion bribed Flower to go to Consul so that no one could hear the attack. Probably he told Verc to wait until Consul had gone, and then to attack near the gate, where there would be no guard to hear. It was sheer misfortune that Pugio had heard them and bellowed to them to shut up.

When it was dark, Verc heard the conversation between Consul and his Flower, and knew that the coast was clear for him. When he was sure that the guard at the gate had left his post, he stole over to the boy with the javelin point in his hand. The boy woke to find a dark figure over him. Overwhelmed with terror, he ran to the stockade wall, but died before he could scream for help, he was so petrified with terror. And as soon as he fell, Verc hurled the weapon over the wall. It fell among trees, startling some bats or birds, while As wondered whether they could speak to each other. If they could, they were only complaining about being stirred so early.

I looked at the Centurion, who met my gaze resolutely.

"Sir, this man killed a hostage purely for his own advancement, and put the legion in danger. We could be attacked at any time, but if the tribes think that we have harmed their hostages, freely given to us as a token of peace, they will attack us in force. Our safety is under threat. We must make an example of this man."

"What if it was the other one, the fellow you called 'Trin'?"

"I think we could discount that. Why should he want to kill his cousin? It would bring him no advantage."

The Centurion rose and motioned for the hostages to be returned to their pen. When he spoke to me, his voice was only a little above a whisper. "Very well. Think like this. I do not admit anything, but what if the tribes were to learn that a hostage of such importance had died? They would attack, as you say, and those who defended this place would win a place in Rome's history."

"Unless we are all killed," I pointed out somewhat sorely.

"That is unlikely. And the next leader of the tribe will be a sworn ally of Rome."

There it was. He'd done a deal: attack us, we'll kill your leader, and you become the new leader and our ally. "*Him?*" I asked, staring at Verc's back. "You think *he's* a safe ally?"

"Next year we will be back here again. This is only a short reconnaissance. Next year we land in force," my Centurion said, his eyes gleaming. "This tribe may attack, but we can beat them off. We will annihilate them. Verc will be the new chieftain, and we will win much praise for our courage! Perhaps even *you* will be rewarded with honour," he added slyly. He seriously thought that it could motivate me to support him, even though he was risking my neck and the other men's.

As though there was any need, he added dreamily, "*Or*, as a sleeping guard yourself, perhaps you prefer to be beaten to death?"

What could I say? I wanted to make sure that I lived, and trying to accuse my own leader of such insane dealings was a short trip to a charge of mutiny and a not so swift death. So I did what I had to. I smiled knowingly, understandingly, and smarmed my way out of his presence. Jesus, it was like trying to placate a snake. His venom was never so deadly as when you weren't sure where he was or what he was doing.

I did the best I could. I received his assurance that the lads were safe from any accusations. Pugio wouldn't be under threat, and nor would As. Instead we would put all the blame on Trin and let him carry the can. I felt a bit sorry for the fellow, but there was no choice. I couldn't win against the word of a Centurion. Armies work like that.

*　　*　　*

Well, the tribes attacked only a couple of days later. We were out collecting corn from a nearby field, when the enemy suddenly sprang out from the surrounding trees. They were on us, killing several before we knew what was happening. We couldn't do much, because our weapons were all on the ground while we gathered the corn, and it was a mad scramble to collect them up again. I can vividly remember the long javelin plopping into the soil beside me as I grabbed for my *gladius*, staring at it in horror, imagining what it could have done to my back, and then I grabbed it, turned, and hurled it on.

Later, of course, the body was found. Do I feel guilt?

It was his machinations which had caused the attack in the first place. He was prepared to risk all our lives, even the whole army. And he was happy to see Pugio die to support his plan – it was only my own guesses which had stopped that and saved Pugio. If the Centurion had succeeded, he would certainly have won renown and the praise of our general, but that wouldn't have helped us, would it? The mad bastard.

Verc the politician died, happily, on that battlefield. Perhaps it's bad to lose a potential ally, but I don't think so. He was prepared to sell his own people, so how trustworthy was he for us? So Verc died, a Roman javelin in his guts, ironically, rather like the tip that he used to murder his nephew, just one more unmissed and unlamented politician. And not far from him, there lay a dead Centurion.

He won't be missed either. There are enough ambitious men in the world for one Centurion to go unrecorded.

De Crimine

Miriam Allen deFord

We have already met Cicero in Steven Saylor's story. Here we meet him again, twenty-eight years later, but still a force to be reckoned with. In fact we'll meet him again in the next story. The work of Miriam Allen deFord (1888– 1975) is not as well remembered today as it should be, even though she had a career spanning some fifty years and was a popular writer of mysteries, science fiction and true crime. Her books include The Real Bonnie and Clyde *(1968) and* The Real Ma Baker *(1970). Her short mysteries were collected as* The Theme is Murder *(1967).*

When this story was first published in 1952, Miss deFord remarked: "You can rely absolutely on the authenticity of this story; besides the work I have done in Latin translation and Roman biography, I even consulted the world's greatest authority on Roman law and did a lot of reading to make no mistake in clothing, furniture, architecture or anything else. Cicero (and Tullia), Clodia and Dolabella are, of course, real people; the others (except Tiro) are fictitious."

Tiro, Cicero's faithful freedman and secretary, brought him word that a lady who had come all the way from

Rome begged to be permitted to see him. She was Favilla, the wife of Gnaeus Manlius Ordo.

The great old advocate frowned. He had recovered from his first overwhelming grief at the death of his adored daughter; had even been able to move from Lanuvium back to his villa of Tusculanum where she had died; but he was trying to drug his sorrow by the writing of philosophy, and he desired and allowed no visitors.

"I know the family, of course," he said to Tiro. "They belong to the late opponents of our benevolent master in Rome – just as I did, until it was too hopeless. I believe Manlius is still in Spain, hesitant about coming home since the final defeat of the Pompeians, unless Caesar issues an amnesty. And I have a vague memory that I once knew the wife, though I can't quite place her. I have met too many people in the past forty years."

"She asked me to say," the secretary interposed deferentially, "that she was a dear friend of Tullia's when they were girls together, and that she pleads for an interview with you for Tullia's sake."

The tears started to Cicero's eyes, as always at the mention of that beloved name. He turned his head for a moment; not even Tiro knew what he had suffered.

"I will see her," he said brusquely.

He half-recognized her as she entered, and automatically he turned on all the charm that, as much as his oratory, his patriotism, or his legal wisdom, had won his way to the front when he had entered public life, a "knight", a "new man" among the old patrician leaders of the Republic.

"Favilla!" He took both her hands in his. "It has been very long since we have met. It is good of you to come this long journey to see me."

"No, it is good of *you* to be willing to see *me*," she contradicted him. She was tall and slender, not exactly beautiful, but with the unmistakable distinction of her aristocratic heritage. She must be about thirty – of an age with Tullia – but she was childless and she had kept her figure.

"I must be frank, Cicero," she went on. "Tullia *was* my close friend all through our girlhood, as you may remember – though I saw her seldom after we were both married – and I did love her dearly. My heart aches for you; I wish there were something I could say that would comfort you. But I came here today to ask for help, not to offer it. I have a difficult problem before me, and I need your advice."

Cicero played with the stylus with which he had been writing when Tiro had entered.

"Since you have come so far just to consult me," he began doubtfully, "if I can help you at all I shall do so gladly. But of course you know that at present – perhaps permanently – I have withdrawn from both politics and the law. If your problem is anything of that nature, you should go to Caesar, not come to me."

"It isn't political," said Favilla. "It's a family matter, and with my husband away – you know about him, I suppose?"

Cicero nodded.

"I have no idea how soon it will be safe for him to come home, even though he never held a prominent post in Pompey's army, either in Africa or in Spain. While he's gone, everything – his home, his estate, even his honour and good standing – all are in my charge; I represent him and must safeguard his interests. And now –"

"Now something endangers them?"

"In a way. A month ago his old aunt, who lived with us, died – died suddenly. Aufidia – you may recall her. She wasn't really his aunt, but his uncle's widow; but when her husband died she had no living relative left, so naturally Gnaeus took her in with us. She wasn't much of a burden; sometimes we hardly realized she was there. In late years she had grown very heavy, and she seldom left her own rooms, and practically never left the house. We aren't rich, you know – we have lost most of our fortune during the disturbances of the past ten years, like so many others – but we could always give Aufidia a home, and plenty to eat, and a servant to wait on her. I tried to keep her from feeling neglected; I visited her at least once a day, and I think she was fond of us both."

"She had no property of her own?"

"That's what I'm coming to. Unfortunately – perhaps you remember her husband, Titus Manlius Ordo? He loved good living, and he always lived beyond his means. By the time he died, he had nothing left; his wife's dowry had gone with the rest – there was nothing for her to recover. Even their slaves had to be sold for his debts."

"Then Aufidia came to you penniless? Poor old thing – I remember her when I was a very young man, and when she was a striking woman and a famous hostess."

"It's hard to realize now. She had grown very lame as well as being so fat, her heart was bad, and she was becoming just a bit – well, foolish, mentally. She did save one thing out of the wreckage, and that was some of her jewels. She had some very valuable and very beautiful pieces. They were given to her in the early days of her marriage by her husband, and most of them were heirlooms – from the Manlius ancestors, not from hers. So we were the natural heirs, though of course while she lived they remained her property. It wasn't just their monetary value, though that was very high, but they were part of my husband's inheritance – you understand?"

"Perfectly." Cicero winced a little; even after all those years he could still be hurt by the most innocent implication that, naturally, he wouldn't comprehend the ideas and customs of high society. "And now, since her death, they are not in your possession?"

"How did you know that?"

"My dear lady, otherwise why would you have mentioned them? What happened?"

"I'll try to tell you." Favilla's voice shook a little.

To spare her, Cicero rose and stood looking out at the soft October landscape. Favilla went on.

"It was just a month ago. I was in the atrium, writing a letter to my husband. Aufidia's maid – a Cappadocian woman who had been with her ever since my aunt came to our house, and who was devoted to her – came running in, screaming that something was wrong with her mistress. It seems Aufidia had sent her to launder and mend some old tunics – she was very careful of her clothes, and we scarcely ever had to buy her anything new – and it had taken the woman half an hour or so. When she came back to Aufidia's bedroom, where she had left her mistress napping, she found – well, her breath gave out at that point, and she could only gesture to me to come.

"I ran as fast as I could. There was the old lady, lying half on the bed, half off it. Her face was a queer, sickly purple, her mouth was open, and I could see at a glance that she wasn't breathing.

"Her right arm lay stretched out towards the cabinet where she kept her jewels. The doors of the cabinet were open, the drawers pulled out, and most of them were empty. There was nothing left except a few worthless trinkets. We found the key later, under the bed.

"I thought at first Aufidia had had a stroke, and might still have a spark of life left. The servant and I managed to get her great weight back on the bed – I couldn't be sure, under all that fat, whether her heart was still beating or not – and I sent another slave running for the Greek physician, Callidoros, who had tended her before when she was ill. He came quickly, but as I had feared, it was too late. She had been dead for nearly an hour by then, he told me."

"What did he say was the cause of her death?" Cicero asked.

"He couldn't tell – they never do know, really, do they? He said her heart had stopped, which I knew without his announcement. By the time he arrived I had closed the cabinet; I didn't want any gossip started, and I gave the maid strict orders to say nothing to anyone without my permission. She was so frightened for herself that I'm sure she obeyed me."

"You thought, of course," Cicero suggested, "that there had been foul play. Someone had killed her and stolen the jewels – or frightened her to death – a fat old woman with a weak, over-labouring heart – and then stolen them. Isn't the next step, in great households like yours, to put all the slaves to the torture to find out who is guilty?"

He was sorry for the malice of his remark as soon as he saw Favilla's painful flush, but he had been unable to resist that minute revenge.

"It was probably the custom in our parents' time," she said with asperity, "but I hope we're a little more civilized today. Besides, we don't have a great household in that sense; we have only twenty house slaves in all, and I know every one of them. We have been barely able to keep up appearances in recent years. Naturally, the first thing I thought of was that someone who knew about the jewels had bribed one of my servants to do the deed – for no one could enter the house past our doorkeeper without my knowing it. But as it happened, I knew where every one of the servants had been during that half-hour. The details don't matter, but some were out on errands, others were in my sight from the atrium, the doorkeeper was chained to his door as usual, and so on."

"The Cappadocian woman?"

"Most unlikely; she was too terrified, it would have taken a skilled actor to imitate her astonishment and horror. Besides –"

Favilla broke off, and herself looked a little frightened, as if she had said too much.

They had been sitting in the peristyle of the house, with the fountain playing in its middle and the soft breeze ruffling the plants set against the painted columns. Now Cicero clapped his hands for a servant, and ordered him to bring wine.

"Talking dries the tongue," he said with a smile. "And you will, of course, stay the night before you begin the long journey back. I must give orders for dinner, and see that your escort is properly cared for. I am afraid I am an awkward host; it has been so long since I entertained a guest."

He sighed deeply, and Favilla, with exquisite tact, only looked the quick sympathy she felt. Here at Tusculanum the great lawyer and orator had once given banquets to the most important men in Rome; here, in some cubicle beyond the *cavum caedum*, his Tullia had died in his arms, only eight months before.

The slave had gone again, leaving them alone, and they had drunk a cup of wine together, before Cicero spoke again.

"You are not telling me all, Favilla," he said gently. "I can't help you if you hide things from me."

"I know." She toyed with her wine cup. "It's my brother – Sextus."

"Sextus Favillus?" Cicero sounded surprised. "Why, he's a child."

"He is nineteen. He would be furious to hear you call him a child." She smiled briefly. "He is very handsome, and very brilliant – he wants to be a poet, he has set Catullus and your old opponent Calvus as his models – and he is quite unmanageable. You know, I'm sure, that we were left orphans when I was a very young girl and he was little more than a baby. We had a good guardian, who looked after our estate and saw that we were well cared for. But we were very lonely, both of us, and we had no one to love but each other. I loved him very deeply, Cicero – I have no children, and in a sense he has been almost like my son."

"You are not so close now?"

"How could we be, after I was married? – though, of course, I love him just the same. He has fallen in with a wild crowd, young men with far more money than he ever had. He's anticipated most of his inheritance, and squandered the money in their company – wine and gambling and girls. His trustee has just thrown up his hands in despair. I tried hard to save and help Sextus – my husband did his best while he was at home – but to my young brother I suppose we were a pair of croaking old meddlers. He refused to live with us any longer when I wouldn't welcome his friends. We have never quarrelled, but he has long since ceased to pay any attention to anything I might say."

"And so?"

"And so a few months ago he fell headlong in love – madly, crazily in love – with just the wrong woman. She is more than twice his age – though she is beautiful still, and rich, and of a very good family. Of course she laughed at him and snubbed him, which made him only more ardent. He has even" – her voice trembled – "he has threatened to kill himself if he cannot have her – or at least have a share of her, which is all any man ever has," she added bitterly.

"I see." Cicero's heart fell; only one woman in Rome exactly fitted that description.

"No, forgive me, but you can't see it all. Let me tell you in my own way. Because – because I didn't want a scandal, because I had to make all the decisions alone, and the honour of my family and my husband's family was in my hands, and because as things are now, a criminal trial would only be a

farce – I should have had to find a man to act as accuser, I
should have had to name somebody to accuse, and give the
reasons –" Favilla's pale face grew even paler; who was there
to be accused but her brother? "And then of course the
witnesses and the jury and even the praetor would be bribed
– they always are nowadays –"

"Not always. I've won a few cases without bribery myself,
Favilla," Cicero interrupted dryly. Where, he wondered
forlornly, was the great incorruptible Republic of his youth?
And yet in his heart he felt relieved by Favilla's last words;
ever since she had started telling about Aufidia's death, until
she had got out that revelation about her brother, he had
been afraid she was going to ask him to act for her as
somebody's accuser, or to defend somebody, and there
was nothing he was surer of than that it would be most
indiscreet of him to make any public appearance, or even to
go to Rome at all, at this juncture of political affairs. Besides,
he thought cynically, if the woman concerned were the one
he thought it was, there would indeed be plenty of her money
put out in bribery, if only because she loved a row, with
herself in the centre of it.

Favilla was speaking again.

"Of course you have," she answered him crisply. "And
nobody knows better than you how different conditions are
at present. Anyway, right or wrong, I decided to keep things
to myself if possible. Officially, Aufidia had died of a stroke,
or of heart disease. After all, she was nearly eighty. I wrote
my husband of her sudden death, and in his name I gave her
the funeral to which her birth entitled her. And nobody but
myself – and now you – knows about the jewels. Except, of
course, the person who took them, and the person who has
them now."

"And the Cappadocian woman."

"Who doesn't count. I've taken her over to help my own

maid, and she's so grateful not to be involved that she would die before she would talk. You didn't notice what I said last – 'the person who has them now.'"

"I noticed. You mean they are no longer in the possession of the thief."

Favilla shivered at the word.

"I swear to you, I never even thought of my brother until I saw –" She took a deep breath. "I don't, naturally, associate with the group surrounding his – lady-love. But four days ago I was at the baths. She was there, in full panoply, with all her entourage. I imagine Sextus was somewhere on the outskirts, but he must have seen me and vanished. He hasn't been near me since Aufidia died."

"He was with you at that time?"

"He had spent an hour with me, just before," she said reluctantly. "And whenever he came to see me, he dropped in for a chat with Aufidia. He was a great pet of hers – had been since I was married, nine years ago, before her husband died, when Sextus was only a little boy. But this is what I want to tell you. We came face to face in the corridor at the baths. We didn't speak, of course – after all, we have never actually met socially, though she belongs to a greater family than either my husband's or mine, and as society is nowadays she isn't even exiled from it. But I've led a quiet life, and I don't frequent the kind of parties she gives or attends. Still, I've got eyes, and I used them. She had on a magnificent gold arm-band, set in the design of a peacock, in rubies, pearls, and emeralds. She wore a necklace to match. She wore two great pearls in her ears. Those, I suppose, could not be identified, but the necklace and the arm-band could. They were Aufidia's."

There was a silence. Then Cicero asked mildly: "Who is she?"

"Clodia."

"That is what I had guessed. 'The ox-eyed one', the sister – and probably more – of the man who had me exiled and had my home torn down. The woman I shamed and excoriated in public in words no Roman lady had ever had applied to her before, when she had young Furius up on the charge of attempting to poison her – and she sat there and gloried in the sensational publicity. My bitterest enemy on earth . . . Why have you come to me, Favilla? What could I do for you where Clodia is concerned? Twenty years ago, perhaps, when she cast those ox-eyes on me and wouldn't believe they couldn't move me – No, you should apply to Caesar to help you; he, I believe, is still in her good graces. But not I."

"Yes, you," said Favilla earnestly. "Just *because* you hate her and she hates you – because you know her so well, know her weaknesses, her real self behind the beauty and the wit and arrogance and self-will. I don't ask you to do anything – just to tell me what to do. I must, I must get those jewels back, quietly and without a scandal. And I will not take any means that might expose or imperil Sextus."

"If you will forgive me for saying so, my dear," Cicero commented, "your young brother seems to me to be considerable of a fool. I presume he thinks of himself as a second Catullus, and because our Clodia was Catullus's 'Lesbia', she must be his as well. He forgets that she broke the heart of the loveliest lyric poet Rome has ever produced. And Catullus never stole any jewels for her, either."

"Don't use that word! My brother isn't a thief."

"No? What do you call it? Think of the very least that he could be guilty of, Favilla. Suppose he cajoled the old lady into giving him the jewels; he knew they weren't hers to give, in right and equity, and he knows now that excitement and remorse killed her afterwards. Or think of what is much more likely – that he found Aufidia dead or dying of a heart attack and then rifled the cabinet. Or – you might as well face it –

that he demanded the jewels from her and she resisted physically – that she died from the effects – or that he smothered her or strangled her –"

"Oh, no, no! That's impossible! He couldn't – it isn't in his nature."

"Who knows what is in the nature of a youngster crazy with frustrated desire? I don't even say, as you might expect, that Clodia put him up to it. I doubt if she has the remotest idea where the jewels came from, though she must have a shrewd notion that he stole them from someone – from someone who doesn't know about it yet or for personal reasons doesn't wish to claim them. What could a boy like Favillus mean to her? He would be a bore and a pest, and to get rid of him she might very well say, 'All right, bring me a gift worthy of my favours and we'll see', thinking that would be the last of him."

Cicero sighed, and went on. "Poor lad, if I know my Clodia, he hasn't even had value received for them. But she would accept them, and wear them openly, just because she loves beautiful jewels, and laugh at him all the time. That woman doesn't know the meaning of fear – either physical fear or fear of notoriety. Favilla, this is a serious business. I'm speaking to you now, not only as your friend, but as a lawyer. Theft – and perhaps murder – are dreadful crimes, not boyish pranks. You can't get those jewels back without exposing your brother. You can't get them back anyway, to my way of thinking. Clodia is neither decent enough to return them voluntarily, nor capable of being scared into returning them under threats of disclosure."

Favilla's eyes filled with tears.

"There *must* be a way," she murmured. "And believe me, I'm not the doting imbecile you take me for. I know Sextus has been very, very wrong. For my husband's sake as well as for my brother's, I have to avoid publicity, but once I have the jewels back I intend to confront Sextus with the whole thing, and to see that he makes what amends he can. Only, I must get them back first, for if I talked to him now he would only protect Clodia instead of listening to me. Surely, Cicero, you who know her so well can tell me some way in which she can be coerced, if she can't be appealed to and can't be threatened? Surely there is a weak spot somewhere through which she can be reached?"

"There may be," said Cicero slowly after a pause. "Yes, there just possibly may be."

Publius Cornelius Dolabella had been Cicero's son-in-law. Tullia had married him against her father's advice and wish, and she had remained passionately in love with him, though finally his unfaithfulness, extravagance, and profligacy had forced her to divorce him shortly before the birth of their second son – the child of whose parturition she had died. In spite of this, he and his father-in-law had remained on friendly terms; Dolabella was one of those worthless but utterly charming scamps of whom nobody approves but whom nobody can help liking. Now Cicero wrote, asking him to come to Tusculanum as soon as possible. There was nothing Dolabella would not do to oblige – especially if the obligation gave him no trouble and might afford him a bit of cynical amusement. He moved in Clodia's circle; he had just returned from Spain with Caesar; no one could be better fitted for the business Cicero had in mind.

The afternoon following Dolabella's return to Rome from Tusculanum, Clodia, whose beauty seemed timeless and whose daring and flouting of convention only grew with the years, was at home to her acquaintances – which meant practically all Roman upper society with the exception of the women of a few austere and old-fashioned families. Clodia had never cared for women, anyway. Dolabella was there, the bubbling centre of gayety as usual, under the influence of his hostess's excellent Falernian wine.

And young Sextus Favillus hovered as near as he could get to his beloved, who paid little attention to him outside of an occasional enigmatic smile. Once in a while, casually, as if by accident, he touched a fold of Clodia's violet stola, in the new and rather flashy style of coloured garments for ladies. So far as he could be, when he had to share her with so many others, he was content, for once more she wore the most precious of the gems he had given her, the earrings and necklace and arm-band, and when he greeted her she had laid a polished fingernail for a moment on the ruby-and-emerald peacock at her throat, and whispered, "Soon, I promise you."

Here in the open sunshine, with wine under his tunic and the sound of laughing voices all about him, Sextus could look at those jewels and think only of the woman who wore them. At night, in the rented rooms which were all he could afford since most of his borrowed money had gone in careless living, it was different.

And then, with senses half-dulled by drinking and lack of sleep, he heard Dolabella say: "My dear lady, where *did* you get those ornaments you are wearing?"

Clodia tapped him smartly on the hand.

"What a question!" she exclaimed in that rich, throaty voice of hers. "Do you always make such personal remarks, Dolabella? Where do you think I got them? I bought them, of course. Or perhaps they were a gift."

"Then, my dear, somebody has taken a gross advantage of you."

"What do you mean? They aren't false, are they?" Her voice was suddenly sharp.

"Not so far as I know – I believe they are very valuable. But if *I* recognized them, as I did, so will a lot of other

people. You are too trusting, Clodia my love. Some rascally
merchant has taken you in, or one of your acquaintances is
trying to play a trick on you. If I hadn't seen those things
today and warned you, you would soon be the laughing-stock
of all Rome."

Sextus, very white, was unable to move. How *could* Dolabella have recognized the gems? They had never been
outside of Aufidia's bedroom for twenty years.

And now everybody was listening. The boy felt himself
tremble. In a sudden flash of despair he wished desperately
and vainly that time would unroll and obliterate the past six
weeks of his life.

"Explain yourself, my friend," said Clodia coldly.

Dolabella laughed.

"I couldn't possibly mistake them," he answered lightly.
"I must be growing old; when I was a young man everybody
would have known them at sight, and there are plenty of us
left who will. I'm surprised you didn't recognize them
yourself. Why, Clodia, those are the famous jewels which
Lucius Torrentius Afer, that freedman who grew so enormously rich in slave-trading, bought to adorn his pet monkey! It was the joke of the whole city. When the creature
died, he gave the baubles to one of his servants, and the
fellow must have sold them to some trader."

Clodia turned ashen with anger.

"You wretched puppy!" she spat at the miserable Sextus.
"So you thought you could make me ridiculous, did you?
You dirty, misbegotten ape! How dared you do such a thing
to me – how *dared* you?"

Sextus forced his thick tongue to a few stammered words.

"It's not true!" he whispered. "They aren't – they came
from –"

He fell abruptly silent.

Clodia snatched the band from her arm, the circlet from

her neck, the pearls from her ears, and threw them at the stricken boy's feet.

"Get out of my house!" she screeched. "Get out of my sight and never come near me again as long as you live!"

White to the lips, Sextus turned awkwardly and fled.

With clenched fists, Clodia paraded the atrium, cursing Sextus Favillus in words seldom heard outside the Subura, and not often, even there, on a woman's lips. She was in one of her magnificent rages, usually witnessed only by her unhappy lady's maid. The guests felt uncomfortable and embarrassed. One by one they slipped away without their hostess's even noting their murmured excuses and farewells. Unobtrusively Dolabella stooped and picked up the jewels, and placed them carefully in a fold of his toga.

That night he sent them by a trusty slave to Tusculanum. Cicero wrapped them in a package of his own to despatch to Favilla. He felt full of amused satisfaction. His sensitive vanity was pleased that even now he was still the clever man of influence to whom those in difficulties turned naturally for aid. Dolabella had written the full details of the scene at Clodia's. Cicero's lips twitched. If only he had someone with whom he could share this delicious gossip! How his darling Tulliola would have delighted in the story! The ready tears blurred his eyes again as he affixed his seal to the parcel.

Three days later the jewels were back in Aufidia's cabinet, and the cabinet itself was in Favilla's bedroom.

Sextus had disappeared. For a week nobody saw or had news of him. Then, haggard and sick from days of drinking, he turned up shamefacedly at his sister's house.

Her heart smote her at his woebegone appearance, but for the boy's own sake she made herself speak sternly.

"So you have come to me at last, have you?" she said. "And now, little brother, we must have a reckoning."

She led him to a room where they would be out of sight or

hearing of the servants. Sextus threw himself dejectedly onto a couch.

"I know," he muttered. "You think I'm the world's worst fool, and I suppose I am. I don't know how you managed it, but I'm sure that what happened will be no news to you. Well, if it's any consolation to you, I'm cured – cured of women forever," he proclaimed, with the extravagance of nineteen years. "But the jewels are gone – I don't know what became of them."

"The jewels, which were the property of my husband's family, are back in my possession," said Favilla severely. "There will be no public scandal about how you got them – though I have no doubt everybody in Rome knows by now what occurred at Clodia's house," she added cruelly. "But that doesn't mean that everything is forgiven and forgotten." How was it Cicero had phrased it? "Theft and murder aren't boyish pranks – they are dreadful crimes."

"Murder!" cried Sextus sharply. "What do you mean? You don't think I *killed* Aufidia, do you?" To his shame and horror, he burst into tears.

Favilla let him weep in silence. When he had stifled his sobs at last, she said gently, "Tell me what happened, Sextus."

"I dropped in to see her, as usual," he answered in a muffled voice, his gaze averted. "And there she was just as you must have found her. The cabinet was open, and the key was on the floor by her hand. She must have tried to reach for the jewels without leaving the bed, and with all her fat the exertion was too much for her heart.

"For a second I was too shocked to think. Then, of course, I knew I ought to call you at once. But the drawers of the cabinet were open – and I saw the gold and the gems – and I had no money to give Clodia the kind of presents other people gave her – oh, what's the use, Favilla? You know what I did."

Favilla's voice softened in spite of herself; it was such a relief to know that her worst suspicions had not been true. But she had had a week to prepare for her brother's eventual return, and she must not weaken now.

"Sextus," she said, "you know as well as I do the kind of people from whom we are descended. Can you imagine our father, or any of our family, stooping to steal a dead woman's jewels, no matter what the provocation? It's no wonder the Republic is in danger, when the sons of its oldest and proudest families can so lower their standards – or the daughters, either, for that matter. Think of Appius Claudius Caecus, for instance, and then think of his descendant Clodia!"

"Don't, Favilla!" Sextus was abjectly humble now. "I never want to think of her again! Just tell me what I can do to atone for the wrong I did. Do you want me to go away – to Spain, to Asia, anywhere you say? I'm so ashamed that I'd be only too willing to die, if that would do any good."

"Stop being a child!" his sister snapped. "It's about time you grew up, Sextus. No, I don't want you to die – I want you to live, to live to be of some use to your family and your country."

"I promise, sister," the boy said earnestly. "Indeed I do. I'm sick of that whole lot. And I'll never look at another woman as long as I live."

"Oh, what utter nonsense! Of course you will, and I wouldn't think much of you if you didn't. Just so it isn't another like Clodia, that's all I ask. I hope to live to see you married to the right sort of girl and the father of a fine family."

Sextus shook his head obstinately. Favilla could not repress a smile. But she had one more task to perform.

"I want to show you something, Sextus," she said in a low voice. "I have used every connection I had to prevent an open scandal – both for Gnaeus's sake, to keep his name from being smirched through me and mine, and for yours, to save you from the disgrace of a public trial. But don't think people haven't suspected that there was something peculiar going on here, what with Aufidia's sudden death, and your carryings-on, and now that affair at Clodia's, with half of Rome as witness. Well, Sextus, yesterday one of the slaves called me and showed me an inscription that somebody had scrawled on the wall of our house. I had it removed at once, but I copied it first so that you could see with your own eyes the kind of thing to which you have exposed your sister."

She went to a chest and drew out a wax tablet. She held it out for Sextus to read what was written on it.

> Clodia, they say, was noted for
> Devotion to her brother:
> Her case, it seems, has set the style,
> For here we find another.
>
> While Manlius hides away in Spain,
> His lady looks on blandly
> And showers her brother with the means
> To play the rich fool grandly.
>
> And when the husband's money's low,
> You still can trust the ladies –
> The heirs can ship an aged aunt
> Quite suddenly to Hades!

Sextus shook with anger.

"Oh, vile!" he breathed. "Vile and false! We both know you never gave me a penny. And Aufidia had no money – she was a burden to you, not a prospective benefactress. And then to hint that *you* had anything to do with her death –!"

Favilla took the tablet from him.

"It's not worth getting too upset about," she said calmly. "From the allusion to Gnaeus, I take it that one of our political enemies is just being nasty."

"Give it to me, Favilla," exclaimed Sextus, reaching for the tablet. "I'm going to find out who wrote this outrageous thing and when I do, I'm going to thrash him roundly."

"You're going to do no such thing. I copied this for you to see, and now I'm going to destroy it. We've had enough gossip around here, and right now life is disturbed enough as it is. I only hoped that if you realized what you had let me in for, you would strengthen your resolve to make up for it by being a different person."

"Oh, I will, Favilla – believe me, I will! This clinches it – I'll never forget that disgusting libel. You, who've been more like my mother than my sister! Listen, Favilla, come with me to the atrium, and I'll swear on the images of our ancestors that to the day I die I'll never again do anything to make you ashamed of me!"

"Idiot!" laughed Favilla, tears in her eyes. "They're Gnaeus's ancestral images there, not ours. Ours, as you very well know, are in safekeeping till you have a wife and home of your own. And I don't want you to swear; I have faith in your bare word. Wait a minute till I wipe off this tablet, and then I'll have them bring in some wine to drink to your new life – and in memory of poor Aufidia, good old soul!"

Her heart was light as she seized the stylus and scraped the tablet clean. The slanderous verses had accomplished their purpose.

Yet she could not help a faint auctorial pang. Those verses had never been written on the wall of Gnaeus Manlius's or any other house. It had taken her many laborious hours, while she planned that interview with her brother, to compose them herself.

The Will

John Maddox Roberts

Though set just two years after the previous story, Roman life has changed forever, with the murder of Julius Caesar. Trying to survive through these turbulent years is Decius Metellus, a Roman administrator and lawyer, who features in the SPQR series by John Maddox Roberts. Starting with SPQR (1990), the series has now reached eleven volumes, though only the first seven have appeared in English, the latest being The Tribune's Curse *(2003).*

"We're trying to find his father's will," the big, soldierly-looking fellow informed me. The odd youth seated next to him just looked at me with a wide-eyed, reptilian stare. I detested him without even knowing who he was.

· "I see, and who might this father be?"

"Caesar," said the big man. A closer look told me he was little older than the other. His size and his tough looks made him seem the elder.

I contributed to the silence that followed. This was not the sort of thing one expected to hear on an otherwise unexceptionable morning in Rome. Now I gave the wide-eyed boy a closer look. He was scrawny, with a big head on a thin neck and a shock of unruly, light-coloured hair. I couldn't see much family resemblance. He had the beginnings of a straggly beard and wore a dark, dingy toga, both tokens of mourning. A lot of Romans were wearing mourning at that time.

"Then you would be young Octavius?" I said.

"I am Caius Julius Caesar," he said stiffly, then added, "Octavianus." He gestured to the larger man. "And this is Marcus Agrippa. I am Caesar's son and I have come to Rome to receive my legacy."

"Good luck," I told him. "I hear that Antonius has pretty well laid hands on all of Caesar's property and he's not a man to provoke. I'd advise you to go back to Athens or wherever you were and write him a nice letter. He might let you have some of the land and Caesar's library. Antonius doesn't have much use for books."

"It was Appolonia," Agrippa growled. "It's in Illyria."

Of course I knew where Appolonia was. I'd been there. I also knew that young Octavian had been sent there. There was just something about the boy that made me want to needle him. A character failing of mine, I suppose, but nothing that happened later caused me to alter my first impression.

"I am Caesar's heir and I've come to claim what it mine by right!" The way he said this was profoundly unsettling. In spite of myself, I was reminded of our recently deceased Dictator.

"You were Caesar's friend," Agrippa said. "You are married to his niece. You should want to see his will carried out."

"I would very much like to see the provisions of Caesar's will carried out," I told them. "He left me a generous bequest. But what I really, truly want above all is not to be murdered like he was. Being murdered is a messy business and it can ruin a perfectly good toga. Defying Antonius is a good way to get murdered. He's a nice enough fellow, don't get me wrong. I've always gotten on well with him and I've helped him out of a few scrapes. But he *is* an Antonius and the Antonii are a family of hereditary criminals. He likes to keep what he's seized and he's surrounded by friends who love to put obstacles out of his path."

Agrippa snorted. "In Greece we were told that Metellus was a man who could get things done, that he's a man who doesn't frighten easily." I was getting to be known by a single name in those days, mainly because the prominent men of my family had been killed or exiled in the last round of civil wars. They had backed Pompey and that was the sort of mistake you didn't make twice. I was about the only prominent Caecilius Metellus left in Rome, and trying to keep my head down.

"Listen," I said. "I was there when Caesar's will was read at the house of Calpurnius Piso. Believe me, it was almost worth not getting my bequest just to see the look on Antonius's face when he learned that the vast bulk of the estate was going to you," I nodded at Octavian, "and your little brother. And of course there were the 300 sesterces per citizen and the great gardens, which he left to the public: Antonius didn't dare interfere with those. He does love being the darling of the people." I could see the boy's jaw clench at mention of the gardens and the money. Clearly he thought it should all be his, no matter what his adoptive father had wished.

I was getting tired of this. "Rome has always been a hazardous place," I told them. "Right now it is a very deadly place, especially for men of ambition. Soon, I fear, we shall see the old days of Marius and Sulla again: proscription lists and paid informers and blood in the streets. Only this time there will be no men of the stature of those two, just a pack of second-raters tearing at Rome and at each other like dogs fighting over a carcass. At least Marius whipped the barbarians and Sulla gave us a fine constitution. The current lot will ruin the empire through pure incompetence."

"None of that matters," Octavian said.

"What do you mean?" I asked, puzzled.

"All the property, the money, even the provinces they are so busy apportioning to themselves. Caesar's strength wasn't in his wealth but in his soldiers. The one who commands their loyalty will be the new master of Rome." Agrippa cut an impatient look at him, obviously wishing he'd keep his mouth shut. But, for some reason, the boy was the dominant of the two.

For my own part, I just gaped. We seldom encounter such presumption in one so young. Clodius at his worst wasn't a match for this one. "I don't think we need –" I was cut short by the timely arrival of my wife, Julia.

"Caius!" she cried delightedly, clapping her hands. She rushed to embrace the little lout. "And you must be Marcus Agrippa. Why, you've both grown so much since I last saw you!" As if that were some sort of accomplishment.

"How wonderful to see you, cousin!" said the boy, and to my amazement his face lit up with unfeigned pleasure. Well, Julia could charm a Parthian off his horse. "We've been speaking with this – with your distinguished husband, who seems to have been out of Rome on my previous visits." This was not quite the case. I'd just never bothered to go to any of his appearances and Caesar had packed him off to Illyria when things got lively at home.

"We think your husband could help us with a difficulty we have," Agrippa added.

"And I am sure he will be most happy to render you every assistance," said my ever-helpful wife. I tried to signal her, but as usual she ignored me. "What is the problem?"

"It's Antonius," Octavian said. "He's confiscated

Caesar's will and all his other papers. The provisions of the will are public knowledge but that isn't worth much without the original document. Besides, I believe that in his other writings, my father makes it known that I am to succeed to his other offices and powers."

I couldn't help wincing every time he referred to Caesar as his father. I had had a decidedly mixed experience with that strange and difficult person, but he was the one truly great man I had ever known; as close to being a demigod as a mortal ever gets. To hear this little wretch claim paternity of such a father was ludicrous. And among Caesar's many offices was that of Dictator. Surely he wasn't claiming that, too?

"Intolerable!" cried Julia. "Antonius is such an odious man! I never understood Caesar's regard for him, except as a soldier. He should have taken action against the assassins and other conspirators instantly. Instead, he has made peace with them. It is a dishonour and a disgrace!" I had explained to her the many very good reasons why Antonius had been unable to do so, but she refused to accept them. Julia had a blind spot where her beloved uncle was concerned.

"I could not agree more, cousin," the boy said, with Agrippa nodding grimly beside him. "He is a vicious, rapacious villain and he aspires to all of Caesar's honours."

"Don't be too rough on him," I said, pouring myself a Falernian. "He gave Caesar a wonderful funeral speech. Lied through his teeth, of course, but he made the old boy look good and the conspirators look bad." All three of them glared at me, for some reason. That called for yet more Falernian.

"The fact is, my lady," Agrippa said, "we must have those documents to show the soldiers. They are simple men, very impressed by official documents, and they revere the memory of Caesar. Just now Antonius commands their loyalty, as the commander nearest to Caesar at the time of his death, but they are confused just now and could be swayed by lies of the conspirators, or they could attach themselves firmly to Antonius. To press our Caesar's claims, we must have his father's papers."

"I understand," Julia told him. "And I am sure that my husband can get them for you. Don't mind his gruff manner, it's just his way. He will do whatever needs be to set things right." No question of consulting me about this, you will notice.

"Very well," I said. It had occurred to me that, if I made a nuisance of myself, Antonius might simply do away with the brat. "I'll see what's to be done." I saw them to the door. "I knew your father, you know," I told Octavian. "He once threatened me with execution. One day I was brawling with Clodius and practically cut his throat right in front of your father's court. We'd been rolling through the streets and I finally had him down, had his head jerked back and my dagger applied to his jugular, when I looked up and there was the *praetor urbanus* Caius Octavius, big as day, seated on his curule chair and a Vestal sitting right beside him. Would've been death for me to kill Clodius right in front of those two, and I never got another chance as good." I chuckled at the memory. Those were the good old days.

The boy turned at the door and said, coldly, "My father was Julius Caesar." And they left.

I went back to the courtyard. "Why did you tell them I'd help them?" I demanded of Julia. "It should be enough that I don't like him. More to the point, if I want to stay alive, I have to walk carefully around Antonius. He has no quarrel with me now, but if he even suspects I'm plotting against him with some rival —"

"Oh, don't be so timid," she said. "You'll just be pursuing a legal matter, just like any senator. And young Octavian is the coming man, did Rome but know it. You'll do well to put him in your debt."

"That child? What makes you think he's ever going to amount to anything?"

"First, because Caesar adopted him. He wouldn't have done that for anyone he didn't consider a worthy heir. Second, what did you think of Marcus Agrippa?"

That took me aback. "Very impressive: soldierly, capable, tough and intelligent. He's the one that looks like consular material, not the boy."

"Yet you can see he all but worships Octavian. He is devoted and loyal. Doesn't that tell you anything?"

She had a point, not that I was willing to concede it. "What of it? Clodius inspired loyalty in better men. Did that make him great?"

"Clodius came of the family of the Claudia Nerones, who are insane. Octavian's heritage is that of Octavius and Atius and, most importantly, Caesar, all fine and sensible families." She had a patrician's grasp of family connections. She also had their blindness to the fact that it is wealth that determines any family's importance, not any splendid qualities they are fancied to have inherited.

"He'll be nothing but trouble. Listen to the way he uses that name, as if he had a right to it!"

"Caesar did adopt him," she said.

"He adopted him in his will," I pointed out. "Such a testamentary adoption has to be ratified by a praetor and a court. That's not likely to happen while Antonius holds the whip."

"Dear," Julia said, "just go find those papers. I will handle relations with young Octavian. He's my cousin, after all." She poured me another cup of Falernian, rather than attempt to curb my intake in her usual fashion. I took this as an ominous sign.

★   ★   ★

My first call was upon Cicero. He possessed the finest legal mind in Rome, though his political acumen was deserting him. At this time he was engaged in making a series of mistakes which would culminate in his death a few years later. He had taken no part in the conspiracy to murder Caesar, but he had made no secret of his approval of it. This was understandable if he had intended to throw himself wholeheartedly into the cause of Brutus and Cassius, but he tried to hew to a middle course and please everybody, a sure recipe for suicide.

He received me hospitably, as always. "Decius Caecilius! How good of you to call. Come join me." We went into his library and indulged in the usual refreshments and small talk, then I broached the cause of my visit.

"Ah, yes, that remarkable young man. I spoke with him just yesterday, and assured him of my good will and support." This was typical of Cicero in those days. First, approve of the murderers of Caesar, then try to befriend his adopted son.

"I gave him no such assurance," I told him, "but Julia prodded me into helping him."

He laughed dryly. "The things we men do to assure domestic harmony, eh? As a matter of fact, I recommended you to him. You've undertaken many odd projects in the past."

"I wish you hadn't. But it seems I have to try. By what right does Antonius retain the papers?"

He laced his fingers across his small paunch and gazed at his ceiling. "Let me see – how many soldiers does Antonius command?"

"Several legions seem loyal to him," I answered.

"And how many soldiers have you, or Octavian?"

"None."

He spread his hands, his point made.

"And yet," I said, "Antonius has never been, shall we say, one to place a high value on paper, be the contents poetry or a will. Why is he so determined to retain these?"

"Probably because he knows that simple, common men hold written documents in awe. The rabble of the city and the soldiers of the legions are just such men."

"There has to be something else," I objected. "Antonius can charm the populace and the legions alike. It's his specialty."

"It is true that he has few other talents," Cicero sniffed. "He is a fine soldier, but Rome has many such. To hear him speak in public, one would never guess that he has the mind of an ox. Rome has seen many mediocre men in the ascendant, though few have risen as high as Antonius. Mind you, he had to wrap himself in Caesar's bloody toga to do it."

"So there is no legal pretext I can use to pry the papers from him?"

"You have the law on your side," Cicero assured me. "But the law does not apply to a Dictator, and that is what Antonius is, though without constitutional precedent. He is what he is by threat and force of arms."

So, having found no help from that quarter, I went to call on the next man on my list: the great Marcus Antonius himself.

I found him in the mansion he had built for himself on the Palatine. It was a gaudy place, worthy of Lucullus at his most ostentatious. Antonius had been noted for personal extravagance in his youth. Caesar had made him comport himself with greater dignity and simplicity, but now Caesar's constraints were off. I practically had to kick aside the peacocks and other exotic fowl as I crossed his formal gardens, where scores of slaves planted and tended imported trees and shrubs, culled flowers, dug new beds, hauled water and so forth. Artisans installed fountains that showered perfumed water or even wine; others inlaid the walkways with picture-mosaics. Everywhere stood fine Greek statues, stolen from the cities of Asia or seized from his Roman enemies. In short, everything was being done to create a setting worthy of Rome's most splendid man, Marcus Antonius.

The house was full of his sycophants. They paid decent respect to my ancient and illustrious name, if not to me personally. Everyone remembered that my family had taken sides against Caesar, though I had not. A few were his legates and senior commanders; serious military men. Most, however, were merely the sort who always attach themselves to any man whose star seems to be in the ascendant, and who desert him as swiftly when his star sets. I have forgotten almost all of their names.

One of the few I do remember came to greet me. "Decius Caecilius! We haven't seen you in too long!" It was Sallustius Crispus, a man I always despised. "Have you come to pledge your loyalty to Marcus Antonius at last?"

"Why?" I asked him. "Has he been voted king while my back was turned?"

He sidled closer. That was the way Sallustius was: he sidled. "Don't be foolish, Metellus. I advise you for your own good: make peace with Antonius and give him your loyalty."

"I was never at odds with him in the first place," I insisted, wondering even as I said it why I bothered explaining myself to this worm. It was just the sort of man he was. Sallustius could infuriate me by wishing me a good day.

"Didn't say you were, I assure you. It's just that lines are being drawn just now. A man must take sides."

"True. I've decided to side with young Octavian." I don't know why I said it. Perhaps I just wanted to see the expression on his ugly face change, which indeed it did.

"Octavian? He's a nobody!"

"Well, I've always liked long odds at the Circus," I told him.

"In this game, it's not chariots," he spat. "It's more like pitting a fifth-rate tyro against a champion of the arena."

This man Sallustius was an especially egregious specimen of the sort of senator we had in those days, the ones who contributed so much to the downfall of the Republic. He had served as an ineffective Tribune of the Plebs, been kicked out of the Senate by the censor Appius Claudius, wormed his way into Caesar's favour and got reinstated with his help. After that he clung to Caesar like a limpet and rode that man's fortunes to the top. He was given Africa to govern and plundered the place thoroughly and at that time was accounted one of the richest men in Rome. But in a time of contending warlords a man of no family only kept his wealth by adhering to a powerful man, and Sallustius had chosen Antonius. He also had pretensions to being an historian and man of letters.

"I'm here to see him on a legal matter," I said impatiently.

"Oh, well. I'll take you to see him." Apparently, he had appointed himself Antonius's steward or major-domo, an office usually occupied by a slave. But some men are slaves by nature, and love to ingratiate themselves by servile acts.

We found Antonius amidst his cronies, and the sight of him took me somewhat aback. They were in a courtyard, enjoying the sunshine, some of them wrestling or fencing with wooden weapons, as if this were the *palaestra*. In the midst of this athletic throng Antonius held forth, dressed in a brief tunic that appeared to be made largely of silk, a fabric so precious that it was forbidden by the censors from time to time, and forbidden to women at that. Men weren't even supposed to think of wearing the stuff.

Under pretext of mourning, he cultivated a full beard.

Antonius never needed much excuse to go bearded. He fancied that it increased his resemblance to Hercules, the supposed ancestor of his family. The name supposedly came from Anton, a son of Hercules. His hands gleamed with golden rings and he even wore a necklace of heavy gold links.

This whole rig would have been thought effeminate, had Antonius not been such a hulking brute of a man. He caught sight of me and waved me over. I complied and he draped a massive arm over my shoulder, making me a present of some of his manly sweat. He'd been wrestling despite his priceless clothing, and sand still clung to his limbs and dusted his beard and hair.

"Metellus!" he roared. "What an honour! I haven't seen you in far too long! Come to join me, have you? Well, there's work to be done! War with Parthia, for one thing!" As you may guess, he had a declamatory style. "Plenty of positions for experienced soldiers. Gallic cavalry's your specialty, Metellus. Do you want a command? I've recruited whole troops of Gallic horsemen."

"Decius Caecilius tells me he has decided to support Octavian," Sallustius said nastily. I expected Antonius to fly into a rage, but he shot me a calculating look instead. The rest of the men fell silent and some of them tried to put distance between themselves and me.

"And why not?" Antonius grumbled at last. "Octavian's his wife's cousin, and we all know Caesar thought the world of the boy." He glared around him and the rest shuffled about, uncertain how to react.

"Actually, I've come to confer with you on a legal matter, Marcus," I told him.

"Well, let's go inside. I'm sure these gentlemen can spare us for a few minutes." He swept the others with his gaze and they drew away to talk among themselves in little knots. Sallustius looked as if he wanted to follow us, but he held back as we went into the house, the sandy, sweaty arm still around my shoulders.

Antonius had a study of sorts, though I am not sure how he could reach his books, what with the great clutter of armour, swords, horse-gear and other masculine objects. His helmet sat on the head of a marble Apollo carved by Praxiteles and he kept daggers in a priceless Corinthian vase. The nearest thing to scholarly appurtenances close to hand were some maps, most of them depicting the east from Greece to Egypt. I noted a single desk with the usual honeycomb-style book holder with all but two or three of its cells empty. Its writing table was clear except for inkpots and a penholder.

Antonius bawled for wine. Then, unlike most arrogant men, he waited until the slaves had withdrawn before he spoke.

"The papers, right?" he said.

"Exactly. As Caesar's adopted son, they belong to Octavian."

"Adopted only provisionally. And the will was read publicly, everyone knows what was in it. Why should the boy want the document itself?"

"Why do you wish to retain it? And why the other papers as well?" I tried the wine, which was predictably splendid.

"I need them for research," he said. "I'm writing the life of Caesar."

It is greatly to my credit that my nose did not erupt with expensive wine.

He shook his head. "Listen, Metellus. I am doing all I can to avert another civil war. People take it ill that I haven't avenged Caesar as I should have. I've driven Brutus and Cassius and the others from the city. But they are alive, and they shouldn't be. The last thing we need is another contender for the loyalty of Caesar's men. You know perfectly well that is what the ambitious little monster wants the papers for."

This was true enough. "You know as well as I that he has no chance of gaining power," I assured him. "Why not let him have the will?"

"In time, in time," he said airily. "When I am through with it and the other items. There are projects to finish, alliances to be made and, eventually, wars to be fought."

"You mean the Parthian campaign?" I asked. Caesar had been about to depart for the war with Parthia when he was murdered. He wanted to avenge his old friend Crassus and take back the eagles lost at Carrhae. That defeat still rankled, though the whole war had been stupendously unpopular and most people thought Crassus got what he deserved. Still, the loss of the better part of seven legions was a humiliation hard to bear.

"Yes, that one – and others."

"Others?" This sounded ominous. "You don't mean another civil war, do you?"

"Not necessarily," he hedged. "Sextus Pompey is still active in Spain, you know." As if fighting yet another Roman army, led by a son of Pompey the Great, did not constitute civil war.

"Excellent," I said, "because you just said that you were trying to avoid one."

"It's not a good time for a civil war," he affirmed, meaning that he didn't feel himself strong enough just yet. Either he was less foolhardy than in his younger years, or he knew something I didn't. I suspected the latter. Nothing ever taught Antonius good sense but he could sometimes be impressed by bald facts.

Something had struck me. "Just what else is there, besides the will?"

"A great heap of paper," he said. "You know how Caesar was – you were practically his secretary for a while, in Gaul. Always scribbling stuff: campaign histories, observations of the natives and their customs, letters, even a few poems. It will take my librarian a while to go through it all."

"Librarian? I didn't know you had one."

"Sallustius volunteered to take care of my paperwork. He's arranging those things now."

This was more like it. "There is no way that you are going to give Octavian those papers?"

"I'm afraid not."

I rose. "Then I won't trouble you further."

"You had to try. I understand. He is a relation, after all."

"Don't remind me." I stepped to the little desk, as if to admire its fine woodwork. On the few scrolls it held I could see Caesar's unmistakably terrible handwriting. "I'll be going."

"Come back soon," he urged. "That offer stands open. I'll need all the good officers I can get." He didn't know the half of it, as events later proved.

I made my way home and summoned my freedman, Hermes. I gave him a brief account of my mission and its failure. He nodded grimly; bored as usual by anything that did not portend danger and violence.

"You remember when we first went to Gaul and I acted as Caesar's secretary?"

"Quite well," he said. "You got in bad with all those officers and Caesar put you to desk work to get you away from them. And there was that German princess –"

"Quiet!" I whispered, knowing that Julia might be eavesdropping. "What I was getting at, is that Caesar *needed* a secretary because he had that strange affliction that makes it so difficult for a man to write. He wrote things backwards and transposed letters and so forth."

He nodded. "You told me."

"Well, I think I know who his secretary may have been in the last days of his life."

"Why do you care about secretaries?"

"Shut up. Just because you're a citizen and can't be flogged doesn't mean I can't make your life miserable. Who was closest to Caesar in the last days? Aside from Calpurnia, I mean.

"Octavian?"

"No. I mean what man toadied up to him the closest? What man sucked up to him and kissed the hem of his toga and flattered him and laughed loudest at his jokes and wiped his —"

"Oh. You're talking about Sallustius Crispus."

"Exactly. He has volunteered to be Antonius's secretary and librarian and I'll wager he did the same for Caesar."

"So what of it?"

"So tonight we are going to burgle his house."

The smile that spread across his face warmed my heart.

That night we went out in dingy tunics and soft-soled Gallic shoes, prepared to skulk and steal. It wasn't the first time we'd done this, although we never did it often enough to keep Hermes happy. He was a criminal by inclination and this made him a very valuable resource, because the times called for a great deal of criminality, some of it on my own part. As a senator and occasional magistrate I understood the importance of rule of law and good civic order, but many distinguished philosophers had told me that one ought always to avoid extremes, so I was not extremely law-abiding.

To approach the townhouse of Sallustius we crossed his huge and very beautiful gardens, which I could admire even in the gloomy night. "He bought himself some good taste to build this," I commented in a whisper.

"He could afford it," Hermes whispered back, "what with the way he squeezed Africa. Now be quiet." Ordinarily I did not take orders from Hermes, but in this activity he was my superior, and I followed his advice. A good thing I did because moments later we came upon a watchman. Before he could make a sound, Hermes was on him like a ghost and we left him under a myrrh-bush, gagged and trussed like a roasting hare with his own tunic and belt. We had to take care of two or three more in the same way before we reached the house. Sallustius was a distrustful man, for some reason. Soon we were at the east wall.

"How do you know we'll find his study here?" Hermes said as we examined the wall.

"In order to catch the morning light," I told him patiently. "Haven't you been with me long enough to know that? You take care of personal and public business in the morning. The afternoon is for the baths and the evening is for eating, drinking and debauchery." He acknowledged my greater mastery in this field. "You see that balcony? That's where his study is. He'll use the balcony to work outside in fine weather. I hope you didn't forget the rope and grapples."

Without a word he reached into his satchel and drew out the rope and the iron hooks. The leather pouch also contained small hammers and chisels, finely crafted prybars and exquisite mechanical spreaders, all made by an artisan in Alexandria. He was a Gaul, and Gauls are the finest iron-workers in the world. They know nothing of housebreaking, but this one had lived most of his life in Alexandria, where the art is appreciated. The tools had cost dearly, but I wanted Hermes to have the best, when he carried out the duties I assigned him.

Ordinarily, I did not go along on these little escapades, but this time I was the one who could recognize what I wanted. I had never been able to teach Hermes an appreciation for literary matters. Besides, I was bored.

With the deceptive ease of the true expert, Hermes cast the

hook up to the balcony, where it landed with the merest tick of sound. He drew it back slowly, coaxing its direction with little tugs, until it lodged firmly. "Got it," he announced.

"You go up first," I told him. "Make sure the room is empty. You know the rules: no noise, no blood, and don't kill anyone who isn't attacking you with a weapon."

He went up the rope with a lightness and ease that was a pleasure to watch. He went over the balcony rail and into the room with no more noise than his own shadow. Moments later he was back at the railing, signalling me to come on up.

I tried to keep in good condition, since I might be called to war at any time and life in Rome frequently called for agility and a fast pair of feet, but I was puffing and wheezing by the time I scrambled awkwardly over the balcony rail.

Hermes' teeth flashed white in his face. "You're getting old."

"You'll know the feeling soon enough," I assured him. "Now, let's get some light in here." Hermes tiptoed out to find a lamp while I waited and got my breath back. The place was new and smelled of fresh wood and plaster, with a subtle, unmistakable tinge of papyrus.

A few minutes later Hermes was back with a small lamp, the sort that are used to illuminate stairways. With it he lighted some of the many elaborate lamps that stood by the reading table and soon I had enough light to read. I told Hermes to stand by the door and catch anyone who might interrupt me.

The library was a fine one, befitting a rich sycophant with literary pretensions. Its walls were decorated with portraits of the great writers of Greek and Latin, with pride of place going to Caesar himself. Great racks of cubbyholes held hundreds of scrolls. But I knew what I was looking for would be in a prominent place, easily accessed, since they would constitute the materials for the wretch's latest project.

Sure enough, I found them stacked on a writing desk beneath a window next to the balcony door: a whole stack of scrolls bearing Caesar's own seal. I began going through them. By the scrolls stood a stack of recent notes written by Sallustius for future reference. I tossed them to the floor, except for a single sheet.

First I separated the documents by handwriting. Some of them I recognized as my own, written by me when I served as Caesar's secretary in Gaul. Others were written in various hands, a few in Caesar's own wretched scrawl. Using the sheet I had retained, I found the ones in Sallustius's own writing. These would be the most recent, written in the last months before Caesar's death. Tags on the ends of two small scrolls identified them as Caesar's will. *Two* wills?

"Somebody coming!" Hermes hissed.

"Gag him," I said, absorbed in the contents of the two little scrolls. I ignored the minor scuffle behind me, unable to believe what I was reading. In time I turned to see Hermes holding a dagger at a man's throat. The fellow's eyes bulged like a toad's, which was rather fitting.

"Good evening, Sallustius," I said pleasantly. The toad-eyes darted about, saw what I had been examining and he wilted. "Now, if I allow you to live will you speak in pleasant, conversational tones and not wake the slaves?" The dagger point scraped his neck and he nodded gingerly. I signalled Hermes to let him go.

"Metellus, this is low even for you," Sallustius said, without much heat. "You've been accused of all sorts of vile behaviour, but I didn't know housebreaking was one of your practices."

"No help for it. I knew what had to be here and just now there's no legal means available to get you to cough these up, so extra-legal measures were called for. I knew where to look when Antonius all but served you up on a platter this afternoon."

He rolled his eyes. "That lunkhead! What tipped you?"

"He said he was writing a biography of Caesar. The very idea was ludicrous, but I knew that something had to have put the idea in his head. He said you'd volunteered to handle his papers and you fancy yourself a historian, therefore, you must have the relevant documents, including *both* wills. You wrote them at Caesar's dictation, didn't you?"

"Of course. Including the one that *wasn't* read at Piso's house."

"How did you accomplish that? Piso was executor. Was he in on this?"

"Of course not! He never saw it. I copied it out and Caesar appended his seal. I was to deliver it to Piso and tell him it superseded the other."

"Why didn't you?" I demanded.

"Because Caesar was dead before the ink had a chance to dry. I wrote it down in the early hours of the Ides."

I marvelled at the document, chuckling. "My Julia just has to see this. Sallustius, you are going to be my guest tonight. You will escort us out the front door and we'll have a little drink while I decide what to do with you. Hermes, gather up all these papers."

"Do with me? Metellus, you are going to do whatever will keep you safe, and that means keeping your mouth shut and leaving me strictly alone." It pains me to say it, but the man wasn't entirely without intelligence or courage.

"That's to be seen. Let's go." And so we went out through the darkened streets of Rome to my house in the Subura.

"Brutus!" Julia all but shrieked. "He left everything to Brutus! I can't believe it! He adopted Octavian!"

"Caesar had a way of changing his mind," Sallustius said,

holding a silver goblet that held heated wine with a dash of vinegar, just the thing to take the edge off a chilly night in April.

"And," I said, "there are those old stories that he fathered Brutus. Caesar and Servilia were quite close, you know."

"Nonsense!" she said. "He'd have had to father Brutus when he was only fourteen years old! It's not –" she looked at us, but we just looked back with that expression of bland innocence we always give to our women. "I still don't believe it!"

"You don't have to," I assured her. "This was not to be the last will, surely. One day it was Octavian, the next Brutus, probably Antonius soon enough. He was a calculating man and he wanted all his cronies to keep guessing who would receive his favour. It bound them to him."

"But how would they know?" she asked.

I looked at Sallustius. "Oh, I think he had reason to believe that word would get whispered in the right ears." He studied the decoration on my wall. Not as splendid as his own, of course.

Now Julia glared at him. "So you went to Antonius and told him about the second will, and he bribed you to keep it secret."

"Bribed me?" he said, offended. "I am already as rich as he is. I wanted all of Caesar's papers for my biography."

"To which Antonius graciously assented, since he can barely read. Sallustius, you'll have to talk to Octavian if you want to use them for your work. They're going to him, as I agreed."

"Metellus," he said, "Antonius greatly preferred the earlier will, because he knew he could dominate a callow boy like Octavian. And Caesar adopted the boy. But if you let it be known that Caesar favoured Brutus above Antonius, he'll regard you as his mortal enemy."

"Let me worry about that. As for you, Sallustius, I advise you to retire from political life and stick to your scribbling. We're about to have another round of squabbling warlords, and to them such men as you are eminently disposable. One or another of them will denounce you just to lay hands on your wealth. Now be off with you." With a sour look he slunk from my house. He took my advice, too.

"What are we going to do with this?" Julia said, shaking her head at the will. "We can't let the world know that Caesar willed everything to his own murderer."

"Nor shall we," I said, pouring myself another cup with great satisfaction. "Tomorrow, I will go to the house of Antonius again, and this time I will burn that document in front of him. Not to keep your uncle from looking like a gullible fool, but to save my own neck. It's all he wants, anyway. He never had any use for the other papers and this will put him in my debt once again. That could come in handy, soon. Let Octavian have them."

Besides, I knew that the little nobody would never amount to anything.

These things happened in the year 710 of the city of Rome, during the unconstitutional rule of the *Magister Equitum* Marcus Antonius.

Honey Moon

Marilyn Todd

*We move on a little over thirty years to the early days of
the Roman Empire. The young Octavian of the previous
story has become the all powerful Emperor Augustus. It
was Augustus who brought peace to the Roman world and
established a brief Golden Age. It was during this time that
Marilyn Todd set the books about her scheming minx
Claudia Seferius, who first appeared in* I, Claudia
*(1995). Fans of Claudia may be surprised to find she is
getting married again, but those who know Claudia know
there's more to this than meets the eye.*

The roar of the crowds followed Claudia as her procession
wound its way down the Via Sacra, past the Temple of
the Divine Julius into the Forum. Hardly the quickest route to
Arlon's house – but, by Jupiter, it was the one that would
attract the most attention! She'd hired the best for today.
Jugglers, tumblers, musicians and dancers, with a stilt-walker
to bring up the rear. But that was only half of the story.

"My dear child."

Claudia had been buffing her fingernails in the peristyle
when the priest burst in, his long white robes billowing in his
wake.

"You do realise that only brides on their wedding day are entitled to wear the orange veil?"

"So?" she had asked, without glancing up.

"So this is *sacrilege*!" he exploded, as much at her disdain as the religious outrage. "I cannot allow it."

Claudia examined her cuticles, buffed again, then, satisfied with the shine, adjusted her pendant, checked her pearl ear-studs and picked up the small, battered bowl from the marble bench beside her. Finally, she tossed the veil nonchalantly over her head.

"This dye isn't orange," she said levelly. "It's flame." She watched the priest's eyes narrow in fury before adding cheerfully, "The valance which veils the top of my litter is orange."

Imbecile. Did he imagine she didn't know what she was doing? Did he think she'd let an occasion like this pass, without having half of Rome turn out to witness it? And what a feast the procession was for their eyes! The young widow of the wine merchant Gaius Seferius being transported shoulder-high on an open litter through the streets of Rome by eight of the most handsome and muscular bearers in the whole of the Empire, accompanied by the finest entertainers in town.

"For gods' sake, slow down," she told the bearers. "This isn't a bloody foot race." Dammit, any faster and they'd be there in ten minutes, with an Olympic medal to boot. "There's an extra denarius apiece if you take another half-hour."

The bearers eased up so quickly, she was almost thrown off the cushions. The crowd laughed, believing it was part of the act. She laughed back. And made a mental note to reduce the bearers' tip to only half a denarius.

"Good luck, love!" cheered the throng.

"All the best!"

"May the gods smile on you, darlin'!"

They were all there. Coppersmiths, perfumers, mule doctors and rent boys, cleaving a path for her noisy cavalcade. Auctioneers, surveyors, stonemasons and barbers stepped aside to watch her pass. Fishwives, sack-makers, tax collectors and chandlers whistling and clapping their hands. Claudia returned every wave with equal vigour. Dear me, so many well-wishers, it brought a mist to her eyes. Young and old, rich and poor, sick and healthy, they stopped what they were doing to cheer her on. Cradling the battered bowl to her breast, she didn't realize she'd been rubbing it until:

"In my country," an Arab with rings in his ears called out from the crowd, "we use lamps to conjure up jinni."

Thank Croesus her face was hidden by the veil. She adjusted her expression, lifted the linen, a perfect smile pasted in place.

"My good luck charm," she retorted. "I never go anywhere important without it."

"Looks like an old begging bowl to me," someone else shouted.

"It is," she laughed, waving the battered bronze cup in the air. "I begged Apollo for sunshine and look! Not a cloud in the sky."

As she planted an ostentatious kiss on the metalwork, she felt her stomach churn and quickly dropped the veil back over her face. *But there was no going back now –*

"Be happy, love!" the crowd chanted.

"May you and your husband be blessed!"

Ah. Husband. On her soft swansdown pillows scented with chamomile, Claudia shifted position.

Tall as a Dacian, lean as an athlete, bronzed as Adonis himself, Arlon was one of Rome's most eligible bachelors. With his glossy blond hair and marble quarries spread across Africa and the Aegean, not to mention a flush of stud farms

down south, Arlon had it all. The big house in Rome. Villa in
the country. Winners galore at the Circus Maximus racetrack. And today, on this twenty-first day of June, on the
shortest night of the year and under a clear sky when a full
moon would transmute blackness into silver, Claudia Seferius would be plighting her troth to this man.

*Widow and widower, bound together until death do them
part.*

She considered the gifts she was bringing. Most, like the
ivory inlaid chair and the thick Persian carpet, had been
despatched separately, but others, like the beads of Arabian
frankincense resin and the heavy gold betrothal medallion,
were not the kind of presents which should be delivered by
an anonymous household slave. Neither – she patted the
onyx perfume phial and the engraved silver hip flask in her
lap – were these. Such treasures were to be handed over
personally. When the occasion demanded.

Having circled the Forum, the procession now left the way
it had come. Behind the Temple of the Divine Julius, back
up the Via Sacra, then branching off towards Arlon's great
sprawling mansion on the Esquiline Hill. There were no
crowds lining these elegant, patrician streets, but Claudia
didn't care. She had done what she set out to do. The orange
drapes round her litter and the orange veil on her head might
have contravened the odd convention or two, but since when
had conventions mattered to Claudia Seferius? She had been
noticed today. *That's* what mattered.

For the men in the crowds, there had been only goodwill
wished upon her. In the women, though, she had seen mixed
emotions. Most of them, of course, had turned out for no
other reason than to enjoy the acrobats, give their toddlers
their first sight of a stilt-walker and to cheer on the bride-to-
be.

Others had a different agenda. They were the ones standing

pinch-lipped and smug. Brought to book at last, the uppity
bitch. I mean, who did she think she was, taking over her
husband's wine business, indeed! These women had lined the
route, arms folded over their chests in grim satisfaction that
everything she owned (or at least, everything the gold-digging
bitch had inherited!) would pass to Arlon after the wedding.
Arlon would see she kept her place. Arlon would make sure
she'd do what she should have been doing a long time ago.
Keeping house and dropping babies like everyone else. To
that section of the crowd, not fooled by her misuse of the veil,
Claudia waved harder than ever.

But there was a third group of women which had caught
her attention. A minority, true, but they were the ones who
weren't smiling either in joy or schadenfreude. Who hadn't
thrown rose petals into her path.

You had a chance, said their sad, accusing eyes. *You had
the chance to pave the way for other women to take on the men in
their own world. Instead, you betrayed us. You sold the sisterhood out.*

The litter drew to a halt outside Arlon's villa. Trumpets
sounded. A carpet of red shot with gold thread was thrown
out across the pavement to welcome her. Rainbow ribbons
soaked in lavender and cedar wood oil streamed down from
the rooftops. In a vestibule lined with lilies in tall silver pots
and elegant floral frescoes, liveried slaves carried her in on
their hands to an atrium gleaming in marble and gold. Here,
light streamed in through the roof, fountains danced, and
bronze charioteers guided Arlon's bronze stallions in an
eternal victory lap. Surrounded by priests, family, friends,
business colleagues and neighbours, the man of the house
stepped proudly forward.

Claudia stretched out both hands to greet her blond
Adonis and smiled. I ask you. *What* sisterhood?

★   ★   ★

"I shall cherish this moment for the rest of my life." With great tenderness, Arlon rubbed the ring he had just slipped on Claudia's finger and brought it gently to his lips.

"Ah," sighed the congregation, and one or two of the women surreptitiously dabbed at their eyes.

"The physicians tell us there's a nerve which runs from the ring finger direct to the heart," Arlon murmured, smiling deep into Claudia's eyes, "and that it is this nerve which governs our happiness. Sealed for eternity by this gold band of love, may the gods strike me dead if I ever have cause to harm you." This time he raised both her hands to his lips. "I love you, Claudia. I love you with all my heart and with all my soul, and nothing and no one can change the way that I feel. You do know that, don't you?"

Claudia felt an unaccustomed rush of colour to her face. "Yes," she said quietly. "I know that, Arlon."

Now the women were sobbing quite openly, and there were a few sniffs from the men in the audience as well. Even the priest had to swallow.

"Let us make sacrifice with offerings of spelt," he intoned solemnly, "that the gods may bless this joyful betrothal."

They made such a good-looking couple, he thought, so in love, that he had forgiven Claudia her transgressions over the veil. Her previous husband had been old when they'd wed. Fat as a pig, if he recalled correctly, with bad teeth and a bald spot. A marriage of convenience for both parties, and now that the husband was dead, and looking at a lifetime of happiness with a dashing and virile young blade, what woman wouldn't want to advertise her wedding twice over? The priest, laying spelt cakes on the altar and pouring libations, couldn't begrudge her the orange veil for her betrothal, as well as her marriage.

All the same, he wondered why she hung on to that battered bronze bowl, even during the ceremony, when tradition decreed both hands should be free. It had made his task of exchanging rings and medallions virtually impossible, and he'd had to call one of his acolytes to assist. Most unusual woman, this beautiful young widow, and the priest resolved to have a word with Arlon before the wedding. Intractability is no asset in a wife and if this wilfulness looked like it was persisting, the priest would recommend a jolly good beating. A tactic which had certainly brought his own wife to heel.

"When did you sweethearts meet?" one old hen clucked.

"Yes, do tell us. And where?" clucked another.

"It was last Saturnalia," Claudia told the middle-aged female crowd which had knotted around her. "I'd laid on a sumptuous banquet and invited a select group of merchants round, in the hope of persuading them to sign up for barrel loads of Seferius wine, when —"

"When Arlon persuaded you to love him, instead!" the hens shrieked.

"Well, no, actually," Claudia said. "His first words were, 'How much would you take for your cook?'"

Everyone laughed.

Claudia slipped away.

Outside in the garden, it was hotter, not cooler. The mosaics and marble, the honeycomb screens and gently waving ostrich feather fans conspired to keep the atrium at an ambient temperature, despite the crush of the revellers. But there were too many people talking at once. She needed the space. And the quiet.

Her gown trailing over the path, she found a secluded bench in the shade, overhung by clusters of fragrant pink damask roses. Jewel-coloured birds chirruped and preened in an aviary set in the wall, and marble nymphs danced round fountains which splashed prettily and made prisms as the drops caught the sun. She sat down on the marble bench and stretched out feet shod in the softest white leather. The air was heavy with birdsong and the buzzing of bees, and scented from swathes of bright purple lavender, with valerian, pinks, and a thousand sweet-smelling herbs.

Why, then, could she feel no peace in her heart?

"I suppose there's no point in my asking what you're up to this time?" the bay tree to her left asked in a melodious baritone.

Claudia spun round. The bay tree was grinning.

"Marcus Cornelius Orbilio, don't you ever think of approaching people in a normal fashion, instead of creeping up on them?"

"If you'd seen me coming, you'd have run off."

"Doesn't everyone?"

He stepped out from behind the bush, his dark eyes twinkling. *All the better to see you with* . . . "I'll have you know, there are some people who actually like me," he said, settling himself beside her on the bench.

"Name one, and your mother doesn't count."

"Not everyone sees the Security Police in a sinister light," he laughed, tugging at his right ear lobe. *All the better to hear you with* . . . "There are those who actually believe we're an asset to the Empire, rooting out assassins, rapists and thieves."

"Oh well, then. If it's gardening you're into, the potting shed's over there."

The grin broadened, to show white, even teeth. *All the better to eat you with* . . . "Trowel by jury, you mean?"

Orbilio folded his arms behind his head, leaned back against the trunk of the sycamore tree in whose shade they were sitting and closed his eyes. Claudia did not fall into the trap of believing he was asleep. And now she knew that his sandalwood unguent was truly the scent of the hunter.

Time passed. It could have been minutes. Then again, lifetimes might have elapsed.

"Tell me about Arlon," he said at last. "Tell me why you're playing this particular charade."

Until Claudia exhaled, she hadn't realized she'd been holding her breath. She counted to five. Then –

"You're the law," she said brightly. "You know how the system works."

Rome needed babies. As the Empire swelled, so did its population, but it was swelling with the offspring of slaves, not baby citizens. A victim of its own success. With peace came prosperity, and with prosperity came luxury goods, gourmet foods, safer streets, marble temples, libraries, sewers and the dole. It provided everyone with better education and better health. Which, for women, led to improved contraception. Oh, come on. When the risk of dying in childbirth was one in ten, who could blame the poor cows? So a law was passed to reverse the downward trend.

Widows of childbearing age had two years in which to find themselves a new husband. And if it wasn't a man of her choosing, then by Jupiter, she would be forced to accept the choice of the State.

Claudia shot Orbilio a radiant smile. "My two years are nearly up," she said cheerfully. "Arlon is the man I have chosen."

He grunted and closed his eyes again. Cicadas rasped, bees hummed and the heat in the garden pulsed harder. She watched his profile. The patrician nose. The decisive jaw. The vein that beat at the side of his neck. She swallowed. Watched a bumblebee scour the pink blooms of hyssop in its quest for nectar. And found her gaze locked on the flowers long after the bee had flown off.

"Tell me how you two got together," he said.

"It was last Saturnalia," Claudia began. "I'd laid on a sumptuous banquet and –"

"That," he murmured, "is word for word what you told

those old ducks indoors, and an investigator always mistrusts the account which never varies."

"You don't trust your own shadow," she snapped.

A muscle twitched at the side of his mouth. "Flattery will get you nowhere," he said. "Tell me what happened *after* that."

One. Two. Three. "Very simple. I told Arlon, 'I can't sell just one slave. If you want my cook, you'll have to take his wife, his three daughters, his mother-in-law and an aunt, I won't have the family broken up.'"

"Claudia," he growled warningly. One eye opened. "Explain to me – *please* – how it was that several months passed before you and Arlon met up again."

Something tightened beneath Claudia's rib cage. He was the Security Police. What did he know? Correction. How *much* did he know . . . ? Lies formed into a plausible story, but before she could open her mouth, Marcus said,

"You do know the rumours about his late wife?"

Again, Claudia breathed out. "Rumours? Good grief, Orbilio, the woman committed suicide nine months ago. That's hardly a secret."

No one throws themselves off the Tarpeian Rock without the whole of Rome knowing, much less a rich merchant's wife. After all, if you want privacy when you die, you don't leap from the Capitol Hill, right in the heart of the city.

"She jumped at night," Orbilio reminded her. "There were no witnesses to the suicide."

"So?"

"So she wasn't a pauper," he said dryly. "She brought considerable capital to her marriage, and she had no heirs to claim on the estate. Arlon inherited the lot."

Claudia reached up and plucked a rosebud from the truss. "You have my undivided disinterest, Orbilio."

One eyebrow rose in scepticism, but he did not presume to

contradict her. Instead he said, "Just humour me, and tell me how exactly you and Arlon got together. How soon it was, after Saturnalia, that he started to court you?"

A weight lifted from Claudia's stomach. She felt light. Free. Free as the birds in the dovecot.

"Arlon court me?" She tossed the rosebud into his lap and danced off down the path. "My dear Marcus, for an investigator, you really do have a long way to go."

"Excuse me?" He was alert now. Tense and poised.

"Maybe you should follow the family tradition and become a lawyer instead."

"I don't understand." He was on his feet now. Frowning.

"I'm the one who pursued Arlon," she trilled over her shoulder. "Like a terrier, if you must know."

He caught up with her after the betrothal feast, after most of the guests had gone home. Claudia wasn't surprised to see Orbilio at the banquet. Being an aristocrat himself, his own house was a mere stone's throw from Arlon's superlative mansion and he'd probably have been on the invitation list as a matter of course. Neighbour to neighbour, and all that. But Claudia knew that he would have inveigled an invitation anyhow. It was his nature.

As the last guest stumbled out on distinctly unsteady legs and a bawdy song on his lips, she stared around the banqueting hall. Crab claws, lobster shells, cherry pips and meat bones littered the floor between the couches, and a couple of kitchen cats were probing the debris with delicate paws in search of tasty titbits. The sun was sinking fast, casting a vermilion glow over the dining hall and turning the bronze couches to the colour of molten gold. It had been a memorable feast, Claudia reflected with satisfaction. The affianced couple linking arms as they drank a loving cup between courses. Musicians. Poets. Performing apes. Plus a tightrope walker who walked backwards as well as forwards whilst entertaining the gawping diners with ballads. The food had been exquisite. Sucking pig, honeyed dormice, venison and boar, served with asparagus, milk-fed snails and white truffles which had been fetched from the Istrian peninsula. From time to time during the meal, rose petals showered the guests with their fragrance from a mechanical contraption overhead, and iced wine flowed down a river into a pool from which female slaves dressed as water sprites filled the jugs.

Now Claudia watched as, with a snarl and a hiss and with thrashing wide tails, the tabby and the tortoiseshell squared up to one another over a prawn. Too late. The porter's rangy mongrel strolled in through the open windows, scattering felines to the four winds as it proceeded to snaffle up everything in sight, shells and all.

"That dog needs worming," Orbilio said.

"And you need a bell on your collar."

He leaned against the side of a couch, one hand resting lightly on the carved antelope armrest. "That," he said looking round, "was a very good show."

"I thought the snake charmer rather went a bit off-key, but the fire-eater was pretty impressive."

"I'm talking about you," he said. "If you ever fancy a career in the theatre . . ." He let his voice trail off. Then: "What's behind this chicanery, Claudia?"

She scooped up a handful of petals and tossed them in the air, watching as they floated down like pale pink snowflakes. "You're just worried that, once I'm married to Arlon, I'll set your career back a year."

Know your enemy. It was a good rule to live by. And Claudia Seferius knew that this fiercely ambitious young investigator only kept such close tabs on her, because she sailed so close to the wind. She was his fast track to the

Senate. The more results he clocked up, the closer his seat in the Assembly. Why else would he dog her every step?

"Or is it merely a question of dented pride?" she added. "That your hundred percent success record will be broken, if I wriggle off your investigative hook?"

Orbilio sucked in his cheeks. "Whatever you do, Claudia Seferius, and wherever you go, it will always involve some degree of illegality. Believe me, my career is not in jeopardy here."

She stared at the bowl in her hand. He was probably right. She was destined to live life on the edge, pushing herself to the limits, because danger was as vital to Claudia's constitution as oxygen. Without testing yourself, how can you be truly alive?

Outside, the sun had sunk below the rooftops and the sky was the colour of blood. Cicadas buzzed like blunt saws, the heat pulsed, and bats darted round the eaves of the building. Soon, slaves would come to light the oil lamps, but for now the twilight and Claudia were one.

An age passed before he pushed himself away from the couch. She could not make out his expression in the dusk, but she knew without looking that the dancing light in his eyes had died.

"He's a sleaze ball, Claudia."

Something changed inside her, too. "What do you know about Arlon?" she sneered.

She saw his fists clench. "I know that no one gets that rich, that fast, without being a ruthless, callous, grade-A bastard – and Arlon's all that, in spades."

"Strangely enough, Marcus, I'm inclined to agree with you." Claudia scooped her bronze begging bowl into the wine pool. The ice had long melted, making the wine warm, but not unpleasant. "And bloody sexy it makes him, too."

Orbilio frowned. Spiked his hands through his fringe.

"Claudia, if this truly *is* about you needing to find a husband before the State imposes –"

"Why? Are you offering?"

He cleared his throat. Stared at his feet. Shuffled. "You could do worse."

Now who's talking about careers in the theatre? Him, an aristocrat with a lineage going back to Apollo, marry a girl from the slums who'd adopted the identity of a woman who died in the plague in order to hook a wealthy, if ancient, wine merchant? Hades would take day-trippers first. Welcome to my atrium, said the spider to the fly. Oh, really, Marcus Cornelius. Do I *look* like I have wings?

"You don't get it, do you?" she said over the rim of her bowl. "I love Arlon."

"Bullshit. And don't give me that crap about him loving you, either. Arlon wants to get his hands on your assets, Claudia. Nothing more."

Did he really think she hadn't done her homework? Her agents had dug and dug until they hit bedrock and one of the first things that Claudia discovered was that, like herself, Arlon had also married for money the first time around. His wife's fortune had enabled him to buy a marble quarry in Euboea, then another in Alexandria, then another on the island of Chios, until one way and another he'd acquired quite a collection. When the Emperor was hell bent on turning Rome into a city of marble monuments, from temples to baths, statues to fountains, Arlon's quarries worked round the clock to meet the demand. This income in turn funded a string of stud farms round Apulia and Lucania, which, wouldn't you know it, simply couldn't stop turning out winners. At the age of thirty-three, Arlon was rich beyond his wildest dreams. Good grief, by the time he hit forty, he'd have amassed so much wealth, even Midas would turn green with envy!

But that wasn't the issue here.

Claudia cleared her throat. Turned to face the ardent patrician.

"Trust me, Orbilio, there's only one thing Arlon wants to get his hands on," she said pointedly. "And I've promised him that as a betrothal gift."

Even in the twilight, she could see the colour drain from Orbilio's face. "You aren't serious?"

Her heart was drumming. Her mouth was dry. "Never more so," she assured him.

"For gods' sake!" He spun her round to face him. "Claudia, you *can't* sleep with that bastard. He's a monster. A fiend. He killed his wife, for Croesussakes."

She shook off his hands, turned away, but could still smell the sandalwood in her nostrils, taste his minty sweet breath in the back of her throat. And where he had touched her, two handprints burned a hole in her gown.

"He was dining with friends the night his wife committed suicide," she said levelly.

But then, as an investigator, he must surely know that.

"Claudia, please, anything but that. I couldn't bear –"

Enough. "I'm not asking you to bare anything, Orbilio. Now, the betrothal party is over. The music's ended, it's late, the wine's warm, and you're the last guest left, so I'd be obliged if you'd kindly leave me and my husband-to-be in peace."

"Don't go to his bed, Claudia." His voice was ragged with an emotion she couldn't place.

A bad oyster. It must be. She felt nauseous. Faint. Her legs wouldn't support her. But they had to. By all that was holy, *they had to . . .*

"What I do or don't do is none of your goddamned business," she snapped, and there was no quaver in her voice, none at all. Attagirl. "Now get out, before I have the guards throw you out."

She put a hand on the couch to steady herself. Please, Marcus. Please. Go. Go now –

"I'm not going anywhere," he said, and his voice was a rasp. "Unless you come with me."

The room swayed. I can't, Marcus. Don't you understand? I can't walk away. I have to go through with this. *Have* to. Something wet trickled down her cheek.

"What?" she sneered. "Sneak off with some uptight, prissy law-enforcer on a penny-pinching salary, when I've got all this?"

Now will you bloody well go?

He prised the begging bowl out of her grasp and threw it onto the floor, where it clattered and bounced under a couch. "For gods' sake, you've proved your point." He grabbed both her wrists. "You don't have to go through with this –"

The skin burned, she pulled away so fast. "Oh, but I do," she said dully.

As the moon started to rise, its light picked out the burnished metal among the crab claws and chop bones. Scooping it up, Claudia spat on the bowl, polished it on the hem of her gown. Saw the full face of the midsummer moon reflected in the bronze.

"Believe me, Marcus," talking to herself as much as him, "I do have to go through with this."

"So that's where you're hiding!"

Laughing, Arlon stepped through the open double windows from the garden. In the moonlight, his fair hair shone like silk, and corded muscles bulged out the sleeves of his tunic. There was wine on his breath. Perhaps one goblet too many.

"What in Jupiter's name are you doing in the banqueting hall at this hour on your own?"

So then. He hadn't yet noticed that she wasn't alone. From

the corner of her eye, Claudia watched Orbilio step backwards into the shadows, as silently as a fox.

"Sorry, darling, I lost all track of time re-living the banquet," she said, turning her back on the shadows. "Arlon, it was an absolutely wonderful party. Thank you."

"Mmm." His attention was no longer on the betrothal feast. "You know, you've showered me with everything from rugs to rubies to Arabian resins, but –" One bronzed hand slid round her waist and pulled her close as the other brushed a strand of hair from her eyes. "There's one gift you still haven't given me."

"Don't sell yourself short," she laughed, releasing a curl from its ivory hair pin. "I'm banking on you enjoying more than one, if you don't mind!"

"Then let me unwrap it," he said thickly. "Right here, and right now."

With a backwards sweep of his hand, the plates and bowls went flying off the low table. At home, everything would have smashed to smithereens, but being Arlon, of course, the metal merely clanged, rolled and bounced.

"I've been celibate for two years," Claudia said huskily, arching her back as his hand travelled slowly, expertly, down her backbone. "I don't intend to rush this. Quite the reverse, in fact, darling. I intend to savour every delicious moment, both in the comfort of a soft bed and –" she walked her fingertips lightly down his chest "– all night."

"That's cheating," he laughed. "You know damn well this is the shortest night of the year."

"Then we mustn't waste another minute," Claudia said, and felt something burning into her back from the shadows.

"Absolutely," Arlon agreed, releasing the rest of her hair from its pins.

Slowly, his lips closed on hers, and the kiss was deep and unyielding. In the inescapable light of the moon, Claudia could not control the shudder that rippled over her body when his hand moved to her breast. As his passion intensified, she squeezed her eyes shut and surrendered to Arlon's embrace.

Therefore, she did not see Orbilio slip out of the shadows.

Or the mist that clouded his vision.

The windows in Arlon's bedroom had not been shuttered and, high in the heavens, the moon flooded the room with its silvery blue light. Standing in the limbo land of doorway between bedroom and peristyle, Claudia inhaled the scent of the night stocks and listened to the soft tune played by the fountain. From here, she could see clearly the bench beneath the sycamore tree where she had been run to ground by an investigator in whose veins ambition coursed as fast as his blue blood. For a second, she thought she caught a movement in the bay tree to the left. But she was mistaken. He would be long gone.

"Come to bed," Arlon whispered.

"Soon," she promised.

"My family think you're after my money," he chuckled.

"Not true," she assured him.

"I know that, but all the same, you're a complex woman, Claudia Seferius. You tell me that stupid bowl in your hand is a good luck charm, that you refuse to be parted from it, yet I've never see the bloody thing before in my life."

"After tonight, Arlon, I promise you won't see it again."

She might not have spoken. "And then you woo me and pursue me until I fall helplessly in love at your feet, and promptly withhold all your treasures."

He was right. She had used every trick in the book, every feminine wile, to win Arlon over. It hadn't been easy. It had taken weeks of relentless and painstaking effort, ensuring she was accidentally seated beside him at the theatre, at the

Circus, at banquets, at parties, coincidentally bumping into him at temples, libraries, in the Forum, on the Field of Mars, by the bonnie, bonnie banks of the Tiber. But Claudia knew her man. Had researched him like a thesis. Knew exactly which strings to pull, and which to let go . . .

"Then it's time I gave you my final three gifts," she whispered. From the depths of her gown, she withdrew the onyx phial. "First," she said, removing the delicate glass stopper. "Balm of Gilead."

"Claudia!" he gasped. "That's the most precious oil in the world."

"If it was good enough for the Queen of Sheba to give Solomon, then it's good enough for my bridegroom," she said. "Lie back while I rub it over your chest."

His muscles were hard from working out in the gymnasium, his flesh firm. He groaned in pleasure as she applied the pungent oil.

"Next comes the mead." She held out the engraved silver hip flask. "Brewed by a small tribe in the Peloponnese, its principal ingredient is fermented honey. What the Immortals call nectar," she added.

"Something of an acquired taste," he grimaced, and then grinned. "But to paraphrase a certain young lady, if it's good enough for Ganymede to serve to the King of the Gods, then it's good enough for the bridegroom." He upended the flask and wiped his mouth with the back of his hand. "That, my darling, is one strong brew they mix up there in Greece."

You don't know the half of it. My darling.

"This is the old country proverb, isn't it?" he said. "When it comes to oil, the oil scooped off the top is the best. With honey, the sweetest lies at the bottom. But wine –" he reached out to her, but his hand missed "– of wine, it is the middle which is unsurpassed." He tried to prop himself up on his elbow, but his body seemed weighted. "God, I can't wait to taste Seferius wine. Take your clothes off. Let me gaze at the vessel."

"In your dreams, you bastard."

Consternation flickered in his eyes. He couldn't decide whether he was hearing correctly. Venom? From the luscious lips of his beloved? Surely not. "Enough teasing tonight, Claudia. Come to bed."

There was no mistaking, however, the snort of derision. The contempt which blazed from her eyes. "Arlon, I would go to my grave before I went to your bed."

Again, he tried to sit up. Again, his muscles failed him. "I – I don't understand."

"See this bowl?" She pushed the bronze into his face. "It's a begging bowl, you bastard. It belongs to a crippled, broken, old woman, blind in one eye, who is unlikely to live to see another full moon."

And the story came out.

It was April. Colder than usual, wetter than anyone could ever recall. Claudia had been hurrying along the Via Nova, the part where the road narrowed into a high, vaulted passage, when she almost tripped over the beggar. Hardly surprising. They tended to cluster there, as well as under the porticoes and aqueducts, to shelter from the rain. She was about to move on, when there seemed something familiar about the voice of the cripple. She stopped for a closer look.

"Phyllis?" It was. It was one of *her* slaves. "Phyllis, is that you?"

The weeping sore that was the woman's one good eye narrowed to focus. "Mistress Claudia?"

And another story came tumbling out.

A story that started on the day of Claudia's Saturnalia banquet –

As she told the old hens, she'd invited a select band of merchants, with a view to converting them to the produce of her vineyards. The idea was simple. Lay on lavish entertainment, ply them with gourmet food, unlimited vintage Seferius wine – dear me, the contracts had been drawn up long in advance, they were all ready to be witnessed and signed!

Certainly, marble merchants with quarries dotted over Africa and the Aegean were high on Claudia's priority list. Especially when those merchants had access to hundreds of contacts in the racing world, too! But it was no joke, despite what she'd told the old hens. Arlon's first words to her were indeed,

"*How much would you take for your cook?*"

And her reply was exactly what she'd repeated to Orbilio on the bench. "*I can't sell just one slave. If you want my cook, you'll have to take his wife, his three daughters, his mother-in-law and an aunt. I won't have the family broken up.*"

Arlon hadn't bought Seferius wine, but he did pay a good price for the slaves, and Claudia had thought no more of it. Before handing them over to their new owner, she had established that none of his slaves, not even those in the quarries, were harshly treated. The subject had passed from her mind, especially since the cook had been a stand-in for Verres, her permanent chef, who had been laid up with a broken leg at the time.

But the tale Phyllis told had made her blood run cold.

Phyllis was the cook's mother-in-law, sold as part of the family unit. Grandmother to his three young daughters, aged nine, eleven and thirteen. Arlon, she quickly discovered, had no need of a cook. The first thing he did was despatch the poor man to Africa, his wife to Chios and the aunt to Alexandria. The old woman he did not think would be a problem. He merely sent her to Apulia in the south.

The three children he took to his stud farm in Lucania. Stud being the operative word . . .

"You like them young, don't you, Arlon?" Claudia said. As he struggled to bring his vision into focus, she pressed on. "Oh, not you personally. Your tastes are far too refined. But you know plenty of men who like little girls. Officials at the Circus, for instance. Magistrates, judges. Those who decide who wins by a nose – and who doesn't."

As she said, know your enemy. Claudia had done her homework on Arlon. Didn't take a broken old woman's word. She had checked up on the men who officiated and judged the race winners. Those who were in a position to dope Arlon's competitors. *For a sweetener of their own –*

"From a position of respectability, you procured innocent young children and passed them to men who abuse and debauch them without conscience, and have no conscience about the foul deed yourself."

"You don't understand," he gulped. "You don't know what it's like to be poor. To grow up in the slums, half-starved, wearing rags, watching your siblings die in the cradle, your parents grow old before their time."

Don't I? Claudia swallowed. Said nothing. And had the small comfort that at least her parents hadn't suffered from premature ageing. They were both dead before they'd reached thirty.

"I vowed to myself, that I'd never be poor again. Never," he said. "That I'd do anything, *anything*, not to go back to the gutter."

How rich does a man have to be, she wondered? How high is the price of a man's soul?

Arlon recoiled at the contempt in her eyes. "I love you," he insisted.

"Purely because I fed you drugs that would make you addicted to me."

Or the smell of her, to be precise. (Oh, she had a lot to thank those cunning Orientals for!) But Arlon, completely indifferent to his Saturnalia hostess, could not possibly become addicted unless Claudia contrived to be regularly by his side, slipping the drug day after day into his wine –

"Your mistake," she said, "was sending Phyllis to another stud farm. You should have sent her to Africa with the others."

In his complacency, he had forgotten the overlap among the racing fraternity. Gossip quickly spread to Lucania about the scandal that had to be hushed up. How the cook's middle daughter fought, and died, for her virtue. Prompting the eldest to hold a pillow over the face of the youngest, before slitting her own wrists. At thirteen . . .

"Phyllis confronted one of the paedophiles, and his idea of remorse was to have her beaten and left for dead. But Phyllis is an indomitable old woman. She survived."

For how much longer, though, was debatable. Her lungs were ulcerated, she was coughing up blood, growing weaker and weaker every day. But at least she was growing weaker under Claudia's roof, with the attentions of Claudia's physician. And, Juno willing, she would not die before the ships docked, bringing her daughter and son-in-law home.

"You can't prove it," Arlon said, and his voice was weak now, his limbs leaden. "You can't prove any of this."

"I know. Just as I can't prove that you killed your wife or that fifty other small girls have been raped and defiled before conveniently disappearing."

He must know. Orbilio must know about this. He called him a fiend. A monster. Oh, he knows –

"Then what do you gain by this betrothal?" Arlon asked.

Claudia stood up, shook out her sleeves, adjusted her girdle. "Haven't you guessed?"

The moon was still full, but this was the shortest night of the year. Already the sun was starting to rise, prompting the birds in the aviary to sing their hearts out.

"Well, you're a clever man, Arlon. You worked out the country proverb, and I'm sure you'll work this out, too." She tucked the phial and the hip flask back in the folds of her gown. "Sooner or later."

Nine days later and the heat had not abated. The moon, shrinking fast, still cast a silvery light over Claudia's garden, accentuating the feathery foliage of the wormwood, but now the constellations could be seen bright in the heavens. The great bear, the little bear, the dragon, the lynx. And from the northern horizon to the east, the great white swathe of the Milky Way stretched into infinity.

Claudia sat on the edge of the pool with her gown hitched up to her knees, dangling her feet in the cool water. Beside her, gnawing on a fresh sardine, her blue-eyed, cross-eyed, dark Egyptian cat, Drusilla, stiffened. Half a sardine dropped from her mouth, and a low growl emitted from the back of her throat.

"I know, poppet." Claudia stroked the hackles flat. "I smelled him, too."

Sandalwood among roses and pinks.

His tall frame cast a shadow over the papyrus as he untied his high, patrician boots and eased himself down on to the marble rim adjacent to Claudia, his toes making slow ripples over the surface of the pool. Moths fluttered round the night stocks and herbs, and Drusilla fused with the night.

"You didn't attend the funeral, then?"

"Prostrate with grief," she replied.

"It must be tough," Orbilio said, and it might have been

the moonlight, but she could have sworn she saw a flash of white teeth.

"You have no idea," she said honestly. Stuck indoors for nine days, she'd missed out on the Festival of Fortune, two days of bull fights and the Celebration of the bloody Muses.

"Still." He plucked an orange marigold and twirled it slowly between his fingers. "The period of mourning is up now. I'm sure you'll be fully recovered by tomorrow."

"Sarcasm," she said, snatching the bloom out of his hand, because the significance of its colour hadn't escaped her, "doesn't suit you."

He snatched it back. "Any more than black suits you. Which," he added mildly, "I presume is the reason the grieving bride-to-be isn't wearing it . . . ?"

"Cut to the chase, Orbilio. What do you want?"

His eyes took a leisurely journey over the tumble of dark curls round her shoulders as he inhaled her spicy Judean perfume, watched the rhythmic heave of her breasts. "What do you think I want?" he murmured.

"Oh, I rather imagine it entails handcuffs and chains. Things like that."

He pinged a pebble into the pool. "I never do bondage on a first date," he said. "But you should have come to me with your suspicions about Arlon, not take the law into your own hands."

Claudia held out her hands, first palms downwards, then palms up. "I see no law." Several minutes passed, cicadas rasped, and the heat of the night intensified. "Are you going to charge me?" she asked, and her voice was so quiet, and so much time elapsed, that she wondered whether he had heard her.

"With what?" he asked eventually. "Arlon died alone in his own bed on midsummer night, choking to death on his own vomit after drinking too much."

But he knew, she thought. He knows everything. And in the moonlight, she waited.

"It was a dangerous ploy, Claudia." Marcus stretched out on his elbows on the marble path, his legs still dangling in the pool, and stared up at the night sky. "It could have backfired, and badly."

"What could?" she asked innocently.

"The honey trap you set for Arlon."

Classic in its own way. Girl lures man. Sets him up. The perfect entrapment. Like a fly in amber, there's no escape. Men are such fools when it comes to sex.

"Honey*moon*," she corrected, stretching out beside him. Up there, Polaris twinkled the brightest.

"Whatever," he laughed. "But it was clever. Immoral, mind you. But clever."

Pfft. How can rubbing a pungent oil on a man's chest to disguise the bitter soporific with which she'd laced his mead compare to the terror of fifty young children? Immoral, my eye! Yes, of course she knew Arlon would choke. Everyone saw how much he'd drunk, it might have happened anyway, all it needed was a slight nudge. One less scumbag, fifty children avenged, hundreds more spared the same sickening fate.

The celestial zoo tramped across the heavens. A pink light began to tinge the sky to the east. The first blackbird broke into song from an apple tree already swelling with tiny green fruits.

"Let me at least reimburse you for the expense," Orbilio said sleepily.

"No need," she replied.

Rugs? Gold medallions? Balm of Gilead? Ivory chairs? Cheap at half the price, she reflected, as the first bees began to buzz round the lavender.

The State understood grief. Accommodated the bereaved. Made allowances.

Thanks to one bright orange veil, a noisy procession and an ostentatious plighting of her troth, Claudia Seferius had two more fabulous years of freedom stretching ahead of her.

"Breakfast?" she said.

Damnum Fatale

Philip Boast

The seventy years since the last story have seen the decline in the Roman imperial family through Tiberius and Caligula to Claudius and now Nero. It was during Nero's mad reign that the Christians began to make their presence known in Rome and that is the background for the following story, which has to be the ultimate Whodunnit. Philip Boast is known for his historical epics, especially those with a Biblical background, including Sion *(1999) the story of Jesus and Mary Magdalene, and* City *(1994), the story of a former Druid prince, baptised by Jesus, who returns to Britain with a terrible treasure.*

Rome, AD 63

"Bar the door closed," he ordered. "Let them burn."

The flames kindled by the Guard erupted through the roof of the house, illuminating the tall apartment blocks standing around it against the night sky, setting the lower washing lines strung between them alight. Tunics left to dry overnight blazed like fiery ghosts, evil portents, as the wind gusted. He smiled while the screaming of the men and women trapped inside grew louder, more painful. Let their god save them now.

"Rebels." He inhaled smoke. "It's good to smell them burn."

But fire, as always, struck fear into the hearts of Romans, citizens or not, rich and poor alike. The horns blew, lamps were lit, children scampered for loot in the confusion and dogs yapped, but although it was an hour until dawn the municipal fire team turned out with buckets, organizing a chain from the fountain, dousing the flames before they took hold.

He watched without emotion, the winter gale tugging his cloak. It suited his purpose just as well. There would be survivors. The rebels would have hidden down in the cellar. They always did. Or even deeper, mired to their guts in the shitpit, praying their heads off.

"Sergeant," he ordered. "Fish me out a live one."

The Guard drew their swords and kicked down the door, setting the screaming off again. A couple of women were dragged out by their hair. The elder of the vicious creatures, Pedilla, recognized him and called out, "I forgive you. You do not know what you are doing."

"You're wrong, traitor." He gave her a broad grin from his scarred, seamed face. "I do know."

His grin widened, showing his blunt brown broken teeth, as a rebel was dragged to him between two soldiers. An intellectual; and not poor either, by his clothes. "If you kill me," the man quavered, stinking with dung, "I shall live forever."

"Kill you? It would be a waste to kill you today." Matrusus drew his sword. The blade glinted in the dawn light, razor-sharp. "I have something much better in mind."

He pressed the tip to the man's forehead.

"My name is Matrusus," he said. "You will remember me."

*   *   *

"Master," called her deep throaty voice from his bedroom, "How much longer must I warm your bed? I need sleep!"

"Go to your quarters, Omba," Quistus called absently, working at his desk. He wore a plain cream tunic, and was that age which is anywhere between thirty-five and fifty-five. Standing he would be tall for a Roman; sitting made him look a little awkward, his legs and arms too long. "I'm stopping," he lied. "You are released for this evening."

After a while she called, "It's morning. Your bath's cold too. Stop working for once, Septimus Severus Quistus!"

"Mmm," he muttered, and forgot her.

It was a windy night outside the Villa Marcia. The shutters rattled, setting the candles flickering as he bent over the books. Fascinating. A new invention, far easier to read than scrolls. A whole new class of book-writers had sprung up almost overnight, seizing the new medium to air crazy personal views about – anything. Anything at all. Saving the world, eternal life, recipes for *gustatio* appetisers ("fry 5 dormice in Apicius's finest olive oil, sprinkle with honey and poppy seeds"), face creams ("take ten female dog roses"), revolting medical lotions ("insert finger slowly"), crackpot religious opinions, absurd political prejudices, amateur philosophy. The list was long. People who rarely bothered to read scrolls read these books avidly. That made them dangerous.

"*Master!*"

"Coming!" he called, realizing how low the candles had burned.

Books. Easy to hand round, quick to slip under clothes, small enough to be taken out and read aloud to men of the low sort, women, even slaves. Fashionable enough to impress the well-off, often written in the form of personal letters to increase the reader's sense of self-importance, of being party to a privileged communication. Letter to the Tarsans. Letter to the Jebusites. Knowledge, ideas, information. There was going to be trouble.

He jerked guiltily, his mind turning to more immediate trouble as he heard the bath-furnace roar, re-heating. Pots were clattered bad-temperedly. Omba was not the sort of slave to tolerate rebellion from her master. Quistus, Senator, *always* took a bath before bed, therefore he always must. Quickly he pushed the books in the drawer, turned the key, and hurried from his office to the marble bathroom. A pang struck him. This echoing room with its aquatic murals had comfortably contained his active, noisy young family of ten; one by one their happy calls and cries faded into his memory and there was only him. And, now, Omba.

"Master," the slave tutted massively, her gold ringlets and earrings and bracelets tinkling, flashing by lamplight as she waddled forwards. "You'll catch your death of cold when you get out of this water, don't you know it's January?" She took his sandals. "Anyway, bathing's an obscene idea at this time of night." Bathing was an obscene idea to Omba at any time of day or night; she avoided water like the plague, rubbed her skin with fruit oil, and gleamed like a Walrus of living jet. (Quistus had seen a fabled Walrus with his own eyes in the land of the Norvaaks, and been obliged to run from it for his life.)

He said mildly, "The sight of naked men isn't obscene to your people. You encouraged them, I recall." He tested the hypocaust-heated pool with his toe, then hopped. "Ouch!"

"Master, you *know* we *loved* the sight of our naked warriors, male or female. But our lovely men weren't skinny and scrawny and fishbelly-white like you. Your nose is too big and your" – she gestured – "is too small." Omba studied her master critically. "You'd never make an Oromos. I'd be ashamed to have you in my tribe, Senator. We'd feed you up

and make you a lusty fighter and seducer and father of fat
babies." She shrugged: "Not a mere brain-thinker, a phi-
soloph . . ." she gave up on the word. "Whatever you call
it."

"Logician." He relaxed sleepily. "Pupil of Epictetus.
Himself."

"Thinking's an excuse for doing nothing. Boredom's exhausted you. You've retired from everything important, you
don't even talk to your friends since your wife and . . ."
Omba bit her tongue. "Anyway, bathing makes you un-
healthy. You don't know where that's water's been."

"Piped very expensively from outside the city."

"Tastes of lead, Senator."

Quistus gazed up through the steam at the dark, gleaming
mountain of his gold-encrusted slave. Omba had never
forgiven him for his abrupt resignation from the Senate;
she believed in rank, the higher the better. Three years ago,
in Africa, he'd saved Princess Omba from a particularly
nastily thought-out execution by the new queen in Kefa's
palace, finding the enormously naked princess staked out on
an anthill with her mouth held open by thorns, her tongue
smeared with honey, and the ants getting busy. Princess
Omba, eyes rolling, groaning, made her only possible choice,
better to be a live slave than a dead princess; but after
nineteen days alone in the desert with her, he'd appreciated
why her tongue was the first part of Omba her enemies
wanted silenced. Not once did she stop talking – not in the
desert, not in Alexandria, not aboard ship, not during the
shipwreck, not on the island, not in Rome, not once since
he'd owned her and her Latin became horribly fluent had she
stopped talking (except the time the Aryans tossed them both
in the Black Sea with stones tied to their feet). It shouldn't be
this way between master and slave. By Roman law everything that was hers was his: her gold, even her tongue, was

his property – he had every right to steal one and cut off the other. It was tempting. But.

But Omba was Omba. Black as starless Nubian night, no shorter than he yet almost as wide as she was tall, she draped herself in ornaments of solid gold instead of clothes, except the loincloth of gold beads and fancy gold tassels swinging from her breasts. To have seized her gold and forbidden her ceaseless chatter would have killed her. He wouldn't harm a hair of Omba's head, had she got hair.

Quistus's life had been a bleak and terrible emptiness – a desert – since his wife was murdered and his son was (not dead, not dead!) was gone. Gone.

Then in the desert, the real desert, he'd found Omba. This dark, shining, exotic, magnificent, cruel, expansive creature with her endless booming gossip irritated him unbearably, yet filled his emptiness – or was, at least, the single light shining in the darkness of his despair.

Omba was nothing like Marcia. No reminders, no echoes, no pain –

He sat up, spraying water. "What?"

"You slept. You weren't listening to me. Someone at the door."

He rubbed his face. "At this hour? Who?"

"A girl."

He yawned. Omba would have given the prostitute a penny, a lecture, and sent her away. Instead she said: "She's waiting in the entrance hall. Something's wrong."

He scrambled to his feet, grabbed the towel. "You let a woman in my house?"

"You can't hide for ever in books and scrolls. She's beautiful and she's crying. I was sorry for her. There's more."

She held out his toga, knowing when to say nothing for just one moment.

"What?" he said testily, adjusting the folds.

"When you see her, it'll tear your heart out."

He stopped. "My heart is already torn, as you know."

"I don't reckon," Omba said. "You look dog-tired, you've been up all night brain-thinking, wasting your time. Well, think this. Do some good. I'll take her to your office and bring you both some *Kefa* while you talk. It's just what you need, Master."

He sat, covering his shock at her appearance with an effort, as the young lady removed her cloak. Even for a Stoic forced since his schooldays to conceal his feelings, it was a big effort. He said quickly, "Please, sit down," before she fell down.

The stool would require cleaning. This room would require fumigation.

"Septimus Severus Quistus?" She half-collapsed, half-sat, dripping. Her eyes were blue, more than enough to make most dark-eyed Romans stare. A foreigner. Yet she struggled to bear herself with dignity, and her Latin was good. Perhaps even a Roman citizen, then, but not from Rome. "My name is Volusia Faustina. My mother is Pedilla Exuperata, and my father is Faustinus."

Provincial names: probably British. Her accent reminded him of his time in Britannia with Emperor Claudius, a river-crossing called Londinium. Hardly more than a wooden bridge and some army tents back then, but such places grew fast.

Gods, she stank.

He opened the window but papers blew off the desk. He closed the window and took breath through his mouth. "What brings you to my house in this desperate condition, Volusia Faustina?"

Like many women, she wore several layers of tunics one over the other, and a scarf over her head – very British. Now she put back the scarf. Volusia was indeed beautiful, once you got used to those eyes. But her face was splashed with blood and dung, her clothes saturated with slime. She looked like she'd spent the night in an abattoir.

She said: "I have come because you're the one man in Rome who is not afraid."

He said nothing for a while. This could be a very dangerous conversation. The Emperor Nero was subtle and devious and believed himself all-powerful; his mother had murdered his adopted father the Emperor Claudius, and Nero himself had murdered Claudius's young son, and then his own mother, then his wife. No doubt he had not stopped there. Any man in Rome with sense was afraid. "Am I unafraid?" he said. "Perhaps you know more than I do."

But she responded fiercely. "Everyone knows you are a lost man. You do not fear the Beast because you have nothing more to lose. You know what they call this house in the slums, in the Subura, the Cloaca? The ivory tower. Even the children know the story. Your life ended when your family was murdered. No one knows who did it. The Emperor's Guard. A street gang. Unknown. A terrible mystery. You live here alone, caring for nothing. A dead man breathing."

He covered his mouth, then said, "Go on."

"You alone can help me, Septimus Severus Quistus. You alone can understand, you alone will help. My family is . . . I escaped. I make no apology for running to you like this. Just by letting me into your house, you have implicated yourself. But I need you to see me as I am. This is my father's blood." She swayed, exhausted.

She had called the emperor the Beast. She was undoubtedly a rebel. Their lives were forfeit if they were overheard.

Omba came in with a tray. "Oh, you poor thing," she gushed, fussing over Volusia. "Here, this will perk you up."

She waved Quistus away, spoke low-voiced. "You can see what a state she's in. Whatever it's about, it's serious."

"I know. I also know that I should throw her out before I hear another word. It's your life too, Omba."

"At least let her wash. I'll find her something clean to wear."

"Let him see me as I am." Volusia would not be moved. "I'm not ashamed." Those fierce blue eyes, unblinking. "I won't change these clothes or wash until he's heard what I have to say."

Quistus sat again. "You should know I am no longer a politician in Nero's Senate. I have no powers or influence. I cannot offer you political help –"

"I do not care what you are not!" she burst out. "Only what you are."

"He still knows all the right people, don't worry." Omba pushed one of the small fatty balls of *Kefa*, or coffee, into the girl's hand. "Eat, it's my own recipe. Now, why don't you tell him what's on your mind?"

Volusia struggled to collect her thoughts. "I don't know where to begin –" She nibbled the coffee-ball and made a face, then continued in a stronger voice. "You see, I was born in Britannia, in Londinium. My father grew rich as a merchant trading goods with Hibernia where, as you know, there is much trade with Egypt. On his voyages my father became interested in the Egyptian religion, in fact fascinated. Baptized. My brother is an Hibernian priest, my elder sister has modelled her life on the Virgin."

Quistus nibbled his coffee. "The Egyptians worshipped many gods of their own once, but now they prefer obedience to the gods of Rome, and the Emperor who is a god, of course."

Volusia shook her head. "Some time ago the Egyptian traders took to the Jewish God, yet kept their ancient rituals of spring-birth and winter-death of Amen, their own most powerful god. Now the two religions have come together, fused. The Egyptians believe that the Jewish God has had a Son. They *know*."

"The Jews of Judea believe in one god, called God. Not two."

"The traders *know* the Son was born to a virgin of the Jerusalem Temple. About sixty years ago. He was educated in Egypt, just as Isaiah prophesied. They *know* He walked among us on this earth, in the flesh. It's proven – His sayings have been written down and are the Truth which guides us." She reached under her clothes, pulled out a slim book. "This is the gospel truth." She held it out.

Dangerous even to touch it.

Quistus reached out and took the book in his hand.

He leafed a few pages. Latin, but not in the difficult joined-up Roman style; this writing was presented in short verses for easy reading aloud, to a small circle or congregation perhaps. He chose a verse at random. "'Blessed are you that you did not waver at the sight of me.'"

"From the Gospel of Mary Magdalene." Volusia leaned forwards, her eyes alight with devotion. "One day Paul hopes to assemble these many scriptures into one great Bible."

"Paul?"

"Our leader, a Roman citizen. So does Peter, too, plan a book of books, a Bible – but they argue about which gospel is truest."

He laid the book carefully on his desk. "The author of these sayings is the Son of God? What's his name?"

"The Jerusalem priests mocked Him as Yehoshua ben-Mary. But some Greeks, a few, reverence His name as Iesous Christos. In Latin, Iacimus Christus. But all mean Jesus Christ."

Quistus, bright-eyed, helped himself to another ball of coffee. "Fifteen or twenty years ago troublemakers, followers of someone called Chrestus, rioted in Rome. Is that the same man?"

"We are not troublemakers."

"But trouble follows you."

"We believe in peace, in love. We die rather than kill. Christ teaches us by His example. He allowed Himself to be crucified that we may learn how to live."

"So," Quistus said, "if your Christ is dead, and you're not troublemakers, what's the problem? There are hundreds of gods in Rome."

"Christ is not dead. He was crucified and entombed, yes, but He arose, resurrected, *redivivus*, after three days. Now Jesus Christ is alive inside me and inside everyone who believes in Him. In His own words He tells us" – she touched the book, but knew the words by heart – "'Beware that no one lead you astray, ordering Go here or Go there! For the Son of Man is within you.'"

"Your god is inside you, so you need no public temple or statues?"

"We worship in small families of friends, in secret. Often underground, for safety, in private houses. But they find us even there."

"They?"

"The devils of the Beast."

"How many of you are there?"

"So many, Paul says, that because Christ is within each one of us we should call ourselves Christians. There are many Christians."

Omba said, "Sometimes I swear by Jupiter, but I'm not a Jupiteran. And Janus looks after every door in my master's house, but I'm not a Janusian."

"Christians have a new way of believing," Volusia said.

Quistus steepled his fingers thoughtfully. "New beliefs attract persecution from old beliefs."

"We Christians are given no peace. We are hounded from house to house by the imperial interrogator, Matrusus. Thug, bully, torturer, destroyer, he is the chief devil sent by Satan, the Beast, to try us."

"And this morning he found you?" Quistus said gently, "I cannot protect you from Matrusus."

"I do not ask you to. This morning Matrusus ordered the house of Pudens, where we had gathered in prayer, burnt over our heads. Some Christians were burnt alive, afterwards others were tortured by Matrusus, horribly tortured. He carves the sign of the Cross, which is holy to us, upside-down, in blood . . ." She shuddered. "I hear Pudens screaming still."

Heedless of her filth, Quistus took her hand. "But something even worse than that has happened, hasn't it?"

She nodded, squeezing his fingers tight.

"Matrusus has been murdered."

"Omba, stay here." Quistus crossed the courtyard of the Villa Marcia.

"Me, stay?" she called. "I'm not staying. Who would look after you?"

He whistled from the gate. The Vicus Armilustri was a wealthy street and at once a waiting sedan chair of the Subura cartel, the "family" of Vitellius, was lifted and run smartly to him. The slaves hefting the poles were the usual hairy barbarians, broken-down warriors from forgotten wars, the blind one at the back, and at the front the one with eyes but no arms, lifting with a neck-sling. There was nothing wrong with their muscle-strapped legs.

"Pomegranate Street." Quistus handed Volusia aboard. "The house of Pudens, near the Basilica Opimia." The blind one nodded eagerly, carrying a map of Rome in his head. "Run all the way and there's an extra penny for you, each. And I won't tell Vitellius."

The men heaved the weight, taking the uphill slope at a run. Volusia sat on the narrow bench opposite him, their knees almost touching. He looked out. "They'll take away Matrusus's body soon. The *praetor urbanus* will decide if there is a case to answer. A prosecutor will be appointed. I've got to get there first."

"Why?"

Still he wouldn't look at her. "There may be signs that tell us what really happened. Perhaps that Matrusus was indeed murdered by Pudens, or by your father. Or not, as you say."

"We believe in peace. It is impossible for a Christian to commit murder. We are the Lambs."

He said nothing.

"What's the matter?" she asked. "You're so pale."

He gazed at the crowds pushing and shoving. "Your clean clothes. Omba gave you my wife's clothes to wear."

"Does it offend you?"

He looked from the window. "It . . . reminds me."

"Marcia."

"Yes. That was her name."

"You have no idea at all?"

"Not one clue. Death is not reasonable, perhaps."

"In your military career and as a diplomat you must have known many men die." The coffee would not let Volusia go. "Perhaps death follows you," she blurted. "That must be hard for a logician to accept."

"Logic is simply a way of discovering the truth."

"To discover truth you must become a Christian."

"I believe death always has a reason." No sign of Omba following them, but he knew she'd be close, no one knew the back ways of Rome like Omba. He closed the curtains,

suddenly hating the crowds. "Sometimes a reason is so hard
to discover. I am *Septimus* because I am my father's seventh
son, it was his pet name for me. Now I can hardly bear to
hear it said. My own seventh son is Septimus."

"Is?"

"His body was not found with the others."

"What does that tell a logician?"

"That Septimus is still alive."

"Isn't that a father's faith, desperate hope, not logic?"

The curtains blew open in the wind and he closed them.
"Logic says perhaps he killed them."

"All of them?"

"His sister was not found. Perhaps they both killed their
brothers and their mother and ran away together." He
shrugged. "Perhaps there is no reason or logic to be found.
Perhaps it just . . . happened."

"My father did not kill Matrusus."

"Then," Quistus said, "in order to prove that, we have to
prove who did." And he ignored her angry stare.

The sedan stopped, dropped. A knock on the roof. "No
further can we go," called the blind man's heavy German
accent. "My penny now please sir."

Quistus gazed across the heads of the crowd as he paid the
fare, tossed the men an extra penny each. The house of
Pudens was burned out. A flapping sound in the sky: the
apartment blocks on each side attracted the wind, setting the
washing flying and twisting on the ropes strung between
them. "Keep close." Towing Volusia after him, muttering
an apology to the bald-headed man he knocked aside, Quistus pushed to the front. He tapped the Guard on his greasy
shoulder. "Let me pass."

"Piss off."

Sword clenched in hand, the body of Matrusus lay where

it fell, outstretched on the cobbles, rubbish blowing past it, cloak rippling like living blood. The spear-shaft standing between his eyes nodded gently in the wind, its movement making Matrusus appear oddly alive, wisely nodding at his own death. "I want carts! And carpenters!" A squat man gave orders to soldiers and scribes. "I want crosses. Yes, crosses."

Quistus murmured, "Stigmus. I feared it." He called, "Stigmus!"

"You?" The squat man turned. "Are you mad? Are you with these people?"

"Let me through."

"Stay away, Septimus Severus Quistus. You can do no good here."

"I am merely curious."

"Curious? I thought you were dead. Yes, pass him." He beckoned.

"Stay out of sight," Quistus whispered to Volusia. "Stigmus and I go back." But she exclaimed, seeing her father lined up with the other Christian rebels by the wall, their clothes torn, trembling and nervous. They had not been lightly treated. Several men had the shape of a cross cut into their heads, still trickling. Their wives held the wounds closed.

"Father! Mother!" Volusia twisted from his grasp, ran to Pedilla and Faustinus, embraced them. Stigmus watched attentively, saw enough, then moved his hand lightly in command. Two soldiers dragged Volusia to the end of the line, threw her down. "A touching reunion. Thank you, my dear Quistus. Another fish drawn into my net to wait her turn."

"She's done nothing wrong, Stigmus."

"Fish, yet another secret name of these Christian martyrs, did you not know? Graffiti of the Fish are scrawled on street corners everywhere. It will stop. I will stop them."

If any man could, Quistus knew, that man was Stigmus. The prosecutor was forty-five years old, thickset, powerful, determined, ambitious. His grey hair was tightly curled across his forehead, his square face surprisingly intelligent, slightly too red, faintly debauched. His eyes were cold, dark stones.

"Let her go, Stigmus. She doesn't belong here."

"She's a Christian. Promise me she hasn't involved you. This is a bad place."

"Do you know what happened?"

"A Christian riot."

"You know Matrusus better than that."

"Knew." Stigmus moved one hand from the folds of his toga, gestured at the body, but his eyes did not move. "Murdered."

"He was a murderer many times over."

"Killed by a single spear thrust through the face. Directly between the eyes. Perfect symmetry. One can only admire these Christians' skill and strength and astonishing precision, as well as their viciousness."

"He won't be missed."

"The Emperor will miss him. Nero cried when he heard. Do not get mixed up with Christians, my friend." By friend Stigmus meant enemy. "I warn you, the Emperor is interested. Personally. I have full powers of investigation."

"I can guess what the result will be."

"I'm a fair man. As usual they will be asked to invoke our gods, worship the image of Nero, and curse Christ. If they refuse they are guilty and I shall crucify them as their god was crucified, except upside-down. They hate that. They believe in an underworld, a place of fire and torture called Hell, and they don't want to fall to it head-first."

"All of them? A spear can fly from only one pair of hands."

"They say they're all guilty. In the next breath they say

they're all innocent." He shook his head in disgust. "They want to die. It's the same in all these pagan religions, they all believe in death. Die, be happy. You know their Christ preached revolution? Destruction of the Jerusalem Temple. His closest advisers were zealots, assassins, the poor – desperate enough to do anything. Don't believe a word Christians say."

"Why does Nero hate them so?"

"Because he is tolerant and they are not. Their God excludes all other gods – including the Emperor, who is of course a god, *pater*, Pope, *Pontifex Maximus*, the bridge between this world and the next, married to immortal Rome. When Nero dies he will rise again, *redivivus* – an idea the Christians have actually stolen for their own Christ! Blasphemy."

"Stigmus –"

"You know what your Christians call our Emperor? The Beast. Worse names. 666. Satan. You can't expect him to love them for it."

"Who carved the cross on their foreheads?"

"Matrusus's signature. You know his sense of fun. A blood cross. They call it the mark of the Beast."

"I need to examine the body."

"They killed him, and that's that. Matrusus died unnecessarily, they will die legally and horribly. Now, I have an interrogation to conduct." Stigmus threw back over his shoulder, "You're wasting your time!"

Quistus knelt. Matrusus stared at the sky. The spear had pierced him exactly between his eyes – as Stigmus said, with absolute precision. Almost eerie precision. Very skilled. Would Faustinus the merchant, thin and looking the far side of fifty, have such strength, such skill? Pedilla his wife, or Volusia? One of the soldiers was calling their names, a scribe writing them down. Linus might be strong enough. What about Timothy, who crouched away from the women? The one called Peter was too old. Pudens looked like an intellectual, a poet, but he sat beside a strong-looking red-headed woman.

"Claudia, his wife." Omba grunted, kneeling. "I checked, Master. Everyone's eager to talk. The daughter of old King Caractacus of Britannia, they say."

"A Roman citizen?"

"Pudens is, so she married one, she's protected by citizen law."

"Not much protection for long." Quistus closed his hands around the shaft of the spear. "Are you thinking what I'm thinking?"

"It's too thick, too long, too heavy."

"That's because" – Quistus placed his sandalled foot on Matrusus, tugged hard on the shaft, withdrawing it with a soggy sucking sound – "it isn't a spear."

He wiped the brains off the end. Blunt sawn wood. "It's a pole." Omba shook her head, impressed. "Someone very strong threw that thing. Phew."

Quistus turned his gaze from the Christians, raised his eyes to the washing flapping in the sky between the apartment blocks, the Exelsius on one side, the Imperium on the other. "It's a washing-pole." He pointed at a rope, still with washing attached, hanging down from the top corner of the Exelsius, then turned back to the Imperium. No pole, no rope.

"No," Omba said. "I'm not climbing up there, not me."

The Imperium doorkeeper had fled. Light in the lobby came from above, down the light-well in the centre of the building. Quistus climbed the stairs past sturdy apartment doors, came out on the flat roof. He hung on as the wind gusted, about eighty feet above the street. The roof of the

Imperium was laid out like a small garden, carefully-tended shrubs, a trellis, a few benches, a pleasant place to relax on a summer evening but cold and breezy now. At each corner a washing-pole stood bedded in mortar, an endless line leading from the tip to another apartment block.

Except this corner. Quistus leaned out. Even Omba looked small, far below. He narrowed his eyes, peering across at the cream stucco of the Exelsius's seven storeys. A mark on the corner just over half way down. He returned downstairs.

"Well? Thrown from up there?" Omba asked.

Without a word Quistus crossed to the Exelsius. He climbed three floors, orientated himself, then knocked on a door. It swung open. An old woman sat with a cat on her lap. "I thought you were my breakfast," she said. "But you don't sound like my daughter."

"Did you hear the trouble last night, mother?"

"No, nothing."

He stepped onto the balcony, reached out past the dangling, frayed end of the line to the gash in the stucco. Fresh. The end of something rounded had struck against the wall here, very hard – hard enough to break the line. He stared down, eyes searching. "Nothing at all?"

"No." The blind woman stroked her cat. "At night I sleep. With my ears closed. It's safer."

"Thank you, mother."

He closed the door and went downstairs to the street. He stood by Matrusus's feet, on the exact spot Matrusus was standing when he was hit. It didn't make sense. Then he saw the slope-roofed outhouse leaning against the ground floor of the Imperium. His eye traced an imaginary line. It beggared belief; but it had to be true.

He looked round, realizing everyone was watching.

"Don't keep me waiting," Stigmus said.

Quistus gathered his thoughts. "Let him think!" Omba

sounded proud, almost maternal. "That's what my master does best, he does."

"Keep her quiet," Stigmus said.

"You can't keep me quiet," Omba said.

Quistus spoke. "The fact is, none of the Christians was strong enough to do this to Matrusus on the ground. To have shoved this blunt pole – not a spear – through his face would have required someone as strong as Matrusus himself. And why didn't Matrusus defend himself? His sword was drawn."

"Everyone can see the pole was thrown from a distance," Stigmus said. "His sword was no defence."

"The pole was thrown from up there." Quistus moved a few steps from Matrusus, pointing up at the top corner of the Imperium that came into view.

Stigmus said, "The killer couldn't even have seen his target! How could he aim? This is nonsense!"

"The wind killed Matrusus." Quistus pointed at the washing line down the wall of the Exelsius. "There was a gust, the line was heavy with washing, the pole broke out of the mortar. As it fell fifty, sixty feet the attached line swung it like a slingshot towards the Exelsius. The pole struck the wall by the balcony with terrific force, breaking the line –"

"This is ridiculous! Still not in sight of Matrusus! How could it hit him?"

"The pole span downward, struck the sloping roof of that outhouse at just the right angle, then span outward on the new trajectory. Matrusus never knew what hit him."

"Hit him with incredible accuracy. How do you account for that?" Stigmus was furious. "It beggars belief. I'll tear the truth out of them."

"Stigmus, it was an accident," Quistus said. "Pure chance."

A voice called out, "No. Stigmus is right."

Quistus turned to the bald-headed man in the crowd who had spoken.

"Stigmus is right," the bald man repeated. "It was no accident. I witnessed what happened." He stepped forward. "I am a Christian. I am the voice of this congregation. I saw —" A soldier whacked him in the belly with the butt of his sword, dropping him.

"Put him with the others," Stigmus said.

"Stop." The bald man struggled to his feet. His clothes were very poor, and his hands were gnarled. "You cannot touch me. I am a citizen of Rome."

Stigmus glared, then waved the soldier away.

Quistus said, "Tell us your name."

The bald man drew himself up with dignity, though he was so short and ragged. "To you Romans my name is Gaius Iulius Paulus," he said. "To the Jews I was Saul. But a great light shone upon me on the road, and now to these folk my Christian name is Paul."

Quistus glanced at Volusia. Paul, leader of the Christians. A man of great faith to risk himself here, or mad.

Quistus said, "Who did it?"

Paul said: "God did it."

"God Himself." Paul raised his voice. "The death of Matrusus the devil was an Act of God. A *Damnum Fatale*. God's justice."

"Dare you testify to this?" Stigmus said dangerously.

"Hear me!" This Paul was a natural orator, the crowd responded to him. "I am Paul of Tarsus, a Roman citizen of good family fallen on hard times, a tentmaker, a Christian. There is no Christian church, no temple, only the Jesus Christ we choose to carry inside our hearts, each of us."

"I'm not listening to this drivel." Stigmus beckoned the

soldier with the eager sword-butt, but Quistus said, "It can't do any harm to hear him out."

"Words are the most powerful weapons," Stigmus hissed, but Paul was speaking.

"Merciful God killed the evil Matrusus just as he killed the evil men before Noah. God killed Matrusus just as surely as He slaughtered the pagan prophets of Baal. God struck down Matrusus just as He struck down the strong of Egypt and drowned their bodies beneath the waves. See!" He swept up his arms towards the roof of the Imperium. "Jesus Christ watches over us and cares for us. He is in our hearts and in the wind and in the sky, He *is* us. There is no chance, no accident. I saw Him blow the wind, I saw His perfect hand guide the pole like a spear through the air so that it struck that building and began a new path, struck the outhouse and was turned afresh again, ordained, so that Matrusus received the spear of God not one hair's breadth to the right or left. How can that be chance? It proves the existence of God. *Damnum Fatale*. Amen."

One by one the Christians spoke, though Stigmus shouted at them.

"I saw it too," Faustinus croaked. "Matrusus carved me with the mocking cross, and died where he stood."

The women shouted that they too had seen.

"*I* saw," Timothy said. "But I don't believe they did, because they are only women."

"We all saw," Volusia said. "Even us women."

Then Peter spoke with dignity. "I am a poor fisherman," he said. "Yet I know what I saw."

"If any tongue speaks more," Stigmus roared, "I shall order it cut out."

Paul lived in the Transtiberium, the Jewish quarter. The wind blew brown waves along the Tiber, breaking white against the bridge. The buildings lining the river were tall but falling down, decayed, and stank of strange food. Eyes watched them from alleyways, bearded men bargained, and talk stopped when Quistus's toga passed: here a sign of rank was an unusual provocation. Footsteps padded after them. There was a masculine cry and a falling sound. Someone had tried to separate Omba from her gold.

"I fear nothing for I have Jesus in my heart," Paul said. "But you should, here."

"I have only curiosity in my heart."

"And me behind you, Master," Omba said.

Peter walked holding his belly where he had been struck; he was frail. "I'm a Jew, but these Jews are too poor to hate me for what I've become. Even they scratch a living sewing tents of forbidden pigskin for the army, as do I, and burn candles of pig-fat. I'm a Jew to the Jews, a Roman to the Romans. In Jerusalem I led riots against the Jerusalem Church to bring them to Christianity, to their senses. The priests arrested me." He gave a cunning chuckle. "But as a Roman citizen I had the right to be tried here. The Roman courts grind slowly."

"But thoroughly."

"I shall be found guilty and killed. But I have bought a little time."

Quistus took a long step over a stinking puddle. "For what?"

"For Jesus to come again."

"Did you truly see Matrusus die by God's hand?"

Paul stopped on the bridge, the river rushing beneath. "There is no other explanation. There was no crime."

"I think there was," Quistus said. "I think Linus escaped out of the back of the house under cover of smoke, climbed that apartment block, cut the rope, broke the washing-pole out of its mount, and ran along the roof until he got a clear view of Matrusus. Then he threw the pole. And he was lucky. Incredibly lucky."

"How do you explain the gashed wall of the other apartment block?"

Quistus was silent.

"He's got you there, Master," Omba said.

"And you told us the rope was not cut but broken," Paul added. "Even Linus is not that strong. I cannot believe you."

"It can't have been the wind, chance. It just can't. The odds are incredible. Unbelievable. A murder requires a murderer."

"You know I am right." Paul smiled for the first time. "It was I who sent Volusia to fetch you. By the way, this fell out of your clothes." He held out a slim book. "The Gospel of Mary Magdalene. My foot covered it before Stigmus saw."

Quistus took it wonderingly. "She must have slipped it to me in the sedan."

"Perhaps you are one of us, a little. You did not mention your suspicion of Linus to Stigmus." Paul shrugged. "They will all die anyway."

"All? But Pudens and Claudia are Roman citizens, and Volusia too —"

"Surely you know Volusia and her parents are not citizens? For Pudens and Claudia death will inch its way through the courts, as it does for me. For Volusia and the others it will come running."

"When Stigmus puts them to the test surely they will agree to curse Christ, and live."

"The only way to live," Paul said, "is to die in Christ."

Quistus shook his head. "Get out of Rome, Paul. Go. Save yourself."

"No, my friend. I am a citizen of Rome. Rome is the centre. If Rome is Christian, all the Empire is Christian. I stay." He shrugged. "Perhaps not all will die. Peter may be allowed to live. He heads a different sect from mine, one that believes in churches and priests, not Christ within each heart. The Emperor may dream of placing himself at the head of such an organization as Pope."

"But Volusia will die for a crime she did not commit."

"There was no crime, there is no death. Only eternal life with Jesus Christ."

"But still she will die in agony."

Paul turned, frowning. "Does it matter?"

Septimus Severus Quistus sat in his office reading a book. He turned the pages, his lips moving as he read.

Omba sat silently behind him, arms massively crossed. For days her tongue had not spoken. Even the many gold ornaments and bangles that clothed her body were silent.

He spoke without turning.

"I know," he said.

Night. At the centre of the square four crosses stood, dimly lit by red firelight from below, blue moonlight from above.

The crosses had been planted upside-down. The crossbars were nailed, not near the top, but close to the base.

The Christian rebels were crucified head-down, their feet against Heaven, their heads towards Hell. Upturned, they had screamed as the nails were hammered home.

By now the crowd of thousands that mocked them and roared its pleasure at their cries had gone as though it never was.

The screams had died down to low, gasping moans. Almost no one heard them; only two footsoldiers on guard, and the old madwoman, a scarf over her head, bent double by arthritis, feeding crumbs to the birds. "Here birdie birdie." Her low cackling voice got on the soldiers' nerves. They exchanged glances.

Suddenly soldiers of the Imperial Guard trod steadily into the square, forming a circle facing outward from the crosses. They drew their swords and touched them to their foreheads in obeisance, as though to an approaching god.

The imperial palanquin of gold and purple was carried into the square. The curtains were reverently opened by slaves, and a god stepped down.

The Emperor Nero, *pontifex maximus*, his hair tightly oiled, a gold stick in his hand, his tunic dusted with chalk so that it was a perfect holy white, unsoiled by any earthly imperfection, walked to the crosses. A purple carpet was unrolled before him so his sandals did not touch the bloody, filthy stones.

He stared down at the faces, then raised his little finger. "Stigmus."

Stigmus ran forwards. "Your Grace."

"This one is already dead."

Stigmus crouched. "The one called Faustinus, your Grace."

"*Damnum Fatale*." The God-Emperor smiled. "Well, this is Emperor's justice. Let their god save them now, eh?" He touched a face with his stick, tutted. "This one's gone too."

"Pedilla. The younger ones may be expected to live well past dawn. Three days is the record, I believe."

"Aaah," whispered Volusia.

"Such blue eyes on this one," Nero said idly. "She lives."

"I curse you," Volusia whispered. "Beast, you'll burn for ever in the fires of Hell."

"Silence!" Stigmus added apologetically, "Your Grace, none of them have recanted, or cursed Christ, despite my best efforts to persuade them."

Nero smiled. "I shall return tomorrow night and see how she fares."

Stigmus asked diffidently, "Shall the one known as Peter the Fisherman be crucified, your Grace?"

"No. He may be useful. So may his chief lieutenant, the one called Linus." Bored, Nero returned to the palanquin, then paused. "Stigmus, could it be true? Did the Christian deity murder Matrusus? Did their God really try to save them?"

"I cannot believe so, your Grace."

Nero nodded, relieved. "A God who allowed His own Son to be murdered . . . even I am not that ruthless, Stigmus. That would be a God to be feared, indeed." Whatever else was said between them the old woman did not hear; the palanquin was lifted and borne away, the Guard marching on each side, and the square fell silent once more.

"Here, birdie birdie."

"You stupid old woman!" shouted the second of the two soldiers. "It's night, there aren't any stupid birds! Get away from us!"

"Birdie birdie birdie."

The two soldiers exchanged looks and drew their swords. There was a loud bang as their helmets were knocked together from behind. Black hands gleaming with gold rings and bangles gripped their throats, dropping them where they stood.

"Well done, Omba." The old woman threw off her scarf and stood straight, kicked away the swords. "Don't kill them, let them sleep. There's enough death."

"Master," Omba grumbled, returning the dagger to her gold wrist-guard.

Quistus ran to Volusia. While Omba lifted the girl's weight he took pincers from the bag of crumbs, gripped the nail-heads, pulled. Omba carried Volusia to the sedan chair waiting in the shadows. "I'm not doing this for pennies," the blind man said.

Omba sat Volusia on the bench and stepped back. "I'll be by the Transtiberium wharf as you ordered, Master, with the captain in my pocket."

"Good. Well done, Omba. Run."

Quistus climbed into the sedan. It bumped, lifting, then set off immediately through the dark streets. He closed the curtains and lit the candle.

Volusia watched him, the flame making her eyes very blue. She murmured, "Omba has no pockets."

"Oh, she has all sorts of places to keep stuff." Quistus bandaged Volusia's feet. "Is the pain very bad?"

"No. I suppose." She stared at her hands. "The marks of Christ. I was ready to live, Septimus."

"You know better than to call me that."

"Why did you do it?"

"Because I believe you should live fully in this world before being in too much of a hurry to live in the next."

She gazed at him steadily.

"Because I am wearing your wife's clothes," she said. "Do I look like her?"

He shook his head.

She asked, "Do I make her alive again for you, a little?"

He said, "The Transtiberium boat is small. You'll transfer to a bigger vessel at Ostia."

"And where will that bigger vessel take me, Quistus?"

"Britannia. Londinium. Learn how to live, Volusia, not die."

"Did you read that little book?"

He shrugged.

"So," she said. "I live, and I take Christianity to Britannia."

The sedan-chair weaved through alleys, was hurried across a broad thoroughfare, then came swaying downhill. They smelt the river.

"But you are not coming with me," she said.

"No."

The sedan-chair bumped as it was set down. He blew out the candle and they sat in the dark.

Then he got out. He paid the runners with gold.

Volusia stood up. "Nothing like her at all?"

He shook his head.

She kissed his lips. "Goodbye. And thank you."

Omba helped her down to the boat. He watched with tears in his eyes. Volusia looked back from the deck, moonlight glowing on her pale robes.

Omba returned as the sail was hoisted. "What's wrong, Master?"

"Nothing's wrong, Omba. You could not have known." He watched the moonlit sail shrinking on the moonlit waters. "They are the clothes Marcia wore on her wedding day."

He stared until he could no longer see Volusia's sail, only moonlight.

"*Redivivus*," he said.

Heads You Lose

Simon Scarrow

After Nero's death came the turbulent year of the Four Emperors in AD 69, from which Vespasian emerged victorious, establishing a new, albeit shortlived, dynasty. Vespasian came to glory because he was a superb general and he set his sights on Rome while on campaign in Palestine. He left his eldest son, Titus, in command, and Titus successfully completed the siege of Jerusalem in AD 70. This story is set during that siege. Simon Scarrow shot into the front rank of historical novelists with Under the Eagle *(2000), the first in a series that charts the Roman conquest of Britain under Emperor Claudius.*

Soon after sunrise the morning hate began. The heavy thud of catapult arms striking home against their packed leather buffers was accompanied by the sharper thwack of the bolt throwers. Overhead the sky was laced with the smudged black arcs of incendiary pots and punctuated with the dots of stones and the dashes of the heavy iron tipped spears flashing in much lower trajectories towards the old city.

Jerusalem would fall before the month was out. That was

certain. Both sides knew it. The four legions of General Titus Flavius had battered their way into the city, taken the fortress of Antonia and had, at last, forced their way into the temple complex. But every stage had cost far too many lives, and now the exhausted legionaries were bracing themselves for the final assault on the old city; the rebels' last line of defence. Once that was breached, as it would be, then – Titus had promised his men – they could do as they wished when they burst in upon the starving remnants of Jerusalem's population. According to the intelligence gathered from those Jews who had managed to escape from the old city, conditions inside were appalling. Faction had turned on faction, and all had turned on anyone who even mentioned negotiating a surrender. The huge grain stores that had been gathered to see the defenders through the siege had gone up in smoke; deliberately fired by the leader of one sect to deprive his rivals of rations. Now, it was said, the long suffering bystanders were reduced to eating the bodies of their own children. The Romans sat outside this horror, biding their time, waiting for the day when they would enter and lay waste a city of walking skeletons.

Even this chance to slake their bloodlust and taste for booty had failed to rally the legions. They knew that they would pay a high price before this siege was over. The surviving factions of the Judaean rebels were a game lot, and knew that they could expect no mercy from the Romans. They would fight with the grim desperation of the already dead, each one determined to take as many legionaries as possible with them to whatever afterlife the Jews believed in.

No wonder the men were quiet, chief centurion Figulus reflected, as he gazed towards the thin pall of smoke hanging over the old city. His legion, the Tenth, was quartered amid the ruined streets surrounding the Antonia, most of which had been razed to form the artillery platform. The task of

guarding the temple complex had been trusted to the First
Cohort of the legion, Figulus's cohort. Each watch eighty
men trailed up through the breach in the temple wall to
replace their tired comrades who struggled down the rubble
slope and collapsed in exhaustion in their goatskin tents.
Under normal conditions those on night watch suffered from
the most strained nerves as they struggled to hear what their
eyes could not detect. But conditions were not normal. Far
from it.

For three nights now something had been killing those
men posted on the blackened walls of the inner court of the
temple, which sheltered the sanctum of the most holy of
holies. It was a large chamber, perhaps thirty feet square,
which no man had entered since its construction. Until the
legions arrived. Many had passed through the space with the
usual soldierly indifference. In truth it was bare and smelled
musty and the only thing inside it was a plain dark wooden
chest sealed from the outside world. Despite the intense heat
of the fire that had consumed much of the temple complex,
the chamber in which the chest rested had been spared. One
of his centurions, Quintus Marius, had forced the top but
had only discovered a few dusty scrolls inside after he had
hacked through the glassy sheen of the centuries' old wood.
Marius had found an old priest guarding the chamber, and
once the man had been disarmed, with contemptuous ease,
the centurion had tried to force him to reveal what was in the
chest.

"Bunch of sacred scripts, my arse!" Marius had snorted as
he looked around the temple complex. "Place like this has to
be worth a few denarii."

He looked at his interpreter, a weasily prisoner who had
quickly volunteered his services to the Romans. "Josephus!
Tell the old man to cough it up, now, or he's dog meat."

The Judaeans exchanged a few words in their gutteral

tongue before the interpreter turned back. "He says there's nothing in there but scrolls. And no treasure. There's no treasure anywhere."

"We'll see about that!"

Marius had seized the old man and dragged him inside the chamber. For a while Figulus only heard the odd cry of pain, and then there was a short thin scream and it was all over. Marius came out, wiping the blood from his dagger on the old priest's head cloth.

"Any luck?"

"No, sir. Stubborn bastard just kept shaking his head, like, and uttering his gibberish. Got tired of it and knocked him on the head."

"Very well."

That had been several days ago, and any euphoria the men might have had about finding something valuable in the temple had long since dried up, like everything else in this dusty arid husk of a province. And now, to add to the chief centurion's problems, something was murdering his men. Figulus watched as the first legionaries from the night watch appeared in the breach, silhouetted against the dawn sky, as they began to pick their way down the slope towards the Cohort's tent lines. One of the figures was hurriedly picking his way down the rubble slope, making towards the chief centurion. Figulus felt his heart sink like a rock; there could only be one explanation for the man's hurry. He turned towards one of his orderlies.

"Send for Centurion Marius. Tell him to meet me up there. In the inner temple."

The body of the sentry, like all the others killed that night, and the previous two days, was missing its head. The man was lying forwards in a pool of his own blood. Most of it had dried to a dark, dim purple but patches still glistened and had drawn a noisy droning cloud of flies. Figulus knelt down by the man's shoulders and cocked his head to look at the ugly mass of muscle, artery and bone where the neck had been cut through.

"What the hell did that?" Marius asked, squatting beside his superior, but slightly further away from the body.

"Looks like a sword blow. Maybe several sword blows. Look there." Figulus pointed to a cut in the flesh that angled away from the edge of the skin. "Took our man a few attempts to get the head off."

"Our man?" Marius looked at him with raised eyebrows. "What makes you think a man did this? And all the others?"

"What else would it be?"

Marius looked at him silently for a moment before speaking. "So how did he get past the sentries on the outer wall? How'd he get inside the inner walls, sir? It's not possible."

"Of course it's possible. It's a certainty. Some of those bloody sicarii must have found a way back into the temple," Figulus said quietly. "They're picking off our sentries."

"Then why take the heads, sir? What's the point of that?"

"Trophies," Figulus suggested, remembering when he had served as a raw recruit in the Second legion during the early years of the invasion of Britain. The Celtic warriors built their reputations on the number of enemy heads they managed to accumulate. "Or maybe there's some kind of bounty on offer."

"Or maybe it's just the work of some demon . . ." Marius muttered, casting a wary glance towards the chief centurion, a man who had little time for petty superstitions.

"Demon?"

"It's just what the lads are saying, sir."

"Is that right? A demon . . . What kind of bollocks is that?"

"What do you expect them to think, when we lose men night after night? And every one of them has lost his head?"

"Seems to be catching," Figulus sniffed with contempt. "I don't want to hear any more of this nonsense, especially from you, Marius. I've never had you down as being gullible. This is the work of a man. A flesh and blood man. There are no spooks involved. Got that? Make sure that the rest of our lads get the message. There'll be no more talk about demons."

"Yes, sir."

Despite his order, Figulus was well aware that the rumour of a demon preying on the sentries of the First Cohort was spreading through the rest of the legion like the plague. Everywhere he went the men fell silent and sullen at his approach and only continued talking in muted whispers after he had passed. Nor was the rumour any respecter of rank. As the sun dipped into the haze of smoke hanging over the city at the end of the day Figulus arrived at the legion's headquarters for the evening briefing. The legate, Flavius Silva, had occupied a wealthy merchant's house, abandoned long before the siege when its owner had been condemned to the galleys for an attempt on the life of a Roman official. Silva had made himself quite at home in the faded opulence and now conferred with his senior officers in a shuttered dining room overlooking the dead plants of the roof garden. Beyond the crumbling parapet of the garden, the house had a magnificent view towards the old town. In a more peaceful time the vista would have been fascinating and relaxing. But now Silva's staff used the roof garden as an observation point to signal the fall of shot to the prefect of artillery on the huge earthworks close to the Antonia. As the briefing started the observers signalled the last fall of shot, and then tied the signalling arms down for the night and returned to the camp, leaving the roof garden to the legate and his officers. Once the usual strength returns, supply levels and intelligence reports had been discussed the senior centurions and tribunes were dismissed. With a scraping of chairs, the officers eased themselves back from the trestle table and rose to leave.

"Figulus," the legate called out. "A word in private, if you please."

"Of course, sir."

Conscious that they were no longer wanted the other men hurried their departure and then the door to the stairway closed behind the last man, leaving Legate Silva and his chief centurion alone. The dying glow of the sun diffused the air with a faint red glow, burnishing the polished medallions on Figulus's harness.

"Sit yourself back down," the legate waved him to a chair on the opposite side of the table to his own. "Figulus, what's the situation up in the temple?"

"Situation?" Figulus shrugged. "We've no problems there. The walls are in good nick; no chance of any breakout through the temple complex."

Silva smiled. "That's not quite what I meant. One of my tribunes says he heard some of your men talking about a spate of bizarre killings up there."

"It's true, sir," Figulus nodded. "We've lost a number of sentries the last few nights."

"Lost? That's putting it mildly from what I'm told."

"The circumstances are unusual," Figulus admitted. "But it's nothing more than a handful of the enemy trying to put the frighteners on my lads. Playing on their fears, like."

"And you're not afraid?"

Figulus tightened his lips in an expression of contempt.

"I see," continued the legate with a smile. "You're not worried then. Trouble is, the men evidently are. Unless we put a stop to these deaths, and the unfortunate rumours, the men won't be able to press home the next assault with full hearts. That'll cost even more lives."

"Yes, sir."

Silva paused to look out over the city, slowly sinking into shadows as only the tallest roofs and towers glowed in the last rays of the setting sun.

"I want this matter resolved as soon as possible, Centurion. General Titus has ordered our legion to lead the assault on the old city. We will be successful. I will not tolerate any failure and I will not have my men going into battle with their heads filled with ridiculous fears about demons fighting on the enemy side. Do I make myself clear?"

"Yes, sir."

"So, I want you to find out how the rebels are getting into the temple. Find their tunnel, or whatever it is, and seal it."

"I've already looked, sir. Thoroughly."

"Then look again, thoroughly, and keep looking until you find it. Because if there is no way into the temple complex then it can only lend credence to these stories about a demon."

An unpleasant thought struck Figulus. "If there is no way in, and no demon, then whoever is killing my men might be on our side, sir."

"Maybe." Silva shrugged. "Just deal with it."

"I'll deal with it, sir," Figulus said firmly. "Tonight."

The smoke from the fires still burning in the old city obscured the stars and even though the moon had risen it only appeared as a wan yellow disc in the gloom. Figulus, wrapped in a black cloak, set out to make a stealthy inspection of the sentries posted on the walls of the inner court of the temple. He had considered taking a few good men with him, but more men meant more noise. The chief centurion wanted to avoid drawing any attention to himself as he observed his sentries. For the same reason he had not told anyone where he was going when he had slipped out of his tent earlier. Beneath the cloak he wore only his tunic, and sword belt, so that he could move easily and silently through the ruins. There was always the chance that he might be mistaken for the enemy in the darkness by one of the more alert of his men, but Figulus was counting on his experience and guile to remain invisible.

Picking his way up the rubble-strewn ramp Figulus looked up at the dark mass of the temple walls towering over him and a cool breath of air made him shiver. He wondered, for an instant, if there might be some supernatural forces at work after all. Then, chiding himself angrily for being such a weak-minded fool, Figulus pulled the wool folds of his cloak more tightly about him and crept forwards. The loose masonry and shattered tiles made tough going and he had to pick his way carefully to avoid slipping or turning his ankle. At length he reached the wide breach in the wall and entered the remains of the temple enclosure. Beyond the breach the vast outer courtyard stretched out in the darkness. The inner court lay ahead, and beyond, dimly visible, was the massive wall that looked down on the old town. Figulus stayed close to the wall, making good use of the shadows there as he crept towards the midpoint, directly opposite the walls of the inner court, where his men had been murdered.

The chief centurion waited a while until the moon was obscured by a thick pall of smoke, slowly billowing across the night sky. Then he ran across to the wall and entered through one of the small fissures that had been left as a result of the fire a few days earlier. The opening still carried the bitter reek of charred timber as Figulus crept through, carefully avoiding any of the wooden beams and their load of pre-cariously balanced blackened stone. He paused a moment, heart beating quickly against his chest, but no one seemed to have noticed him so far. That was not a good sign, and tomorrow there would be a few harsh words to be said to those on the night watch. But, with the murders of their comrades firmly on their minds, they would be spending as much time looking into the shadows immediately around them as they did watching the approaches to the inner court. On the other hand, Figulus smiled, they would be less likely to be suborned by the usual monotony of guard duty. Sleeping on duty, according to the harsh laws of the legions, was punishable by death. Death meted out by wooden clubs in the hands of the soldier's mess mates. Thought of which made Figulus wonder about his earlier suspicion about the killer.

Slowly he made his way along the inside of the wall, watching the walkway for sign of his men, and whoever, or whatever, seemed to be stalking them. It was hard to spot most of the sentries, even though he had chosen their stations. Usually the men on duty would be moving around to keep themselves wide awake, but this night they were keeping to the shadows, motionless and alert as they no longer had the luxury of knowing the direction from which any danger would emerge. Even so, the chief centurion was only challenged once, and the exchange of challenge and password was carried out in low voices that would not carry far. After a few hours his eyes were aching from the strain and he decided to find somewhere to rest a while.

As the trumpets down in the camp sounded the middle of the watch, Figulus sat down in the remains of a small portico in the centre of the inner court. Around him, in the darkness, were the four sentries tasked with keeping watch. For the moment they were still alive. Figulus wondered if he had been wasting his time, and yearned for the basic comfort of his camp bed and a decent blanket. His cloak provided poor shelter from the cold night and a numbing chill was slowly working its way into his joints. Ten years ago this would not have bothered him and Figulus smiled grimly at yet another sign of his aging. But he dare not get up and walk the stiffness off.

A sharp cry snapped him out of his self-absorption. Though the sound was gone in an instant, Figulus was sure that it had been human, and close at hand. Throwing back his cape he quickly drew his sword and ran in the direction the sound had come from. There was a flight of blackened stairs, almost invisible in the darkness, and he sprinted up them, leaping three steps at a time, until he reached the parapet. Immediately to his left the walkway had collapsed and Figulus turned to run in the other direction. Thick clouds obscured the moon and only the faintest silvery shimmer showed that it was there at all. Ahead, in the gloom, he saw a darker mass; a man sprawled on the ground and a figure looming over.

Man or demon, there was no sense in taking it on alone.

"To me!" Figulus shouted. "Sentries, to me!"

The figure snapped upright at the sound of his voice. Figulus saw the dim line of a legionary short sword and then the man dropped a small bundle, turned and ran off into the darkness. The chief centurion ran after him, but stumbled over the body and crashed down on his knee. A red-hot stab of pain shot up his leg. He tried to rise, but the joint gave out and with a shouted curse of agony and frustration he slumped down beside the body. The sentry was quite dead, and his head, dropped by the fleeing attacker, lay on one ear, eyes wide open in shock as blood dribbled from contorted lips. There were shouts in the darkness as the other sentries hurried towards Figulus. The chief centurion was struck by a sudden fear that they might miss him in the darkness, and that the killer might return.

"Get up here! Up here! Smartly does it, lads!"

Close by there was the grating crunch of iron studded boots as the sentries clambered up the stairs and ran along the parapet. Dim forms thickened into the substantial shapes of legionaries and Figulus at last let himself relax the grip on his sword handle.

"Shit . . ." muttered one of the sentries when they reached the chief centurion and their dead comrade. "What the fuck's happened here?"

The three sentries were young, nervous and horrified. Their chests heaved with the exertion of sprinting from their posts, and they darted anxious glances into the darkness that wrapped itself about them.

"Did you see it, sir?"

"It?" Figulus looked up.

"The demon, sir. Did you see it?"

"At least we know it's not some kind of devil," Figulus said to Legate Silva, gritting his teeth as the legion's surgeon tightened the dressing around his knee. With neat movements of his fingers the surgeon tied the two ends of cloth together, and then eased himself back on his heels and stood up.

"Nasty gash, that. Keep your weight off the knee for a few days and get the dressing changed dawn and dusk. Should mend soon enough, sir."

"Keep my weight off it?" Figulus frowned. "Are you mad? I'm a bloody chief centurion, not some pampered tax-collector."

"I'm sure the empire will survive a few days without your support, sir," the surgeon smiled humourlessly.

"Look here . . ."

"He's right, Figulus," the legate intervened. "I need you in a fit state when we launch the final assault on the old town."

"What about the killer?"

"You've probably scared him off. We'll double the sentries. That should be the end of it, now we know what we're dealing with. We can have an investigation after the city falls. Now, at least, we know it's one of our own. The Jews haven't found a way through our lines. That's a comfort."

"Not to those lads of mine who died," Figulus replied quietly. "It'd be bad enough if they'd been killed by the enemy. It's a shitty way to die, murdered by someone on your own side. Murdered and mutilated. And what for? That's what I want to know . . . What I need to know."

"We'll catch him." The legate nodded sympathetically. "As soon as there's time."

"Unless he covers his tracks in the time that we allow him."

"Maybe. But that can't be helped," Silva concluded firmly. "Now, you rest that knee, Centurion. That's an order."

Figulus nodded reluctantly, and the legate, satisfied that he had made his point, turned and left the dressing station. Silva marched down the edge of the parade-ground, a former market square that had been cleared of rubble, and Figulus watched him until the legate turned up a side street and disappeared from view. Then he swung his legs over the side of the trestle bed and flexed his knee. It was painful, but would not prevent him walking. He had endured worse. The surgeon eyed him warily.

"Hope you're going to obey orders."

"I'll do what I must," Figulus replied through clenched teeth as a jet of pain seared up his thigh. "Now mind your bloody business."

The surgeon shrugged. "Suit yourself, sir."

"I will. Now piss off."

"Yes, sir!"

Figulus stayed seated and watched a century drilling on the parade ground. No matter what duty the legion was engaged with, whether building roads or assaulting enemy fortresses, there was always drilling. Endless repetition of barked commands and instant responses. The men became as cogs in a giant machine, each one interlocked with his companions as they all worked in smooth harmony. There was nothing quite like it on this earth, Figulus decided. A legionary obeyed without thought, instinctively and absolutely, with no regard to the danger. That was the real secret of the legions' success. The enemy might have a bigger build, like those bloody Britons Figulus had fought so many years ago. The enemy might even be more fearless and adept with weapons, but the iron efficiency of the legions was a rock on which the greatest of Neptune's waves would only be dashed.

The chief centurion smiled at the bathetic turn of thought, then his mind quickly turned back to recent events. There was little doubt that the killer was Roman. But that knowledge only released a torrent of further questions. Why would a Roman kill his comrades? Why would he take their heads? What would he do with them? Above all, how could he achieve this? One sentry might be surprised, but four each night? Such a killer would have to possess superhuman stealth.

A screaming tirade of abuse from the parade ground drew the chief centurion's mind away from such troubled thoughts. He looked over the dusty ground to where the men of the century stood to attention as their commander tore into a hapless legionary.

"You disgusting little turd!" the centurion screamed into the man's face. "You make me puke! You dare come onto *my* parade ground with one of your fucking boots undone? You worthless piece of shit, drop your kit and get it tied up before I rip your dick off and beat you to death with it!"

Figulus smiled approvingly. The centurion was on fine form and the legionary would not forget this dressing down for a long time. The centurion stood back a pace and irritably slapped his vine cane into the palm of his other hand. The legionary dropped his shield and javelin to one side and dropped to his knee, head bent down to look at his boot. His neck guard rose up and flashed in the brilliant sunshine, the reflection momentarily dazzling Figulus.

Then the chief centurion felt an icy chill tickle its way up his spine and into the flesh at the back of his neck. He frowned for a moment, angry and bitter that the thought had not occurred to him sooner. Some lives might have been spared then. Before he had proved that the deaths were the work of no demon . . . Figulus eased himself up onto his feet and limped towards the edge of the dressing station. The surgeon saw him rise and, leaving a patient to one of his orderlies, he moved to intercept.

"Don't say a word!" Figulus warned him. "Unless you want to be treating yourself for a broken jaw."

The surgeon opened his mouth to protest, thought better of it, closed his mouth and nodded meekly.

"That's better. I'm off to my tent. I want you to send my respects to Centurion Marius. Tell him to come to my tent at once. Tell him we're going to end these killings tonight."

Shortly after sunset Figulus and Marius clambered up the long slope of rubble. A thin band of clouds had appeared on the horizon at noon and had now thickened into a towering mass that threatened rain. The underside of the cloud mass was awash with a deep red glow from the invisible sun, but here on the shattered remains of the Antonia deep shadows made the going treacherous. The chief centurion was glad for his companion's help as they picked their way towards the breach in the vast walls of the temple complex. Besides their swords Marius had brought along two small wineskins to help keep them warm through the coming night as they watched the sentries and waited for the killer to make his appearance.

"What makes you think he'll be there tonight?" asked Marius.

"He's not missed one yet," Figulus smiled. "Our man is a creature of habit."

"If it is a man."

Figulus turned to his companion with a faint look of disappointment. "Surely you don't still think he's some kind of spook? Not you."

"We'll see."

"Yes, we'll see. Now let's keep it quiet, we're almost inside and I don't want to attract any attention."

Marius shot him a sidelong glance. "Why the big secret, sir?"

"Don't want to give the killer any advance warning. Especially if he might be one of our own men."

"Who knows we're here?"

"Just you and me."

Marius sucked in a breath between his teeth with a faint hissing sound. "Isn't that a bit risky, sir?"

"Why should it be? Think we can't take him on ourselves?"

"No. If he's flesh and blood, we can sort him out well enough."

"That's the spirit! Now just give me a hand here . . ."

Once inside the temple complex the two officers stealthily made their way to the inner court, slipping through the shadows of the main gate where all the sentries had been found. Dead and headless.

"What now?" Marius whispered.

"Inside here." Figulus indicated a small shrine, scarcely

bigger than a section tent. "We'll dump the wineskins and make a quiet tour of the lads – make sure they're all right. Then we go back to the shrine and wait."

Marius looked at him with a scathing expression. "Call that a plan?"

"You think of anything better?"

"Yes." Marius nodded. "Not being here in the first place."

"Too late for that. Come on."

The chief centurion led the way inside the shrine, carefully feeling his way over the charred timbers and chunks of plaster that littered the floor. On one side a section of the wall had fallen in and now offered a view of the ramparts along the inner court. On the opposite wall, a small barred window looked out over the flag-stoned expanse towards the vast wall facing the part of the city still held by the Jewish rebels. Figulus dropped his wineskin by the window.

"I'll take this side. You're over there."

"Right."

They set their wineskins down and were turning back towards the entrance when Figulus snagged his boot on a sliver of wood.

"Shit!"

"You all right, sir?"

"Fine. Just caught my boot lace. You go on and keep watch."

Marius nodded and then softly crunched his way outside. The chief centurion joined him a moment later and then beckoned him towards the wall that looked out onto the old town. The night was dark as pitch under the heavy clouds. A cold breeze had picked up, lifting ash and dust into the air in small whirling vortices, so that the two men had to squint and raise their neckerchiefs over their mouths. They moved slowly along the perimeter of the inner court, checking that each of the four sentries was still in position, and still alive. The dark silhouettes of the men with their helmets, shields and javelins were just visible in the gloom and, satisfied that all was well, Figulus led the way back to the shrine. As they crept over the inner court the first spots of rain pattered around them, and a white flash in the sky over the old town momentarily lit up the temple ruins. Then it was dark, and almost at once a deafening crack of thunder sounded across the city, slowly dying away in an angry rumble. The rain began to slash down, frozen, mid-air, in glinting steel-grey lances as the next burst of lightning filled the sky.

The two officers hurried back to the shrine, Figulus jogging carefully to favour his wounded knee. Inside they made their way to their positions and looked out as the storm lashed the war-torn city. Figulus pitied the men on sentry duty; there would be little shelter for them up on the walls, and he could picture them soaked and shivering in the rising wind that now howled over the battlements.

"Only a fool would be out on a night like this!" grumbled Marius. "I'd wager the killer is tucked up in his tent keeping himself dry and warm."

"I'd take that bet." Figulus smiled. "Shall we say a gold piece?"

Marius considered it for a moment, and then nodded. "If he doesn't show, you pay up."

"Surely."

As the night dragged on the two men kept watch over the inner court, occasionally sipping from their wineskins. The storm eventually passed and left a steady, dreary downpour in its wake. From time to time the sentries were visible as their beat brought them into view on the wall. But there was no sign of the killer, and at last, when the first faint hints of dawn gathered on the skyline Figulus slumped down and reached for his wineskin.

"Seems you may start the day a richer man, Marius. Let me toast you."

The centurion chuckled as his superior pulled out the stopper, raised the wineskin to his lips and squirted a jet of dark liquid into his mouth. When Figulus lowered the wineskin his face relaxed into a look of contentment as the last mouthful of fiery liquid passed down his throat. Marius started to drink from his own wineskin and Figulus waited for him to finish his first draught before speaking.

"Rough stuff, that! Where'd you get it?"

"Samaritan wine-seller. Comes to the camp gate each day with a small mule-train loaded with wine. Not cheap, mind you."

"Nothing ever is on active service."

"No . . . No, that's true."

"They're like bloody vultures. Selling us crap like this for a small fortune. There's hardly a man in the legion who isn't dipping into his savings right now. Unless the general lets us loose on Jerusalem when the rebels finally give in we're all going to be a lot poorer."

"True."

Figulus looked at his subordinate as Marius took another swig. "You must be worried."

Marius lowered the wineskin. "Worried? Me? Why's that, sir?"

"You've less than a year's service to go, haven't you?"

"Yes. So?"

"So, this is your last chance to get hold of some loot, to see you through your old age. I doubt you've been finding this campaign cheap. If you're like me, you've spent a good deal on those merchants."

Marius watched the chief centurion silently for a moment, and then shrugged. "I'll be all right. Even if there's not much left in my savings there's the gratuity to look forward to . . . I'll be all right."

"I'm sure you will," Figulus replied quietly. "How much have you found so far?"

Marius stared at him. "Sir?"

"How much of the temple treasure have you found so far?"

"I don't understand, sir."

"Come now, Centurion, don't be coy. I just wanted to know how much you've discovered. You've been hard at it. Three nights' work, not to mention twelve murders. I don't know how you keep going. Must be even tougher than you look. So, how much?" asked Figulus, before he drank some more wine.

"All right then," Marius's craggy face slowly smiled. "Enough for a small estate at Baiae."

"Nice!" Figulus whistled. "Where have you been putting it?"

"Somewhere safe. Somewhere secret from the Jews, and our side. Somewhere not a million miles from where we're sitting, as it happens."

"Really?"

"Yes, really. You're almost on top of it." Marius nodded towards the floor in the centre of the shrine. "Of course it's taken a lot of hard work to haul it across from the temple."

"The kind of work that draws unwanted attention."

"Precisely."

Figulus suddenly shivered. "Shit! It's getting cold."

"Isn't it?" Marius grinned. "And it'll get colder yet."

"It was a neat idea to take the heads. I suppose you started the rumour about the demon?"

"Didn't have to. Knew I could count on the more superstitious amongst us to do that for me. Worked like a dream. Apart from the sentries everyone's been keeping well away from the inner court, leaving me to get on in peace."

"Didn't it bother you, killing your own men?"

"I've had a lifetime of killing. Got used to it. The first one was a little difficult, but they stood in the way of a fortune. It became easy . . . How did you find out?"

"Took a while," Figulus admitted. "I never believed in the demon. But the problem was how any killer could take all his victims by surprise. One sentry might be a bit dopey and not detect the killer, but all twelve? Somehow, he managed to get them to stand still while he took a free swing at the back of their heads with a club . . . or maybe a centurion's vine staff. Then, once they were down the killer could cut the head off easily enough. As you say, you've had practice. Thing is, the neck guard on a legionary helmet should prevent any blow to the back of the neck, yet the head you were good enough to leave behind yesterday had a bruise right on the hairline, above the ragged flesh where the head had been severed. Looked to me like someone had knocked the sentry down before removing the head. Incidentally, where are all the heads?"

Marius nodded towards the floor again.

"Good. We'll need them back so the lads can have a proper funeral. Be a bit unseemly for them to enter the Underworld minus a head."

"What makes you think you're going to live to tell anyone about this?" Marius said evenly. His hand trembled a little as it rested on the pommel of his short sword.

"You'll see," Figulus replied, nodding towards the centurion's sword. "You won't need to use that."

"No, I won't," said Marius. "Do go on."

"As I was saying, how could it be that any sentry would willingly bare their neck to a killer? Unless they were ordered to do it. Ordered by a centurion. The sestertius dropped this afternoon while I was watching some men on the parade ground. Must have been awfully easy for you."

"It was. I just turned up, told them to stand to attention, gave them a bollocking for not tying their laces properly and told them to sort it out. Once they were bent over looking down it was easier than taking sweet cakes from a baby. When they were all dealt with I could get on with it."

"How did you know where to look?"

"That rabbi told me."

"Thought you didn't speak their tongue?"

"I don't. But there are other ways of making people very eloquent indeed. The old man couldn't take me to the treasure fast enough."

"I see." Figulus was suddenly very tired of playing this game. Tired, and finally very angry. Life in the legions was precarious. The chief centurion had served with thousands of men over the years. Most, he knew, were dead. Killed in action, killed in accidents, killed by disease. Only a few had been killed by their comrades, and even then it was mostly as a result of a drunken brawl. Those who served with the eagles knew the odds were against them. The prospect of death was far more certain than the chance of retirement to a small farm and the slow, fading serenity of old age. Living face to face with death, in its many guises, the men of the legions formed a peculiarly close bond with each other. Beneath the rough, hard exterior of the soldier burned a compassion and sentimentality that most civilians never guessed at, as the chief centurion well knew. Men who could kill with merciless ferocity one day, could act with great compassion and gentleness the following day. But valued above all other qualities was loyalty to your comrades. Which is what made Figulus sick to the pit of his stomach as he sat opposite Centurion Marius in the thin cold light of dawn.

"You'll die for this, Marius. It'll be painful, and you'll deserve it."

The centurion laughed, and Figulus smiled grimly as he

saw that the man was shivering. Marius laughed again, this time edged with a distinct sneer. "I deserve it, all right. But it's not going to happen to me. Not for a while at least. You should be more worried about yourself, sir."

"I presume you're referring to this crap." Figulus raised his nearly empty wineskin. "From the symptoms, I'd say you used hemlock, or something very similar."

Marius stared at him. "You knew? You knew and you still drank it?"

"Yes, of course . . . After I'd switched the wineskins round."

"Switched them?" Marius whispered. "When?"

"Before we checked on the sentries. Remember my boot-lace? Must admit I was worried that you might try to do to me what you did to the others, but I was ready to react if you'd made a move. Unlike those poor bastards. Anyway, I had my suspicions about the wine. When you came clean about the killings I knew it had to be poisoned. I'm glad you had the chance to confess before you died."

Marius glared at him, and there was no hiding the cold trembling that had taken charge of his limbs. There was a terrible apprehension in the centurion's expression now, and his glance darted towards his hands, shaking uncontrollably as they clenched in his lap. He looked up.

"You bastard . . . You bastard. You'll pay for this!"

Marius reached for his sword, and in the faint light his face looked ashen. His fingers wrapped round the handle and with a great effort he wrenched the blade free of its scabbard and the sword quavered as the point struggled to rise in the direction of the chief centurion. Figulus watched it all with an expression of cold contempt.

"I don't think so."

"Bastard!" Marius spat, and suddenly lunged forwards. But the chief centurion was ready for him and ducked the blow, knocking the other man's arm to one side. The blade clattered to the rubble-strewn ground and its owner collapsed beside it, struggling for breath with ragged shallow gasps. Figulus stood over him for a moment, watching the icy hand of death tighten its grasp on the centurion. Then he bent down and stretched his hand towards the purse hanging from Marius's belt.

"I think you owe me something."

Marius reached down towards his belt, shaking fingers scrabbling to defend his purse, but Figulus calmly knocked the dying man's hand aside, then helped himself to one gold coin.

Great Caesar's Ghost

Michael Kurland

This story follows on just a year after the last one and we find Vespasian still trying to settle into his rôle as Emperor. Vespasian was a no-nonsense man, not one who felt comfortable with all the trappings of high rank. His sons Titus and, especially, Domitian were far more smitten with the imperial life. The following story features the great orator Quintilian, who lived from about AD 34 to AD 95. In later years he became the tutor of Pliny the Younger who appears in a later story. Michael Kurland has established a solid reputation in the fields of science fiction, crime fiction and rock music – he edited the music paper Crawdaddy *for some years. He has also written a short detective series set in the 1930s starting with* Too Soon Dead *(1997) as well as the useful guides* How to Solve a Murder *(1995) and* How to Try a Murder *(1997). His earlier story about Quintilian, "Blind Justice", will be found in my anthology* The Mammoth Book of Historical Whodunnits.

I t was on the Nones of September in the second year of
the reign of Emperor Vespasian, many years ago now,
that our involvement in the events that I am recounting

here began. For reasons that will become clear as I continue my narrative, I could not record this at the time, as is my custom – as, indeed, is my task. As is, I fear, my excuse for being.

I am Plautus Maximilianus Aureus, a member of the household of the great orator and barrister Marcus Fabius Quintilianus and, as I describe myself, his perpetual student. Somewhat higher than a servant, and somewhat lower than a protégé, I earn my keep by taking down on wax tablets, in my own special shorthand, such speeches, comments, and ideas of Quintilian as are worth recording for use in the series of texts for the training of youth that Quintilian is writing, intends to write, or may someday get around to writing. When I am not attending my patron Quintilian, I transcribe my shorthand onto scraps of parchment or papyrus and organize the comments into a variety of different categories, such as: oratory, law, government, nature, music, human conduct, instruction for the young, instruction for those who would teach the young, and humour. The humour category is not overly crowded.

The fame of my patron as a barrister and rhetorician had been on the rise for the past few years, but I don't believe that even he had any idea just how high it had risen until that morning, when a squad of the praetorian guard appeared at the gate of Quintilian's villa. "I would speak with Fabius Quintilianus the orator," the decurion in charge told Peris, our gatekeeper.

Peris yawned and stretched, and tried to act as if having six men in bright, shiny armour appear at our gate was an everyday affair. "It is barely past sunrise," he told the decurion. "I doubt whether my master is yet up."

"I am on the emperor's business," the decurion replied sternly. "For me, he will arise."

There was a time, and not so long ago, when having a

squad of the emperor's praetorian guard appear at your front gate was a good reason for fleeing out the back gate, no matter how noble your family or how high your position. But the days of Caligula and Nero are in the past, and our present emperor is not known for intemperate rages or random murders. Still, the gods themselves have been known to fly into sudden fits over minor misunderstandings, so to my mind a sudden summons from Emperor Vespasian might not be cause for flight, but a little moment of sheer terror might be understandable.

The decurion told my mentor, who came grumbling to the door of his bedroom, that his orders were to take Quintilian directly to the emperor, and as quickly as possible. With that, Quintilian dressed, splashed some water on his face, threw a cloak on over his toga, and said, "Lead on!"

I was already dressed, so I grabbed my sack of fresh wax tablets and fell in behind my mentor. I was so accustomed to accompanying Quintilian everywhere he went that we were halfway to the imperial palace before I realized that I had not been included in the summons, and Quintilian had not actually asked me to join him. Quintilian strode along, impatient with the measured tread of the guardsmen. I scurried to keep up, the sensation in my left leg, crippled from a childhood illness, progressing from a dull ache to a sharp, jarring pain with each step. But I have learned to live with pain.

The thoughts that were a great jumble in my head were of more concern than the pain in my leg, and I will admit they were unworthy of the lessons I have learned at the feet of the great Quintilian. If my mentor had somehow incurred the emperor's displeasure, would Vespasian throw him into a dungeon, or send him home to commit honourable suicide, or have him dispatched by the short sword of, perhaps, this very decurion that was taking us to the court? And, since I was with him, would the emperor include me in his displeasure, however expressed, as a matter of course?

We arrived at the east gate of the Golden House, the great palace that Nero had built (although he had died before it was finished, to the relief of all Rome), and were rushed through a series of rooms and courtyards, going deeper and deeper into the inner palace. At each doorway the decurion lifted his left hand, exposing to the guard a sigil he kept cupped in his palm, and announced, "At the emperor's command!" And the guards stood aside as we hurried through. Shortly we reached what I assumed were the private living quarters of the emperor himself. There were guards scattered all through the vast structure, like golden raisins in a porridge, but here they were clustered closer together and they stood straighter, and their armour was even more highly polished.

The decurion handed us off to a gold-plated centurion, amid much saluting and foot-stomping, and the centurion clasped hands with Quintilian. "They call me Sabatinus," the centurion told him. "I am to take you directly to the emperor."

"Do you know what this is about?" Quintilian asked.

"Not a clue. Have you met Vespasian before?"

"Once, briefly. A ceremonial occasion."

"Then for your information: he dislikes being called 'emperor', or 'Caesar', or 'princeps', or any of the other titles he has to use in public. Call him 'General Vespasian', or just 'General'."

Centurion Sabatinus took us through a great hall and we entered a corridor wide enough for a goods wagon to pass along without scraping the sides and long enough to require a lusty shout to be heard at the far end. Not that I attempted a lusty shout – that was just my impression. There were a pair of great bronze doors a comfortable distance along the corridor, flanked by two glittering guardsmen, but the centurion skirted by them and took us instead to a small black door near the corridor's end. The guardsman at the door intoned, "They are both in there," under his breath, and pulled it open.

We entered. The room was small, plainly furnished with a flat board for a desk, several camp chairs, and a nest of cubbyholes along one wall filled with scrolls and rolled documents of various sorts. And *they* were indeed in the room. Sitting behind the flat board of a desk, bent over a lengthy scroll, his body squat and hard, his face the square, blunt, honest face admired by his legionaries, was Titus Flavius Vespasianus, subduer of the Britains under Emperor Claudius; conqueror of the Jews under Emperor Nero; and now himself Emperor of Rome and sole ruler of the Roman Empire, which encompassed most of the known world. Standing by his side, holding a partially unrolled scroll, was his 20-year-old son Domitian, Titus Flavius Domitianus, who had been his father's presence in Rome while his father was in Judea, and was now Vespasian's trusted right hand.

I looked over Domitian carefully, for I had heard much about him. He was young; younger even than I. He was handsome, with a square jaw and a shock of dark, curly hair. His feelings, whatever they might be, were reserved and did not show on his face, which was a mask on which a slight, disdainful smile was the only visible emotion.

Some say Domitian was jealous of his brother's success. Vespasian's older son Titus had been left behind in Judea to finish the job of subduing the Jews, and had taken and sacked their capital city of Jerusalem and burned their temple the year before, ending once and for all the incessant bothersome revolts of these religious zealots with their "Our god is better than any of your gods" fanaticism.

Some of those who claimed to have an ear into what happened inside the palace walls, those who studied the currents within the imperial household with the diligence of nervous lovers interpreting their beloved's every sigh and gesture, said with a sneer that Domitian was just as glad not to be facing the rigours – and dangers – of a martial campaign.

There are many who seem to know, and will be glad to whisper to you in great detail, the secrets of the palace; yet I have observed that those who actually do know seldom can be persuaded to speak. That last sentence has a nice flow. I believe I have just written an aphorism of some worth. I would read it aloud to Quintilian, but he would assuredly first compliment me on it and then spend some time telling me how to improve it. And most galling of all: he would be right. I think I shall not show it to him at this time.

The centurion came to attention by Vespasian's desk. "Marcus Fabius Quintilianus, as directed, General."

Vespasian looked up. "Ah!" Then he turned to look at me, and I believe I turned white with fright. "And who is this?"

Quintilian stared at me, I swear by Janus, as though he had never seen me before "My scribe Plautus, General," he said finally.

"A scribe, eh?"

"I also use him as my personal assistant," Quintilian added.

"I see." Vespasian glared at me. "You may assist the honourable Quintilian, if he needs your assistance," he told me sternly. "But you are not to scribe a single word of what transpires here. Is that clear?"

"Yes, your, ah, general," I managed to get out.

"Good." Vespasian made a gesture, and the centurion saluted and left the room. "I have a problem," the emperor of all the known world told Quintilian, lacing his hands behind his head, leaning back in his chair, and staring at Quintilian through half-closed eyes, "and, from all I have heard of you, I am depending on you to discover the solution for me. Pull over one of those camp chairs, and enlighten my son and me with your wisdom." He spoke in a measured voice, as though each word were weighed before it was uttered. I suppose that if I knew that my every word would be dissected, parsed, examined and discussed by a sycophantic, back-stabbing collection of Roman courtiers, I, too, would get into the habit of speaking with great care.

Quintilian moved one of the leather-covered camp chairs over to the desk and sat. I squatted on the floor next to him and restrained myself from pulling a wax tablet from my bag.

"I thank you for your faith in my judgment," my master said, "but I'm not sure I should thank whoever passed on such a glowing account of my small abilities. I am a rhetorician, with some success in pleading cases before the courts of Rome. If it is skill with words you require, I shall be honoured to write speeches for you, as Seneca is said to have done for Nero. But I know nothing of statecraft, or of warfare, or of the numerous intrigues that doubtless cloud the imperial court."

"And yet when I ask the courtiers who infest this place to find me the wisest man in Rome, those who did not immediately drop to the floor and chant 'you are, oh mighty Caesar,' seemed to think that, since Seneca died, it is probably one Marcus Fabius Quintilianus. I also had my staff ask of various learned men whom they would recommend for solving an arcane problem, and your name was mentioned frequently."

Quintilian smiled a thin smile. "These must not have been friends of mine, General," he said. "My friends would have assured you of my almost invincible stupidity."

"He is the one!" Domitian interrupted, leaning forwards,

his knuckles on the desk. "I told you, father, what the Sybil said." He turned to Quintilian. "My father and I have chosen you for this task. You are expected to comply!"

Vespasian raised a hand. "I apologize for my son," he said. "He has not yet learned that there are some people to whom you must give orders, and others from whom you may request, but not require, assistance. If you do not feel you are fit for the task, it would waste both of our time for you to attempt it."

Domitian swallowed and sat down by the side of the desk.

"And just what is the task, General?" Quintilian asked.

"People here in the palace; guards, courtiers, and others, recount that they have been seeing a ghost wandering about these halls. Or so they say. I want you to find out just what it is they are seeing and, if it is a ghost, convince it to go away. And, for that matter, if it isn't a ghost, convince it to go away."

"A ghost?"

"Just so," Vespasian said, looking annoyed. "And not just any ghost. The shade, to be precise, of Gaius Julius Caesar."

I stifled an exclamation.

"Julius Caesar? He's been with his fellow gods for over a century now," Quintilian said.

"A hundred and twelve years," Vespasian affirmed. "Why, you may ask, if he were to come back, would he return to Nero's palace; a place he'd never seen in his life built by a man he'd most assuredly despise? I have no answer. But that doesn't stop him from walking these halls, at least according to those who have seen him."

Quintilian nodded. "Reports of ghosts should be taken seriously," he said. "But would it not be better to get Pliny the naturalist to investigate this? I understand he's writing some sort of vast book on these sorts of natural phenomena."

"We sent someone to ask his advice," Domitian said. "He's at his estate in Como. He recommended you."

"Ah!" My master nodded thoughtfully. "And just what was it that the Sybil said?"

Vespasian sighed. "My son went to Cumae to consult the Sybil about two weeks ago. He asked my permission, and I complied. I thought a favourable prediction would end the mutterings."

"The mutterings?"

Vespasian made a gesture to his son, who took up the story. "A figure wearing a senatorial toga with a laurel wreath circling his head has been seen wandering throughout this building at all times of the day and night – but mostly at night. He disappears when anyone attempts to approach. Those who have seen him report that he looks like the busts of Julius Caesar. I think every Roman has a good idea of what the great Caesar looked like."

Even so," Quintilian agreed.

"Some even report seeing open wounds on the figure, such as Caesar received on that fateful Ides of March," Domitian continued. "And the blood dripping on the ground. But no blood has been found when the area was examined."

"I see," Quintilian said. "So we have a disappearing spectre who looks like great Caesar. How long has this been going on?"

"At least two months. Perhaps longer."

"Have either of you ever seen it?"

Vespasian shook his head. His son said, "No, we have not been so fortunate."

"So. And why are the ruler of the Roman Empire and his son so concerned about this spectre flitting about the palace that they feel the need to ask for my poor services?"

"Two things," Vespasian said. "First, the shade has begun to speak."

"Speak?"

Domitian stood up and leaned over the desk. " 'Beware the

Ides of October,'" he recited. "That's what the fool thing has started to say. Bah! If it *was* Caesar, it'd probably be saying 'where are the girls,' or more likely, 'where are the boys?'"

"Now, son," Vespasian fixed his younger son with a stony glare. "Those are vile calumnies spread by Caesar's enemies when he had joined the gods and was no longer around to defend himself. Jove only knows what they'll be saying about me when I, ah, ascend."

"Beware the Ides of October," Quintilian repeated. "Not good."

"No." Vespasian grimaced. "And you know how superstitious the average Roman is; always looking for portents and appealing for help from one god or another. When I embark on a campaign I must have the legion's soothsayer inspect the entrails of a pigeon and a rabbit to make sure the signs are favourable. My troops might refuse to move if I did not."

Something about Vespasian's glare as he said that told me that the soothsayer knew in advance just what he'd better find in those entrails.

"It makes me a prisoner in this blasted palace of Nero's," Vespasian continued. "I want to move out. I *planned* to move out. This gilded claptrap is too ornate – too Nero – for me. Now that it's finally finished, I plan to turn it into an imperial forum, or a series of temples to the more important gods, or something. I plan to build myself a simple – well, comparatively simple – imperial abode by the Field of Mars. But I cannot move with this spectre hanging over me. I cannot seem to be moving from fear. If I leave while this is going on, my troops will lose respect for me. And there are still followers of Otho or Vitellius about who would just as soon see me dead. And if that happens we'll have another year with three or four emperors, one after the other, bim, bam, like that, fighting to stay in power. And Rome couldn't stand it."

"So the ghost of Julius Caesar is keeping you in Nero's palace by threatening your death. I assume that's how you interpret the 'Ides of October' business?"

Vespasian shrugged his broad shoulders. "How else?"

Quintilian nodded. "And that's why your son consulted the Sybil?"

"It was right after I first heard of the 'Ides of October'," Domitian said. "I went to Cumae with a small bodyguard, and paid the priests for an audience with the Sybil. I did not tell them who I was."

Sure, I thought, *just some random nobleman guarded by a troop of the praetorian guard*. But I kept my mouth shut.

Domitian continued, "The priests kept me waiting for most of the day. Then, as dusk fell, I was taken into the cave. 'Sybil,' the priest said, 'this is Vergilus,' for such is what I had told them was my name."

"What did the Sybil look like?" Quintilian asked.

"The cave was dark, and lit by torches, and it was difficult to tell," Domitian said. "One moment she looked young and beautiful – unbelievably beautiful – with long, dark hair, and a slender, sinuous body. And the next moment she looked old, unbelievably old, and wise beyond the knowledge of mortal men."

"Ah!" Quintilian said, running his forefinger along the side of his nose. "Tell me, did you smell anything?"

Domitian thought for a moment. "Some kind of incense. Perhaps it was from the smoke coming from a vent in the rock. It made my head spin."

"Ah!" Quintilian said again.

"She looked at me for a long moment. And then she said to me, 'Hail, ruler of men.'

"'I am no ruler of men,' I told her.

" 'You are what I say you are,' she said. " 'You have come about a Caesar,' she said, 'the Caesar that is yet to be concerned about the Caesar that was.' "

"Indeed?" Quintilian said.

Domitian nodded. "I was startled. I am no fool; I know the priests could have guessed who I was from my raiment, or from the guards I travelled with. But I told no man the purpose of my quest."

"And what was it she told you?"

"She seemed to go into a trance. For a long while she said nothing. Finally she said, she sort of chanted,

The past returns through the wiles of men
It is not hard to die
Saying does not make it so
The highly regarded ignorant one will cleave the knot
And Caesar shall create a school in his answer"

"This verse," Quintilian asked, "is it precisely what she said?"

Domitian nodded. "A priest sort of hides in a corner and writes down everything she says. He wrote out a copy for me."

"I don't know what else it may mean," Vespasian said, "but you are marked by your own words. It is clear that you are the highly regarded ignorant one who will cleave the knot."

Quintilian thought for a moment and then looked up. "You said there were two things."

"I did." Vespasian turned to his son. "Domitian, show our learned friend the other, ah, thing."

"Very well." Domitian stood up and gestured for us to accompany him. We went a short way down the corridor and entered a short separate hallway leading to a single door. A guardsman before the door stiffened into a living statue of The Perfect Guardsman At Attention at our approach.

"At ease, guardsman," Domitian said. "Has anything happened during your watch? Anything at all?"

"No, sir," the guardsman spat out between clenched teeth, his face turning red from the effort of talking without moving his lips.

"Thank you. Remain at ease." Domitian pushed open the door. "This is – was – the anteroom to Nero's throne room," he told us. "My father chooses not to use a throne room, but has a small audience chamber in another part of the palace."

The anteroom was small, the walls decorated with a continuous painted scene of woodland beauty, including several scantily clad nymphs darting among the trees. There were two doors: the door we had come in, and a door across the room leading to the throne room. Whatever furnishings the chamber had held during Nero's time had been removed. It was now bare, except for one, lone, corpse lying in a grotesque heap in the middle of the floor.

"He was found early this morning," Domitian said. "The throne room is occupied through the night. It is used as the guardroom for posting the night guards. The hallway is under guard all night. Nobody saw the lad go in or out. And yet, here he is."

The corpse was a young man in a white tunic and sandals; by his dress not a slave, but not a high-status Roman either. Possibly a freedman servant. He had been stabbed several times in the chest and neck. There was surprisingly little blood, but the victim had apparently used what there was to draw the number XIII on the floor above his head with his right forefinger as he was dying.

"Thirteen," Quintilian said.

"The Ides of October fall on the thirteenth," Domitian said.

"Yes," my mentor agreed. "That would be it, of course. Who is the dead lad?"

"One of the pages. Name was, I believe, Septius."

"What were his duties?"

"I have no idea. You can ask."

"Who saw him last, that is, when he was alive?"

"You may ask that, too."

Vespasian appeared in the doorway behind us. "Well?" he asked.

Quintilian turned to him. "This lad was not killed by a ghost," he said.

Vespasian sighed. "You know that, citizen Quintilian, and I know that. But when word of this gets out, it will be hard to convince the mob. Including, I am afraid, most of my guardsmen."

"All right, General. I will try to resolve this ghostly business for you. After all, we cannot make a liar of the Sybil. First I must spend some time examining this poor lad's body. Then I must see the various places where this apparition has appeared. And then I will speak with all those who claim to have seen Caesar's ghost, and particularly those who have heard it speak."

"Yes," Vespasian agreed. "And I must find out who the lad's parents are. They must be notified. Death is always cruel and often unnecessary, even in battle. This –" he gestured at the body "– this is a waste." He looked down at the corpse and shook his head. "I sometimes think that the only death that is not difficult to accept is your own."

"It is not hard to die," Quintilian said.

We all looked at him. "It is not hard to die," he repeated. "That's what the Sybil said."

"So it is," Vespasian remembered.

"When Nero was escaping the mob he hid himself in this palace for a day and pleaded with the head of his guards, to save him. The guard declined, saying, 'Is it so hard, then, to die?' which is a line from one of Virgil's plays, I believe. Upon which, Nero fled to the countryside."

"The theatre does not interest me," Vespasian said.

"But it might explain the Sybil's quote," Domitian offered.

"How?"

"I don't know yet," Quintilian said. "Give me some time."

Vespasian and Domitian left us alone in the room. Domitian said that he would arrange for the centurion to be waiting outside for us when we were ready.

Quintilian examined the corpse slowly and carefully, from head to foot, taking an oil lamp from its fixture on the wall to give himself better light. I watched as best I could, but I confess I am not yet hardened to the sight of dead bodies. "Notice how little blood there is," he commented.

"Indeed," I agreed.

He rolled the body over. "The back is completely clear of wounds, and of blood. The boy was attacked only from the front."

"Even so," I agreed.

"He has a small sheath here on his belt," Quintilian commented, "but the knife is missing."

"Perhaps he was killed by his own knife," I suggested.

"Perhaps," Quintilian said, "but I think a larger weapon was used, judging by the size of the wounds. I would that you could take notes but, as that is forbidden, try to remember what you see and what I tell you."

"Yes, mentor," I said. "I will do my best."

"The boy was not killed here," Quintilian said. "He died elsewhere, and was carried here. If he had been stabbed repeatedly here, the strokes of the knife would have splattered blood over the floor and walls."

"But both entrances were watched."

"No one was assigned the task of actually watching the entrances to this room," Quintilian said. "Besides, he came here somehow, alive or dead, despite the possible watchers."

"True," I said.

Quintilian went to the door and opened it. The young centurion was waiting patiently outside with two guardsmen, who snapped to attention when they saw Quintilian emerge. My master was, if only for the moment, a person of some stature in the palace. "Sabatinus," Quintilian called.

The centurion came over to the door and looked curiously at the body lying inside.

"Did you know about this?" Quintilian asked, indicating the corpse.

"Oh, yes," Sabatinus said. "News travels fast within the palace walls. There are, I believe, few secrets."

"I assume no bloody room has been noticed about the palace this morning?"

Sabatinus thought for a second. "It could be that some of the servants found such a room, and thought to clean it up without mentioning it to anyone. I will have enquiries made."

"Also there is a small knife missing from the dead lad's sheath. See if anyone found it."

"I didn't notice the missing knife. I shall have a search made."

We left the room and closed the door behind us. "Do you know of the ghost said to be wandering these corridors?" Quintilian asked the centurion.

"Great Caesar's ghost? Yes, I have heard tell."

"But you have never seen it yourself?"

"No."

"What do you think of the stories?"

Sabatinus thought for a moment. "I thought it was an

amusing thing for us to have our own personal ghost – and that of Great Caesar, at that. But when it was reported that the spectre had begun to speak, then I began to wonder if it might have greater portent."

"Then you believe the stories?"

"No, in truth I can't say I believe them." Sabatinus smiled. "But were I to come face-to-face with this spectre, I might rapidly change my opinion."

Quintilian nodded. "Can you gather the people who claim to have actually seen this wraith and send them in to speak with me?"

"I will make a list of names, and then send some of my guardsmen in search of the people you require."

"Fine. Let not status be considered in your search. From slave to senator; if the person claims to have seen the spectre, I would like to speak with him – or her."

"Very good. It will take some time."

"Also bring me whoever saw this page last when he was alive, and someone who knows what he was supposed to be doing at the time. They may well be the same person."

"Very good. I will put some men on it."

"Find me a suitable room in which to wait, provided with chairs, a desk of some sort if possible, and refreshments. We have not yet eaten this morning."

"It shall be as you wish."

"And tell – whoever – to remove that poor young man's body."

"And clean the blood from the floor. That, also, shall be done."

Centurion Sabatinus showed us to a room about the size of a large bedroom. It was lit by a skylight, and had wide benches strewn with cushions around three of the walls. What it had originally been intended for, I have no idea. After a few minutes a couple of guardsmen brought in a slab-top desk, much like the one Vespasian had been working on, and several folding chairs. And some time after that two serving girls came in bearing trays of food: dried fish and several sorts of olives and bread and olive oil and little pastries filled with lentils and spinach and figs and slices of melon, and a pitcher of a good Falernian wine. My master was hungry. He ate. After a moment he pushed a plate my way. I was hungry. I ate.

"How do you suppose," I asked my mentor, who was staring thoughtfully at a fig, "the Sybil knows what she knows?"

Quintilian turned to stare thoughtfully at me. "What, exactly, does she know?" he asked.

"I don't know," I said.

"Neither do I." He ate the fig.

The first witness was brought in shortly after that. A short, round man who worked in the kitchens, he was very nervous and kept fiddling with his white cap, dropping it several times during the brief interview.

"Your name?" Quintilian asked.

"Osterius, if it please your excellency."

"Relax, Osterius; you have been brought here merely to tell us what you saw."

"About the ghost, your excellency?"

"Just so. About the ghost."

"I didn't see nothing I shouldn't have seen, your excellency." He dropped his cap and bent over, trying to snare it without looking down.

"Of course not," Quintilian said, waiting patiently for him to retrieve the cap. "But, just what did you see?"

"It wasn't my fault. I didn't want to see it. It was just there."

"Yes. Where?"

"What?"

"Where did you see it? Where were you when you saw it?"

"In the storeroom sir, where we keep the jars of pickled foodstuffs."

"Ah. You saw it in the storeroom?"

"Well, I was, like, in the storeroom. The ghost was outside, in the corridor."

Quintilian nodded and smiled an encouraging smile. "Very good. You're very observant. What was it doing?"

"Eating, sir. A chicken leg, I think."

"And then what happened?"

"Well, he saw me about when I saw him. He looked just like the great Julius Caesar looked on some of them old coins, and on the busts in the Forum. And he looked kind of – ghostly. He kind of smiled, and waved at me. And then he went around the corner. But when Scullius and me went around the corner – he was gone."

"Scullius?"

"Yes, your honour. My mate who was waiting for me in the small preparation room."

"So you didn't go right after this ghost?"

"No way, your excellency. I went to get Scullius first. Then the two of us, we went back and followed him around the corner. And he was gone. And there wasn't noplace for him to go. The only room around that corner is locked with a special lock, to which only the wine master has the key, 'cause it contains the amphorae of Greek wine what come in special wagons from way up North."

"Ah!" Quintilian said. "When was this?"

Osterius thought for a moment. "About six weeks ago."

"Did you ever see the ghost again?"

"No, sir. Once were enough."

"Indeed. Thank you for your help."

*   *   *

Osterius was our interviewee number I, and his story was not that different from numbers II, III, IV or V. Man or woman sees figure who looks like what they imagine Julius Caesar to look like standing in some place where no human ought to be standing – down an empty corridor, or sitting on a bench in a closed courtyard, or at the far end of a deserted room; and they stay frozen in astonishment, or sheer fright, while the figure ambles out of sight, often going into some area from which there is no exit, and disappears.

Number VI, a stocky overseer named Lipato, had the first real variant to the usual story. "It was about two weeks ago," he told my master, helping himself to one of the smoked sprats that were heaped on the food tray. "We were in the third courtyard, which has been turned into a garden, planting some flowers, or I think maybe vines of some sort. It was at night because the gardener says that these particular horticultures has got to be planted at night to grow right. Then I hears it."

"What?"

"This voice. High and squeaky, it was. 'Vespasian,' it says. Beg pardon, and I hope his mightiness the emperor will forgive me, but that's what it says. 'Vespasian – oh woe unto you Vespasian! Beware the Ides of October,' it says. Fairly scared me so much I couldn't eat my breakfast."

"And did you see anything to connect with this voice?"

"Oh, yes. Otherwise it might have been like a joke, you know. But there he was, standing there, as clear as daylight. Julius Caesar himself, in the flesh. Well, maybe not the flesh, but in the whatever-he-was-in. Big nose, laurel wreath around his head, and everything. His toga looked kind of loose and flappy, like maybe there wasn't too much flesh under it."

"This was at night?"

"Yes, but we had maybe a dozen torches stuck in the

ground all around – so the slaves could see what they were planting, after all."

"So it was you and some slaves –"

"That's right. Maybe half a dozen slaves. And Master Funitus, the assistant to the chief assistant head gardener."

"And you all saw and heard this?"

"Indeed."

"And you didn't run after this apparition and try to grab it?"

"Couldn't."

"You couldn't?"

"That's right. It was on the balcony which runs around the courtyard. And by the time Master Funitus yelled something – he claims he yelled, 'let's get it,' but it sounded more to me like, 'let's get out of here.' Anyways, when he yelled, the thing, whatever it was, took a step backwards, gave out with another squeaky, 'Beware the Ides of October!' and disappeared."

Quintilian leaned back in his chair and stared across the desk at the stocky foreman. "I take it that you were not overly impressed with this phantom. Don't you believe in ghosts?"

Lipato shrugged. "Might have been a ghost, might not. At any rate, it wasn't any danger to me, nor was it going to do me any good, as I saw it. Anyway, if it was a ghost, and it wanted to talk to the emperor, why didn't it just flit through a couple of walls and do it properly? It don't make sense."

"The ways of the spirit world are beyond human understanding," Quintilian said. "Or so I've always heard."

"It did put the fear of the gods in the slaves that were in the garden, I'll tell you that," Lipato said.

Lipato left and was replaced by a slim young man who, by the drape of his toga and the inclination of his chin, proclaimed himself to be from an old and noble family. His bearing and attitude filled me with an instant dislike, but the feeling was as instantly dispelled by his first words.

"You're the famous Marcus Fabius Quintilianus," he said, with a sweeping bow. "I am the orator Aopilis Romulus Laius, and I tremble with delight to meet you."

"Tremble with delight?" Quintilian asked, looking slightly startled.

"It is a Greek pleasantry," Laius said. "Perhaps a bit effulgent when translated into Latin, but the emotion is sincere. I teach oratory and rhetoric and whenever I hear that you are going to speak, in a trial or a public debate, I hasten to be in the audience so that I may learn from the master."

Quintilian frowned, but I think it was to disguise a pleased smile. "You have a school here in Rome?" he asked.

"Not precisely a school," Laius said. "I do not teach children. My efforts are directed towards those adults who would improve their Latin, their deportment, and their rhetorical skills to enable them to better fit in with their, ah, new-found place in society."

"Ah, I see," Quintilian said, and he did smile. "You teach the newly rich to, as some would put it, ape their betters."

"Some might put it that way," Laius said defensively. "It is true that my students are, for the most part, freedmen and former slaves who have succeeded in making their fortunes in trade, or other occupations frowned upon by the patrician landowners. But some of those same landowners . . . well, never mind; I'm sure you don't want to hear my protests about the social order."

"Perhaps some other time," Quintilian said. "Right now I'm more interested in ghosts."

"Yes, of course. That's why I'm here." Laius hitched up his toga and sat down. "I saw this supposed ghost, it would be, four days ago. Here in the palace."

"Just when and where, if you can remember."

"Remember? How could I forget? I was waiting in a courtyard – I'm not sure just which courtyard, there are so many of them in this place, but I could find it again if you like – when this person appeared in the middle of a tree about twelve feet off the ground."

"A tree?" I exclaimed.

They both looked at me. "It turns out that it was a potted tree," Laius explained, "and the pot had been moved so that it concealed a balcony. The person was on this balcony. 'Vespasian,' he said, 'Vespasian, beware the Ides of October! Mind what I say!' And then he screeched, and stepped backwards until he was out of sight."

"Your description," Quintilian said, "makes it sound as though you do not believe the person was a ghost. Is this so?"

The teacher of oratory thought for a moment and then nodded. "I am being cautious about calling it a ghost, because I do not think it was a ghost," he admitted. "Although the three or four other people in the courtyard at the time seemed to have no such doubts. They trembled and fell on their knees, and one of them went screaming out the entrance. But for me, I saw nothing ghostly about the figure. True, it did resemble Gaius Julius Caesar, but my uncle Timidus bears an uncanny resemblance to the god Bacchus, as may be seen by comparing him to many a mural in the various houses of joy about the city."

"I see."

"And besides, the person spoke with the slight hint of a foreign accent."

"Really? You are the first to note that."

"Most people wouldn't. You see, the problem was that his Latin was a hair too perfect, as though it had been learned as an adult. Much like some of the people I teach."

"So you couldn't say what sort of accent?"

Laius shook his head. "From the East, rather than the North, I would say; but aside from that, no."

Quintilian nodded. "Thank you, citizen Laius. One last question: What were you doing in that courtyard?"

"Waiting to see the imperial procurator. My father's estates were confiscated by Nero, and I am engaged in a continuing struggle to get them back."

"With what luck?"

"None – absolutely none. It matters not that most of the policies of Nero have been rescinded. In matters of property, the government is most reluctant to retrace its steps. I suppose they're afraid to open the box. I mean, if an estate grabbed by Nero is returned, then what about one confiscated by Claudius, or even Augustus?"

"There is something in what you say. But, if it is so hopeless, then why do you keep trying?"

"It gives me an air of moral authority among my patrons. Knowing that there's a chance, however small, that I may one day once again be as rich as they are causes them to treat me with ever-so-slightly more respect than they would otherwise."

"Thank you again, citizen Laius."

"Have I been of some help?"

"You have added to our store of information, and that is always helpful."

Our next guest was a senator, Marius Trabitus by name. Sort of round, but none the less solidly built, and definitely past middle age, he had sharp eyes and a crisp, yet measured way of speaking, as though no words passed his lips until he had examined them carefully to make sure they conveyed just what he wanted them to convey, and no more.

"Glad to be of help," he said, his eyes taking in the room, with more than one glance towards the platters of food on the table. "Glad to be of help. You want me to tell you about my encounter with the shade of Julius Caesar?"

"Yes, Senator. If you please."

"It was frightening, frightening," Trabitus said, sitting down across from my master and helping himself to a couple of dates from the platter. "It happened about a week ago now. It was late, quite late. I was in the anteroom to General Vespasian's audience chamber – the general dislikes calling it a throne room, and indeed he has no throne in the room – waiting to speak with the general, when suddenly he appeared before me. Just – appeared – like that –" he waved a pudgy hand through the air to show what it was like.

"Who?"

"Why great Caesar's ghost, that's who. One second the room was empty, and the next, there he was. 'Vespasianus,' he called, 'beware the Ides of October.' And he sighed mightily, and dripped blood from gaping wounds in his toga. He stared at me, and I stared at him. I thought of trying to go and touch him, but I seemed to be rooted to the floor. I did not feel fear, but a sort of tremendous awe, as though I were in the presence of something greater than a mere mortal. And then all at once he disappeared, like blowing out a candle. And – you won't believe this – when I went to look, there was no blood on the floor! It was then that I felt fear. And then, like an echo from beyond, came the words again, 'Beware the Ides of October!'"

Quintilian leaned forwards. "And what did you do?"

"I just stood there. I mean, after all, what could I do?"

Quintilian nodded. "What, indeed?"

"Shortly thereafter a page came for me to take me in to speak with General Vespasian, and I told him what had transpired."

"The page or General Vespasian?"

"Both, I'm afraid. And probably everyone else I saw for the next few days. I tell you, it quite unnerved me."

"I can believe that. And what did you make of it?"

"What did I make of it?"

"Yes. What do you think it meant?"

Trabitus looked as if he were about to say something, and then thought better of it. "I don't know," he said finally. "I mean – it's not for me to say."

Quintilian nodded. "Yes," he said. "Very wise. You just report what has happened; let others mull over its possible meaning."

Trabitus stood up and took one last fig. "I heard about the young lad who was killed," he said, shaking his head. "A small knife is of no use against a ghost." He ate the fig. "I suppose a large knife wouldn't be much help, either."

"I think certain sorts of incense and the reciting of the proper prayers are usually regarded as efficacious," Quintilian said. "But there is a lack of general agreement on just which sorts of incense and which prayers to use."

Trabitus looked dubious. "I suppose you're right," he said. "I hope I've been of some help."

"I believe you have," Quintilian told him. Trabitus glided from the room, and Quintilian turned to look at me.

"Yes?" I asked.

He put his knuckle to his lips and stared off into space, working on the phrasing of what he was about to tell me; I recognized the signs. "When the improbable passes over into the impossible, the wall of truth has been breached," he said.

"I can't write it down," I told him. "Very nice, whatever it means, but I can't write it down."

"But it doesn't have . . . yes, I suppose you're right. See if you can remember it to include it in my collection of aphorisms for the young."

"Yes, sir," I told him.

Our next guest stomped in and declared "Decurion Carlus to see Investigator Quintilian as directed!" and then came to attention, standing as rigid as a marble column before the makeshift desk. He was a big man – not tall, but big in every other dimension. His arms were as big around as a wrestler's thighs. It would take two normal men with their arms outstretched to encompass his chest. His neck was so thick that his head seemed to emerge from it instead of being supported by it. His nose was flat, his ears were small and hugged the side of his head, and an ancient scar that ran from his chin to his right temple made his face look lopsided.

"Sit down, Decurion Carlus," my master said, gesturing towards the chair Carlus stood next to.

The massive decurion lowered himself gingerly into the chair. "I am here about the lad who got killed last night," he said.

"Septius?" Quintilian asked.

"That was his name, yes."

"Do you know how he died?"

"I do not, unfortunately. He was a good lad. Wanted to be a legionary. Would have made a good one, too; intelligent, cool-headed, took orders well. The last I saw of him, he was chasing a ghost." A plain, matter-of-fact statement, with no more emotion behind it than if he'd said, "The last time I saw him he was eating a fig."

"Ah," Quintilian said. "When and where was this?"

"At the start of second watch. I had assembled the guards to post them – relieving the first watch, you know – when a figure that looked a lot like Julius Caesar, from the busts and coins and such, you know, appeared above us –"

"Above you?"

"On this sort of balcony. Our guard room was Nero's music room, or some such, and there's this small balcony sticking out of one wall. Well, this apparition, or whatever, starts yelling about the Ides of October, or some such. I pay it little attention, as I have to get my men posted. And besides, the way I figure it, if I act like it don't mean anything, why then the lads won't take it seriously. They'll think it's some sort of joke, like. Otherwise, if they take it serious, well, it could mean trouble. Most of the lads are from the northern provinces, and they're a superstitious lot."

"You don't believe in ghosts?"

"I don't know about that," Carlus said. "But I don't believe they've got any business interfering with my men, when I'm trying to get them posted for guard duty."

"A sensible attitude," Quintilian said, nodding.

"Well, I give the men an 'eyes forwards', and start marching them to their posts, when young Septius, who was in there repairing some lacings on his sandals, suddenly jumps up and says, 'That ain't no ghost! I'll see about that!' and goes racing out of the room. I don't know what got into him. Maybe he saw something that I didn't."

"That could be. Do you know where he went?"

"He was heading towards the stairs to the balcony when last I saw him. When I got back from posting the guard, he was gone, and I didn't hear any more about him until somebody came in this morning and said they'd found him dead."

"What did you think?"

"I didn't think it was no ghost. What use would a ghost have in stabbing a man to death? Not the way of ghosts at all, from what I hear."

Quintilian smiled. "What use, indeed," he said. "You've been a big help, and I thank you."

"A nice lad," Carlus said. "Sorry about whatever happened to him. You bring that ghost forward and my lads and I will take care of him good."

"I'll try to do just that," Quintilian told him.

*   *   *

We saw several more people in the next hour or so, but they added nothing to what we already knew. Of course, as far as I could see, what we already knew added nothing to what we already knew. On reviewing that sentence I can see that it makes little sense, and Quintilian would chastise me for writing it and tell me to write, clearly and concisely, exactly what I mean. What I mean is that we had interviewed over a dozen people, and learned that the ghost of Julius Caesar appeared at times, gave a doleful warning about the Ides of October, and then disappeared. Which is what we knew before we interviewed the first person.

When the last person had been interviewed, Quintilian rose from his seat and began pacing back and forth across the room, his head down, looking at the floor in front of him. I scurried over to the side of the room and sat on the floor, my back against the wall, to keep out of his way. My mentor thinks best in motion, and I try to do nothing to disturb his thinking.

He stayed in motion for some time, gesticulating in strange and wonderful ways as he paced, grabbing thoughts and ideas from the air and assembling them into various patterns, until he found one that made sense out of the facts of the case. He had explained this to me many times, and I had watched him perform this magic in many different cases, usually shortly before the start of a trial. I say "magic" because, when I try a similar process, all I grab is thin air, and all I get is a headache.

Finally he stopped pacing and sat down. "If something is impossible," he said, "why then, it is impossible. Discard it, and you are left with the truth."

"What does that mean?" I asked.

He turned, seeming a bit surprised to see me squatting there against the wall. "It means I see a way to catch a ghost."

I shuddered. And, mind you, I'm not at all sure I believe in ghosts. But after the stories we had just heard . . . "Is that wise?" I asked.

"Not only wise, but necessary," he told me. "It will require a long strand of wool, and, just in case, a man with an axe."

"Pardon me?" I said.

"That centurion – Sabatinus – should be waiting somewhere outside the door. Fetch him for me."

I went into the corridor and beckoned to the centurion, who was sitting on a chair he had acquired from somewhere, talking with two of his troopers. Sabatinus fairly trotted into the room. "It's approaching dinner time," he said. "I would like to let my men go for their meal, if you can spare them for an hour or so."

Quintilian pushed himself to his feet. "Let us wind up this business," he said, "and then, no doubt, your men will be able to feast."

"Ah!" Centurion Sabatinus said. "Then, honourable Quintilian, you have been able to make some sense of the stories you have been listening to?"

"Send one of your men for an axe," Quintilian told him, "and have him meet us at the anteroom where that poor lad was found dead."

Sabatinus sent one of his men off to find an axe, and he led the rest of us back to the door to the anteroom. Which was a good thing as, with all the twists and turns we took in this gigantic maze of a palace, I doubt whether we could have found it on our own.

"You wait out here," Quintilian told us. "I don't want you disturbing the air in the room." And with the final comment, "I could be wrong, but I think not," he went inside the little room by himself.

We waited. We could hear pounding, tapping and thumping from inside for a while, and then my master stuck his head out the door. "I need more light," he said. "Bring me some lamps."

Sabatinus's men scattered about and found four lamps, returning with them about the same time as the trooper who had gone for the axe rejoined our little band. Quintilian took the lamps inside the room and closed the door. We waited some more. This time there was nothing but silence from inside the room.

Quintilian opened the door. "Come in," he said. "We won't need the axe. Well, perhaps we will need the axe; bring it along."

We followed him back into the room. "Well, I'll be –" Centurion Sabatinus said.

At first I didn't see anything different, except for the circle of oil lamps burning on the floor, casting their varied shadows on the walls. And then I saw that what I had taken to be a shadow was actually an opening in the side wall. Starting at the floor, it was about two feet square, and seemed to lead into some sort of tunnel. The part of the wall that had concealed the tunnel had opened inward, and was now flat against the tunnel's side.

"Did you know there were secret passages within the palace?" my master asked Sabatinus.

"There was a secret exit," the centurion told him. "It was the way that Nero escaped the mob that was hunting him, after hiding for a day. We have closed it up. How did you find this one?"

"Logic said there had to be an entrance to this room aside from the two doors. Even a ghost couldn't take a body through solid walls."

"But a man could have passed the guards without attracting much attention," Sabatinus said. "Besides, in the middle of the night, there was a good chance the guards would be asleep – or at least dozing."

"Yes, and a man might chance it. But I doubt whether a man carrying a body would feel the same. So the most logical answer was that there's a hidden entrance to this room. At first I tapped all the walls, but I couldn't detect any difference in sound. So then I pulled a strand of wool from the hem of my toga and lighted the end from one of the lamps. It burned with a thin wisp of black smoke. I slowly moved it about the room, near the walls, until I saw the smoke deflected by a slight draught. After some experimentation I found that the panel unlocked by pushing in on a leaf in the wall painting, and then I could slide it open. So I didn't have to call on the axeman."

Centurion Sabatinus nodded. "Very logical," he said.

"Let's see where this doorway leads," Quintilian said.

"Wait," said Sabatinus. "I'll go first – that's my job." Pulling his gladius from its scabbard, he held the short sword in front of him in his right hand and an oil lamp in his left, and crawled head-first into the tunnel. Quintilian followed, and then the three troopers, each with one of the oil lamps, and the last carrying the great double-bladed axe that he had brought. I followed in the rear, and glad of it. I am not made for fighting. And yet nothing could have stopped me from following along to see the end to this ghostly mystery.

After a short distance the tunnel turned to the left, and then rose steeply some six or eight feet and continued on. A little way further – it's hard to judge distance when you're crawling – the ceiling rose and it was possible to walk upright. There was a steady breeze blowing through the tunnel; I could feel it on my face, and it made the flame in my lamp flicker.

The tunnel went down again, and then turned to the left, and we could see light ahead of us. After a few moments we came to a room, octagonal in shape, perhaps twelve or fourteen feet across, lighted by a sort of covered skylight, so that light came in from the sides but not from directly overhead. There was a table in the room with a pitcher of water and a mug, and there, on a chair by the table, sat Julius Caesar. His toga was soiled, and his fringe of hair was dishevelled, but the resemblance was unmistakable. Several laurel wreaths hung from pegs on the wall.

"Don't kill me," Caesar screeched, throwing himself under the table and cowering as we entered the room. "Please don't kill me! It wasn't my fault. It wasn't my idea. Don't kill me!"

A quarter of an hour later we all stood before Vespasian and his son in the audience hall that the emperor – excuse me, the general – used for state business. "Secret passages," Vespasian said, "running all through the palace. Who could have guessed?"

"Apparently Nero had them constructed as the palace was being built," Quintilian told him. "He used workers from the far provinces and then sent them home again, so the work would stay secret. That's according to our ghost, here." He indicated the soiled Caesar, who was doing his best to stand straight and unafraid, despite the leather restraints with which he had been bound, still not convinced that he was not about to be beheaded.

Vespasian nodded. "I suppose, knowing Nero, I should have thought of something like that," he said.

"If you want to put stock in the sayings of the Sybil," Quintilian said, "you could take her first two lines:

The past returns through the wiles of men
    It is not hard to die

as referring to the hidden passages. 'It is not hard to die,' should remind us of the day Nero spent hiding in this palace, and we should have asked ourselves just where it was that he hid."

Vespasian nodded thoughtfully, and then turned his attention to the ghost. "I await your story impatiently," he said.

Caesar fell to his knees. "My name, so it please your honour, is Lysidamus. I am from the island of Crete. I was brought here as a child and sold to a company of touring actors. It was never clear which of them actually owned me, and I suppose it didn't matter. I was eventually given small parts to play, usually girls or women. When my voice changed, I played the insolent slave, or on occasion the young lover –"

"Let's get to the part where you're hiding in secret passages in this palace," Domitian interrupted.

"Yes, your honour. Of course, your honour. The emperor Nero saw me in a production of Plautus's *The Boy From Carthage* – I played the boy – and immediately purchased me and made me a freedman. I joined the imperial troupe of actors, and became Nero's voice coach. For when he played parts in Greek. He spoke Greek with a terrible Latin accent. I became adept at not quite telling him that."

"Get to the secret passages," Domitian said.

"Yes, your honour. The hidden corridors were used by Nero to spy on his enemies and, I suppose, his friends. There are tubes in the walls that can be uncapped and, if you put your ear to them, you can hear what is being said in the room outside. On that horrible day when the people turned against him, he hid at first in the secret rooms. I went with him, but when the next day he fled the palace, I remained behind. I have been living in these secret places ever since, coming out only for food and to, ah, borrow clean garments."

"Three, almost four, years?" Vespasian asked, incredulously.

"I believe so. One loses track of time in, ah, my situation."

"Why did you stay?"

"At first through fear, I thought the subsequent emperors would just as soon eliminate all memories of Nero, and I was one of those memories. And then because I really had no place else to go."

"You've been listening to what goes on here for all that time?" Domitian demanded.

"Oh, no!" Lysidamus said, sounding shocked. "I never took the caps from the listening tubes. That wouldn't be right."

"And just when did you become a ghost?" Vespasian asked.

"It must be over a year ago now. I was, let's see, in the pastry kitchen, I believe. Someone walked in on me while I was gathering a few pastries to take back to my lair. I raised my arms in fright, and much to my surprise, he was more frightened than I. He raced from the room screaming that he'd seen a ghost – Great Caesar's ghost, to be precise. And, of course, when the others came in to see, I was back in the wall."

"Great Caesar's ghost?" Quintilian asked. "Even that first time?"

"That's what the man said – yelled. I did not realize how much I had come to resemble the great Gaius Julius with the passage of time. I still thought of myself as the young lover. But I decided to take advantage of this chance resemblance and never leave my hidey-hole without wearing an imperial toga and a laurel wreath, and dusting my face with a little flour."

Domitian glared at the sad little man. "Sneaking into the imperial palace," he said. "That's a serious offence."

"I don't know if we can get him for that," Vespasian said, smiling. "After all, he was here before we were."

"Yes? Well, what about that 'Ides of October' nonsense?"

"I don't think he's responsible for that," Quintilian said. "Are you?" he asked Lysidamus.

"Well, I –"

"I mean you did it, of course, but you're not responsible for it."

"Yes," Domitian said, "but murdering that lad . . ."

Quintilian turned back to Domitian. "Oh, that he didn't do."

"Then what did he do?"

"He was discovered," Quintilian said. "Weren't you?" He leaned over Lysidamus. "Weren't you?"

"Yes, yes."

"By whom?" asked Vespasian.

"I don't know his name. He caught me about a month ago, while I was making my nightly foray for a loaf of bread, and ever since I've been living in fear. He told me that, were he to turn me in, I would be instantly executed. But he said he had use for me. He explored the secret ways and found places for me to appear. He told me what to say. Last night, when a young lad almost caught me he – he took away the lad's little knife, and jabbed at him with a long stiletto that he kept concealed in his toga. I think he killed him."

"You don't know?"

"He told me to go back to my room. I went."

"He did kill the lad," Quintilian told Lysidamus.

The actor burst out sobbing and fell to the floor. "What a pity, what a pity," he cried. "And he was such a handsome lad!"

"Who did this?" Vespasian asked.

"I swear, I don't know his name," Lysidamus sobbed. "He wears a senatorial toga."

"His name is Marius Trabitus," Quintilian told Vespasian. "He is a senator."

"Trabitus?" Vespasian repeated. "Why, I know him. He told me he actually saw the ghost, I remember. He has been spending a lot of time in the palace. He knows of my intention to move, and has an interest in taking the building over to turn it into an I-don't-know-what. Some sort of forum, or such. Or so he told me."

"I think you'll find he's associated with one of the groups you mentioned that has its own ideas about who should be emperor," Quintilian said. "Perhaps he thought that if he made enough noise about the 'Ides of October', some superstitious guardsman or courtier would think the gods were giving him instructions?"

"And why do you name this Trabitus as the instigator?"

"And as the murderer of young Septius. He would have been better served by keeping the youth's body hidden. Ghostly appearances are one thing, who knows about ghosts? But a corpse lying in a room has to have arrived there somehow. I knew it was he when he told me of seeing bloody wounds on the ghost of Caesar; an obvious, ah, exaggeration. Why would he make such things up were he not involved? And then he told me that little knives are no defence against ghosts. But nobody knew that lad had a knife, since the sheath was concealed under his body until I turned him over. Bring Trabitus here and let our actor friend identify him."

"I shall," Vespasian said, and gave the order.

Trabitus was not found in the palace and, by the time a squad of the praetorian guard reached his villa, he had committed suicide by slitting his wrists in the bath. When Lysidamus was taken to look at the body, he identified Trabitus as the man who had caught him, and who murdered Septius.

It was about a month later that Vespasian created the Imperial Office of Teaching Rhetoric to the Young, and appointed my master Quintilian to be its head.

The highly regarded ignorant one will cleave the knot
And Caesar shall create a school in his answer

How does the Sybil know these things?

The Cleopatra Game

Jane Finnis

This story is set during the prosperous and relatively peaceful reign of Vespasian when Rome could bask once again in its military glory and look back to its glorious past. The influence of Cleopatra lives on, a hundred years after her death, her flamboyant life as intriguing to the Roman as to us. Jane Finnis was for many years a free-lance broadcaster for BBC Radio, and still undertakes occasional radio assignments but she now spends most of her time researching and writing about the Roman Empire. Her first novel, Get Out or Die, *is a mystery set in Roman Britain. "Human nature hasn't changed much in two thousand years," she commented, "so the tensions and motives that generated murder and mayhem in the first century AD can strike a chord today, too."*

I don't know why, but when you're unusually big and strong, people tend to think you're stupid. "All brawn and no brain," they say, and treat you like a mindless bull – good for strength and courage, but no use for thinking.

My patron doesn't make that mistake about me though. Tadius Sabinus knows better. I'm head and shoulders taller than him, and I've been his bodyguard for years now, ever since he bought me as a slave in the Emperor Nero's time. After he'd owned me for a couple of months I saved his life, and he said to me, "Rufus, you've got a good head on those broad shoulders. Make sure you use it, that's all I ask."

That's why I stayed with him even after he gave me my freedom, and he became my patron instead of my master. He has other bodyguards now; I'm a kind of chief guard-cum-personal assistant, and I – but you don't want to know all that; I only mention it to explain what I was doing at a family banquet given by my patron's mother, the Lady Cornelia. She probably didn't like it, but she knew that if she invited my patron, she'd have to invite me too.

Of course I didn't sit near Sabinus – I was in a distant corner with the other freedmen – but before it all started, he took me aside. "Rufus, I want you to be on the alert tonight. I'm sure Cleopatra is up to mischief. She says she's planning a surprise for my brother, and I don't trust her. Keep an eye on her, will you?"

"It'll be a pleasure!" The young lady was well worth looking at. "I promise I'll watch her every move. And if you want me to sit near her and offer her my personal protection . . ."

He laughed. "I wish I could arrange it. I think you could control that little madam. I'm not so sure Marcus can," he added in an undertone.

Marcus, the patron's young brother, would soon be marrying this Cleopatra – no, of course that wasn't her real name, she was actually Chloe; but Cleopatra was what she insisted on being called. Ever since childhood – and she couldn't have been more than eighteen even now – she'd been fascinated by stories about the celebrated Queen of Egypt, and wanted to be like her. She was from Alexandria, and Marcus had met her there and fallen as completely in love with her as Mark Antony did with the famous queen. They'd come to Rome for the wedding, and this was the first chance his mother had to show off the bride-to-be to all the friends and relatives in the city.

It was quite a party – glittering I think is the word. The forty or so guests were in for a treat, and her ladyship wanted them to realize the fact as soon as they arrived at her house, which was a grand one just outside Rome. Rooms and passages were all decked out with vast bouquets of flowers and wreaths of laurel, and the big dining-room was as bright as day with dozens of silver lamps hanging from ornate carved stands; in fact there were so many lamp-standards they were getting in the way of the table-slaves, coming and going among the dining-couches with food and wine. The meal itself was wonderful (I remember the swans stuffed with peaches in saffron sauce were especially good), and the wine was the best, from Campania. There was some lively flute music played by nearly naked little girls, and between courses there were dancers, acrobats, and an Egyptian lad with a clever performing monkey. Glittering, as I say. But to me it was like a gaudy painting concealing a crack in a wall. It deceives your eye, but the crack is still there underneath.

This Cleopatra, like her namesake, was beautiful, intelligent, and charming when she chose; Marcus was handsome, romantic, and besotted; and both families were happy. Cleopatra's, who were rich but only equestrian in rank, were thrilled by a marriage into a powerful senatorial clan, and Marcus' dear mama, having met Cleopatra at her most charming, declared she was "just the right sort of girl to help his political career." Actually her father's fortune was the real attraction. The Tadius family were well-born but constantly short of cash; Cleopatra's could have built themselves a gold pyramid.

Sabinus was the only person who wasn't happy about the marriage. (Well, I wasn't either, nor were the slaves, but our views hardly counted.)

"She has him running around like a puppy-dog," he complained to me, after she'd been in the house only a couple of days. "I don't like to see her taking advantage of him like that. And as for all this Cleopatra nonsense – it's a childish game, and it's time she grew out of it. Egyptian clothes and eastern perfumes are all very well, but going on about how she wants to live her life just as Cleopatra did . . . I keep expecting her to emerge from a rolled-up carpet one fine day!"

"That would spoil her fancy imitation-Isis hairstyle," I said. "She might try sailing up the Tiber in a golden barge, I suppose."

He didn't smile. "Oh, well, I expect he'll learn to stand up for himself a bit better once they're married."

But I doubted it. Marcus was a gentle young man – affectionate, idealistic, wanted to be a poet – not over-bright, but then he didn't have to be; his family influence and the Egyptian money would get him into the Senate when the time came. Maybe he was a bit too soft, and I reckon that's what his mother thought, and Cleopatra was supposed to toughen him up.

The young madam lost no time in showing everyone how devoted was her adoring Mark Antony, as she called him. She bossed him about almost the way she ordered her slaves, only in a honey-sweet tone that he was incapable of resisting. "Oh, Markie dearest, I've left my stole in the garden. Would you just . . . ?" "Antony, sweetheart, my sandal's come undone. Would you be a dear . . . ?" And then the big one: "Marcus darling, I really need some new pearls to wear at the banquet your mama is giving for us. Won't you take your little Cleopatra shopping?" And whatever she asked, he did willingly, lovingly. Including buy her a lovely necklace, with pearls the size of walnuts.

But what even my patron didn't see was the way she

laughed at Marcus in private, mocking his dog-like devotion, and boasting about the hoops she would make him jump through once they were married. I heard all about how she behaved from my own girl, Amanda. She was one of the slaves lent by Marcus' mother to look after the bride-to-be, who seemed to need three times as many servants as any other female in the house.

"She's evil," Amanda said to me on the day of the banquet. "She enjoys humiliating him, and he's such a sweet gentle boy. I wish there was some way we could stop the marriage, Rufus. Master Marcus deserves better."

I pretended to be annoyed. "You've always had a soft spot for Marcus, haven't you? Now he's found himself a beautiful girl, and you're jealous!"

She kissed me. "You really are a big stupid lump, some-times."

"Stupid, am I?" I kissed her back.

"Only sometimes." For a while we were too busy for talking.

Eventually she said, "I'll tell you someone who *is* jealous of Lady Cleopatra. Her cousin Phoebe."

"Her cousin? Oh yes, the attractive dark girl. Some sort of poor relation, isn't she?"

"That's right. She's got looks, but no money. Her maid says she more or less threw herself at Marcus in Alexandria, but he ignored her. Still, if Cleopatra ever pushes her Mark Antony too hard, he won't have to look far for a sympathetic admirer."

The banquet began, and I can't deny Cleopatra looked truly like a queen, as she reclined on her couch next to Marcus. The necklace of pearls glowed against her lovely fair skin, and there was plenty of skin showing, because her white gown was cut fashionably low. She used face-paint, but it was very discreetly done, enhancing her big luminous eyes.

Her fair hair was bound with a sort of gold diadem. If the real Queen Cleopatra looked half as radiant, it explains a lot about the way Mark Antony carried on – not to mention old Julius Caesar.

Watching from my table in the far corner, I saw what Amanda meant about the cousin not being happy. Phoebe looked beautiful and she had expensive clothes and jewels; but her brittle smile and over-ebullient manner told anyone with half an eye that she was trying just a bit too hard. She was sharing Sabinus' couch, and he was doing his best to make her relax, but without much success. And she was drinking more than was either ladylike or sensible.

She wasn't the only one either. Antony and Cleopatra were knocking back the wine at a fair old rate. Well, why not? It was their party. Lady Cornelia didn't drink much, and neither did Sabinus – and neither did I. A drunken body-guard is as useless as a wax javelin. And I knew I'd have a chance to make up for it later.

When everyone was suitably mellow, Marcus' mother signalled for quiet, and delivered a few well-chosen words of greeting and congratulation. They didn't go on for long, thank the gods. Young Marcus rose to his feet and read a love-poem he had written "to the Queen of my heart". Everyone applauded warmly – it wasn't a bad poem really – and then as Marcus sat down, his Cleopatra arose elegantly from her couch and started to speak.

"I'm overwhelmed by your kindness," she simpered. "Especially from my Lady Cornelia – my new mother to be! – and my darling Mark Antony. And tonight I'm going to prove just how great is my love, as great as the love that bound our famous predecessors."

She suddenly lifted the beautiful pearl necklace right over her head and held it out in front of her so that it gleamed in the lamplight. "This most wonderful gift is a symbol of our union. I'm sure you all know how the great Queen Cleopatra showed her feelings for Mark Antony – by providing him with the most costly banquet ever seen, and the most precious drink in the world." She looked down at her elaborate silver wine-goblet, half full of red wine. "Wonderful wine – such as we have tonight – with just a little something added."

She gave a strong tug and snapped the necklace. There was a collective gasp – everyone realised what was coming. Everybody knows the tale of how Cleopatra had a bet with Mark Antony, and how she won it . . . But surely this silly child wasn't going to . . .

Marcus looked half-amused and half-baffled, as she held the broken necklace in one hand, careful not to lose any pearls. Then slowly, dramatically, she took five of them off their thin cord, and dropped them one by one into the silver goblet. The plop that each one made as it splashed into the wine resounded like a drumbeat in the horrified silence.

"And now," she cried out, triumph showing in every curve of her face and every syllable she spoke, "I'll drink a toast – to my darling Mark Antony, and to a love that will last for ever!" She laid down the necklace, lifted up the goblet, and drank.

But she didn't drain the cup; she took a good swallow, and then lowered the goblet and turned to Marcus, smiling into his eyes. "Now you, my dear," she said. "Drink to me, and to our love."

Marcus was looking perplexed and rather hurt, as well he might. The pearls had cost him a consul's ransom; presumably he'd only been able to afford them on a promise of riches to come after the wedding, and he can't have expected his magnificent gift to be abused like this. A stronger man would have put a stop to the nonsense, but he wasn't the one to resist her now, in front of all the family. He stood up and took the goblet. "To our love, my Queen Cleopatra," he declaimed, and he drained the lot.

I caught a glimpse of his mother's face, disapproval written all over it, and Sabinus was looking furious. There'd be ructions in the family's private rooms tonight, for sure.

Marcus sat down, and a buzz of rather subdued conversation started up around the room. I felt a bit subdued myself, but at least I could relax now the surprise was over.

Suddenly Marcus began to choke. His whole body shook with it. Gods, I thought, perhaps he's swallowed a pearl. They would take some time to dissolve completely in the wine; maybe one had caught in his throat. He flopped back on the couch, dropped the wine-cup, and tried to throw up, but nothing came out. Then he doubled over, clutching his stomach. His face was a horrible grey colour, his eyes staring out of his head, still with a slightly baffled air. I jumped up to go to him, but by the time I reached him he was dead.

For a couple of heartbeats we were all statue-still. Everybody was appalled, his mother especially, half-risen from her couch, her features frozen in horror. Cleopatra looked amazed, and then terrified. She was the first to move; she bent over Marcus, straightened up again, and shrieked out, "No! Oh, no!"

She put her head in her hands and began to wail. Her cousin Phoebe was sobbing noisily, and before long half the women in the place were crying too.

"Rufus!" It was Sabinus, beckoning me a few paces away from his brother's body. "Rufus, did you see all that? What a ridiculous, outrageous thing to do! To make Marcus drink that concoction – surely she must have realized it might poison him? All that nonsense about Cleopatra . . ." He tailed off, too angry to speak, and then he growled, "By the gods, if she poisoned him on purpose . . ."

"I doubt that she did," I said. "Why would she? She was

all set for marriage and living happily ever after. I don't like the lady, sir, any more than you do, but I can't see her killing your brother deliberately. Out of foolishness, now that I *could* believe."

He looked at Marcus' grey face, then went to him and closed his eyes. At the same time a couple of Cleopatra's maids appeared beside their mistress, and half-led, half-carried her from the room. Sabinus angrily watched her go, then turned back to me.

"Maybe he choked on one of the pearls?" he suggested. "They couldn't have dissolved in the wine that quickly, surely?"

"No, they couldn't." But I'd seen the way he had clutched at his belly. Still, easy enough to check. The goblet lay on its side under the table, and I bent to pick it up, but haste made me clumsy and it rolled away as I touched it, spilling out dregs of red wine and several pearls. They skittered across the mosaic floor, and as I tried to catch them, the performing monkey from the entertainment suddenly leapt past me and grabbed one in his small fist. His master was close behind, and snatched the animal up, holding him tight and making him drop the pearl.

"'Scuse me, my lord," he murmured in his broken Latin. "Bad monkey! Not to touch!" He tapped the little animal sharply on the nose.

I swore at the pair of them as he darted away, and counted the pearls. Five. Marcus had not swallowed any.

"So the mixture itself must have killed him," I said. "I still don't think it was deliberate though." But deliberate or not, something about the mixture of wine and pearls had been poisonous enough to kill a grown man. Did that mean the legend about Cleopatra drinking her pearl to amuse Mark Antony was false? Surely Chloe believed it was true; she'd even swallowed some of the wine herself, before demonstrating to the world how easily she could make Marcus do any stupid thing she wanted.

There was a commotion at the Lady Cornelia's couch, and I saw that the old dame had fainted. Sabinus grasped my shoulder, pressing it hard. "I must go to my mother. Find out what happened here tonight, Rufus. I want to know if she did this on purpose, or if it was just a tragic stupid accident. So use that head of yours."

The next few hours were chaos. The old lady soon recovered from her faint, but she took to her bed, leaving my patron in charge of the arrangements for mourning his brother, the ritual cleansing that the priests had to carry out, and the hundred and one other tasks that need attention when someone suddenly dies. Soon the house resounded with the keening notes of the mourners. They grew louder as I made my way through the atrium, where the body was being laid out, and diminished again as I headed for the suite of rooms that Chloe and Phoebe and their entourage were using.

I must admit I wasn't looking forwards to the next step. "Find out what happened," Sabinus had ordered, but it was a great deal easier to say than do. I could talk to Chloe, and she couldn't deny that she had been the instrument of Marcus' death; we'd all seen him take the cup from her. But she'd presumably deny that she'd intended it, even if . . . I hesitated outside the door, trying to think of the best approach. Then fortune smiled on me; Amanda came hurrying along the corridor, carrying a tray with an earthenware flask and a small cup. She paused and smiled at me.

"Rufus, thank the gods! It's awful in there – like a nightmare. All Chloe's people are terrified, saying she's poisoned the master and she'll be putting the blame on one of them. And as for Chloe herself – first she was as sick as a dog, and you can imagine the drama . . ."

"Sick, you say? Is it serious?"

"Not really. I suppose the wine's made her ill, but at least she didn't drink enough to kill her, like poor Master Marcus. The wine was poisoned, presumably?"

"It was the pearls and wine that made a poisonous mixture," I said. "That's what Sabinus thinks, and so do I. The point is, did Chloe know it would happen like that? I need to talk to her. Is she in a state to see me?"

Amanda shrugged. "I expect so, if you insist loudly enough. Use the Lady Cornelia's name, I should; that'll scare them all. And make it quick. I've got some medicine here to make her sleep, something the old lady's doctor has made up for her. She's hysterical, howling the place down like a child that's lost its favourite doll." She sniffed scornfully. "She keeps saying 'I didn't mean to kill him', over and over again. He's dead just the same, poor boy."

"I don't think she did mean to," I answered. "After all, she drank the wine herself before she gave it to him. If she'd known it was poisonous . . ."

"Yes, that's true," Amanda conceded. "And originally she meant to drink it all herself."

"You knew she was going to make that silly scene? You knew *beforehand*?"

"Oh, yes, all the servants did. She'd been planning it for ages, that's why she made him buy the pearls. She went on and on about it, going over what she'd say, how it was so romantic . . . we were all sworn to secrecy on pain of a serious flogging, so I couldn't tell you. But she was determined to drink it all herself. She never mentioned making Master Marcus drink any. That must have been a sudden whim, not in the original plan."

"Unless she was being really cunning, and planning to poison Marcus but telling you all she would be drinking the mixture . . . no, that's too far-fetched. Why would she kill a man who adored her, when she was all set to marry him? Still, it's a funny way to treat a fabulously expensive present from your lover. Didn't she like the necklace?"

"Oh, she loved it. The way she stroked it and played with it and kept it safe . . ."

"Kept it safe?" I repeated. "I wondered about that. Granted she didn't poison the drink on purpose, could the pearls have had some kind of dirt on them, picked up from the shop where they were bought, or from someone handling them?"

Amanda shook her head. "None of us were allowed to touch them. Cousin Phoebe offered to polish them once or twice, but Madam said she was too rough, and after that nobody but Chloe herself went near them."

The door into Chloe's suite opened abruptly, and Phoebe stood there. She'd been crying, which made her lovely face look ugly and hard.

"Amanda! Don't stand gossiping, girl. Hurry up with that sleeping-draught! My poor cousin's beside herself. She must have some medicine to calm her down."

"Coming, my lady," Amanda stepped through the door; I followed, and Phoebe was too preoccupied to stop me.

I don't often go into ladies' private apartments and, whenever I do, I feel like a bull in a glassware shop, several sizes too big and clumsy for the delicate furniture and feminine frippery all around me. I took refuge in being brusque and to the point, and said, "Where's the Lady Chloe?"

"In her bedroom," Phoebe answered, noticing me now. "And who might you be, barging in here without a by-your-leave?"

"Lady Cornelia sent me to ask after your cousin," I said.

The lie worked. "Oh, I see. It's not a good time, but . . . how is her ladyship?"

"She's recovered from her fainting fit, but she's in extreme distress over this whole tragedy. She's ordered me to enquire after Lady Chloe, and get to the truth of what happened."

"I'd have thought it was obvious, even to a stupid hulk like you," she retorted, tossing back her dark hair and fixing me with an angry stare. "My poor cousin wanted to make a romantic gesture, and it went tragically wrong. The pearls somehow poisoned the wine. The story of Queen Cleopatra and her banquet is so well known, nobody questioned that it's true. Obviously it can't be."

"That's certainly how it seems," I agreed, softening my tone a bit. "But I still would like to talk to your cousin. Please. Won't you ask her if she'll see me, just for a little while?"

"It's all right, Phoebe." Chloe herself appeared from one of the inner rooms and came towards me. "I'll see him if I must. Ah – you're one of Marcus' brother's people, aren't you?"

"I'm his assistant, my lady. Rufus, at your service." I had trouble not staring rudely at her; she was changed out of all recognition from the glamorous beauty of the banquet. Her skin was blotchy, her eyes were swollen, and some strands of golden hair had come loose and hung down untidily. She had torn her lovely dress in the ritual gesture of mourning, and there were stains down the front of it where she'd been sick.

"Lady Cornelia asked me to come and see you," I said. "I'm sorry to disturb you, but . . . we're all so deeply sorry about this tragic accident."

"Accident?" She almost shrieked the word. "Yes, I suppose you can call it that. I killed him. I know I did. But I didn't mean to. *I didn't mean to.* Gods, I've been so stupid, so incredibly stupid, and now *I've killed him!* I didn't want the marriage, or him, but – may the gods witness, I didn't want him dead!" She flopped down onto a couch and started sobbing.

I sat down beside her. Normally I would wait to be asked, but I was towering over her like a granite obelisk, and I thought it might intimidate her.

"You didn't want to marry Marcus?" I asked gently.

"Of course I didn't!" Cleopatra was back in control for a few heartbeats, then Chloe began crying again. "There was a man in Alexandria, I loved him, and he loved me. But my father insisted it had to be Marcus, and he loved me too, the poor sweet idiot. Only I couldn't love him. Why else d'you suppose I gave him such a hard time?"

"You were hoping he'd fall out of love? But the marriage would have gone ahead, surely. Love and marriage don't have to go together." Nobody knows that better than we Romans.

"I thought – I don't know *what* I thought. I was trying to make him hate me, that would have been a start. Only he went on loving me! And I didn't want him dead. You must believe that!"

"So you didn't realize," I said softly, "that dissolving pearls in wine would make the wine poisonous?"

She shook her head sadly. "I thought that anything Cleopatra did, I could do too."

I got away eventually, and went with a heavy heart to tell Sabinus. I found him in the garden, gazing moodily into the pool.

He nodded as I came up, then turned back to stare into the water, which was full of starry reflections. "I can't do any more till daylight," he said. "But dawn won't be long. Rufus, this is all such a mess, such a tragic waste." He turned and looked at me. "Well, tell me the worst. What have you found out?"

He wasn't surprised by what I told him, except for the bit

about Chloe not wanting to marry Marcus. He seemed even a little relieved that she was a thoughtless irresponsible child, but at least not a calculating murderess. "After the funeral, we'll ship her back to Egypt," he said. "I expect she can make a decent marriage there."

And your dear mama will have to find some other way of refilling the family coffers, I thought, as I left him and headed for my sleeping-quarters. Amanda would still be with Chloe; I'd be alone for what remained of the night. As I walked down the badly lighted narrow corridor that led to the rooms where we freedmen slept, a dark figure moved in the shadows. My hand went to my knife, but it was only the Egyptian boy, still clutching his monkey. He stood in front of me, blocking my way.

"Please, my lord," he said. "My monkey sick."

"Sick? Well then, fetch an animal doctor, and get out of my way." I made to brush him aside, but he stood his ground.

"My lord, please. Something bad is." His dark thin face was serious, and his eyes were big and intense. Whatever he was trying to tell me, it was important. I didn't want to be bothered with him or his monkey, but I could remember the days when I was a slave-boy and nobody listened.

"Tell me then," I said. "Only if you're not quick, I'll be asleep on my feet."

"Monkey sick from touch pearl out of wine-cup. He only just lick paw, so he not die. But wine was –" he searched for a word "– was dirty."

"Dirty?" I couldn't make sense of it. "Look, if you've got something to say, boy, speak Greek if it's easier, but for the gods' sake get on with it."

He nodded. "Good. For Egyptian boy, Greek is better. I want to make you understand. Poor monkey sick because the wine was poison."

"Actually we worked that out," I snapped. "The pearls poisoned it."

"No, pearls not poison."

Curse the boy, his Greek seemed no better than his Latin. "Pearls," I said loudly, in slow, simple Greek, "dissolve in wine. The wine – eats them up. You understand? When the pearls have been in the wine, the wine is changed into poison."

"No, no!" he gestured excitedly, making the monkey wriggle. "I seen it done before. Pearls and wine. The Cleopatra game."

"The *what?*"

He grinned suddenly. "I worked for master who did magic tricks. Very quick hands. Turn gentleman's cup into dove, or take snake out from under lady's cloak. You know?"

"Yes, I know the kind of thing." In Egypt, magic-show entertainers are plentiful, and often very good.

"He use to put pearl in cup of wine, pretend to make it dis–dissolve in the wine. But it never."

I looked at him sharply. "Go on."

"Pearl not dissolve in good wine. In sour wine, in vinegar, yes, it get slowly eat up." He screwed up his mouth to indicate a bad taste. "Not in good stuff. Master use to leave pearl in wine little time, then he drink all wine, tell the people he drink pearl too. Cup empty – pearl hid in hand. Then he fill another cup, make pearl come out of that. Pearl not hurt, a little dull maybe, but soon polish. He call it the Cleopatra Game. And it never make him sick to drink. Once only it make him sleepy."

"Why?"

"I play joke on him. I rub sleeping stuff on outside of pearl. It wash off into wine, and he drink it, and he sleep. When he waked up, he beat me."

"Gods alive!" My mind was racing. Now I knew how Marcus had been killed – but I still didn't know the killer. Or rather, I didn't know which one of two . . .

"My lord?" The boy interrupted my thoughts. "Did I explain it clear?"

"Yes, lad. And thank you – you were right to tell me. Off you go now. I need to think." I threw him a silver piece, and he scampered off, grinning. I stood alone in the passageway, staring at nothing, just thinking hard.

Either Chloe or Phoebe had poisoned the pearls. Both had had the chance; even though Phoebe wasn't supposed to touch the necklace, I felt sure she could have found a way. Chloe was the more likely though. She hadn't wanted to marry Marcus; by using the pearls and wine she could make his death look like a tragic accident. And she'd been clever, talking about how she intended to drink all the wine, giving no hint that she planned to offer it to Marcus.

But then Phoebe also had a reason to kill – not Marcus, but her cousin, who was marrying the man she herself loved. Phoebe had heard Chloe boasting that she would drink the pearls, and knew that she'd forbidden everyone else to touch them; so if Chloe died, here again it would appear to be a terrible accident, or if the poison was discovered, we would conclude that Chloe had chosen suicide to escape her wedding.

Standing there in the near-dark, I worked out a way to discover which of them had perpetrated this cunning, premeditated killing. All it needed was a little play-acting, and two small items which I went and collected from my sleeping-room nearby: a large linen cloth, and an empty leather money-bag.

Then I ran back through the house to Chloe's suite. I hammered on the door, but nobody answered my knock, so I walked in.

The outer room looked dim and deserted, with only one small lamp burning. Presumably the ladies, and their maids, were in their bed-chambers.

"Lady Chloe! Lady Phoebe!" I called loudly. "It's Rufus, and I'm sorry to disturb you, but I need to talk with you both now. Come out, please. I'm afraid this is urgent."

There was silence. I looked at the two bedchamber doors. I'd have to go in and rouse the women, but maybe I should fetch a couple of our household maids to help me.

"Rufus?" a voice said. "So you've come back." And then I saw Phoebe, sitting on a reading-couch in a dark alcove. She looked flushed; I wondered how much more she'd drunk. "What do you want?"

"Lady Phoebe." I came and stood over her, and this time I didn't worry about towering above her, because a granite obelisk was what I felt like. "Will you please fetch your cousin? I need to talk to both of you urgently."

"You can't talk to Chloe," she snapped, not troubling to hide her hostility. "She's in bed, and sound asleep by now, I hope. She's taken a strong sleeping-draught, and she's not to be disturbed. You can talk to me, if you must."

"Very well then. I've discovered," I said carefully, "that Marcus' death wasn't an accident. The wine was deliberately poisoned."

"Deliberately? But – how dreadful! It wasn't just the mixing of the pearls and the wine?"

"No. Pearls and good wine don't form a poison. Where are the pearls, please? I must lock them away. They're extremely dangerous."

"They're safe enough now." She gestured towards a small table beside her couch. It had a silver cup of red wine on it, and a covered silver fruit dish. She lifted off the lid, and revealed the pearls in a loose pile, gleaming richly even in this dim light. "So pure, aren't they? So perfect . . ." She picked up a handful, and let them run slowly through her fingers.

"Put them down!" I exclaimed. "I tell you, they're dangerous. They've been poisoned. Even just touching them could be deadly." I produced my cloth, and used it to scoop the pearls into my leather bag, making a great show of not letting the jewels touch my fingers.

"What nonsense!" she retorted. "Chloe wore the necklace all through the banquet, right against her skin . . ."

"The pearls were dry then. It's wetting them that brings the poison out. The effect of liquid . . ."

She was following my movements intently as I gathered the last of the pearls. I've long ago perfected the knack of watching someone without appearing to, so I didn't miss her quick glance down at her hands. And she had said the pearls were safe enough *now*. I felt the tingle of excitement a hunter knows when he has laid his bait, and watches the quarry approaching his trap.

"Marcus was murdered," I went on, pulling the bag's drawstring tight. "Poison was smeared onto your cousin's necklace, and it was a special kind that only becomes lethal when it touches liquid. If you drink the liquid it kills you – as it killed poor Marcus. And if you touch it, it kills you too, only more slowly."

"How?"

"Say you washed the pearls. The water would be poisonous, and it would eat into your skin – not immediately, but in an hour, maybe two, you'd feel it start to burn and blister. And then . . ." I let it hang.

She had gone white. "And then?"

"The poison would work through the blisters, and seep into your body. You'd be dead inside half a day."

"But I've dried my hands!" she cried. She spread her hands out and stared at them; they were quite unharmed – of course they were. I was making this up as I went along. But my bait had trapped her, and when she looked up at me again, I saw that she knew it.

"You washed the pearls, Lady Phoebe," I said. "To clean off the poison you had smeared on them."

She said nothing.

"Did you hate your cousin so much?"

She sat unmoving; I thought she wasn't going to answer. Then she said, so quietly it was almost a whisper, "I loved Marcus."

I waited.

"I loved him from the first time I saw him. He didn't want me, I knew that, but I couldn't not love him. And I hated Chloe for the way she treated him. *I'd* have given him love, kindness, respect – I'd never have humiliated him the way she did."

"Yet you killed him."

"But I didn't mean to!" she exclaimed. "*She* was the one I wanted dead! I was trying to protect him from her. I knew if she was dead he still might not love me, but at least he could live his life without her trampling all over him!"

"Wasn't there any other way out? Your cousin didn't want to marry Marcus, after all."

"Both families insisted on it. Marcus and Chloe – a union of rank with riches. The perfect Roman marriage." Her tone was like a bitter wind.

"But deciding to kill her . . ."

"Ah, no! She would have killed herself, by the choice she made. I worked it out carefully. If she died, she'd die by her own hand, and she'd deserve it."

"I don't understand."

"I tried to talk her out of her plan to drink the pearls, but of course that only made her more determined. I suppose I should have known it would. But it was cruel – and wasteful.

Such lovely pearls! If Marcus had given me pearls like that . . . So I thought, let her wear them, but not destroy them. I contracted a man who – never mind; it isn't hard to find such people. He supplied a poison that wouldn't harm her skin, but would kill her if she swallowed it. I rubbed it on the necklace this afternoon, while she was taking her bath. And then it was her decision. If she wore the pearls, she'd be safe. If she drank them, she would die."

Suddenly she began to cry. Not the loud, dramatic weeping I'd seen earlier; this was agonising, gut-wrenching sorrow. "How was I to know she'd give the wine to Marcus? She said she would drink it all . . . but she had to go one better, and humiliate him yet again! And poor Marcus . . . !"

She wiped her eyes, getting herself under control. "I sat at that banquet, and I vowed in my heart, I'll get you yet, you vicious little snake. And now I have."

"What? You can't mean . . ."

"I mean," she said calmly, "that when she took her sleeping-drought, she drank it with – as she put it – just a little something added." She actually smiled. "Oh, not my special poison this time; just good old hemlock, so she'd fall quietly asleep and never wake up. I wanted it to look like suicide. It was a better death than she deserved!"

I stared down at her, appalled; she gazed back unblinking. Two murders – two poisons – she surely must be mad, and she could be capable of anything. There could still be danger.

"Have you any poison left?" I asked. "If so, you must give it to me now. We must have no more killing."

Quick as a snake, she snatched the wine-cup from the table, and drained it in three rapid swallows. I reached out to grab it from her, but she flung it across the room, and exclaimed triumphantly, "There – all gone now!" She began to laugh, a shrill crazed laugh that soon turned into a fit of choking.

She fell forwards onto the floor, curling up into a ball, and I knew there was nothing I could do for her, even if I wanted to.

But Chloe . . . Hemlock works slowly. Might I be in time? I rushed into her bedchamber. She lay on her back on the bed, looking as if she was sleeping peacefully, but when I looked closer, I saw she was dead.

And then terror stabbed me like a knife in the heart. Beside the bed, sprawled limply in a chair, was my Amanda, lying deathly still.

"Amanda!" I shouted, in rising panic. Phoebe had proved she would stop at nothing. Suppose Amanda had discovered about the poison, and accused her . . .

"Amanda!" I yelled, shaking her by the shoulders. She didn't move.

"*Amanda! Wake up! Wake up, Amanda!*" I shook her hard, and she stirred, and looked at me half-awake; and then she smiled.

"Rufus, you big stupid lump, what's all the noise about?"

I've never been so glad to hear somebody call me stupid.

Bread and Circuses

Caroline Lawrence

This story is set just months after the death of Vespasian when his son Titus was Emperor. It is the latest story in the series of Roman Mysteries written for younger readers by Caroline Lawrence, which began with The Thieves of Ostia *(2001) and now runs to seven books. It takes place in November of 79AD between the events of the fifth and sixth books. Though born in London, Caroline Lawrence is an American and was raised in California, but returned to England to study at Cambridge University and has remained here ever since.*

"**I** *am* a detective!" cried Flavia Gemina, and she almost stamped her foot. "I've solved lots and lots of mysteries!" Because her mother was dead and her father – the sea-captain Marcus Flavius Geminus – was often away on voyages, Flavia was probably the most independent ten-year-old girl in the Roman port of Ostia.

"Detective?" Flavia's tutor Aristo raised an eyebrow. He was a good-looking young Greek with curly hair. "There's no such word in Latin. You made it up."

"I did *not* make it up," said Flavia. "It was in the scroll Admiral Pliny gave me before he died. The one he called

Great Mysteries of the Past. He said a detective is someone who 'uncovers the truth'."

"Show me where it says that."

"I can't. The scroll was lost in the eruption of Vesuvius." Flavia looked out through the columns of the peristyle into the wet green garden. She still felt a pang when she remembered the old admiral dying on the beach a few months earlier. "It was the only scroll in existence," she said, "written in his own teeny tiny handwriting." Flavia looked at Aristo again. "But I remember reading that word: 'detective'. As soon as I saw it, I knew: I'm a detective."

"Well," said Aristo, "being a detective is no excuse for ignoring your homework. So sit down and do that calculation again the way I showed you yesterday."

Flavia sighed – a deep sigh of the unjustly oppressed – and sat down again at the marble table. She took the abacus and stared at it, but its boxwood beads were inscrutable.

Across the table, a brown-eyed boy was mouthing something at her. Jonathan – a Jew about her own age – was her next-door neighbour and friend, as well as her classmate. Flavia looked up at him from under her eyebrows, but she couldn't understand the words he was silently forming.

To her right, a dark-skinned girl was pointing behind her hand at one of the rows of beads. That didn't help either. Flavia's ex-slave-girl Nubia had only been in Italia for a few months but already she was better at maths than Flavia.

Finally Flavia glanced at Lupus, the youngest of them. Although Lupus had been a homeless beggar until recently, his maths was also better than hers. Because he was mute, Lupus depended heavily on a wax tablet to communicate. He was casually writing something on it now and she read:

USE THE TENS COLUMN

But the words on Lupus's tablet may as well have been Etruscan. She would have to admit defeat.

"I didn't do the homework," Flavia said in a small voice.

"Well, then," said Aristo. "You know the punishment."

"No!" she wailed.

"You can't object," said Aristo. "Last month I asked each of you to choose the punishment you thought best if you didn't do your homework. The choice was yours."

"But I hate emptying the latrine bucket!" said Flavia. "I hate it almost as much as I hate maths."

"That's why it's a good punishment," said Aristo mildly.

"A detective shouldn't have to empty latrine buckets." Flavia pouted.

"For the last time: you are not a detective!"

"Yes I am!" Flavia's chair scraped on the marble floor as she stood up again. "I'll prove it! Set me any mystery, any task and I'll solve it for you! And . . . and if I can't do it I'll never mention the word again!"

"And you'll empty the latrine bucket every day for a month? Until the Saturnalia?"

"Yes," said Flavia. "But if I win, if *I* solve the mystery then we don't do any maths for a whole month, we'll just read Greek myths."

Aristo's brown eyes gleamed. "Very well," he said. "If you're a detective, why don't you find out who's been robbing Pistor the baker?"

Flavia's face fell. That was precisely the puzzle she'd been trying to solve for the past few weeks. And Aristo knew that.

"I'll give you three days," said Aristo. "And today counts as the first."

"Am I allowed to ask Jonathan and Nubia and Lupus to help me?" asked Flavia.

Aristo grinned up at her. "Of course. You know I encourage teamwork whenever possible. In fact, if you'd conferred with the three of them yesterday afternoon you'd know how to do those calculations. But I'll bet you had your nose in a scroll, didn't you?"

Flavia nodded. "I've been reading Ovid's *Metamorphoses*," she murmured.

"What?" Aristo's face grew pale. "You've been reading *what*?"

"Ovid's *Metamorphoses*?" said Flavia in a tiny voice.

"Where did you get it?"

Flavia tried to look innocent. "From the top shelf in pater's study. Behind the Catullus," she added.

"And do you have any idea why your father put it up there? Well out of your reach?"

"No," Flavia lied.

"He put it on the top shelf because it's completely unsuitable for a young lady of your class."

"But it's so good."

"Of course it's good," said Aristo. "It's a masterpiece. But it's also extremely violent and full of unsuitable sex scenes."

"If I solve the mystery –" began Flavia.

"No!" cried Aristo.

"If I solve the mystery of who's stealing Pistor's bread in the next three days," Flavia persisted, "then will you let us read bits of it? Just the bits that aren't full of unsuitable sex and violence?"

"I suppose I could choose excerpts," said Aristo slowly. He stood, too.

"If you solve that mystery in the next three days then we'll read carefully selected passages from Ovid instead of doing maths. But if you fail, then you'll empty the latrine bucket for a month, do your homework and never mention the word 'detective' again. Agreed?"

"Agreed!" said Flavia.

They shook on it.

"OK," said Flavia Gemina to Jonathan, Nubia and Lupus. "What do we know so far?"

The four friends and their three dogs were having a conference in Flavia's bedroom. Outside, a soft but steady rain fell on the umbrella pines in the necropolis and dripped from the sill of a small window. The pearly light of a November morning filled the bedroom.

Jonathan sat cross-legged on Nubia's bed next to his puppy Tigris. "Well," he said, "We know that the robberies have been going on for nearly half a year. Alma told us that."

Flavia nodded. Her old nursemaid Alma was cook in the Geminus household.

Jonathan continued. "Last Saturday we watched Pistor's customers from dawn till noon. But that didn't get us anywhere."

"I think I know why, now," said Flavia." Alma just told me that Pistor thinks it's an inside job."

"What is 'inside job'?" asked Nubia. Her first exposure to the Latin language had been Virgil and this was not an idiom he used.

"It means the thief must be someone inside the bakery. One of Pistor's family, or one of his slaves."

"What makes Pistor think it's an inside job?" asked Jonathan.

"Last week he mentioned to Alma that sometimes the rolls go missing from undelivered batches. They were never taken to the shop front. That means it's an inside job, and *that* means we have eight suspects." Flavia counted on her fingers: "Pistor's wife, his daughter, his two sons and their three slaves. Alma told me how many people there are in his household," she added.

THAT'S ONLY VII, wrote Lupus on his wax tablet.

"Yes," agreed Jonathan. "Who's the eighth?"

"Pistor himself," said Flavia. "Pliny's scroll taught me never to discount the person who first brings the crime to light. It told the story of a man whose mule fell into a cistern and broke its neck. The man blamed his neighbour because the fence around the cistern had a gap in it. But it turned out the mule was ill and the mule's owner broke the fence on purpose and pushed the mule towards the cistern. He wanted to make it look like negligence, so that his neighbour would have to compensate him and buy him a healthy new mule. And that," she concluded, "is why we can't even tell Pistor we're trying to solve the mystery."

"OK," said Jonathan. "So we know there are eight suspects and that it's an inside job."

"But we are not even knowing all their names," said Nubia and Lupus nodded.

"And you know what *that* means, don't you." said Flavia. They all looked at her.

"To solve an inside job," said Flavia Gemina, "we'll have to get inside!"

Ostia's Imperial Granary was almost as big as the town's famous theatre just up the road.

But unlike the white, marble-covered theatre, the granary was red. It was red from the top of its terracotta roof tiles to the bottom of its brick thresholds. Even the elegant half columns which flanked the doorways and the triangular pediments above them were made of brick.

Some Ostians called the Imperial Granary a monstrosity. But Jonathan liked the way it looked. And he liked the way it smelled: of freshly baked bread. That was because so many of Ostia's bakeries were situated all around it.

Pistor's was one of the smallest of those bakeries. But size didn't matter: everyone knew Pistor's bread was the best. Especially his poppy-seed white rolls, which were even famous in Rome.

Jonathan's stomach rumbled as he caught the yeasty scent of hot bread. He followed his friend Lupus up the two steps to Pistor's shop front. The rain had stopped, but the stones were still wet.

The boys pressed their faces against the damp wooden shutter. By putting his eye to one of the cracks between the horizontal slats, Jonathan could see the marble counter where bread was sold to the public between dawn and noon. Behind it he could make out the wide doorway which led to the bakery beyond. A dim shape moved briefly into the doorway, then disappeared.

"There are still people in there." Flavia and Nubia had joined the boys at the shutter.

"We know that," said Jonathan. "We can smell the bread baking."

"I wonder if there's a back way in," said Flavia.

"Must be," said Jonathan, and Lupus nodded.

"Hark!" said Nubia. "I am hearing a sound."

They all listened and Jonathan heard a faint donkey's bray. He frowned. "It's coming from inside!"

"They are having a donkey inside the bakery?" said Nubia.

"Yes," said Flavia. "I think they use donkeys to grind the grain."

"Why are you lot nosing around here?" said a voice behind them.

The four friends turned to find a pudgy boy standing on the rain-slicked pavement below them. He wore a long-sleeved tunic under a brown cloak and his arms were folded across his chest. Jonathan guessed the boy was about his age. Perhaps a little younger.

"Can't you see we're closed?" said the boy.

"Hello," said Flavia. "Do you work here?"

"*Work* here?" the boy snorted. "Do I look like a slave? My father *owns* this bakery."

"Oh. I'm sorry," said Flavia, and then brightly introduced herself. "My name is Flavia Gemina. This is Jonathan, and Nubia and that's Lupus. Um . . . our tutor asked us to do a project on bread. 'From the harvest to the loaf'. And we wanted to see how bread was made."

"Bakeries close at noon when the baths open," said the boy. "Everybody knows that."

"But we smelled bread," said Jonathan.

"And we are hearing the donkey," added Nubia.

The boy looked at Nubia again. "What did you say your name was?" he asked her.

"My name is Nubia."

"I'm Sextus Nasenius Pistor," said the boy. "But you can call me Porcius. Everyone does."

"Nice to meet you, Porcius," said Flavia.

Porcius ignored her. "I suppose I could give you a tour," he said to Nubia and unfolded his arms. "Would that help you with your project?"

"That would delight us," said Nubia solemnly.

"Right," said Porcius with a nod. "Come on, then."

Nubia looked around the first room of the bakery – a small storeroom filled with sacks of grain and flour. She liked the low vaulted roof overhead and the pretty herringbone pattern of bricks on the floor.

"The first stage of baking bread," Porcius told her, "is getting the best Egyptian grain. We get our grain from the horrea down the street."

"The horror?" asked Nubia. "Do they name it thus because it is scary?"

Porcius corrected her patiently. "The horrea," he said. "The granary."

"But the words are related," said Flavia. "*Horrere* means to bristle. So horrea means a place where bristly grain is stored and *horrere* is when your hair bristles because you're scared!"

Nubia nodded. Flavia was one of the cleverest people she knew. Her former mistress loved words and stories, puzzles and codes.

"Whatever." Porcius turned back to Nubia. "After we choose the best grain we grind it to flour. Come into the next room."

"Oh!" Nubia gasped as they moved through the doorway, and her hand went to her throat. "The poor, wretched creatures!"

They had stepped into a spacious room with two big millstones and one smaller one, all made of grey stone. Each was shaped like the hourglass Alma used in the kitchen and around each one paced a blindfolded donkey.

"Why are you blinding them?" Nubia looked at Porcius.

"The blindfold doesn't hurt them," he said. "It's to stop them getting dizzy. They go round and round all day. Look! You can see they're yoked to a beam." He led Nubia to the smaller millstone. The others followed.

A thin slave with hair the colour of dirty straw was pouring grain from a bag into the top of one of the millstones. He nodded respectfully at Porcius.

Porcius ignored him and pointed to the millstone. "It's made of special Etruscan rock. The top stone is called the *catillus* and it fits over the bottom stone: the *meta*. You can't see the *meta*, but it's shaped like a cone: just like the turning-point at the races. There's a gap between them just wide enough to let the grain in. As the donkey pulls the top stone around the grain is crushed between the two stones. Then it comes out as flour." Porcius pointed to a trough.

But Nubia was not looking at the trough. She was looking at the place where years of donkeys' hooves had worn a ring into the stone floor.

"See the flour coming out?" Porcius was saying to her. "This millstone makes the finest flour for our best rolls."

"He seems wretched," whispered Nubia. "Behold where his fur is rubbing off on his shoulders."

"It doesn't hurt them much." Porcius said. "Animals don't feel pain like people do. Come on, Nubia. I'll show you where we mix the flour with water to make the dough."

Lupus followed the others to a room with several large troughs made of the same grey rock as the millstones. A big man stood facing them at one of the troughs. He was turning a vertical wooden bar. As they approached, Lupus could see that the bar rotated blades which mixed the flour and water into an elastic dough.

The slave wore a one-sleeved tunic. As they approached, he looked up at them, and Lupus saw the brand on his forehead: TENEME. Lupus knew it meant "hold me" and that only slaves who had run away were branded on the foreheads like this. The big slave gave Lupus a wink. His muscular chest and arms gleamed with sweat.

Lupus nodded back and then looked down into the trough. The mass of dough was round and smooth and slightly greyish.

"We bake the best bread first," Porcius was saying. "Then in the late morning or afternoon we bake the *panis popularis*."

"What's that?" asked Nubia.

"You know that the Emperor distributes free grain every day? Most people make porridge out of it but some bring it to us to make into bread. It's cheaper because we only charge for the cost of milling and baking. That's *panis popularis*."

"The Emperor is most benevolent," said Nubia, "to give free bread."

"It's not the bread that's free," corrected Porcius. "Just the grain. And the people would revolt if they didn't get it."

"*We* don't get free bread," said Jonathan. "I mean, free grain."

Porcius looked Jonathan up and down. "Are you a Roman citizen?"

"Yes," said Jonathan. "But only recently . . ."

"Then you should get a token soon. For some of our special customers we pick up the grain and bake the bread. You have to give us your token. I'll ask my father to put you on our list. Hey!" Porcius looked around. "Where's Nubia gone?"

Flavia spotted Nubia first: she was standing near the mill with the smallest donkey. The slave with straw-coloured hair stood beside her. He had unharnessed the donkey and Nubia was stroking its soft grey head.

"He is so little." She looked up at them as they came in. "Not even as big as Ferox."

Flavia nodded. Ferox was her uncle's guard dog – a huge mastiff.

"You like animals?" said Porcius. "Would you like to see my pets?"

Nubia's golden eyes lit up and she nodded.

"Come on, then." Porcius led them back through the store room and up a flight of dark stairs.

At the top of the stairs they met two women coming down. The first wore a light blue woollen stola with a dark blue palla draped over her head. Her face was dusted with white powder to make her look very fair. Behind her came a younger woman with frizzy brown hair and bad skin.

"Oh, hello, mater," said Porcius. "Are you going out?"

"Yes, dear," said the woman in blue. "Aren't you going to introduce me?"

"This is my mother: Fausta," said Porcius. "Mother, this is Nubia. And some friends of hers. I've been giving them a tour of the bakery." He didn't bother to introduce the woman behind his mother so Flavia deduced that she must be a slave-girl.

"How nice," said Fausta, patting his arm vaguely. She and her slave-girl continued past them. Flavia lingered at the top of the stairs, and noticed that the slave girl carried a bath-set: a bronze ring with strigil, tweezers, ear-scoop and oil-pot attached. Porcius' mother and her slave-girl were certainly going to the baths.

Flavia watched them out of sight, then turned and ran to catch up with the others.

"This is my room," said Porcius, leading them into a bright room with a small balcony overlooking the road. "And these are my steeds."

Nubia uttered a cry of delight. On the table beside the bed was a delicate wooden cage. Nestled in the sawdust were several mice. Nubia counted at least five of them.

"And this," Porcius gestured towards a big wooden box as long as his bed, "is where they race."

The box was open at the top and as Nubia looked down she saw a wooden model of a racetrack. She recognized the layout because she had been to the races in Rome a few months earlier.

"I call it the Circus Minimus," said Porcius, "because it's the smallest racecourse in the world. Pater helped me build it."

"You race your mice?" Jonathan raised an eyebrow.

"Yes," said Porcius, setting the cage in the middle of the racetrack and opening the door.

One by one the mice emerged from the cage. Some were grey and some were white. With bright eyes and twitching noses, they explored the model racetrack. There was a central island and the wood round the edges was carved in steps to represent the spectator seating.

The four friends knelt beside the track and Nubia picked up one of the white mice. She giggled as his warm little body explored the palm of her hand.

"What are you doing?" came a voice from the doorway. "Racing those silly mice again? Why don't you grow up?"

Nubia and the others looked up. A girl of about fifteen stood there. She wore a sage-green tunic and had tied a lavender palla round her hips in a way Nubia knew was fashionable among young women in Rome. With her pale skin and dark wavy hair she would have been very pretty except for one flaw: she was cross-eyed.

"Who are *you*?" she asked, staring at Nubia and the others.

Flavia jumped to her feet. "I'm Flavia Gemina, and these are my friends: Jonathan, Nubia and Lupus. You must be Titia."

"I know you," said Titia. "You're Aristo's pupils."

"That's right! Do you know him?"

Titia stood in the doorway for a moment without replying. Nubia couldn't tell which of them she was looking at. Abruptly Titia moved away from the doorway and Nubia heard her footsteps disappearing down the hallway.

"How rude!" muttered Flavia, sitting down again.

"Don't mind her," said Porcius. He had brought out two tiny wooden chariots, each with a wooden rider fixed inside. "She's always in a bad mood because she'll never find a husband."

"Why not?" asked Nubia.

Porcius snorted. "Didn't you see her? She's a cross-eyed freak. I think she's in love with your tutor Aristo," he added.

"How did you know that Aristo is our tutor?" asked Flavia.

"Everybody in Ostia knows. Or at least everybody at my school. They're all jealous because you have a private tutor who is nice to you and lets you do projects and doesn't beat you when you get a sum wrong."

"What school do you go to?" asked Jonathan.

"The one in the forum," said Porcius. "But I don't want to talk about school. Here, Nubia," he said, handing her one of the model chariots. "Why don't you harness up the Greens and I'll do the Blues. The Greens are the white ones," he added.

"He is lovely," said Nubia, stroking her white mouse.

"That's Cupido," said Porcius. He had already harnessed a grey mouse to his blue chariot. "You can tell him by the nick on his tail. He's best on the inside, because he's steady. Icarus there – the one climbing into the Emperor's Box – he's the fastest so you should put him on the outside. Castor and Pollux are the other two. They go in between."

"You really like the races, don't you?" said Jonathan, handing Icarus to Nubia. She nodded her thanks and smiled as the mouse nosed into his tiny harness. The little creatures were obviously used to the procedure.

"I love the races," said Porcius, without looking up. "I'm going to go to chariot racing school in Rome next year, when I'm twelve."

"They have a school for that?" asked Jonathan.

Porcius nodded.

"Have you ever been to the races?" asked Flavia.

"Myriads of times," said Porcius. "Pater always takes me up every year for the *Ludi Romani*."

"We've only been once," said Flavia. "But we loved it."

"They've been, but I haven't," said Jonathan glumly.

"OK," said Porcius, breathing heavily as he concentrated on getting his last mouse into the harness. "Before we put them on the starting line we have to place our bets. I wager ten pistachio nuts on the Blues."

"Five on the Greens," cried Flavia.

"Me too five greens," said Nubia.

Lupus held up his wax tablet: *FIVE ON THE BLUES*.

"Lupus! You traitor!" cried Flavia. "Why don't you bet on Nubia?"

Lupus grinned and shrugged.

"He obviously thinks he knows who's going to win," said Jonathan.

"Aren't you going to bet?" Porcius asked Jonathan.

"My father doesn't allow it."

Porcius shrugged. "You can be the Emperor, then. You drop the napkin."

"What?"

"To start the race."

"Oh. All right." Jonathan pulled his handkerchief from his belt and held it up.

"How many circles?" asked Nubia.

"Seven circuits, of course," said Porcius. "Just like the real races. Ready Jonathan? Then give the signal . . ."

Flavia wiped tears of laughter from her eyes. "That was the funniest thing I've ever seen. They're so cute. And so fast!"

"Yes," said Porcius proudly. "They're my boys. Here you go, Nubia and Flavia. Here are your winnings. Well done. Come on Lupus. Pay up."

Lupus scowled. He didn't like losing.

"Well run, boys," Porcius said to the mice as he scattered a handful of sunflower seeds onto the Circus Minimus. The mice had been released from their tiny harnesses and they happily devoured their reward.

"Oh!" said Flavia suddenly. "We're supposed to be solving – I mean studying – how bread is made."

"Do you really want to go down to the boring old bakery again?" Porcius asked Nubia. She was holding Castor and stroking his tiny shoulder blades with her finger.

"Can you show us the ovens?" Flavia asked.

Porcius ignored Flavia. "Nubia?" he said. "Do you want to go back down?"

"You can see the little donkey again," said Flavia.

Nubia's eyes lit up and she nodded firmly.

"Somebody whipped him!" cried Flavia.

The thin slave with straw-coloured hair was removing bread from a wall-oven. His one-armed tunic left a shoulder exposed and she could see the red welts on his back.

Porcius nodded. "Pater beat the slaves yesterday to see if they knew anything about some missing bread rolls." He noticed the look on Nubia's face. "It doesn't hurt them much," Porcius said. "Slaves don't feel pain like other people."

"Can we try some fresh rolls?" asked Jonathan. "They smell delicious. And I love warm bread."

"No," sighed Porcius. "My father keeps strict account of every loaf of bread baked and sold. If even one goes missing he knows about it. He doesn't even let my mother take bread without asking. Oh, hello, pater!" said Porcius. "These are some friends of mine. They're studying how bread is made."

A short man in a flour-dusted apron came through the doorway from the mill room. A tall boy of about thirteen trailed behind him.

"I know you," said the short man to Flavia. He had onion breath. "You're Alma's mistress."

"That's right. I'm Flavia. These are my friends Nubia, Jonathan and Lupus."

"Titus Nasenius Pistor. This is my eldest son Quintus. We call him Ericius."

The tall boy nodded. He was very thin with spiky hair and bluish shadows under his eyes. He coughed.

"Hello," said Flavia. "We're studying how bread is made and Porcius has been showing us around."

"That's my boy!" Pistor hooked his arm round Porcius' neck and gave his son an affectionate squeeze. "He and Ericius here are going to take over the business one day." Porcius squirmed free of his father's hairy arm, but Pistor didn't seem to mind. "Any questions you'd like to ask me about the baking process?"

"How many slaves do you have?" Flavia asked.

"Just the two," said Pistor. "The one we call Teneme and the one by the ovens there: his name is Tertius. He's also our accountant. This is a family business. Quality not quantity. Special loaves, mainly. Some pastries. Our famous poppy-seed rolls. *Panis popularis* for our preferred customers. The slaves do the milling and kneading and baking. I supervise. My family and I sell at the counter."

Ericius coughed again, and Pistor slapped his tall son on the back. "Both my boys do the early shift, before they go to school. Then my daughter Titia takes over."

"You said some bread has been going missing?" said Flavia.

Pistor nodded. "That's been going on for months. At first the amount of disappearing bread was so small that I didn't notice. But I've been keeping strict accounts for the last few weeks and just this morning I calculated that it's almost always a dozen of my special poppy-seed rolls that go missing."

"That's not very much," said Jonathan.

"No, it's not," he scowled. "But it doesn't matter if it's one roll or a hundred. There's a thief in my household. That's what matters." He spat onto the floor. "And you know, it's very strange. The thefts only occur every seventh day."

*   *   *

"Every seventh day," said Flavia to the others as they walked back home. "I know every eighth day we have the *nundinae*: the market days. But why every seventh day?"

"The Sabbath!" said Jonathan.

"Tomorrow's the Sabbath, isn't it?" said Flavia.

"Actually it starts this evening," said Jonathan. "You Romans start the day from sunrise. For us Jews, the day begins at sunset."

"It's good you're Jewish and Aristo lets us off lessons on the Sabbath," said Flavia. "That means we have a free day tomorrow. I think each one of us should follow a member of Pistor's household tomorrow and see where they go."

They all nodded.

"Lupus, you follow the boys to school. And Nubia, you keep an eye on Titia or Fausta, whoever comes out first. Take Caudex as your bodyguard. Jonathan and I will hang around the bakery and see if Pistor or the slaves go anywhere."

"Who'll be *your* bodyguard?" asked Jonathan. "You know your father doesn't like you going out alone."

"I'll take Scuto," said Flavia, and then muttered under her breath. "But you'd better not tell pater."

Early the next morning, just before dawn, the four friends stood watching Pistor's bakery from across the street. The bakery window was a bright square of yellow where a line of hanging oil lamps illuminated Pistor and his two sons. They were already selling bread to a steady stream of customers. Beyond them Flavia could see the slave called Tertius taking bread out of the ovens.

"Look at Pistor," muttered Jonathan. "Porcius and Ericius could eat a whole loaf each and he wouldn't notice."

Titus Nasenius Pistor was resting his forearms on the counter and gossiping with his customers. His two sons were doing most of the work, handing out bread and taking coins. Flavia's door-slave Caudex and her old nurse Alma were among those in the queue. This was their daily routine.

Flavia had rarely been out of the house this early and she was surprised to see how busy it was just before dawn. It was chilly and she could smell the smoke from the torches people held.

She shivered and pulled her woollen palla tighter round her shoulders. Her bare legs were cold, too, so she stood closer to Scuto and let the heat from his furry body warm her calves. He looked up at her, and gave his tail a tentative wag. When Flavia shook her head at him he sighed and lay down on the pavement. Flavia didn't mind: now his body was warming her feet.

Presently Alma stood silhouetted in front of the bright rectangle above the bakery counter. She chatted with Pistor for a few minutes and finally followed the torch-bearing Caudex back across the street to Flavia.

Alma smiled and handed out bread rolls. "There you go, my dears," she said. "Try those."

"Behold!" said Nubia. "They are warm."

Jonathan bit into his. "And delicious!"

Flavia gave half her warm roll to Scuto, who was on his feet again. He devoured it in one gulp and kept his eyes fixed on her face.

Lupus chomped his roll carefully with his molars, then tipped his head back to swallow. He had no tongue and every bite of food threatened to choke him.

"Do you want us to stay with you here, dear?" Alma asked Flavia. "Caudex and I usually go to the meat market next."

"You can carry on shopping," said Flavia. "But can we keep Caudex?"

★   ★   ★

The four friends – plus Scuto and Caudex – had moved further up the road to a place from which they could see anyone coming out the back door of the bakery. The sky was pale in the east when two dark shapes emerged from this door and moved towards the forum.

"There go the boys, Lupus," whispered Flavia. "Follow them!"

Lupus nodded and disappeared after Porcius and Ericius.

A moment later Flavia jumped as the shutter of the caupona behind them rattled open. She turned to see a sleepy-looking man in a pale tunic yawning at them.

"You waiting for me to open? Have a seat and I'll be with you in a moment."

"We may as well," whispered Flavia to the others. "If we sit here and have a cup of hot spiced wine, we'll be less conspicuous."

"Behold," said Nubia, as they sat at a rickety table near the marble bar. "Pistor's wife and daughter are now serving bread."

"And he's still busy chatting to his friends," snorted Flavia.

There was no longer a queue outside the bakery, but a steady trickle of customers still came and went.

Flavia and her friends had drunk two beakers of hot spiced wine – well-watered – before Titia disappeared from the bakery counter and reappeared a few minutes later at the back door.

"There goes Titia!" said Flavia with satisfaction. "Nubia, you and Caudex follow her. And don't let her spot you. She knows who you are."

It was mid-morning, and Jonathan's stomach was growling. He had only eaten one bread roll and drunk some weak spiced wine. He and Flavia sat at the table, warming their feet beneath Scuto's furry stomach.

"I'm hungry," Jonathan remarked. "It seems like I'm always hungry these days."

"Here." Flavia grinned at him and pushed a silver coin across the table. "Buy us a couple of their rolls. We'll see how good they are."

"Not as good as Pistor's," said Jonathan a moment later. He chewed his roll and suddenly he winced. "Ow!" He reached into his mouth and pulled something out.

"What is is?" asked Flavia, her grey eyes wide.

"Bit of grit. I could have broken a tooth. No," he said, "these rolls are definitely not up to Pistor's standards."

"I'm bored," sighed Flavia. She rested her elbows on the table and her chin in her hands. "I guess being a detective involves a lot of waiting. I wish I had a scroll. But if I was reading then I couldn't watch the bakery doorway."

"Shall I recite some poetry for you?" asked Jonathan. "I know lots of it. It's from the *Tanak*."

"What's the *Tanak*?" asked Flavia.

"Our Holy Book," said Jonathan. "The *T* stands for 'torah', the first five scrolls. The *N* stands for 'nevee'eem' which means 'prophets'. And the *K* stands for 'k'tooveem' which means the 'writings'. When you add vowels you get the word *Tanak*, our holy writings."

"And there are some poems?" asked Flavia.

"There are a hundred and fifty, which we call psalms. I can recite them all. Choose a number."

"What?"

"Choose a number between one and one hundred and fifty."

"Um . . . a hundred . . . and four!" said Flavia.

"O Lord my God, you are very great," recited Jonathan, "You are clothed in glory and majesty and you wrap yourself in light like a garment. You stretch out your heavens like a tent and you make the clouds your chariot . . ."

"Jonathan, that's beautiful," said Flavia. "I never knew you could do that."

"I know all the psalms by heart," said Jonathan proudly. "Choose another number and I'll see if I can tell you the last line. That's a bit harder . . ." He laughed at the expression on her face. "Go on," he said. "Test me."

"OK. Sixty-seven. What's the last line of poem sixty-seven?"

"That's a short psalm; only seven verses. I'll tell you the last two lines . . ." He paused for a moment, then looked up and to his left, " 'The earth will yield its harvest and God – our God – will bless us. God will bless us, so let all the ends of the earth be in awe of him.' "

"Teach me!" cried Flavia. "Teach me a psalm!"

"I'll teach you one of our prayers," said Jonathan, "the one our Messiah taught us: *Pater noster*, our father . . ."

"Pater noster," repeated Flavia, and then she pointed: "There goes the runaway slave!"

"What?"

"Teneme. Look how fast he's moving! Quick, Jonathan. Follow him!"

"Good morning, sir," said Flavia casually, and leaned on the cold marble counter of the bakery. "May I try another one of your poppy-seed rolls?"

"Of course," said Pistor. "That will be one *as*. Still working on your project?" he asked, as he slid her change across the counter.

She nodded.

"Then why don't you come on in?"

"Can my dog Scuto come in, too?"

Pistor nodded.

A moment later, Flavia and her dog entered the bakery. It was almost deserted. Apart from Pistor, there was only a slave sitting at a table in a corner.

Pistor had just turned to serve a customer, so Flavia wandered over to the table. Scuto followed her, his toenails tapping on the brick floor. He sniffed the slave's knees and wagged his tail.

The fair-haired slave stopped flicking beads on his abacus and reached down to scratch Scuto behind the ear.

"You're Tertius, aren't you?" said Flavia.

He nodded.

Flavia casually ran her finger over some letters carved into the smooth wooden surface of his small table. "Do you keep all the accounts?"

"I used to," sighed Tertius, picking up his quill pen and making a note on a piece of papyrus. "But now the master insists on going over them. And sometimes he does spot checks. He has to account for every loaf or roll produced. We even have to note how many rolls are burnt in the ovens."

"Why?" asked Flavia. "Why is he so careful?"

Tertius lowered his pen and his voice. "They say his wife's grandmother was the cause of a famine in Ostia, in the days of the Emperor Augustus."

"Really?"

Tertius nodded. "Her name was Fausta, too. When she had quadruplets, the soothsayers were terrified and predicted four years of famine."

"I remember!" cried Flavia. "Didn't Admiral Pliny tell that story in his *Natural History*?"

"You're very well-read," said Tertius. "And do you remember what happened? Was the prophecy fulfilled?"

"It turned out that the famine only lasted four days?"

"Correct," said Tertius. "But ever since, Fausta's branch of the family has been obsessed with keeping records. She makes him do it, in case there is ever another famine and they are accused of wasting grain."

"I see," breathed Flavia. Then she frowned. "What's

this?" she said, running her finger over the inscription in the table.

Tertius flushed. "Oh, that. It's just a game. Like a puzzle."

Flavia turned her head. "What does it say? The sower . . . holds . . . the works?"

```
S A T O R
A R E P O
T E N E T
O P E R A
R O T A S
```

"It says 'The sower, Arepo, holds the wheels at work.'"

"What does that mean?"

"It doesn't really mean anything. But if you write it out . . ." He opened a wax tablet, turned it sideways and wrote in tiny neat letters:

S A T O R A R E P O T E N E T O P E R A R O T A S

"It reads the same backwards as it does forwards," said Tertius.

"Oh!" Flavia hopped with excitement. "I know those kind of codes. They have a special name. It's called a . . . a . . ."

"Palindrome," said Tertius.

"I know what that means! It's a Greek word. *Palin* means 'back' and *drome* means 'runs', so it's a word that runs the same way backwards as it does forwards."

"And there are other ways you can play with it," said Tertius. He looked at Flavia thoughtfully. "You're a very bright girl."

"So are you," said Flavia, and then giggled. "Not a bright girl. But you do know a lot for a baker's slave."

Tertius nodded sadly. "I used to be a schoolteacher," he sighed. "Before I fell into debt and had to sell myself into slavery."

"Did you ever teach Pistor's sons?" asked Flavia.

"No," said Tertius. "Though I'd like to. Pelops and Erysichthon are bright boys."

"Who?"

"Oh, those are just my private nicknames for Porcius and Ericius. No," sighed Tertius. "I was never a private tutor. Before they let me go, I used to be schoolmaster at the Forum School."

I'M GLAD I DON'T GO TO THE FORUM SCHOOL, wrote Lupus on his wax tablet.

"Why not?" asked Flavia, taking a cube of white goats' cheese. It was noon and they were having a light lunch back at her house.

Lupus took his brass stylus in his right hand and pretended to bring it down hard on the knuckles of his left.

"They beat you?" asked Jonathan.

Lupus nodded. Then he twisted his own ear and grimaced.

"And they twist your ear?" asked Flavia.

Lupus nodded again and wrote on his tablet:
THEY RECITE EVERYTHING
SO BORING he added.

"Yes," said Flavia glancing at Lupus's tablet. "That's how most children in Italia are taught. We're lucky to have our own tutor."

"Especially one being as nice as Aristo," said Nubia.

"And did Porcius or Ericius pull any bread rolls out of their satchels?" asked Flavia. "Maybe to sell them to their classmates? Or bribe the master not to beat them?"

Lupus shook his head and wrote on the tablet:
NO ROLLS

"So that probably rules out those two," murmured Flavia. "What about you, Nubia? Did Titia notice that you were following her?"

"No," said Nubia. "I and Caudex are very hidden. We follow her to market and then to temple of Venus. Caudex waits outside and I pull palla over my head and go in her behind."

"You mean you went in behind her," Jonathan laughed.

"Yes. Titia gives the lady priest a gift and puts a clay thing on the shrine."

"What clay thing?"

"After Titia leaves I go and quickly look. Behold! It is little clay eyes."

"Oh," said Flavia. "You mean a model of eyes, made of clay?"

Nubia nodded.

"That will be a votive," said Flavia. "A votive is a model of the part of your body you want cured. It reminds the goddess of your prayer."

"Is there something wrong with somebody's eyes?" said Alma, coming into the dining room. She set a platter of bread drizzled with olive oil on the table.

They all reached for a piece and Flavia nodded. "Titia. She has cross eyes and wants to be beautiful to win a husband."

"Oh yes, Titia. The poor thing," said Alma. "Pomegranate juice or barley water?"

"Pomegranate juice, please." As Alma went out Flavia turned back to Nubia. "You said Titia gave the priestess a gift. What was it?"

"I am not certain," said Nubia. "But I think it was small loaf of bread."

They all looked at one another. "A loaf?" asked Flavia. "Not a roll?"

"No," said Nubia. "It was being a loaf."

"What about you, Jonathan? You followed Teneme. Did he run away again?"

"No." Jonathan sighed and spat an olive stone onto his plate. "Teneme just went to the Imperial Granary and stood in a queue and collected a big bag of grain. Then he brought it back to the bakery. He arrived just as you left, Flavia. I saw you and Scuto walking home. Did you find out anything?"

"Not really. I talked to the slave called Tertius. He does the accounts. I found out that Pistor doesn't trust him and has started to check his calculations. But there was one thing . . . I just remembered. It might be a clue."

"What?"

"Tertius is very educated. In fact, he used to be a teacher at the Forum School. He collects puzzles and codes like me, and he's given Porcius and Ericius private nicknames. He calls Porcius Pelops, which makes sense."

"Why?" asked Jonathan. "Who is Pelops?"

"He was an ancient Greek who loved racing chariots," said Flavia. "And we know Porcius is mad for the races so that fits. But Tertius called Ericius something else. Eris-something." She chewed an olive thoughtfully. "Erysichthon. That's it! Now if only I could remember where I saw that name . . ."

Alma came into the dining room with four beakers on a tray.

"You know," said Jonathan, "There are still two people we haven't followed."

Flavia nodded. "Pistor's wife Fausta," she said, "and her slave-girl."

"Oh, my dears, you don't want to follow Fausta," said Alma, setting down the tray and handing out the beakers.

"Why not?" said Flavia, taking a sip of pomegranate juice.

"She's far too preoccupied to steal a dozen bread rolls once a week," said Alma, and then lowered her voice to a scandalized whisper. "It's common knowledge that she and her slave-girl go down to the Forum Baths every afternoon to watch the gladiators work out!"

Flavia stood on tiptoe on her father's table and stretched for the highest shelf.

Nubia looked round nervously. "Flavia. You are not supposed to be reading the Ovid."

"I know," said Flavia, "but I just have to look up one thing. Are you keeping a lookout, boys?"

Jonathan and Lupus each stood in the doorway of the study. Lupus grunted yes.

"Pater or Alma might come home any minute so I need to be quick. If I can just . . . Oh, Pollux!"

A cylindrical leather scroll case tumbled from the top shelf. Nubia caught it deftly in both hands. Then she sneezed; the scroll case was dusty.

"Well caught, Nubia!" Flavia clambered down off the desk. She glanced towards the folding door of the study. "Any sign of Caudex?" she whispered.

"He's in his cubicle," said Jonathan. "I think I can hear him snoring."

Flavia nodded with satisfaction, turned back to the scroll case and lifted off the lid. "Ten. I think it's in scroll ten." Her finger hovered over the open case for a moment and then she pulled out a scroll.

"Ten!" she said, and unrolled it on her father's desk. Nubia watched Flavia expertly twist her hands so that the blocks of writing scrolled past her eyes.

Flavia murmured as she read. "Ugh!" she shuddered as she read one passage.

At last Flavia whispered: "*Eureka*! Here it is: right at the end. I knew it was in Ovid." She glanced around at her friends. "A king named Erysichthon scorned the gods – something you must never do, by the way – and he cut down a sacred tree. He also killed the nymph who lived there, so the goddess Ceres cursed him with a terrible hunger. Listen: 'a desperate craving for food rules his ravenous jaws and his churning stomach . . .'"

Flavia's finger moved down the scroll: "And here: 'His hunger remained untouched and his greed unsatisfied'" Flavia shuddered. "Finally he gets so hungry he devours himself," she said.

Nubia stared at Flavia in horror. "That is a story of Ovid?"

Flavia nodded as she rolled up the scroll and dropped it back into its cylindrical case.

"I'll bet Tertius calls Ericius 'Erysichthon' because he's always hungry." She climbed back up onto the table and replaced the scroll case on the highest shelf.

"Jonathan," she said thoughtfully, as she jumped down off the table again.

"Yes?"

"Do you think your father would mind if I asked him a medical question?"

"Worms," said Mordecai ben Ezra. "Roundworms, tapeworms, whipworms. They are all types of parasites that can make a man ravenously hungry. Other symptoms include coughing, wheezing and vomiting."

"Yes!" cried Flavia. "Ericius coughed a lot. And he doesn't look very well."

"What is parasite?" asked Nubia.

"It's an animal that lives off another animal to survive," said Mordecai.

The girls looked at one another and shuddered.

"Ugh," said Flavia. "I could never be a doctor."

"Why not?" Mordecai smiled at her from beneath his dark turban. "Being a doctor is a lot like being a detective. You have to discover the underlying causes for things that happen."

"I think I have worms," said Jonathan slowly. "I wheeze."

"That's because you have asthma," said Mordecai. "I'm fairly certain you don't have worms."

"But I'm hungry all the time."

"And that's because you're an eleven-year-old boy. Your body is growing faster now than at almost any time in your life. It needs bread to live."

"But how can I tell whether I have worms?"

"Do you really want to know?"

They all nodded.

"After you've been to the latrine, you must take the bucket into bright sunlight and carefully examine your stool."

"My stool?" Jonathan looked puzzled. After a moment understanding dawned in his eyes: "My stool! Ugh!"

Lupus guffawed.

"Yes," said Jonathan's father. "And if you see anything . . . er . . . moving there, well, you probably do have worms."

Flavia looked at Mordecai. "So if I wanted to find out whether Ericius has worms, then I'd have to . . ."

Mordecai nodded. "You'd have to take his latrine bucket and have a good look."

Flavia looked ruefully at her three friends. "I guess," she said, "a detective *does* have to empty latrine buckets after all."

"Yes," said Mordecai, coming into the atrium a few hours later. "I've just been round to Pistor's. I'm afraid young Ericius does have worms. I've prescribed a tincture of pomegranate skins and wormwood, after a three day purge. Poor boy."

"I guess you can't blame him for stealing the bread rolls," said Flavia. "I just hope his father doesn't beat him."

"Oh, he's not your culprit," said Mordecai. "I spoke to him gently and he swore he wasn't the thief."

"And you believed him?" said Jonathan.

"Yes. The poor boy lives in fear of his father."

"Pollux!" muttered Flavia. "If Ericius didn't steal the bread rolls then who in Hades did?"

"Let me have your theories," said Flavia, absently scratching a flea-bite on her forearm. "And remember to give me the motive, means and method. That's what Pliny says in his scroll." They were sitting in the boys' bedroom, the girls on Jonathan's bed, the boys on Lupus's.

Jonathan cleared his throat. "My theory is that Porcius is stealing the bread rolls," he said. "His motive could be to raise enough money so that he can run away to chariot school in Rome. His father obviously wants him to become a baker, not a charioteer."

"That's an excellent motive," said Flavia. "And we know he has the means; he works at the shopfront every morning. But what about his method?"

"I'm not sure," said Jonathan. "Maybe he slips some rolls into his satchel and then sells them to the other boys in his class."

"But remember, it was always a dozen rolls and it's only every seven days."

Jonathan sighed. "I know. That's what I can't figure out."

"Nubia," said Flavia. "Who do you think stole the bread?"

"I think Titia is stealing the bread to give to the lady priest at the temple of Venus. If Titia is giving the lady priest much bread then the god Venus will be favourable to her prayers and make Titia's eyes not crossed any more so she can marry a handsome man."

"Good reasoning," said Flavia. "But again: why every seven days and why a dozen?"

Suddenly Lupus gave a grunt of excitement. *I KNOW WHY XII*, he wrote on his tablet. They all leaned forward eagerly as he wrote: *EACH TRAY FOR ROLLS HOLDS XII*

"Brilliant!" cried Flavia. "Someone could grab a tray and take it. But why just one tray?"

"It's quick!" said Jonathan. "You grab the tray, empty it into a sack or satchel, then put it back."

"And maybe the person's bag holds just about twelve rolls," continued Flavia. She sighed. "That doesn't really help us. Titia could put twelve rolls in her shopping basket but the boys' school satchels could hold about a dozen rolls, too."

Lupus wrote on his tablet: *I THINK TENEME DID IT*

"Motive, means and method," said Flavia briskly. "What motive would he have; why would he steal bread rolls?"

SUPPLIES FOR IF HE RUNS AWAY?

"That's worth considering. But remember, the thefts have been occurring for half a year. If he's been storing up supplies for when he runs away . . . well, some of those rolls will be pretty stale." Flavia sucked a strand of hair which had come unpinned. "And we still come back to that strange clue: why every seven days? I'm certain that's the key to this mystery."

"Tomorrow," said Flavia, "I'd like to post watch on Pistor's bakery again. We'll have to do it before lessons, so we'll need to be up very early." Flavia tore a piece from the last of the special plaited Sabbath loaf. She and Nubia had been invited to eat dinner at Jonathan's and now the four friends were dining with his sister Miriam and his father Mordecai. The six of them sat on floor cushions around a low hexagonal table.

"Tomorrow early?" said Jonathan, with a glance at his father. "I can't tomorrow."

"Why not? The Sabbath is over, isn't it?"

"You know why not."

"No, I don't."

"Flavia," said Mordecai. "Tomorrow is the first day of the week. Jonathan and Miriam and Lupus and I will be celebrating the Lord's supper as we do every week. Some of the other believers on the street will join us."

"I'm sorry," said Flavia. "I forgot you're Christians as well as Jews." She sighed. "Then I guess it's just you and me, Nubia."

That night Flavia couldn't sleep.

She kept thinking of all the mysteries she had solved in her short career as a detective. She thought about the assassin they had exposed in Rome: how his disguise had almost tricked them. She thought about the kidnappers from Pompeii: how the obvious culprit was innocent. She thought about the blacksmith's riddle: how it had turned out to be a secret password.

The night oil-lamp washed the plaster wall with a pale orange light which was swallowed by the shadows above her head.

Presently, to calm her churning thoughts, Flavia closed her eyes and printed the words of Tertius's magic square on an imaginary scroll in her mind. She visualized it as a grid and noticed that the word TENET appeared horizontally as well as vertically, and that there was a pleasing symmetry of letters. That helped. Already she felt her eyelids relaxing.

Next she imagined the black letters were ants, running back and forth across the parchment. She smiled. Now they were forming the palindrome: the sentence which could be read both backwards and forwards. "The sower, Arepo, holds the wheels at work."

What a strange sentence, thought Flavia, but now her body felt heavy and warm; she knew she was drifting into sleep. The letters were moving again, slowly rearranging themselves to form patterns. A circle. A diamond. A cross . . .

Suddenly Flavia was wide awake. She opened her eyes, lifted herself on one elbow and wrote on the wax tablet she always kept beside her bed. The dimly burning night oil-lamp gave her just enough light to see.

"That's it!" she whispered. "I've solved the mystery!"

Nubia did not understand why she and Flavia stood shivering by the shuttered caupona, watching the back door of the bakery. It was cold and damp and it was well before dawn.

Luckily there was a full moon, and although it was low in the west it cast a wash of silver over the deserted streets of Ostia.

"I am so cold," said Nubia. "And sleepy."

"I know," whispered Flavia. "The only time my teeth stop chattering is when I yawn."

"I do not think we should be out at night alone."

"You're absolutely right, Nubia. We shouldn't. We could get kidnapped or murdered. Look! The bakery door is opening!"

A figure moved out of the inky shadows. It was a man in a

hooded cape. He held a flickering oil-lamp. As they watched, he turned towards Ostia's main road, the Decumanus Maximus.

"Come on," hissed Flavia. "Let's follow him."

They slipped out of their protective shadow and moved quietly after him, staying on the pavement close to the shuttered shops. Somewhere in the distance a dog barked. Nubia's heart was pounding but her feet in their leather boots made no sound on the cold stones and no watchdogs nearby barked.

In less than three minutes the man stood before one of the double doors of the Imperial Granary. He glanced around, then knocked softly. The door opened immediately and there was a whispered greeting. Then their culprit slipped inside.

"Pollux!" cursed Flavia under her breath. "We've lost him."

"Behold!" Nubia pointed. "Others come."

The two girls pressed themselves into the black shadows of a doorway and watched two women move quickly across the narrow street. Their pallas covered their heads but Nubia could tell they were poor, perhaps even slaves.

Then another man arrived from the direction of the theatre. The silver moonlight illuminated him, too, and before he slipped inside Nubia saw that he wore the conical hat of a freedman. Next to arrive were a man and woman with three children – presumably a family. The man whispered the password and they disappeared inside. Then all was silent.

"Come on," whispered Flavia after several minutes. "Let's go closer."

The brick walls of the granary were thick enough to keep out fire and damp, and the double wooden doors were heavy, too, but as they stood outside, Nubia could distinctly hear the faint sound of singing.

The moon sank behind the town wall to the west and plunged Ostia into darkness. The girls stood near the double wooden doors, shivering. Inside, the singing had given way to chanting.

"You girls shouldn't be out alone," said a deep voice right behind Flavia.

"Ah!" Flavia and Nubia clutched each other in terror.

The man laughed, stretched out his arm to reach past them and knocked on the door. "Come in out of the cold," he said to them, and to the person who opened the door a few moments later: "The sower, Arepo, holds the wheels at work."

"Welcome, brother Stephanos," said the doorkeeper. "Er . . . and sisters."

Flavia was swept inside with Nubia. She caught a glimpse of a huge dark columned courtyard before the man guided them towards a room on the left.

He pushed open another wooden door and they stepped into a vaulted room, almost bare apart from a few sacks of grain. As they entered, a dozen lamplit faces turned to look at them. Most of the faces relaxed into smiles of welcome and curiosity when they saw the girls, but one face grew pale.

It was the face of the thief.

"How did you know it was me?" Tertius asked them later, as the three of them walked back towards the bakery. The fair-haired slave was holding a sack from the granary, his pretext for being out of the house. In the sack was some of the free grain which would be ground and kneaded and baked into bread for Roman citizens.

"Your magic square was the clue I needed," said Flavia. "The palindrome." Flavia opened her wax tablet and held the clay oil-lamp up to it. "I realized that if you arrange the letters in the shape of a cross, they spell out PATER NOSTER twice with an A and an O left over. Alpha and omega: the beginning and the end."

```
       A          P              O
                  A
                  T
                  E
                  R
   P A T E R N O S T E R
                  O
                  S
                  T
       A          R              O
```

"How do you know about that?" said Tertius. "Do you follow the Way?"

"No, but my friend Jonathan does. They have secret pre-dawn meetings, too."

"Ah! The doctor's son. They're a group of Jewish believers."

"Yes," said Flavia. "Jonathan started to teach me your prayer the other day. The one about the father in heaven giving us bread and forgiving us." She looked at Tertius. "Is Arepo another name for your god?"

He nodded. "It's a secret name for God's son, whom we worship."

"God's son," Flavia repeated. "Stephanos was talking about him after he read from the scroll."

Tertius gave her a shy glance. "Did you like it? Our service, I mean?"

"Yes," said Flavia thoughtfully. "Yes, I did. I didn't understand everything. But that room had a nice feeling. And everybody seemed so happy, even though they were poor."

"And do you see now why I bring a dozen rolls every Sunday? Did you see those little girls' eyes light up when we celebrated the Lord's supper and they each received one of Pistor's finest poppy-seed rolls?"

Flavia nodded, then stopped in the street. Nubia and Tertius stopped, too.

"But Tertius –"

"I know," he interrupted. "I've been stealing and it's wrong. The moment I saw you come in I felt convicted. I knew my God was disappointed in me. I suppose I've been justifying my theft: 'Do not muzzle an ox while it is treading out the grain.'"

"What?"

"Never mind." He shook his head. "You know, some masters give their slaves a few coins, or the odd gift. Pistor doesn't give us anything. Only the lash. But I won't steal the rolls again, Miss Flavia. I promise."

"Good," said Flavia.

"You won't give me away, will you? My master could sell me to the mines of Sicily. Even have me crucified."

Flavia looked at Nubia, who also knew the truth. Jonathan and Lupus would have to be told, too.

But nobody else could know. Not even Aristo.

Flavia sighed at the thought of emptying the latrine bucket for a month and of doing maths instead of reading Ovid. She thought of how smug Aristo would be when she admitted defeat.

But really it didn't matter, because now she knew for certain that she was a detective.

In the dark streets of Ostia, holding her little clay oil-lamp, Flavia Gemina looked up at the slave who stood before her.

"No, Tertius," she said with a smile. "I promise I won't breathe a word."

The Missing Centurion

Anonymous

This story is something of an oddity. I found it in the February 1966 issue of the Edgar Wallace Mystery Magazine, *which had a regular monthly "period piece" feature. Editor Nigel Morland would dig up some long forgotten, rare story from the Victorian era. He cited this story as first published in 1862, but he gave no source for it, neither there nor when he included it in his anthology* Victorian Crime Stories *(1978). I have no idea where this story first appeared and there's part of me that questions its antiquity. It doesn't read quite like the often long-winded and melodramatic stories of the 1860s, but does read like a story someone in the 1960s might produce if trying to write a story from the 1860s. Nevertheless it's an intriguing item, set in Egypt during the days of Domitian, Vespasian's somewhat unbalanced younger son and the successor of Titus. If it really does date from 1862 then it's the earliest crime story with a Roman setting that I have read.*

"How cursedly hot it is," muttered the Centurion Septimius to his lieutenant, grave old Lepidus, as he lay half stripped in the shade of his tent, longing for the Northern wind.

And he might well say so. The place was Syene, the time the month of August, and the almost vertical sun was pouring down his rays with a fierceness such as the Roman officer had never felt before.

Septimius and his cohort had been marched up to Syene to hold in check the inhabitants of the neighbourhood, who, servile in general, and little recking then as now who was their master, provided the taxes were not too heavy, had been stirred up by the priests to a state of most unwonted agitation, in consequence of some insult offered by the Roman soldiery to the sacred animals of the district.

The palm-trees were standing motionless, not a breath stirring their long pendent branches; the broad, swollen Nile was glittering like molten metal as he rolled majestically to the sea. In the background the steep sandy ridges and black crags were baking in the sun, and the only sound that broke the silence was the roar of the distant cataract.

"Curse these Egyptians and their gods," said Septimius. "I only wish I had the bull Apis here to-day, or that lumbering brute Basis which pretty Cleopatra used to worship at Hermonthis and I would see how *he* could stand this weather. I say, Lepidus, a steak cut out of Apis would be a blessed change for us from those eternal scraggy fowls that they feed us on. How snug the fat brute looked in his temple at Memphis. I only wish the Emperor's Centurions were put up half as luxuriously."

"Hush," answered Lepidus, his second in command, "you shouldn't ventilate those free-thinking opinions of yours so openly. Whatever you *think*, keep a check on your tongue, for the old priesthood is jealous and powerful even yet, and strange stories are told of their secret doings."

"A fig for the priesthood! What care I for Apis or Osiris either? I am a Roman citizen and a Roman soldier. I fear no man but my superior officer, and I know no god but the Emperor."

"Mark my words, Antony was a greater man than you, Septimius, and *he* bowed the knee to Apis and Osiris too; why, they say he was consecrated himself, and stood high in the priestly ranks, and yet he crouched like a beaten hound to old Petamon, the priest of Isis, and obeyed his very nod. I have heard strange things of that Petamon; men say he knew the old Egyptian secrets and could raise the very dead from their long sleep to answer him. And his grandson and successor is a mightier enchanter than his sire. It was he that stirred up these poor Egyptian slaves almost to rebellion not ten days ago, because one of the legionaries broke the head of a dirty ape that he caught stealing the stores. They say he is at Philae just now concocting some new plot; so, my good fellow, *do* keep your eyes open and your mouth shut – if you can."

Septimius laughed, half good-naturedly, half contemptuously; and turned in to take a nap, while Lepidus went round the sentries to see that none were sleeping on their posts.

It was evening, the sun had set some half-hour before; and the sky, after melting through all the hues of the rainbow had merged in one delicious violet, in which the clear moon and the planet Venus were shining with a glorious light such as they never attain in duller climes, and throwing long, quivering, silver reflections across the dark waters; the soldiery were preparing for their night's rest, and the country people had already forgotten all their cares in sleep. The silence was broken only by the baying of dogs and the howl of a distant jackal when Septimius, shaking off his drowsiness, left his tent to saunter through the village and see how his troops were faring.

The beauty and stillness of the night tempted him to

extend his ramble. The few dogs he met shrank cowering from before his tall form and the clank of the good sword at his side, and in a few moments he was alone in the desert. He had more than once followed the same track towards the now silent quarries, where the old Egyptians once hewed those blocks of granite which are a wonder to all succeeding ages. When he had marched over the ground once before at the head of his legionaries to check an incursion of one of the marauding desert tribes, the sky seemed brass, the earth iron, the sun was blazing overhead, scorching all colour and life out of the landscape; the heat, reflected from the black basalt and red syenite rocks, had beaten on his armour almost beyond endurance, while his stout soldiers could barely struggle on through the heavy sand, sighing and groaning for one drop of water where none was to be had.

How different it was now; the moon, hanging low in the heavens threw the long black shadows of the craggy rocks over the silvered sand; and the air was deliciously cool and fresh.

So he wandered on till he reached a huge boulder, on which some old Pharaoh, now forgotten, had carved the record of his marches and victories. The figures of gods and kings were half obliterated, but the Centurion stood trying to follow the mouldering lines in idle curiosity.

"Be their gods true or false," muttered he, "they were great men, these Egyptians, and their works are mighty."

As he turned round a huge crag behind him was shaped out by the uncertain moonlight into the figure of a colossus seated on a throne, such as he had seen at Thebes, on his way to Syene, and that so distinctly that he was for a moment fairly startled. Ere long the light changed and the colossus faded away again into an ordinary rock.

From behind the boulder an old man advanced to him, and bowing low, with the cringing servility to which the lower classes of the Egyptians had been reduced by long ages of tyranny, prostrated himself at the feet of the Centurion, and in broken Greek craved a hearing. Septimius was good-natured and at a loss for occupation; he welcomed the interruption, and as he was, like all well-educated men of his time, as well or better acquainted with Greek than with his native tongue, in a few kindly words bade the old man speak on.

"My lord Centurion," said the beggar, "I have followed your steps for days in the hope of obtaining a hearing. My tongue is Greek, but my heart is true. You have heard of the Egyptian priesthood and their wiles; not long ago one of your nation, a Centurion like yourself, fell into their hands, and they hold him captive in the neighbourhood. If you would deliver him come here tomorrow night, and come alone; I will tell you *then* what must be done, but I cannot now – farewell." Then he vanished behind the rocks.

"By Castor and Pollux," muttered Septimius, "it *may* be a trap set for me; yet surely they *dare* not touch a soldier of the Emperor's – a Centurion too," he said. "Ay, poor Claudius vanished a month ago; they said it was a crocodile, but none saw it – yes, it must be Claudius; go I will, let Lepidus say what he likes; but if I tell Lepidus he will have my steps dogged, or some such nonsense. I'll keep my own counsel; I'll go, and go alone." With a brisk step he turned on his heel and headed back to his quarters.

The beggar stood behind the rock, his black eyes glittering with the light of triumph; his long white beard fell off, and the rags dropped from his shoulders as he joined his companion who was lying behind the rock. He drew himself up to his full stature – Petamon, the son of Osorkon, and grandson of Petamon, the High Priest of Isis at Philae.

"Hey, Sheshonk," he said to his subordinate, "I have baited the trap for my eagle right daintily, and the noble bird

shall have his wings clipped ere long. *He* mocks the divine
Apis, does he, and blasphemes the Ape of Thoth! *He* thinks
to come here and lord it over us all with his cursed Roman
pride."

"Well done, Petamon," said Sheshonk, the assistant-
priest, whose low forehead, heavy brow, and sensual lips
were in strange contrast to his companions' face, "what a pity
there is nobody here to listen to you, and that such eloquence
should be thrown away upon me, who know as well as you do
yourself, if the truth were told, that Apis is only a bull after
all, and Thoth's ape is a very dirty troublesome ape; at least
the one I had charge of at Hermopolis was."

"Peace, fool," replied Petamon, "the beasts are but beasts,
that *I* know as well as you: but the beast is only the type of the
divinity, whom the vulgar may not know. Enough."

Next day Septimius was somewhat thoughtful; he retired
early to his tent on the pretence of weariness, and when all
was still he stole out of the town. The hour was the same, but
how different this night was from the last. A tornado had
been blowing from the south all day, raising the sand in huge
clouds, which obscured everything and nearly chocked man
and beast with a penetrating and impalpable dust.

At last he reached the granite boulder, and crouching in its
shade, sat the beggar. He rose as the Centurion approached,
and beckoned him silently to proceed. Septimius obeyed and
followed in silence, plodding through the deep sand. At last
the beggar turned.

"Sir Centurion," he said, "the night is hot and the way
heavy; let me ease you of your sword"; and before Septimius
could remonstrate or resist, his nimble hands had un-
strapped the belt, and slung the sword over his own
shoulder. "What men you Romans are!" he continued
slightly raising his voice as they passed along a narrow track
between high rocks on either side. "You fear nothing in

heaven or on earth. I verily believe you would *make beef-steaks of the Divine Apis*"; and he halted full in the way and seemed to grow before the Centurion's eyes.

The Centurion recoiled, and at the same moment two from each side, four strange white figures, each with the head of a hawk, surmounted by the disc of the sun, glided forth and laid hands on him. Septimius struggled like a snared lion; he threatened them with the wrath of the Emperor, and they answered with mocking laughter. He made one furious rush at the beggar who had betrayed him, and clutched him by the robe. Petamon quietly threw the sword far away over the sand and crossed his arms, while his allies advanced to the rescue. The prisoner was torn away, but not before he had rent off a fragment of the priest's robes, which fell upon the sand. His good sword was gone far beyond his reach, and he was bound and lashed to a rude litter which was brought from behind the rock. The four mysterious phantoms silently raised the litter and bore it across the sands, while Petamon, with a vigour remarkable in one so far advanced in years, led the way.

They had advanced along the sandy tract for some distance when suddenly the eye of Septimius who could just raise his head and look forward by straining painfully against his bonds, caught the glimmer of the moonlight on the water, and before him rose a most unearthly, beautiful scene.

In the midst of a quiet lagoon lay the Sacred Island, Philae, girt in by hills on whose rugged sides the black rocks were piled in the most magnificent confusion – a green spot in the midst of a desert of stone – and, amid the Grove of Palms upon its shore, rose the roofs of temples and the tops of huge pyramidal gateways, while the solemn moonlight poured over all. A boat, manned by four more of the strange hawk-headed beings, was anchored at the shore. Silently the priest embarked, silently Septimius was lifted on board, silently the rowers bent to their oars, and in a few minutes they were passing along under the massy wall which rises sheer out of the water on the western side.

Suddenly the boat stopped and the Priest struck the wall thrice. Silently a portion of the wall swung back and disclosed a narrow stair, up which they carried the Centurion; and by a side door entered the outer court. Before them rose a huge gateway, on each of whose towers was carved the giant semblance of a conqueror grasping with his left hand a group of captives by the hair, while he lifts the right to strike the death-blow. They hurried on through the great Hall of Pillars up a narrow stair, and, opening a small aperture, more like a window than a door, thrust in the Centurion, and left him, bound hand and foot, to his own reflections.

Next morning Lepidus was early astir, and, after going his rounds, entered the tent of Septimius. It was empty, the bed had not been slept on, and there were no signs whatever of the tenant. "Mad boy," muttered Lepidus, "off on some frolic as usual. I must hush it up, or Septimius, great though his family interest be, will get a rough welcome from the General on our return. I must say he is sick. He gives me more trouble than the whole cohort put together, and yet I love the lad for his merry face and his kindly smile."

Noonday and evening came and went, and still Septimius was absent; and next morning, Lepidus, blaming himself much for having delayed so long, gave the alarm that the Centurion had vanished or been spirited away, and instituted a regular inquiry. Little information could be elicited. One of the sentries had noticed Septimius wandering away towards the desert but he was too much accustomed to his officer's little vagaries to take much note of the fact. Doubt and gloom hung over all, for the Centurion, rash as he was, was a brave leader and a kindly, cheerful man. Parties were detached to search the neighbourhood in every direction, and Lepidus could only sit and wait for information, chafing inwardly at every moment's delay.

Towards evening one of the sergeants craved an audience of him, and when they were alone together produced the Centurion's sword and a piece of a heavy golden fringe. He had struck into the desert, come upon a spot where there were evident marks of a struggle, and picked up the sword and torn fringe lying on the ground. Sergeant and officer looked at each other, and the same fear clouded the faces of both.

"Petamon is at Philae?" inquired Lepidus.

"He is, sir."

"Then may Jove the Preserver help the boy, for he will need all his help. I see it now: his foolish scoffs at the gods have reached the ears of the priest, who has hated us Romans bitterly for long, and he has kidnapped the lad. We may be too late to save him. Muster the men at once and let us to Philae – *quick*!"

In half an hour the cohort were tramping through the sand under the still moonlight, and an hour more brought them to the banks of the quiet river. There was no boat, and they had to halt till morning broke.

At sunrise a boat was brought from the neighbouring village and Lepidus, embarking with a portion of his troop, was rowed over to the Sacred Island. He landed at a flight of steps on the northern side, and mounting them, halted, giving the quick imperative, "In the name of the Emperor." Soon a band of priests, headed by Petamon himself, appeared at the great gateway, and the Centurion, advancing briefly demanded to speak with their High Priest.

Petamon, with the rising sun flashing on his leopard-skin cloak and the golden fringe of his girdle, with his head and

beard close shaven, in his linen garments and papyrus
sandals, stepped forward.

"I am Petamon, the grandson of Petamon, High Priest of
Isis. Roman soldier, speak on."

"I seek," commenced Lepidus; but he stopped abruptly.
His eye had caught the glitter of the golden fringe, and he
saw that at one side a piece had been torn away. He sprang
forwards, and grasped the priest's throat. "Petamon, I arrest
you on the charge of kidnapping a Roman citizen. In the
name of Caesar Domitian. Soldiers, secure him!"

Priests and soldiers stood for a moment transfixed with
amazement while Lepidus released his grasp on the priest's
throat, and they stood face to face till the Roman almost
quailed before the fierce glare of the Egyptian's eye. The
other priests began to press forwards with threatening gestures; they outnumbered the Romans three times, and,
though the strength and discipline of the latter would have
proved victorious in the end, might have offered a stout
resistance; but Petamon motioned them back. "Fear not,
children," he said, speaking in the Greek tongue, so that
both parties might understand him, "the gods can protect
their own, and *you*, Sir Roman, that have laid hands on the
servant of Isis, *tremble*!" He walked forwards and surrendered himself to two of the soldiers.

"Rather him than me," muttered Sheshonk. "The gods
are all very well to fool the people with, but I doubt if Isis
herself will save him under the Roman rods."

Petamon raised his eyes and met those of Sheshonk. A few
words in the Egyptian tongue and Sheshonk, with a deep
obeisance retired into the temple and disappeared.

The soldiers were despatched to search the island, and
Septimius heard them several times pass the door of his
prison, but his gaolers had thrust a gag into his mouth, so he
could give no alarm. He lay there sick at heart.

The search was fruitless, as Lepidus had expected; and he commanded Petamon again to be brought before him. "Sir Priest," he said, "I seek Septimius the Centurion, who is or was in your hands; unless he is restored before tomorrow's sun sinks in the west you die the death."

"It is well," said the priest, while the mock submission of his attitude was belied by his eye; "the gods can protect their own."

Towards evening Petamon requested an audience of Lepidus, and when they were again together addressed him with more civility than he had hitherto condescended to use. He explained that it was the practice that the High Priest should, at certain seasons, sleep in the sacred recesses of the temple, and have the decrees of the goddess revealed to him in visions. He craved permission to perform this sacred duty; it might be for the last time. Lepidus mused for a moment and then gave orders that the priest, chained between two soldiers, should have leave to sleep where he would.

The night closed in; the shrine of the goddess was illuminated; and the blaze of a hundred lamps flashed on the rich colours and quaint designs on the walls of the shrine. Before the altar stood Sheshonk, burning incense, while Petamon, chained between his guards, bowed for a time in prayer. By midnight the ceremony was over; Petamon, chained to a soldier on each side, lay down before the altar; the lights, all but one, were extinguished; the great door of the sacred chamber was closed. Lepidus lay down across it with his drawn sword in his hand, and soon fell asleep.

The sun was bright when he awoke and, hastily rising, gave orders to change the guard upon the prisoner, and himself entered the chamber to see that the fetters were properly secured. The lamp was burning dimly, and there lay the two soldiers: but *where* was the prisoner? He was gone – utterly gone. The fetters were there, but Petamon had vanished. Lepidus gave one of his soldiers an angry kick; the man neither stirred nor groaned; he snatched up the lamp and threw its rays upon the soldier's face. It was white and still, and a small stream of blood, which had flowed from a wound over the heart, told too plain a tale. It was the same with the other.

Perplexed beyond measure, Lepidus hastily roused the cohort. It was some minutes before he could get them to comprehend what had happened; and even then the men followed him most unwillingly as he snatched up a torch and hurried back. To his amazement the corpses of the soldiers were gone, and in their place lay two rams newly slaughtered, and bound with palm ropes; the fetters had also vanished. Shuddering and horror-stricken, he left the chamber, followed by the soldiers; and, as he passed out of the temple, met Sheshonk in his priestly robes going in to perform the morning services.

A panic seized the soldiery, in which Lepidus more than half concurred. They were men, they said; why fight against the gods? In half an hour they had left Philae and were marching through the desert to Syene, with weary steps, under the already scorching sun.

Terrified though he was at this tragedy, Lepidus was too honest to abandon the quest. The soldiers refused to assist further in the search, and he was left almost to his own resources. After much thought he published a proclamation in Egyptian and Greek offering a thousand pieces of gold for the Centurion, if alive; five hundred for the conviction of his murderers, if dead; and five hundred more for the head of the priest, Petamon; and threatening the last penalty of the law on all men detaining the Roman a prisoner or sheltering his murderers.

His hopes were faint, but he could do no more; and having despatched a full report of the whole case to the Roman general at Alexandria, he waited, impatiently enough, his heart sickened with alternate hopes and fears.

During the next few days he was much disturbed by the sentiments of disaffection which he heard being muttered among the soldiers. Like all ignorant men they were superstitious, the events which had occurred at Philae had produced a deep impression on their minds, and they murmured almost openly at Lepidus.

This feeling was much increased by an old beggar-man who constantly haunted the camp. He had attracted the attention of the soldiers by some ordinary tricks of magic and was constantly telling fortunes and reciting prophecies all foreboding evil to the cohort if it stayed in the neighbourhood; and, indeed, foretelling the speedy and utter downfall of the Roman power.

Lepidus ordered the beggar to be brought before him, and when he came taxed him with attempting to incite the soldiers to mutiny, and sternly reminded him that the punishment for such an attempt was death. The old man listened quietly and calmly, crossing his arms and fixing his glittering eye, which seemed strangely familiar to Lepidus on the Roman officer.

After a pause he spoke – "My lord," and again the tone struck Lepidus as familiar to his ear, "I serve the gods, and you the Emperor: let us both serve our masters truly. You would have news of Septimius the Centurion? It may be that the gods will permit you to see a vision: shall it be so?"

A curl of contempt was on the Roman's lips as he answered:

"You know the proclamation. I am prepared to fulfil its terms."

The old man shook himself like an awakening lion, and again the gesture struck Lepidus as familiar.

"I seek not gold," he said; "give me your attention, and keep the gold for those that need it."

"It is well," said Lepidus; "proceed."

A small stove was burning in the tent; the old man cast upon the charcoal some drugs that raised a dense smoke, and filled the tent with a heavy perfumed smell.

"Look!" said the old man, pointing to the smoke; and retiring behind Lepidus he crouched upon the ground.

A circle of light formed itself clearly and well defined among the smoke, and in its midst Lepidus suddenly saw the image of the bull Apis, as he had seen him once before in Memphis, with all his gorgeous scarlet and gold trappings, and the golden disc between his horns. A moment and the image suddenly grew smaller and smaller, and vanished from the eyes of the wondering Roman.

Again the circle formed, and this time he saw the Centurion Septimius sitting at his tent door, and, stranger still, he saw himself in converse with him.

But suddenly, whether it was the perfumes or the excitement that overcame him he never knew, but the circle of light, the old man, the tent spun round and round, and he sank fainting to the ground.

When he awoke from his swoon the stove was burnt out, the old man was gone, and he hardly knew whether he had been dreaming or not. He felt dull and heavy and could scarcely rise. His servant entered with a light. He glanced at his finger, on which he wore his signet-ring, with which all important despatches must be sealed, and which marked their authenticity – it was gone. He felt in his bosom for the secret orders which the general had entrusted to him rather than to the headlong Septimius – they were gone too.

Back in Philae – on the fifth day after Lepidus so hurriedly left it – Septimius was still alive. A scanty allowance of bread and water was daily furnished him and his bonds had been somewhat loosed, but he had not seen the light of day since his capture, and his heart sank within him in hopeless despondency. Release seemed impossible, rescue hopeless. He could see no way out of his calamities, but by death. He had never seen or spoken to any one since his capture; invisible were the hands that had relaxed his bonds, and invisible the attendants who supplied his daily food.

Petamon had been stirring here, there, and everywhere, rousing priests and people, reminding them of old wrongs and old memories, and urging them to join in one strong effort, and expel the Roman despots.

The news of Lepidus' proclamation had just reached the Island of Philae. It was the turn of Sheshonk to officiate at the altar of Isis, and, while the incense was burning, he stood for a few moments wrapped in deep thought.

"Petamon is crafty and wise," so his meditations ran; "but Rome is strong, and we can never resist her. Better swim with the flood of the river and release that Centurion – and the gold, ay, the gold! – and the wrath of the gods, what of that? I have helped the trickery here for so many years that I hardly know whether there be gods at all. Petamon believes in them; but I am not Petamon. The gold is my god."

The evening closed, the night was half spent, and Petamon, who had been away all day had not returned, when Sheshonk stole silently up the stair with a bundle under his arm, and, touching the spring, entered the dungeon of Septimius. The Centurion enquired in a languid voice who it was.

"A friend," whispered Sheshonk. "Hush, Sir Centurion, and hearken. Lepidus, your second in command, has offered a thousand pieces of gold for your safe return; do you confirm the offer?"

"Ay, and add a thousand to it," answered the Centurion.

"I have an old father in Rome, who values his son at that sum ten times told."

"Good," said the priest. "Petamon seeks your life and in a few days will take it; you cannot be worse than you are, therefore, you can lose nothing by trusting me – will you do so?"

"I will," said the Centurion.

A knife was drawn across the cords which bound him, and he stretched his limbs. Cautiously the priest struck a light with flint and steel and lighted a small lantern, after which he produced from his bundle a pair of huge hawks' heads, surmounted by the disc of the sun, with great glass eyes, and a pair of white disguises, such as the original captors of Septimius had worn. The Centurion eyed them and muttering to himself, "So much for the hawk demons," proceeded to array himself in the disguise, while Sheshonk did the same. This accomplished the priest opened the door and they cautiously descended the stair. They met a young priest, but at a whispered word from Sheshonk he bowed and passed them by. They entered a small chamber on the west side; the priest touched a mark on the floor, and a trapdoor opened at their feet, showing a dark stair. Down this they made their way, the priest stopping for a moment to draw a heavy bolt on the under side of the trap-door to impede pursuit. After some time the Centurion heard a rushing of water above him, the passage grew damper and damper, and the priest in a whisper explained that they were passing under the bed of the river. In a little while they again ascended a high flight of steps, another trap-door opened at the touch of Sheshonk, and they emerged in a small temple on the island of Snem. The priest silently opened the door, and they stole out.

The moon had set and the night was almost dark. Cautiously picking their steps they crossed the island, and found at the other side a small skiff lying at anchor, and two swarthy Nubian rowers in attendance; a few words passed between them and Sheshonk. "We must wait," he said, "till the day breaks; they dare not pass the cataract by night. Sleep if you can, and I will watch."

Septimius was too glad of the permission; he had slept but ill in his dungeon, and, taking off the heavy mask, he buried his head in his garments and fell fast asleep.

In a few hours the morning broke, and ere the sun was risen Sheshonk and Septimius were on board the boat. The rowers pulled stoutly at their oars, and they soon neared the cataract, whose roar became louder as they advanced. Before them lay a stretch of the river, fenced in on either hand with desolate rocky hills; here, there, everywhere, in the course of the stream jutted out the heads of black rocks, round which the water foamed and raced like the stream of a mill dam. The Centurion shut his eyes and held his breath; the current caught them; they were hurried helplessly along for a moment, stern foremost, and were on the point of being dashed upon a rock, when a dexterous stroke of one of the oars righted them: a rush – a tumult of waters – dashing spray and the roar of the current for a moment, then the boat floated again in calm water and the danger was past.

In a few moments they reached the Roman encampment. The Nubians, at a word from Sheshonk, pulled away up the stream, while the two hawk-headed ones hurried through the camp, to the no small wonderment of several drowsy sentries.

Lepidus was just awakening with the weary disheartened feelings of one who dreads impending misfortune, when the flap of his tent-door was thrown back, and the sleepy officer fancied he must still be dreaming when he saw a strange hawk-headed phantom rush into the room.

It was no phantom, for it hugged him close in his arms,

and a voice – the voice of Septimius – issued, hollow sounding, from the depths of the mask:

"Dear old Lepidus. I never thought to see your face again."

There was little time for greetings and congratulations. Sheshonk was urgent on them to complete their work and the legionaries, their fears dispelled by the reappearance of the young Centurion, hastened again across the desert to Philae, burning so hotly to wipe out the insult that had been offered to the Roman name that they never felt the sun.

Several boats were lying at the shore, and while Lepidus with the main body of the men made for the stairs upon the northern side, Septimius and a few chosen followers, under the guidance of Sheshonk, crept along under the western wall in a small boat and reached the secret door. It opened obedient to the touch of the priest, and silently they mounted the stair – they met the other party in the great Hall of Columns; the island seemed deserted – no living thing was to be seen.

Sheshonk's eye twinkled.

"Five hundred golden pieces for Petamon's head!"

"Ay, and five hundred more," said Septimius.

The priest beckoned them on. They entered the sacred chamber where Petamon had kept his vigil on that memorable night, and Lepidus half shuddered as he looked round at the familiar paintings on the wall. The altar was prepared and the fire burning on it. The priest advanced and set his foot heavily on one side of the step in front. Suddenly altar and step, solid though they seemed, rolled away noiselessly to one side, disclosing a passage beneath. The Romans leapt down, Lepidus hastily lighting a torch at the altar fire as they did so. The passage led them to a small room in the thickness of the wall, and throwing in the light of his torch, he saw the arms and accoutrements of the two murdered soldiers, and the fetters that had bound Petamon lying in a corner. Here the passage apparently terminated abruptly, but the priest raised a stone in the roof with his hand, and they crept up through the narrow aperture thus opened, and upon She-shonk touching another spring, a square aperture opened, through which they glided into a chamber, and gladly hailed the light of day as it glimmered faintly through the door.

They searched the whole temple, but in vain; secret chambers they found more than one; even the dungeon of Septimius was opened, but nothing was discovered, and even the bloodhound sagacity of Sheshonk seemed for a moment at fault.

But his eye soon brightened, and he led them through the court under the high painted pillars, and opening a door in one of the sides of the pyramidal gateway, proceeded up a long narrow stair. Suddenly a rustle of garments was heard above them, and they caught sight of the robes of Petamon, his leopard-skin cloak and his golden fringe, as he fled before them. The two Romans dashed after him like greyhounds on a hare, but as they reached the top of the staircase Septimius stumbled and fell, and so checked the pursuit for an instant. He recovered himself, but in that instant Petamon, casting back on his pursuers a glance of baffled malignity sprang from the tower, and in another moment lay, dashed upon the pavement of the hall.

The soldiers and Sheshonk, horror-struck hastened down, and were standing beside the body – Lepidus had just recovered from the finger of the priest the signet-ring that he had lost, and was in the act of drawing the roll of secret orders from his bosom – Sheshonk had raised his head-dress and was wiping the perspiration from his brow, when from aloft a sharp dagger was hurled with unerring aim. It cleft the skull of the traitor, and he fell, with scarcely a groan, on the top of Petamon's corpse.

The Romans looked up: no one was to be seen. With a party of soldiers they searched the huge gateway towers, but without a guide such a quest was hopeless, and they never traced the hand from which the dagger came.

Their main object was accomplished. Petamon was dead, and with him expired all chances of a revolutionary outbreak. Sheshonk was dead too; but as Lepidus said, *that* saved the good gold pieces.

The same evening they returned to Syene, and next day the camp was broken up, and the cohort embanked on the river and floated down to rejoin the garrison at Memphis.

In six months Septimius and Lepidus left Egypt for good, and when they were fairly out of sight of land they seemed to breathe more freely.

"I owe you many a good turn, Lepidus, old boy," said the Centurion; "but I'll never admit, to the end of time, that Apis would not have made splendid beefsteaks."

"Whoever said he wouldn't?" retorted the other, his grim features relaxing into a smile; "only I think it would need a braver man than either you or I to eat them under the nose of old Petamon."

The wind began to freshen, and the ship headed to the deep sea, and towards home.

Some Unpublished
Correspondence of the Younger Pliny

Darrell Schweitzer

Tragically for the Flavian emperors, under whose rule it started so promisingly with Vespasian, it ended all too familiarly with the reign of terror of Domitian's final years. But thankfully better days were to come and after the brief reign of the elderly Nerva, Trajan became emperor. He would be both popular and successful. Trajan was great friends with the lawyer and writer Pliny the Younger (AD 61–112), the nephew of the elder Pliny, who had died during the eruption of Vesuvius. Many of Pliny's writings survive, including ten volumes of Letters, *the last of which is his correspondence with Trajan during Pliny's governorship of Bithynia. No doubt there was even more correspondence lost over the years and in the following story Darrell Schweitzer, who is better known as a writer of fantasy fiction but who has a passion for the Roman world, rediscovers one such sequence of letters.*

1. Pliny to the Emperor Trajan

I have written to you previously, Sir, about my encounter in
Bithynia with persons vulgarly called "Christians", and have
gratefully received your advice on how such criminals are to
be dealt with, which ones are to be spared, and which offered
up to punishment.

I discovered, in the course of my investigations, as I have
previously mentioned, that these persons comprise a degen-
erate cult carried to ridiculous lengths, but that through the
moderating influence of the law, many persons might be
reformed and directed back to the correct worship of our
gods.

The affair has, however, had a kind of sequel. If I may
trouble you again with a long description of these matters, I
would like to describe the case of a young girl, which seems
to press beyond the bounds of the practical guidelines you
have given me. If I were the right kind of poet I would find
here the material for a tragedy, dealing as it does with the
themes of young lovers and love lost, of conflict between a
father and his child, the delicate balance between justice and
compassion, and the mysteries of the world of the dead.

I shall not waste your time with fancies, however. You,
who bear on your shoulders the responsibility for nothing
less than the welfare of all mankind, will doubtless want to
know only the facts . . .

2. Trajan to Pliny

Before you departed on your mission, my dear Pliny, I took
you aside and requested that you write to me whenever you
felt the impulse to do so, not merely in an official capacity

dealing with finances and waterworks, but as a friend might to another friend, to share the experience of his journey with another who is far away and cannot see and hear what he himself sees and hears.

3. Pliny to Trajan

. . . I proceeded from Nicomedia to the shore of the Euxine Sea, and there my party followed the road through one town after the other, staying at the homes of prominent citizens, dealing with such matters as might need to be dealt with. I am accompanied, as you know, by two very capable men, both of whom you met at least briefly before I departed from Rome. They are my Greek physician, a freedman called Arpocras, a wise and inquisitive fellow, whom I fondly call, when he is not within hearing, Little Aristotle, for, like that philosopher he inquires into all things tirelessly; and, secondly, my assistant Servilius Pudens, a Roman knight of unquestionable reliability and loyalty. This Pudens is, however, of a more choleric disposition, easily excited, and quick to leap to conclusions, but sensible enough (especially when moderated by Arpocras's cooler judgments) not to *act* upon his conclusions until he is more certain of them. I call the pair – when both are out of earshot – my two crows, for their frequent arguments may sound like strident squawking, but in fact they share a kind of philosophical discourse.

It happened on that afternoon when we arrived at Heracleia Pontica, as these two (who shared the carriage with me) were in the middle of some furious sparring-match about which of the heroes of the Trojan War had journeys through these regions in ages past, and whether or not the local monuments to this or that legendary person were of merit or merely a means for the locals to beguile a few coppers out of the gullible traveller . . . as this well-chewed-over argument drifted somewhere between comedy and tedium, sufficient to distract me for the moment from the documents I was glancing through . . . at this juncture a runner from the town approached and announced that he was a servant of one L. Catius Magnus, who most earnestly desired that we dine with him that night.

"Well, I shall be glad to be free of the dust of the road, and other discomforts," said Arpocras, rolling his eyes towards Servilius Pudens.

"*I?* I am classified as a discomfort? I am a hardship of the journey?" said Pudens, mortified, as if he were about to leap out of the carriage and stalk all the way back to Rome, which is an absurdity, because the over-large, ever-sweating Pudens would hardly have lasted a mile in the heat. But this was for show, as always. Their friendship is never threatened by such displays.

"We could afford to relax and spend a pleasant evening," I said.

Arpocras's gaunt – and indeed crow-like – features narrowed, and he spoke in a low voice. "I think there is more than relaxation here. This Catius Magnus seems a trifle over-eager to make our acquaintance."

"It's obvious enough," said Pudens. "He wants to be seen entertaining the Emperor's own representative, to make himself seem more important. It's a great way to impress the natives."

"I don't deny that, friend Pudens. Nevertheless, I think there is more to it than that."

"Indeed, we shall see," I said, in the tone of a judge, hoping to make peace between them, for, indeed, I was weary from the journey, my head had begun to ache, and just now I was not in a humour to be amused by two squawking crows.

It turned out that Lucius Catius Magnus offered us every

possible comfort. He stood at the doorway of his house as our company approached. Indeed, we must have looked to the locals like an invading army, possibly a hundred persons in all, myself, my staff, servants, many carriages and wagons, and a troop of mounted guards bringing up the rear. All were accommodated. The soldiers and most of the servants camped in a vacant space nearby. Catius Magnus, perceptively discerning that Arpocras and Pudens were more than mere functionaries, invited the three of us to bathe and dine with him.

So the hours passed pleasantly enough. After bathing, we strolled in the cool evening breeze beneath a colonnade, at the edge of a vineyard. The scenery was extremely attractive. I could almost imagine myself back in Italy, gazing out, not over the Euxine, but the Bay of Neapolis towards Capreae. This Magnus had made every effort to transplant a bit of home, here in Bithynia, or, perhaps I should put it, to make at least a patch of this foreign soil truly Roman.

Magnus himself turned out to be a man somewhat younger than myself, about thirty-five, the twice-great grandson of a soldier who had served with Pompey and helped colonize the area when he retired. The family had prospered through investments and trade. By the standards, at least, of a provincial town, they had grown great. Magnus, like his father and grandfather before him, was a member of the local senate. His family held several priesthoods. He himself officiated over regular sacrifices to the gods, to the Emperor's genius, and also to the spirit of the Divine Augustus, whose small temple the local senators maintained at their own expense.

Magnus went on in this vein – gods, sacrifices, rites, loyalty – for more than I thought ordinary. It piqued my curiosity. Indeed, when, over dinner, I exchanged a glance with my ever-alert Arpocras, he seemed to reply wordlessly, *Ah, we near the heart of the matter.*

Pudens winked. When he is impatient, one side of his face twitches in an odd way.

So we came to the heart of it, suddenly. Imagine some mishap in the theatre and an actor's mask suddenly falls off. There is his face, revealed, dismayed, and he has no secrets any more.

Catius Magnus interrupted his own small-talk.

"Sir," he burst out, "the reason I've brought you here, what I'm really after . . . is mercy . . . mercy for my only child, my beloved daughter Catia . . ."

"*What?*" exclaimed Pudens, who sounded as if he'd nearly choked.

Arpocras and I exchanged knowing glances.

I bade Catius Magnus explain, trying to be reassuring in my manner. He was almost unmanned by whatever troubled him, close to tears.

Explain he did, somewhat incoherently, though this was, of course, an educated and articulate man. Yes, he had a daughter. I had seen her briefly when we entered the house, a pretty girl of fourteen or fifteen, who had bowed to me demurely, then been led away with apparent haste by two large serving-women. At the time I had wondered if the girl might be ill. Now it was clear.

The girl was, or professed to be, despite her father's every effort to dissuade her, one of "those of Christ", called "Chrestianoi" by the vulgar provincials. She had been led into this vice by a servant – who had since been disposed of – a lewd woman who acted as pander between the headstrong Catia and her lover, one Charicles, son of Damon. Now Catius Magnus knew Damon slightly through his business, a respectable enough fellow, a grain merchant, pious enough in his observances of the gods. Prejudice aside, the match might not have been impossible. True, Damon and his son were not even Roman citizens, but Greeks – and when this was mentioned, my good Arpocras shot me an offended glance, as if to say, *And what is wrong with that?*

Otherwise young Charicles was handsome and pleasant, and his family was rich. Not impossible, though he could be nearly as wild as the girl.

So Charicles and Catia became lovers in secret, and in secret descended into much more serious matters. They became Christians. Using various deceits, with the full connivance of Catia's servant, they secreted themselves, night after night, to a necropolis outside the city, where they participated in the abominable rites of the *Chrestianoi*. The leader of the cult seemed to be some awesome personage, a thaumaturge called the Masked One, who promised, among other things, that his followers would live forever in the flesh and need never fear death. This presumably would allow them to continue in carnal rites until the end of time, when their dead Christ would also rise from the dead, return to them, cast down the gods and rule the world.

"Of course . . . of course . . ." Catius Magnus was almost too beside himself to continue speaking. "It is *complete rubbish*. I knew it. Damon knew it –"

"Damon knew it?" Arpocras asked.

"Yes, yes. He did. *As one father to another*, he came to me. He asked *my* help. He was as appalled as I . . ."

"I should think," interrupted Pudens, "that a father would be able to control his daughter, and another – even if he is a Greek –"

Arpocras cleared his throat irritably. Pudens continued.

"– even if he is a Greek, would be able to control his son."

"Have you any children, sir?" Catius said with surprising sharpness. It put Pudens off his balance.

"No, I don't."

I waved my hand dismissively, and Pudens said nothing

more. To Catius Magnus I said, "Nor do I. Friend Arpocras has two sons, who are far away. But I think we understand –"

"Can you, sir? Can you really? Can you appreciate how a father's love for his child might come into conflict with his duty?"

"Duty must prevail," I said quietly.

"Indeed, sir, it must. Damon and I resolved to do our duty. I ordered my daughter kept under close watch. I got rid of the evil serving-woman. Damon was going to send his son away on a *very* long trading trip away north somewhere – across the sea, wherever they get amber. It seemed like a good idea at the time. But then your instructions were published –"

"I was but repeating those of the Emperor himself, who graciously advised me," I said.

"Of course. Caesar's guidelines cannot be questioned. And, I assure you, none of the local officials did question them. That was Damon's grief. It broke his heart. It killed him well before his time."

"Killed him?" Arpocras asked, "How?"

I could sense the man's true grief, his own fear, his confusion, his desire to fulfil his duty as a Roman citizen, and he had only my deepest sympathy. Here was a man who would do, I was sure, the brave and correct thing at the end.

"It killed him, by the failure of his heart, when the police began to inquire after Christians, and, far from attempting to hide his guilt, the young fool Charicles proclaimed his allegiance openly. He even named Catia as a fellow conspirator. He laughed at the judges, claiming that he had no fear of them at all, because death could not touch him, that if they killed him, he would be resurrected immediately. Now, shocking as all of this was, we couldn't quite put it out of our minds that this was one of our neighbours, a child who had played in our streets, who might yet be saved if properly guided. Damon wept and got down on his knees, begging his son to repent. Others enjoined him. I did. But in the end I had to try to save my daughter. She shrieked like a fury when brought into the court, clawing at the women who restrained her. That, I think, inadvertently helped, because I was able to convince the judges that she was mad. In the end, though, Charicles was crucified, and Damon, with a dignity that would befit even a Roman, merely announced that he would retire to his house and not emerge again. He died within a few days."

There was a long pause. Night had long since fallen. Within the house, we were shielded from both city noises and those of nature. Silence prevailed, in the gathering dark. A servant entered the room, offering to refill everyone's wine cups, but was waved away.

Pudens, large and corpulent fellow as he is, squirmed uneasily as he reclined. The couch creaked.

"A truly terrible story," I said at last, "but I don't see how *I* can actually help you. The girl is under no legal judgment, having been declared insane. Perhaps Arpocras, who is very learned in the medicines of the Greeks, can prepare a potion to calm her mind."

"Thank you," said Catius Magnus. "Thank you . . ." For a moment he seemed too emotionally exhausted to say much more. But then he rallied. "I fear . . . what I am truly afraid of . . . is that this matter is *not over*. Nothing is over with. The Masked One of the *Chrestianoi* still haunts the night. Some of his followers have been caught, but they will not give up his secret. My daughter would tell nothing, even –"

"There are ways, you know," Pudens said, "to get anybody to confess anything."

"Gods!" exclaimed Arpocras. With one savage look he shut up Pudens. I could only concur. We were hardly going to ask Catius Magnus to torture his own daughter!

It took some persuading to get him to continue, but at last I got the extraordinary heart of the story out of him.

"The matter is not over," he said, "not merely because some masked criminal is still on the loose, *but because his promises have turned out to be true. His followers can indeed transcend death. I know this is so. The boy Charicles has come back from the dead and I myself have seen him!*"

Now *that*, I confess, put even me at a loss. I believe there are such things as ghosts. I had a long discussion with Licinius Sura on the matter once. Both of us knew many stories. The one about the philosopher Athenodorus renting the haunted house, wherein he discovered and laid to rest a chained spirit, is rather famous. But *what*, I could only ask myself, was I, as an Imperial representative charged with legal and financial investigations, supposed to do? I wasn't sure I had any jurisdiction over ghosts.

It was Arpocras who came to my rescue, who cut his way through the dark clouds of superstition which were gathered all about us.

"What, exactly, did you see, sir?"

"First I *heard*. The servants told me that the girl was talking to someone in the night, calling out in the darkness. The servants were terrified. They thought she was summoning demons. I thought, alas, that she really was mad, and it wasn't just a convenient plea to save her life for a time. But to be sure I stood by the door to her chamber one night – and I heard her call out, addressing her beloved Charicles – and, incredible though this may seem, I heard the boy reply. I recognized the voice. It *was* Charicles."

"But you didn't see him?"

"Oh, I saw. He said he would return again when the moon was dark. I don't know what that means. Perhaps the *Chrestianoi* fear the Moon Goddess. Anyway, I said nothing to my daughter, but noted how as the time of the dark of the

Moon approached, she grew calmer, but more anxious, as if *expectant*. This time I did what might sound a little ridiculous. I climbed up on the roof of our house. There I was above my daughter's room. Her window looks out over the sheds and stables by our wall, into the street, where there is a broad space at the edge of a few trees, with a stone bench. You've seen the place.

"On the appointed night, then, with all the servants in their rooms at my orders, I watched from the roof. My daughter came to the window right below me. She called out something I couldn't quite make out, some kind of prayer or incantation, and *Charicles* answered. Her words then were of joy, of how much she loved him and wanted to be with him. He promised that she would be soon, despite anything her 'cruel jailer' – meaning me – could possibly do about it, because the power of the Masked One was greater than that of the whole Empire or even the gods. 'How can I know this?' says she. 'Please, give me some proof?' 'Isn't your faith strong enough, even after all we've been through?' 'I am afraid,' says she. 'I am weak. Please.' She wept piteously, and Charicles assented. '*Look at me, Catia. Do you not recognize me?*' There was a light over among those trees, as if someone had uncovered a lantern, and there *sitting on the bench* was the youth Charicles. He looked – though of course it was hard to tell under the circumstances – pale and *strange* in a way I could not quite define. But it was Charicles, all right. He raised his hand.

"At that point Catia let out a cry, and I was so startled, I admit, that I nearly lost my grip on the roof. I slipped. A couple of loose tiles crashed into the paved yard below, and the light among the trees went out. By the time I could clamber down and summon a couple of manservants, and we could get outside to those trees, we found only the empty bench. There was no sign that anyone had been there."

"No sign?" said Arpocras.

"What would you expect? We didn't find the lantern."

"How was your daughter?" I asked.

"The nurse found her on the floor. She had fallen into a swoon, which became a delirium, from which she has only imperfectly recovered."

"How long ago was this?"

"But two nights before you arrived in the city."

Again I wondered how I, who am trained as a lawyer and to some extent as an engineer, could be of any particular assistance. It continued to seem more a matter for a physician – or a priest.

Catius Magnus looked at me, helplessly.

"Couldn't you . . . make up some document . . . declaring her to be innocent because of her illness, now and into the future?"

I explained that no law can absolve someone for a crime they may commit in the future.

"Then I have no hope," said Catius Magnus. "It may take years, but this will destroy my daughter. As long as she thinks her boy is alive – as long as he *is alive* – she will believe in the magic of the *Chrestianoi*. I can only restrain her for so long. When she grows up, as an adult woman . . . perhaps after I am gone . . . she will continue to proclaim her adherence to these cultists. And she will have to be punished, as the Emperor's guidelines have clearly laid down. She will not recant, I am certain of that. So what am I to do? I can only pray uselessly to the gods, and mourn."

Again there was a moment of awkward silence, and again it was my indispensable Arpocras who saved us.

"I think we can help, sir. I think we can look into this."

I saw that for once he and Pudens were of one mind. I didn't let on that *I* was the one who didn't quite follow.

So we remained for several days as the guests of Catius

Magnus. His daughter was kept out of sight. I inquired once of the serving women, and they said that "The Mistress" was sleeping calmly. There was no other mistress in this house, as Magnus's wife had died some years before and he had not remarried.

But she couldn't sleep all the time, could she, even if drugged? Sooner or later she would get into more trouble. I appreciated my host's dilemma.

Nevertheless, I kept myself occupied with official business. The financial records of Heraclia Pontica were in arrears, like those of so many others in this province. There were the usual improprieties, an aqueduct that cost three times as much as it should, a theatre that never seemed to be finished . . .

It was Arpocras who made more intimate inquiries. He asked to see the girl, and said that he found her awake, not at all delirious, but closely guarded by muscular women the size of small oxen, and the look on her face was one of absolute, venomous hatred for him and for all of us.

He went out into the town and asked certain questions.

One afternoon he deposited a small lump of matter on my desk.

"What is that?"

"Wax, sir."

"So it is. What of it?"

"I found it on the bench across the street, by the trees."

"I confess I don't see the significance."

"If someone used the kind of lantern which has a candle in it, as opposed to an oil-lamp, it might leave such droppings."

"So? I am sure many of the citizens possess such lanterns."

"But I do not think they use them while sitting on that bench in the middle of the night."

"Perhaps that is so –"

"It means that someone was actually there, sir, as Catius Magnus reported."

"I didn't think he was lying. You don't mean –?"

"No, sir, I don't," he said, at his most inscrutable.

What we finally decided to do, following a suggestion which came, inevitably, from Arpocras, and to which I assented, was to attend one of the midnight orgies of the *Chrestianoi*. This was the only way to gain the answers we needed, and to bring our host's agony to an end.

It raised a tactical problem. It hadn't been too hard for Arpocras to learn when and roughly where the cultists met. It was an open secret among the lower orders of the town. Some dreaded these meetings as the manifestations of demons, which would bring plague and doom on us all. Others anticipated them. It seemed that the infection was quite widespread . . . and all too many believed the impossible, apocalyptic – a term the *Chrestianoi* used – prophecies of the Masked One. I had to admit that these were not at all like the beliefs of the criminals over whose trials I had presided at Nicomedia, but what respectable Roman can possibly know much about these strange matters? Is it possible that there are differing factions and even various nations of *Chrestianoi* right before our eyes, invisible to all but fellow believers?

But I drift from my theme. The immediate problem was how to attend the meeting without giving alarm. We tried, one last time, to convince the girl to cooperate.

She spat in Arpocras's face.

"You can kill me," she said, "but I will not betray them. I am not afraid of you."

Arpocras, showing a manner I had never before seen in him, yanked the girl's head back by the hair, held a small knife to her throat, and said, "We'll see how fearless you really are."

"Go ahead. I will rise again . . . as Charicles has risen and *you never will.*"

"It's useless, Arpocras," I said.

He let her go and put his knife away. He sighed. "Yes, it is. But I have something here which is not." He revealed a small, stopped phial, which he set on a tabletop.

The two muscular serving-women held the girl Catia firmly while Arpocras forced her mouth open.

"Would you open that for me, please?" he said to Pudens, indicating the phial. Pudens opened it, and, as the Greek nodded, poured the contents down the girl's throat. He held his hand over her nose and mouth, and, struggle though she might, she eventually swallowed.

Her father looked away.

"She is not harmed," said Arpocras. "The potion will merely make her docile. She is unlikely to speak, but if she did, her words would be slurred, as if she were drunk. But if we guide her, she will be able to walk, and if we arrive in her company, and are not ourselves recognized, perhaps it will be enough." He looked at me, as if to say wordlessly, *It's the best I could come up with.*

It would have to do. All there was left for us to do was to disguise ourselves. Arpocras wore a Greek cloak. Catius Magnus, Pudens, and I wore the plain togas of citizens, but without the stripes of a senator or a knight, which might attract too much attention. That the clothing we donned was not entirely clean was for the best.

We draped our togas up over our heads, like hoods, to hide our faces. We could only hope that perhaps the *Chrestianoi* maintained this custom of covering the head when at religious services . . . in any case, luck was with us. It looked like it was going to rain. It was a dark, windy, overcast night.

At the time appointed, we made our way, the girl between us, with her either arm held by Pudens and her father, out of the city of the living, into the city of the dead. There among the many tombs – some of them alleged to be of Homeric heroes; I could imagine Arpocras and Pudens chattering about them under happier circumstances – we waited, seated on a flat stone. We had with us a lantern with a candle inside it, but kept it covered.

I felt a little spray of rain on my face. The night was, indeed, turning foul. A storm approached from across the sea. The air started to turn cold. I saw that the girl Catia's teeth were chattering, even though the expression on her face was completely blank. She stared forward, into nothing.

But it was by following her gaze that I saw the first sign. A cloaked, furtive shape moved among the tombs. Then there was another, and another. They were all around us. I fancied for a second that we had been overwhelmed and surrounded by some army of beasts, something that crawled up out of the earth or out of graves.

Someone whistled. Someone else began to play, very faintly, on a flute.

"We cannot conceal ourselves," whispered Arpocras.

We stood up, Catius Magnus and Pudens holding the girl, Arpocras holding the covered lantern under his cloak.

There were little outcries of surprise, but then the cultists – for so they were, ordinary men and women and even a few children, all of the meaner sort – saw that the girl was with us, and this soothed them.

They parted before us and bade us proceed, and so we did proceed into a low area, where running water had cut away part of a hillside, and some of the tombs seemed about ready to tumble down on our heads. Far away, lightning flashed. Thunder came a while after. The rain was more than spray now, light, but persistent. I will admit that I was afraid, that every superstitious fear which we try to banish away by philosophy and reason came washing back over me like a tide. I feared the wrath of Hecate, absurd as that seemed. I feared hungry, angry ghosts, and the demons of the *Chres-*

tianoi, who might well reach up through the muddy earth and pull me down into that underworld of fire and torment the *Chrestianoi* supposedly believe in.

We proceeded to the mouth of a cave, where a rude tent had been set up, as if to extend the cave mouth out among the tombs. There the *Chrestianoi* seated themselves, on stones or on the bare ground. Some food and wine was passed around. I had heard of this from the prisoners at Nicomedia, the "love feast" of the Christ-followers. It was hardly a feast. We all took a few mouthfuls of whatever was offered, and pretended to give some to the girl Catia, who sat among us as if she had walked in her sleep.

Someone got out – strange as it may seem – a small wooden cross, and reminded those assembled of Christ, who had died on a cross and risen again. Prayers and chants followed, as if to a god. My companions and I mumbled and pretended to follow along. I noticed, to my alarm, that the girl was actually mouthing the words.

Then someone cried out, "Behold! Our prophet comes and brings with him the martyr who has been resurrected!"

There was a flash, like lightning, but *inside the cave*. I don't know what it was, but I smelled a foul, sulphurous smoke. I didn't have time to consider the matter further, because there, illuminated by two uncovered lanterns at the back of the cave, stood the infamous Masked One, who wore a beaten silver mask fashioned like the rising sun – that is, the rays spread out from the sides and the top, but not the bottom, giving it the overall shape of a fan. He wore a black robe. I couldn't see his hands. Either closely-fitting gloves covered them or he had painted his hands black. The effect was to make the mask seem to float in the air.

Then he began to speak, in a loud, resonant voice.

"I, the foremost disciple of the risen and true Christ, of Jesus of Nazareth, who died, as you know, in Judea in the time of Tiberius, but rose again – and I say to you that on the night he rose he came to *my house* to tell me, first of all those he loved, that he had indeed risen; and he bade me go forth into the world and continue his work, raising up our believers from out of their graves, so that they might never die. I was his *most* intimate friend, the only one to whom he revealed *all* his secrets. Those others who claim to have the truth have but part of it. To me *alone* he revealed the mysteries of the inner light, which is in all of us and in all things, which shines through the flesh and will never die. He said to me, *Lo, I am as the risen sun in glory*.

"Now there is one among us here tonight who has suffered a great loss, whose heart has been torn by the seeming murder of one she loved –"

All eyes turned to us, and to the girl. I froze. Pudens and Catius Magnus looked terrified. Arpocras seemed as expressionless as some ancient, grim statue.

The girl struggled and moaned.

"Yes," said the Masked One, "I can offer you another glimpse of your beloved Charicles. He cannot yet lie in your arms, my dear, for the path back from death is long and hard. Every day I must accompany him for a time on his journey. But you may see him again. Look –"

Another lantern was uncovered. A dark curtain was drawn aside, and there, seated in a niche of stone was a young man, naked but for a strip of cloth about his loins. I could see that he had indeed been crucified. The horrible wounds on his wrists and feet were not healed. His eyes were open. His expression was completely blank. Did anyone else notice that his bare chest did not rise and fall, that he was not breathing?

Did anyone? There were exclamations. The girl writhed and began to moan. The congregation shouted prayers and thanks to their god.

Then the boy began to speak, or at least someone spoke. It

was hard to tell. The sound echoed strangely in the little cave.

"*Catia*," came the voice, "*I long for you. I am coming back to you, my love. Soon we will be in one another's arms for ever and ever, and no one can ever separate us –*"

Did *anyone* notice? Yes, my faithful Arpocras did. Once again we exchanged glances. I gave a signal.

Then many things were happening all at once. The girl broke away from her captors, and staggered forwards, screaming. The massive Pudens lumbered forwards like a maddened bull and tackled the Masked One, who went down with an audible crunch. Now everyone was screaming. The cultists swarmed over me, wrestling with me as I got out a clay whistle I wore around my neck and blew on its as hard as I could.

Arpocras uncovered his lantern, and light filled the cave. I saw Pudens on top of the still-struggling Masked One, while cultists scrambled over him, like, indeed, dogs attacking a bull in the arena.

Behind him the corpse of the boy Charicles – for corpse it was – toppled out of its niche.

Lightning flashed. Someone hauled me to the ground. Several more swarmed over me, pushing my face down into the mud. I gasped. I was drowning. Then there came thunder, hoofbeats, and the *Chrestianoi* released me and tried to scatter.

There were shouts and screams among the tombs, but soldiers burst out everywhere, and I do not think very many of the culprits escaped.

I stood up, sputtering, as Catius Magnus held onto his sobbing daughter, and forced her to look long and hard at the Masked One, who without his mask was an ordinary, bearded man, his features distorted by pain from a broken leg. And likewise he made her gaze upon the nearly naked corpse of the unfortunate, fanatic Charicles, which Pudens had dragged out into the rain, into the clear light of reason and Arpocras's lantern.

Subsequent investigations, Emperor, were by more orthodox means. It was soon discovered that this Masked One was a Hellenized Egyptian, whose Greek name was Lysimachus. He had become notorious as a fraud and swindler in Alexandria, where he used sleight of hand and various trick effects – indeed he had the ability to disguise his voice or even cast it elsewhere, so that an invisible spirit might seem to be speaking out of the air. Thus he had relieved the gullible Alexandrians of their money until he was finally uncovered and driven away. He fled, then, to his native district in the heart of Egypt, where he consorted with all manner of magicians and scoundrels. He learned from the priests there *some of the secrets of preserving corpses*, at which the Egyptians are so adept. Again, his reputation caught up with him, so he made his way to Asia, appearing in Bithynia under a variety of assumed names, and presenting himself to his followers in a mask, claiming that his face was too holy to look upon and that he was an actual contemporary of Jesus – which would make him more than a hundred years old, unaged and (so he asserted) immortal.

This much I learned mostly from him during his interrogation, after which he proved quite mortal when I had him executed.

Therefore I am writing to you, sir, to assure you that *this time* the pestilence of *Chrestianoi* has been eradicated, and that the people of Heracleia Pontica are returning in great numbers to the worship of the gods. Sacrifices are offered, as is proper, before your statue and those of your deified predecessors.

I write, too, to ask of you one more thing, a boon perhaps, though hardly a trivial favour, or even anything for myself.

You have instructed me to describe things to you as a friend might, when corresponding with another, not merely as an official reporting to his Emperor. So I have. But as a friend, then, I dare to ask your advice. You have always said to me, "I trust you implicitly. Use your own judgment." But what if I no longer quite trust my own judgment? Catius Magnus is a good and loyal man, and a responsible father. According to the law, as laid down by your own instructions, the girl Catia, who, despite everything, persists in proclaiming herself a Christian, should pay the penalty. But this seems unduly cruel to the father, who would suffer much grief. He has already lost his wife, whom he greatly loved, and he has only this girl, however disordered her mind may be, however outrageous her behaviour, to remind him of her.

Is there any way she may be spared, even if she must be kept under close watch by her father, so that she may not spread her abominable beliefs to others?

4. Trajan to Pliny

Yes, you may spare the girl, because she has clearly departed from reason, and insane people are not to be held entirely liable for their acts. Furthermore it is good to reward the loyalty of Catius Magnus and to spare him further grief.

5. Pliny to Trajan

Sir, before I left Heracleia Pontica to proceed to Amastris, I gave the news of your merciful decision to Catius Magnus, who was moved to tears of joy and thanksgiving.

I am sorry to report that the girl herself is still insane, though Arpocras holds some hope for her eventual cure.

When, in the company of her father, I went to bring the news to the girl herself, she had to be restrained by the two muscular serving-women. Her face was distorted with rage and hatred such as I have never before seen in one so young.

She began to rave and prophesy. She said that one day the *Chrestianoi* would rule the world, that even emperors would bow down before the dead Jesus, and the gods of our country would be overthrown and forgotten, their images broken up into bits and powder.

I repeated to her that her variously named Masked One was a fraud and criminal, who used trickery to deceive, and that her lover was not resurrected. Even now he lay in his family's tomb, beside his father, the virtuous Damon.

Again she spat and cursed, and announced, amazingly, that she didn't care about Lysimachus anymore. She knew he was a liar. (On this Arpocras hangs his hope of her recovery, for her reason is not entirely absent.) Indeed she felt no sympathy for him at all.

"He will burn in Hell," she said, "along with all unbelievers and others like him —" Here she used a word I did not know. "– like all *heretics*."

I can tell you that he burned as he left this world. I ordered his body cremated and his ashes scattered. He did not rise again.

A Golden Opportunity

Jean Davidson

Probably the one emperor we all remember in the years after Nero is Hadrian, and that's because of the remarkable Wall that he commanded be constructed across the north of Britain in AD 122. That is the time of the following story, which takes place at the Roman fort of Isca, known today as Caerleon in South Wales, and was inspired by a recent visit made by the author.

"I was just sweeping through the frigidarium – I always does that last, see, once the duty soldiers have lit the boilers, on account of –"

"Yes, yes, get to the point of it, man." Centurion Brutus twitched his vine stick impatiently at Antheses. The janitor responded by looking at Legate Julius Publius for his nod before continuing.

"Well, as I said, the boilers was stoked up for the morning and I'd cleaned and mopped all through when I saw it."

All eyes followed his dramatically pointing finger to where the stone drain cover had been moved aside. Beside it lay the thick forearm of a man with the hand still attached. Julius noted that the skin was mottled and that the cut had been neatly done.

"Where exactly was the arm when you found it?" he asked.

"Inside the hypocaust. See, I saw straight off the cover'd been moved, 'cos I swept the dirty water through it earlier myself. So I took a look – saw something down there, reached down and pulled this out."

Centurion Brutus grunted and poked at the arm with a sandalled foot. Julius swallowed, still not inured to such sights despite his twenty years of military service. But he hid his weakness.

"You're sure the cover was on when you went through to the caldarium." Julius thought the man might be lying to cover up for his own slipshod-ness.

"'Course! It was all tidy. I didn't hear nothing neither. Well, I was singing, if you must know. Nice echo in them warm rooms."

"How long was this room empty?"

Antheses looked shifty. "'Bout five minutes – maybe ten. I'm thorough, see, not like some of the others. You can rely on me."

"That's enough wasting the Legate's time," Brutus ordered. "If you've nothing else to tell him, get on your way."

"But that's just it. I do have something to say. It's the arm, see." Everyone obediently looked again. "I'd know it any-where. It belongs to old Faustinius."

"Do you want a spell in gaol?" Brutus growled. "I'm severely tempted to lock you up and throw away the key."

"No, no." Antheses wasn't cowed by the threat, Julius noted. He was sure of his ground. "It's the ring he's wearing, see. I recognized it straight away. His personal seal, the eagle engraved on garnet and made of Silurian gold. Very nice, high quality. And if you look inside, you'll see his and his wife's initials."

*   *   *

Julius had ordered everyone else to leave and stood alone in the frigidarium with Brutus. He gazed around at the high vaulted ceiling, the pillared alcoves, the fine mosaics and stone washstands.

"As fine a baths as I've seen this side of Rome," he said.

"And the swimming pool's a good length. You can get a good workout there and in the gymnasium after. If every soldier went in twice a day they'd be at peak fitness. But they've grown soft and lazy, idling about without any action."

"Then make up a roster for increased exercise."

Brutus' brown eyes gleamed with satisfaction. "The men will be brought up to battle readiness. Even though we've had no orders as such?"

"It would take a strong man to shift that drain cover." Julius deliberately did not respond on the subject of future orders. "And I'd guess Antheses was gone a good fifteen to twenty minutes – he was lying about that."

"Or two men working together."

"Hmmm. A conspiracy?"

Brutus frowned. Was the Legate making fun of him?

"I *am* interested in your opinion. You've been here at Isca how long – a year? I've only just arrived. Anything I should know?"

Brutus hesitated then shook his head. "Nothing beyond the usual thieving, gambling and fights you get in a barracks this size. With upwards of five thousand men you're bound to get wrongdoers but we've dealt accordingly – firm but fair. Roman justice."

"The janitor's accent is execrable but his Latin is good. Is he Silurian? Could he have done this?"

Brutus snorted. "No, sir. Antheses is a liar and a cheat but he hasn't the guts for murder, in my opinion. He's from Londinium originally, I believe. No doubt on the run from something."

"Otherwise why end up here in the west on the very borders of civilization. Exactly. Tell me about our victim, if it really is him. After all anyone could have put that ring on the hand – Faustinius himself, if he wanted to flee and delay our finding him gone, for example."

"Import–export. Brings – or brought – supplies up the river Isca from the coast or from Venta Silurum. An older man. A family man. Very successful."

Brutus waited while Julius paced. This was something he could do without. A test of his leadership when he'd only just arrived. Deliberate, perhaps. Could news of his secret orders from Emperor Hadrian have leaked out already?

"First, have your men search the bathhouse and gymnasium to see if the rest of the body is anywhere about. Then move this and anything else you may find to the hospital. After that the ritual purification will have to take place before the bathhouse can revert to normal use again. I will inform Faustinius's family and have the ring confirmed as his, if possible.

"Get to it, then."

Brutus saluted, though Julius sensed again some hesitation, but then he turned and went to carry out his orders.

It was June, a bright summer's day. Although it had been raining when Julius arrived at his new posting a week ago, today only a few white clouds graced the deep blue sky and the day was becoming warm. On his arrival the rounded hills had looked black and misty. Now he saw only lush greenness and an abundance of different types of trees and bushes.

Standing on the fort ramparts looking towards the amphitheatre he strove to catch a glimpse of the river, but the land the fort was built on was too flat and low lying. Not as beautiful as his native hills north of Rome but more to his liking than the dark forests of Germany, where he'd also been Legate of a key fort.

He strode on, absent-mindedly acknowledging the salutes of men coming to attention as he passed. Modestina, his wife, always teased him about the way he liked to walk the perimeter every day: "Surveying your kingdom," she'd say, eyes gleaming, sometimes an invitation to more teasing and perhaps a return to their bedroom together.

Hiding a private smile he continued on more briskly. She was making the best of their move as always, settling the children in at the school and asking no questions. Not that he had any answers. Why had he been chosen for this posting? Tempting to think it was because someone believed he was the best man for the job. But what job? Rome had lived peacefully with the Silurians and other local tribes here in Britain for many years. No, he'd been expecting to be brought back to Rome. Perhaps put up for public service in public works or building, as he'd trained as an engineer when young. Then start looking for a retirement villa with a good stock of vines.

Well, better men than he had come to grief from questioning why. It was better to get on with the job. And now this. The matter of the dead man had to be resolved fast. Not just because he had to show strength and make his mark within the camp but also because of his special orders, due to be opened in three days' time.

Faustinius was a merchant, so greed was a likely motive. Or perhaps he'd double-crossed someone and this was their revenge. A reward might yield up a name, but it could also be used for settling a grudge so he decided not to post one. He regretted he'd not had the opportunity to meet Faustinius himself, but the man had been travelling on business until last night.

He saw that he was almost back at headquarters at the

centre of the fort and the good humour left his face. Now he'd have to deal with Lucan, his second in command. The boy's patrician family was closer to the Emperor than his own and he clearly thought he was above "playing soldiers" as he called it, serving out his time till his recall to the Senate. Well, they were a long way from Rome here and it was he, Julius, who was in charge.

Lucan was lounging in Julius's chair and moved languidly out of the way, yawning. "I hear old Faustinius has breathed his last, a matter for rejoicing I'd say. His prices were scandalous and he didn't let any competition near the fort. He also leaves a lovely widow."

Julius raised a neutral eyebrow. "On the take, was he? I didn't read that in any of the reports."

The young man flushed pink. His skin was baby smooth, his hair fair and silky. "I didn't write those reports, did I?"

"I haven't been able to find fault with the inventory and our stores are fully stocked – not even a case of all left sandals and no right ones. I'm told he was responsible for fulfilling the army's orders. Did you deal with him personally?"

"Me? Hardly." The boy flushed even more and Julius pressed him harder.

"But you knew his wife."

"You could hardly miss her. There's not a man in Isca who hasn't a soft spot for Sahia. It's true I met her socially – not the sort of parties I'd normally attend, but life can be pretty dull here – but that's as far as it went. We were friends."

"Then you'd better come with me to offer our sympathies and to find out more. Maybe the grieving widow will confide in you, her friend."

Together with a detail of soldiers and slaves they left the fort and went among the houses that lay just outside. Lucan led the way to a small, neat home in the style of a Roman villa and built of the highest quality materials. Faustinius's widow, Sahia, had clearly been an exquisitely beautiful young woman. Even though she was becoming fat, her features blurring, the beauty was still there. Lucan had told him she was a freed slave from Egypt whom the merchant had subsequently married and they had three surviving children. Her distress seemed genuine to Julius.

"My Fausti was good man. He was strong, take good care of his family, he don't look at other women. What will we do without him?" She broke down, weeping again. Rings flashed on her fingers, Silurian gold bracelets covered her wrists.

"Look at this." Julius held out the ring taken from the severed arm. "Can you confirm this was your husband's?" He had not told her yet that the body was not intact and hoped gossip would spare her that knowledge until the rest of it had been found.

She uncovered her dark lustrous eyes, nodded, then broke into fresh tears. "He chose the eagle because it soars so high. Such a powerful bird. Oh, I want to kiss him farewell. When can I –"

"Later," Julius said firmly. "When we have carried out our official duties. Tell me again about what happened since his return."

His question distracted her. "He came home last night – such high spirits, so many presents for me and the children. He said the ships bring many good things and give him good prices. Oh, such a reunion . . ." She sighed, recollected herself. "He left me early this morning – very busy, he said, so much to do."

Of course, Julius thought, the merchant would be delighted with the extra orders of shoes, weaponry, and uniforms that he, Julius, had placed to be ready for whatever his secret orders might be. "Did he tell you he was going for a swim at the bathhouse?"

She frowned and shook her head. "No. My Fausti did not swim. He went to the baths, yes, but at the end of the day to talk to his friends, or sometimes lunchtime. Is that where –?"

"Sahia, think carefully, did he say if he was going to meet someone? Did he talk about any enemies he had?" Lucan asked.

She held out her hands to him and he took them, then she shook her head and closed her eyes, overcome by a great weariness. The ritual wailing of the slaves filled the sudden quiet.

"We have to search your house," Lucan said. "Do we have your permission? We may find helpful information in your husband's papers and records." When she'd given her assent Lucan added under his breath to Julius, "No doubt we'll find some sordid secret or evidence of his cheating ways."

"I would not have been able to restrain myself," Modestina declared. "You've such self-control, Julius."

"It was difficult when I felt like punching his snooty little face, but there are plenty of enemies around without having them among my officers as well."

"Enemies a-plenty there too at times – here, try this honeycake. These local bees make wonderful honey."

They were eating lunch together, enjoying the breeze as it had become a hot sunny day again. Julius had told his wife that he felt satisfied that he'd inspected and investigated every inch of Isca Fort and its personnel. "I don't like to speak ill of my predecessor but he was too easy-going for my taste. Repairs not done, training and exercise schedules not kept to. At least the barracks' supplies of tunics, sandals, and arms are all up to date, thanks to the dead man, Faustinius."

"So you don't think he was fiddling the inventory?"

"Not that I could see." They had brought their own slaves and servants with them and felt confident enough of their loyalty to speak openly in front of them as they served wine and food. "Nor is there any sign of the rest of his body. The bathhouse and now the entire fort has been thoroughly searched."

"It amazes me that there wasn't a great pool of blood."

"He was killed somewhere else, but for some obscure reason only the arm was hidden in the underground heating system."

"Unless the whole body was brought and he or they didn't have time to hide it all. But then surely someone would have seen it being carried? It was light very early today."

"And only a few hours of darkness, with it being the longest day of the year." Julius shook his head. "I've asked Centurion Brutus to find out if any of the guards were bribed to silence." He finished his wine and stood up. "Prince Ceryth of the Silures is arriving in only a few hours' time for our first meeting. Bad timing for me."

"The banquet preparations are complete."

"I've decided I will tell him but will make light of it — better that than his hearing exaggerated rumours. The last thing we need is for him to sense weakness here."

Unspoken between them lay the matter of his secret orders from Emperor Hadrian.

Antheses hummed happily to himself as he made his way to Faustinius's villa. He'd made himself wait until the coast was clear of Legates, Centurions and other officials but could contain himself no longer. He pressed his hand against his belt pouch — yes, the ring was still there. It'd been easy to slip into the Legate's office while he was out and palm it while pretending he'd been called for an interview.

The evening sun was casting long shadows. This morning's excitement had died down, though he couldn't say the normal lazy rhythm had been restored to Isca. This new

Legate was a stickler for drill and exercise, as well as cleaning and repairing. The soldiers were grumbling twice as much as usual. Antheses was suspicious about his sudden arrival. The Emperor would hardly send someone just to improve the housekeeping. Still, he wasn't complaining, extra work meant extra denarii.

He didn't waste time trying to enter at the front door but went round to the slaves' quarters. Robinia was busy, bending over a vat of washing. He grabbed her from behind and she gave a satisfying squeal, then slapped his arm good-humouredly.

"Creeping up behind me like that – you nearly made my soul leave my body." Robinia had been captured from the Silurians and enslaved when a baby and had now converted to a peculiar new religion called Christians. She often came out with strange phrases and Antheses played along with her. "Such a terrible day," she sighed now. "He was a good master, as masters go – though I only have one true Master"

"And a wily old devil when it came to business," Antheses interrupted her, not wanting another lecture on her religion. "Did they tell you it was me who found him or, rather," he lowered his voice and told her in juicy detail of his discovery. She covered her mouth in horror then made the sign of the cross.

"My poor mistress, how can she bear it?"

"She doesn't know the full story yet. And you can help her – I've brought her a memento from him that might cheer her up. Do you think you could get me in to see her? It won't be the first time I've carried messages from Faustinius to her."

Robinia's face brightened. "Oh, if only you could lift her load a little. I'll see what I can do." She gave him a sisterly hug.

Sahia was lying on a couch, eyelids and lips swollen from

weeping. The light had left her dark eyes and she could barely lift her head.

"What is it, Antheses?"

He still thought her the most beautiful woman he'd ever seen.

"I bring you my deepest sympathy, lady, and a gift."

She heaved a sigh. "You were a good friend to Fausti. He often said so. What is the gift?"

Antheses rolled his eyes and she understood, gesturing for the slaves to leave the room. She forced herself upright. He held out his hand, the ring lying in his palm. Her expression softened.

"His favourite ring." She lifted it up. "Garnet stone with an eagle in full flight and our initials carved on the gold. I identified it yesterday Antheses, I know he was not – whole. Who could do such a thing?"

"Faustinius was a powerful man," Antheses jumped in quickly before the tears started again. "Other men were jealous. He confided in me, you know." He leaned forwards. "There is another package, yes? I expected there to be one more today."

"Another package?" Sahia was wary.

"Yes – you know the sort, looks like an amphora of olive oil buried in straw, but underneath – well, let's just say, special goods. Let me act as your husband's courier once more. You don't want that stuff lying about in case they come back and search your house again. I don't want you getting any awkward questions. It wouldn't be fair."

"My husband told me you'd been helpful, but not in what way. Sahi, he used to say, you leave the business to me. I take care of you. He was true paterfamilias. But I know he had a special consignment of oil in his office. He said it was a gift – to oil the wheels, he said. But you say it's not oil. Maybe I should look."

"Of course, lady, it's yours – look all you like. Only I'd worry for you. Might be safer to do as Faustinius said and stay ignorant. For the sake of the children. Not that he was up to anything wrong, but you know what these Roman laws are like – anything to send back money to Rome. I say we should keep some of it here. Leave it to me, and I'll make sure there's some more of that," he nodded at the ring, "to come your way."

She closed her hand on the ring and held it to her heart. "Thank you, Antheses. You only want to help me. I will tell Robinia to have the package transported to your house as a reward for bringing me this ring. And Antheses – there will be more rewards if you find his killer."

Antheses' blood stirred at the sudden fire in her eyes. He was bowing low to take his leave when they were startled by shouts and hoofbeats in the street outside.

Huge flies buzzed over the round boat constructed of woven willow laths and tanned animal skin which had been drawn up on the shingle strand. Julius heard their buzzing before he saw them and so prepared himself for the stench.

"Who found the coracle?" he asked.

Lucan looked at Centurion Brutus, who replied, "Silurian fishermen, sir. It was a good mile downstream, caught up on some branches."

Julius approached cautiously. One glance inside was enough to reveal the rest of Faustinius, further dismembered and drained of colour. His head was covered by a cloth.

"Fishermen covered him up. Said his eyes were staring." Julius glanced at the Silurian fishermen who were watching intently. Their flowing hair and moustaches and rough tunics or trousers were no longer strange to him after his meeting with their leader, Ceryth.

"Have you looked? Is it definitely Faustinius?"

"Yes, sir," Brutus said. "I identified him myself."

"Arrange to have this transported to join his arm at the hospital, will you, and I want the surgeon to tell me how he actually died, if he can. If he was dead before these cuts, as we must hope."

"Sir – in my opinion his throat was cut and his blood drained. Look how pale he is. His blood was taken from him."

Stillness settled over the riverbank. Even the horses became motionless. Brutus had said something very significant, but Julius did not know what, so he decided it would be safer to overlook it for now.

Stepping forwards he spoke through an interpreter, thanking the Silurians for bringing the body to Isca. They were not hostile, yet they seemed stirred up by something, and spoke amongst themselves in their strange lilting tongue.

"They say they are not to blame. They want your assurance you will tell Prince Ceryth they did not do this."

"You may give them my assurance."

As they walked away from the river Julius said, "Well, Lucan, what was that all about?"

"It's said that that is the way their priests – wild men called Druids – carry out their sacrifices. Others say that they never made human sacrifice but only worshipped trees and rivers."

"And what do you say?"

Lucan shrugged. "I've never come across one. In fact, I thought they'd all disappeared up north to some little island called Mona since we outlawed the region."

"Brutus must have some knowledge of them. He wouldn't have mentioned it unless there was cause for concern."

"It's the time of year. Yesterday was the longest day. Apparently they need the blood of a man to influence the moon and the sun, or some such nonsense. So I've been told.

But those days are long gone. Silurians worship Roman gods now."

"Indeed. And Prince Ceryth gave every sign of wanting to continue our current position when we met yesterday. If it is Druids, they must be acting on their own. We can only hope they don't have many followers." Julius hid his worry. He could not afford to leave Isca exposed when the Emperor's orders were revealed. With only one day to go before then, he must resolve this matter speedily.

"Julius, did you hear me?" Modestina's voice was concerned rather than accusatory. "Your thoughts must be very full."

Julius laid his hand over his wife's for an instant. "I can't get the sight of that coracle out of my mind. I've seen plenty of bodies in my time, but the smell – well."

"But it's more than that," Modestina observed. "Finding the rest of the body has not helped you, has it?"

"You're right. It's not only having to give the terrible news to his widow but – I've looked at it every way and it's inescapable – I think Brutus may be right. This could be the work of those forbidden priests of nature. The Druids."

"Which means possible confrontation with Ceryth."

"He seemed a reasonable man at our first meeting but if it is the Druids, his tribe must have helped them in this to get access to Isca. Either he's going to defend his people, whoever they may be, and risk conflict with me, or he'll listen to me politely then seethe with resentment secretly – or even attack. Whatever he decides, it'll be well thought out. He's a sensible head for a young man – he's about thirty years old, I think – but he could still react with his heart if provoked. It could even be some internal attempt to undermine his leadership that we know nothing about – the timing of it with his arrival here for our first meeting could be significant."

"Not if it really is the work of Druids. They are operating by the rhythms of nature, not of man. Perhaps it's a secret sect trying to regain power with their own people?"

"It's possible. Religion comes in many forms – look at the rituals of Isis or Dionysus, and there's this new one, Christianity. Then on the other hand, it could be someone here at the fort trying to implicate the Silurians to lead me away from the truth."

"It's the attempt to hide the arm in the bathhouse that doesn't make any sense." She gestured to a slave to pour them some more wine mixed with water. "Why?"

"I know. Lucan suggested that whether it was the Druids or someone else, they killed him and spilled his blood elsewhere and were hiding his body in the bathhouse to throw blame on someone in the fort when they were disturbed by the janitor, so they abandoned the body on the river." He drank some wine. "I am going to have to meet with Ceryth later today. I've sent a messenger ahead to catch up with him before he gets too deep into his own mountainous territory."

He was grateful for Modestina's quick nod, without complaint or fuss. "I shall oversee your travel requirements." She made to get up but he held her back.

"What is it that you were trying to tell me, my love?"

"I don't want to trouble you with this. . . ." At his reassuring nod she went on, "The children brought me a very sad tale from their lessons today. They have played with Sahia's children and they learned from them that she is absolutely overcome. She has withdrawn to her room and speaks to no one, not even her own children. They only know their father is dead, not how, and they are so bewildered in their grief." She blinked tears away. "I suggested they stay with us until their mother is feeling better. Was that wise of me?"

"Very wise," Julius said, kissing his wife, not caring for

the slaves or servants nearby. "They could not be in better hands."

The Silurian encampment was a rough affair by Roman standards. Horses were not tethered in neat lines but allowed to roam in a rough enclosure of hurdles. There were no tents, the men slept on the bare ground, wrapped in their plaid cloaks, even Ceryth. But the campfire was big and cheerful with tasty meat roasting over it and plenty of the sweet and heady honey mead the Silurians drank. Julius felt he and his men were safe enough sharing their hospitality, but he was glad of the stool Modestina had packed for him.

Smoke from the fire wisped up to a sky crusted with stars and firelight shone on men with plenty of red or black hair and rough clothes and his own smart well-shaven soldiers, alike.

After half an hour of banter and drinking – Julius found it hard to get used to the Celt's casual way with their leader, for it appeared these argumentative people could all have their say – Ceryth slapped him on the shoulder and said, "Well, then," in his passable Latin. His men fell silent and Julius felt his heartbeat quicken. "I don't expect you rode after me because you enjoyed my company so much and couldn't bear to part with me." A handful of his men understood and translated for others, and there was a ripple of laughter. "So perhaps it's the death of your trader, Faustinius."

"You no doubt heard the rest of his body was found, floating in a coracle."

"Ah. Then you've come looking for my advice, no doubt. And I'm happy to give it." He grinned, giving Julius's shoulder a firm squeeze, but his eyes were watchful.

"Your knowledge and experience would be of great service," Julius agreed. "We spoke only briefly about Faustinius before. He traded with you?"

Ceryth shook his head. "*I* do not trade – I lead. But some of my people saw fit to exchange our goods for Roman ones. He came and went freely among us."

"I understand. But it is the nature of his death that – I have been told – has been made to look like a ritual from your olden times. Druidic. No doubt to hide the real identity of the murderer." He gave Ceryth a few details.

Ceryth waited until the muttering among his men died away then said, "We do not follow those old rituals. But there are some that still do, I've heard. It could be these men – strangers to us here – who have done this. Perhaps they want to undermine my friendship with the Emperor."

Julius tried not to betray his relief. "Prince Ceryth, if that is the case, I pledge any help I can give to bringing these wrongdoers to justice – to *your* justice."

"I pledge likewise." They clasped hands then talking and drinking began again. Yet Julius still felt uneasy. Ceryth had happily passed the blame on to the Druids, promised to find the killers – it had been almost too easy. He felt Ceryth was one step ahead of him – he had been ready for him. Julius knew that he was working in the dark, in an unknown environment. He longed to be able to get back to military matters. There he felt safe and in command. This death threw up too many woolly questions without answers. He wanted to leave it to Ceryth, but his sense of duty still pricked at him, urging caution.

Sunlight glancing off polished armour, the shouts of men being drilled that morning when he returned to the fort, even the greeting cries of his own children, all conspired to make Julius's headache worse. And now it was going to be the sound of his own voice that would make him wince. The Celts' honey mead should only be drunk in moderation, he thought.

Squinting into bright sunlight he looked across the parade ground, which lay just outside the ramparts, at the massed ranks of Legio Augustus II. All eyes were expectantly turned to him. The only movements were the occasional stamping of horses, and their tails being fanned by the breeze.

He raised the scroll he had brought with him, the Imperial seal now broken.

"Men, your days without purpose are over. Emperor Hadrian has need of your skills, your strengths and your hearts. I have today read his command, as have legates in other forts across Britannicus. We are to march again, shoulder to shoulder, for the might of Rome and to bring civilization to the darkest corners of the Empire.

"The day after tomorrow not one, not two – not even five vexillations, but all of our legion will be marching North, to Caledonia, leaving a few here to run Isca fort.

"It is thirty years since we were north of the River Bodotria, and twenty since we were safe north of Vindolanda. Too long have we been plundered and harried by the tribes of Caledonia. The Emperor's visit to Britannicus earlier this year brought him to a decision. We are going to build a wall. The greatest the world has ever seen, with towers and forts all along it to protect our land. It will stretch from one sea to the other, either side of this island and we, men, are going to help build it.

"And, before we go, I have ordered the best entertainment and games the Isca amphitheatre has ever seen.

"Hail to Rome, hail to the Emperor."

The returning hails from the men were reasonably enthusiastic, he thought as he took his throbbing head home. He knew that in their bunkbeds tonight there would be plenty of grumbles. It was a long way to go. Home comforts would be few, though wives and sweethearts would no doubt follow too. It would be cold and wet.

On the other hand, they would be involved in a magnificent project, and there would be enemy to fight too. Julius was excited at the prospect. He now knew that he was the right man for the job, for hadn't he trained as an engineer when young?

The arena had been swept clean of animal blood and sprinkled with fresh sand and now, in a twilight enlivened by flickering torches, it was the turn of human performers. Acrobats, jugglers, the exotic and the downright bizarre paraded for the entertainment of the audience.

Antheses chewed on a snack he'd just bought before swallowing some wine from his own stone jar. The Legate had promised a good games, and had been true to his word. Man and beast alike had fought fiercely and the crowd had screamed and groaned with the thrill of it. Antheses had joined with them, and afterwards had enjoyed joking with the men and families he knew best, but now he felt something was missing: Sahia.

Of course she was in mourning. It would not be right for her to attend. But he was used to seeing Faustinius and his wife at the games, or about the small town. They made life interesting with a lifestyle to aspire to. Even more, he admired the way Faustinius managed to smuggle goods, jewels – even people – to and fro behind his legitimate trading. He had long suspected that Faustinius must have a secret cache of money or jewels, and then Faustinius had taken him into his confidence – and now he had the cache, the amphora full of gold nuggets, still intact bar one.

He finished his hot snack, cheered as the acrobats performed their most complex manoeuvre yet, then thought of Sahia again. She'd be alone now, with everyone at the games – he'd seen Robinia earlier, here with her Christian friends, come for the acrobats. Yes alone, probably lonely. She might be cheered up by his company. Besides, he'd been unable to resist exchanging just one nugget of gold to buy some good leather shoes for himself and a small piece of ladies' jewellery – perhaps she'd like it.

With a quick glance around, he left his seat and strolled through the encroaching evening towards the villa where he'd so often acted as go-between for Faustinius. Once there it took him some time to wheedle the old and, in his opinion, daft man left as doorkeeper to send to his mistress that Antheses had some information for her. But he knew he was lucky, the usual doorkeeper would have turned him away instantly and had fists he couldn't argue with.

Antheses fidgeted in the doorway, ignoring the superior gaze of the Nubian slave guarding the inner hallway, till they both heard the old man's returning shuffle.

"Oh, the Gods – what are we to do?" he cried tremulously. "My mistress is not in her bedchamber – she is not anywhere to be found!"

In the ensuing melee as the few servants and slaves in the villa argued amongst themselves about what to do, Antheses went to the room where he had last seen Sahia, and then into her bedroom beyond. He quickly lifted the lids of her two wooden and inlaid ivory chests – empty. The bed was undisturbed and he could not see any of her jewellery.

Sahia had gone.

Antheses left through the slaves' quarters and hurried to his own one-room dwelling on the edge of the town. It was dark by now, as dark as his thoughts. Surely she didn't think the Legate believed her guilty of killing her husband? Or could she have lost her reason through grief? Robinia had told him her mistress had shut herself away. Yet she'd taken all her belongings. That didn't look like the action of some-one mad with sorrow.

Once indoors he emptied his jar of wine, wiped his mouth,

and then went to where he'd buried the amphora of gold. Sahia knew he had it – just supposing she had come to his house to look for it, knowing he'd be at the games.

"No, here it is, all right," he exclaimed out loud when his fingers touched the amphora's neck – just as a large hand descended roughly on his shoulder.

"I wonder what can be so special about that jar for it to be buried?" Centurion Brutus said. "Could it be filled with raw gold, I wonder?"

"What d'you want?" Antheses said, trying to move away from the jar. Brutus kept him firmly in place.

"I want answers to some questions I have. First, there's Faustinius's missing ring. Legate thinks Lucan took it to give to the widow because he's sweet on her, but the guards told me you'd been in headquarters too about that time. Then gossip reached my ears that you were splashing money around in the marketplace on fancy goods. Now where does a janitor get that kind of money? So when I saw you leaving the games early, looking over your shoulder all the time, I thought I'd follow. First Widow Sahia's, now this."

"You're right, it is gold – Faustinius entrusted it to me. It was his life savings. I want to give it to Sahia – that's what he'd've wanted. But when I went to see her she'd gone – disappeared without telling anyone. Somebody should be out, looking for her."

"Somebody like you, for instance. You hear the good lady has gone – who knows where, she could be kidnapped, wandering deranged – and what do you do? Come and check your gold is still here. Hardly the action of a friend of the deceased, I'd say."

Antheses hung his head. "I didn't think – too shook up – I thought maybe I could buy information –"

"You thought she might've come and taken what's rightfully hers, you mean. Antheses, I think it's time you came with me and spent some time in our nice comfy prison. See what other stories you can come up with."

"No – I mean, what's the hurry? Look, there's plenty of gold here – plenty for two, if you know what I mean. Some for me, some for you – some for Sahia too, if you say."

"Hmm – interesting proposition. Needs a second opinion. Let's see what the guards say – did you hear that, lads?"

There was an answering shout from outside. Brutus took hold of Antheses' shoulder again. "Time we went. Let someone else finish your digging, then we'll hold the gold for when she returns. Meanwhile, I've got plenty more questions waiting to be answered."

Legio Augustus II, all bar a skeleton staff of men headed by Lucan left to guard Isca, marched out of the fort on their way north. Julius rode beside Centurion Brutus who, he noticed, kept glancing over his shoulder.

"You have an uneasy look about you," he said.

"I know Antheses is locked up and you've given him a good long sentence for duping the widow out of her husband's money – how Faustinius came by it we'll never know, now she's gone. But I have this horrible feeling that he'll manage to give us the slip and get out."

"Well, if he does, he'll go in the opposite direction as us, so he'll be someone else's problem."

"I wanted to tell you as soon as the arm was discovered to keep an eye on him, but I only had gossip and rumour that he was seen coming and going from Faustinius's villa. They were working together on some scheme. But I only thought he might lead us to the killer."

"Every time we questioned him we got a different story. You can forget him now – you've done a good job, Brutus."

"I never suspected he might've killed Faustinius, because I thought he needed the merchant more than the merchant needed him. People like Antheses are ten a penny. Faustinius, he was the clever one."

"And the lucky one, married to Sahia, most would agree. Wherever she is, we wish her well. She knows her children are safe with my wife, and they're good companions for our children. Now Brutus, forget Isca – keep your eyes on the road ahead."

Lucan stretched, luxuriating in the press of Sahia's naked body next to his. When she came to him begging for his help, he knew instantly what to do. A friend of his had left this small dwelling an hour's ride from Isca, and he had helped her flee. As soon as the Legion marched away, he had come to her and they had embraced and – he dropped a kiss on her forehead. For him it was passion, for her – perhaps comfort, at the moment, but who knew where it might lead?

And finally she had revealed to him why she had been so afraid. That foolish husband of hers had double-crossed the Silurians he traded with. He'd given them short measure, increased his prices – he'd been overconfident. No wonder they'd set their Druids on him. And Sahia was terrified they'd come for her too.

Silly girl, he thought, stroking her rounded hip. At least he wouldn't have to double-cross anyone to shower her with gold and presents. His family had money enough to keep Sahia happy. One day they might even send for her children, safe with Modestina Publius, when things had quietened down.

Mind busy with happy plans, Lucan too fell asleep.

Antheses watched the dust settle after the last soldiers marched out of the fort, and felt a great stillness fall. All the hustle and bustle was gone. This was going to be a dull place, he thought. Where should he head for next? Hibernia possibly, or maybe Gaul – yes, Gaul was probably a land of opportunity for men such as himself.

He sat on the hard stone floor and took out his dice and began to play with them. Funny how thoughts kept coming back to you when it was still and quiet. Thoughts you didn't want. Like the look on Faustinius's face when he'd cut his throat. He looked so surprised. Like he didn't believe it was happening. The blood – the blood kept coming . . .

Antheses tossed the dice, scooped them up, tossed again. That's when he'd had the idea – he'd heard all about those wild men and their barbarian ways. Human sacrifices – ugh. At least that had worked. Everyone had fallen for it, even the Silurians. They were just glad Faustinius was dead. If he hadn't got him, they would have, in revenge for his double-dealing.

No, Faustinius had only himself to blame. He'd been just too clever for his own good. Coming back upriver like that, bursting with pride at all his clever deals, boasting to Antheses. Then letting slip about the hoarded gold. The picture of it had burst in Antheses' mind like a rising sun. Such a golden opportunity – to end the life he'd led till then, somehow he would become a man of substance, invent a new Antheses who wouldn't be looked down on, have to do the worst jobs to eke a living. The knife had been in his hand before he even knew it and then –

Then he just had to dispose of the body. The coracle would lead everyone to the Silurians. But the arm in the hypocaust – well, that had been his bit of fun. He couldn't resist it. So close to the truth, and no one even guessed. But the cutting, that had been hard –

No, he would get rid of these thoughts. He tossed the dice again, then called out, "Antoninus, fancy a game? Now, what shall we use for stakes?"

Caveat Emptor

Rosemary Rowe

When I compiled Classical Whodunnits *in 1996 I was delighted to publish the first story featuring Libertus the Pavement-Maker, and he has since gone on to feature in a series of popular novels starting with* The Germanicus Mosaic *(1999). Libertus is a freedman and craftsman who lives in the city of Glevum (what is now Gloucester) in Britain at the end of the second century. This story takes place seventy years from the previous, to a time when Roman Britain was at its most prosperous.*

To most of us an iron knife is just an iron knife. Of course, there are different qualities of blade, which is why some of them become almost magical, though I bought one from a pedlar once which would scarcely cut a piece of cheese. Mostly, however, knives are simply things for carrying in one's belt, useful if one is unexpectedly invited out to dine, or as a scant protection against bandits, wolves or bears while travelling. Scarcely a commodity to risk execution for. Yet there is the curious case of Calvus, who did exactly that.

His real name isn't Calvus, obviously. Few people are called "Baldy" legally, but since he hailed from Gaul and had a name which no one could pronounce, Calvus he

instantly became. And it was as Calvus the meat-butcher that
he sent word to me, when he was captured and locked up in
the Glevum market cells.

I knew him only slightly, and liked him even less. He was a
small, fat swarthy man, bald as a pig, with a smile as
unpleasant as any of his wares. Standing at his *marcellum*,
his market stall, with a hatchet in his hand, spattered from
head to foot with blood and entrails, and surrounded by
bleeding carcasses, he was a fearsome sight. Mothers murmured, "Calvus will get you" when children disobeyed.

It was Junio, my slave, who brought me the news. I'd sent
him to collect water from the town fountain, and when he
returned, he came panting into my rickety workshop to say,
"Master, Calvus the butcher is in jail, and I am sent to ask if
you will speak to him."

I put down my selected tiles with a grunt. I was engaged
on a complex piece of work, a decorative panel in honour of
the impending visit of an ambassador from Rome. I was
assembling it on a piece of hessian and was hoping to take it
to the council chambers on my handcart the next afternoon.
With a little planning, I could take out a section of the
existing tiles and put my insert in, while all the councillors
were busy at the baths. It is a technique I have perfected over
years, and it requires concentration on my part. I was not
pleased to be interrupted by a summons from a common
butcher who had no rank at all.

I bridled. "He sends a message, does he? I wonder how
many guards he had to bribe for that." Common prisoners in
the filthy Glevum jail are not usually privileged to summon
friends.

Junio gave his cheekiest grin. "You forget, master, he is
one of Marcus's *clientes*. No doubt that's why he asked for
you."

It was true, I had forgotten that. Calvus had first come to

Glevum as a gift, to Marcus Aurelius Septimus (one of the most powerful men in the entire province of Britannia) from a friend. He was then a kitchen-slave, but Marcus had permitted him to buy his freedom shortly afterwards – partly, I suspect, because he didn't like Calvus any more than I did. So Calvus was legally Marcus's freeman – which meant that he had lifelong duties to his patron, naturally, but also that Marcus was more or less obliged to offer protection in return. Which, unfortunately, was where I came in. Marcus Aurelius Septimus is my patron too.

"Marcus suggested it?" I said, knowing what the answer was. I've solved a few crimes for Marcus in the past, and he has formed a habit of involving me. I got up resignedly and gestured for my cloak. No question, now, of my refusing this or *I* was likely to end up in the cells.

I didn't take Junio with me to the jail. I'd spent a day and night there once myself. The cells are filthy, stinking, dark and damp and men are shackled to the floor like animals: not a place to take an impressionable boy My decision wasn't very wise perhaps, since, seeing me turn up at the gates tunic-clad and without an attendant slave, the guard on duty almost refused to let me in.

I almost pointed out that I was a full Roman citizen, but remembered that, in that case, I was supposed to wear a toga on business at all times. I let the matter rest. I said, humbly, "His Excellency Marcus Aurelius Septimus required me to come. One of his clientes is in jail."

The soldier looked me up and down. "Calvus the butcher, is it? I was warned to expect somebody for him. Through that door there, in the jailer's house."

I should have predicted that. Having a powerful patron won you certain rights. It wasn't like being a citizen, of course (Calvus wasn't born in Glevum, which would have given him automatic rights) but Marcus's name was sufficient to ensure that our interview would not take place in the foul darkness of a cell. Indeed, the room I was shown into was a pleasant one, with a shuttered window space and a rough stool and table set for me. There was even a jug of cheap watered wine, and a few battered-looking dates.

Calvus looked in worse condition than the fruit. His legs were bruised, his clothes were torn, and a bloodied blackness round his eyes and mouth suggested a less-than-gentle arrest. Before they found out who his patron was, the jailers had obviously chained him up "slave-wise", with a collar around the neck linked to his arms and feet. The victim cannot stand upright, nor move without half-strangling himself. Of course, these bonds had been removed by now, but Calvus still walked painfully.

The big guard who had brought him in prodded him towards me with his sword and winked. "All yours," he said. "And welcome to him, too. I was told that you could talk to him alone, on His Excellency's orders, but I'll be right outside the door. If he's any trouble, just give me a shout." He patted his dagger cheerfully and left. I heard the heavy key grate in the lock.

"Well," I said to Calvus, "What's this all about?"

He half-raised his head. "An . . . n . . .," he managed, in a voice still cracked with thirst.

I knew I would get nothing from him in this state. I let him have the wine-jug. He lifted it two-handed and drank, straight from the lip, in deep grateful gulps. When he had half-emptied it, I took it from him and said, "Well?" again.

He looked at me. "A knife," he gabbled. "It all started with an argument about a knife. I admit that. But it wasn't me who kidnapped him and tied him up . . ."

I interrupted him. "Suppose you start at the beginning, Calvus. Who did you have this argument with, and where?"

The butcher heaved a huge sigh. "It was like this . . ." he

said, and launched into his tale. It was a long and rambling version of events, but this – effectively – was what he said.

It happened some months earlier, in Corinium. Calvus had gone there to try and buy a slave to help him with his trade. The slave market at Corinium is a lively one, with slaves from all corners of the Empire – much better than the weekly one held in the forum here. So, Calvus left his brother-in-law to mind the stall, hired a mule, and went to Corinium overnight – to another relative who kept an inn. He wanted to be at the market shortly after dawn to get the best choice of slaves available, and perhaps to make some other purchases.

He didn't find a slave to suit, he said, but he was haggling with the vendor of some wool when an itinerant cutler came into the market-place – a dramatic figure, in a multi-coloured robe, with an impressive beard, long hooked nose, and a huge red turban wrapped round his head. I have seen such men in Corinium myself; they come from the North African Province, and their very appearance draws a crowd at once.

This man did. People were already crowding round as he drew a coloured blanket from his handcart, spread it out, and then reverently lifted down a big, carved box.

He didn't open it at once, but stood admiring it, which only made his audience more curious. They jostled closer.

At last, he opened up the front. It hinged apart like a pair of double doors. The watchers gave a gasp. Inside were knives, cleavers, hatchets, every kind of blade. Then, in a high-pitched sing-song kind of voice, he began his cry – holding a piece of linen in one hand and running a blade down it so it fell in two. "Best knives. Finest in the Empire. Feel the weight. What do you offer me for these amazing blades? Just like those used by the Emperor himself. Twenty denarii? Fifteen? You won't believe it, gentlemen, I'm asking only five denarii. It is a crime. I'm robbing myself at the price. Only twenty left. Who'll buy the first?"

As Calvus described the scene I could imagine it too well. Five denarii was a fair price for a good knife, and some credulous fool in a tunic was soon pressing forwards, eager to part with his hard-earned coin. Then there was another, and another, until all the knives were gone.

"You bought one of them?" I said.

Calvus shook his head. "Not then. I was still bargaining at the buckle stall. But I was listening all the time. Nicodemus – that's what he called himself – sold off the cleavers next. I wanted one of those, but they disappeared more quickly than the knives. Then the hatchets went. By the time I'd finished my business and could get across, there was only one knife remaining in the box. It had a carved bone handle and a wicked blade. He didn't even try to sell us that. Somebody wanted it, but Nicodemus shook his head. That knife was not for sale at all, he said. It was the only one like it in the world, forged in the fires of Vulcan himself."

"You believed that?"

"Of course not, but then he picked it up and started cutting things. It was incredible. I've never seen anything like it in my life, and I've owned scores of knives. Straight through a chicken, bones and all, as if it was a piece of honeycake." Calvus gazed glumly at the stone flagstones on the floor. "I don't know what came over me, but I wanted that knife more than I've ever wanted anything. And Nicodemus knew it. I offered him all the silver in my purse, but he just smiled and shook his head, and made as if to put the knife away."

"So you made him an offer?" I began to see where this might lead.

"A hundred denarii," Calvus admitted.

I gasped. The fact of agreeing on a price – however high – made that a contract enforceable in law.

Calvus shuffled his still-shackled feet. "Of course, it was more than I could realistically afford. But I did want that knife. I had the money saved, to buy a slave, but I wasn't carrying it with me in the market-place – it's always full of pickpockets and thieves. I'd left it, hidden in my mule-pack at the inn, where my relatives could keep an eye on it, but where I could get it if I needed it. And I was desperate to have that knife. Perhaps it really was a magic blade. Certainly it put a spell on me."

I thought I could see what was coming next. "But when you went to get the coins he switched the knife?"

Calvus looked at me indignantly. "I am not quite a fool," he said. "Of course I realized that he might do that. But equally he couldn't let me take it till I'd paid. In the end he offered to put it in the box, under my very eyes, and get one of the townsfolk to sit on it – in full view of everyone – until I came back. I couldn't see the flaw in that. I even picked out the bystander – a young man I slightly knew – so there was no possibility of fraud."

"But . . .?" I said. There had to be a but.

"I don't know how he did it to this day, but somehow he played a trick on me!" Calvus groaned. "I got the money: came back: he opened the box and gave me the knife – the only one there was. I was delighted. But when I got back to the inn and went to use the blade – merely to cut a piece of barley-loaf – I knew at once that it was not the same. Oh, it looked identical – ornate carved handle and everything – but it hardly cut. I took it to the ironsmith straight away – his shop is not so very far away – and he tried to grind a decent edge on it – but to no avail. It was just useless, and I'd paid a hundred denarii for it! I've discarded better knives than that!"

I was beginning to feel quite sorry for the man. "So what did you do then?"

"Went back and confronted him, of course – he was still packing up his things – but the crowd had drifted off by then and he just laughed at me. I was not going to put up with that. I called on the *aediles*, the market police, to have him charged before the magistrates that day."

I nodded. Though a vendor is not liable under the law for the quality of what he sells, a purchaser can sometimes get his money back if he can prove that he was wilfully deceived. "What happened?" I said sympathetically. "Did he avoid arrest?"

That is not unknown. It is the responsibility of the man who brings a case to ensure that both he and the accused appear in person at the town *curia* before noon on the appointed day, otherwise there's no case to be heard. Not as easy as it sounds, if the accused is reluctant to appear!

Calvus surprised me. He smiled, a little bitterly. "Oh, I'd paid the *aediles*. It cost me something, naturally, to have it all rushed through like that, but they seized him and dragged him in before the trumpet blew. They made very sure of that."

I could imagine that. The market police are armed, and – since they are on the first step to higher things – anxious to be noticed by the authorities for their efficiency. They would ensure that Nicodemus came to court "before the trumpet blew".

That was often the hardest part of all. The Romans have this convention of dividing the hours of daylight into twelve equal parts and calling the resultant divisions "hours" – (and the same thing for the hours of darkness too). But since most of us humbler citizens have no water-clocks, "the start of the seventh hour" is hard to calculate. So, to mark the official middle of the day, a trumpeter comes out onto the court-house steps and blows – and if you come in after that, you're late. But it seemed that hadn't happened here.

"Did he find some legal quibble, then? Persuade them that they needn't hear the case?"

"On the contrary," Calvus said bitterly, "They heard the case. I lost, that's all."

"But you had witnesses?"

"That was the trouble, in the end. Nicodemus didn't deny the knife was valueless. Instead he turned the whole case on its head. That was the knife that I'd contracted for, he said – contracted properly in front of witnesses – 'Do you solemnly swear to buy this knife for one hundred denarii?' – Which, of course, I had. He didn't ask me to swear the contract till I brought the money back. So technically it was *that* knife that I'd agreed to buy, whatever it was like! The magistrates simply laughed at me and threw me out of court – and I had to pay the *aediles* all the same. It cost me every coin I possessed."

I frowned. "But you did pay?"

"Of course."

"Then I don't understand. This was months ago. Why are you in prison now?"

He gulped, and I thought for a moment he was going to cry. "This is a much more serious affair. They arrested me today. I'm charged with robbery on a public road. Nicodemus's revenge, I suppose."

No wonder he was looking so distraught. If they found him guilty now, that was a crucifying offence. It cost me the remnants of the wine, which he seemed to require to fortify himself, but in the end I got the story of the day.

Calvus had been at his Glevum market stall, as usual – when who should come into the market-place, but Nicodemus, with his box of knives. Calvus was busy with his customers and couldn't leave the stall, but he watched, and it was exactly the same as in Corinium. In no time at all a crowd had formed, and Nicodemus was selling off his knives. Even the patter was identical.

Calvus watched till he could bear no more. The memory of Corinium was still raw. He left his brother-in-law to mind his stall again and made his way to where the cutler was. Nicodemus was selling hatchets by this time – but Calvus noticed there was still a single knife left in the box.

"The same knife?" I interrupted.

"I'm sure of it. The box had been repaired, but the knife looked just the same. I would have known it anywhere – that carved bone handle – it was a work of art. I intended to wait till he began to show it off, and then announce that it was not for sale."

"Because it had been forged in Vulcan's furnaces?"

"Perhaps it was. The way it sliced through everything, it was miraculous. But then someone started bidding for the knife, although the hatchets had not all been sold. The price went up and up, just like before. I don't know what came over me – I was still furious at being made to look a fool. I started shouting that he was a cheat, and people turned to look at me. But the man bidding for the knife was too intent. Then Nicodemus looked up himself. He didn't even recognize my face. It was too much. I strode over and picked up the coloured blanket from the ground, tipped up the box, and sent the whole stand flying." Calvus looked animated, even now, recalling it.

"So *he* called the *aediles*, this time?" I suggested.

Calvus shook his head. "He had no need to call them, they were there. And I was ready with my story too – and then Nicodemus realized who I was. And that's when he sprang his next surprise. He claimed that after the trial in Corinium, when he'd won, he'd gone off to the baths to celebrate before he set off for an *oppidum*, a little village several miles away. But no sooner had he started on the road, than someone came up behind him silently, held a dagger to his ribs and pulled the outer folds of his turban down around his eyes, so that he couldn't see. Then his attacker dragged him off into the trees, stripped him of his purse, pulled off his robes, and left him tied up against a tree. When he came back to his handcart again, he found it had been ransacked, and his knife-box broken into and dashed on the ground."

"It had two compartments, I presume?"

Calvus stared at me. "How did you know that?"

"What other explanation could there be? And what about the knife? The proper knife, that is?"

"He must have had it hidden somewhere else. In any case, it seems it wasn't found. He had it this morning in the market-place, so who knows where it was? But his purse was taken, and he was attacked. And of course, he claims that it was me."

"And was it?"

Under the bruising Calvus turned an ugly shade of puce. "I've been telling them all morning that it wasn't me. I don't have a dagger, anyway. But of course, I'd half-condemned myself by shouting out – in front of everyone in the market-place today – that he'd cheated me in Corinium. And then I turned his knife-stall upside down. That made me seem a violent man. And then he said he recognized my voice."

"Does he have any proof that he was robbed that day?"

Calvus laughed bitterly. "Apparently. A soldier from a passing unit heard his cries – that's how they came and found him stripped and tied up against the tree. The whole detachment thought it was hilarious. No doubt they could be found as witnesses. Oh, Nicodemus was attacked, all right."

I was calculating rapidly. "And what time did you leave Corinium?"

He looked abashed. "That is the trouble, citizen, I can't be sure. A little after the trial finished I suppose. After I'd spent my money at his stall and paid the fine, there was no point in staying any more. In any case, I'd hired a mule – and I had to return that before the town-gates closed."

"That might be important. Where did you hire the mule?"

He gave me the name. Stortus Maximus. I knew the man. He kept a hiring stable just outside the walls. Most of his animals were old and wheezing – as he was himself – but they were cheap. And Stortus was a decent sort of man. He bought his mules and horses broken-down, but he looked after them – some of them went on for years and years. And he was honest too – the town wags said he lacked the intelligence to cheat.

"Very well," I said. "I'll see what I can do. I'll go and talk to Stortus now. And Calvus, when they question you again, give them the answer but say as little as you can. Otherwise you'll talk yourself to death."

He had turned pale now. "What do you mean?"

I looked at him. "You say you had no dagger, Calvus, but you had a knife. You spent all your money on it, didn't you?"

He looked sullen. "That! It would hardly cut a loaf o' bread."

"But a man could hardly see that from behind. Take my advice, Calvus, watch your tongue. Nicodemus is a cunning man. He'll twist your words, just as he did before. Now, I must go if I'm to save your skin. Guard!"

The warder was opening the door, almost before the word was out. "All right, Citizen? He isn't causing any trouble here?"

I shook my head. "Not at all. But you may show me out and take him to the cells."

From the pathetic look on Calvus's face, he must have hoped I'd somehow contrive to free him then and there. But naturally there was no chance of that. I left him to his miserable lot, and made my way – with some relief – back to the freedom of the world outside.

The soldier at the gate grunted a greeting as he let me out. "There's a message for you from His Excellency. You're to call on him, and tell him how things stand."

"I will," I promised, but I did not go direct. I went first to where Stortus kept his mules.

It was a tumble-down affair, merely a sort of large roofed wooden shed, with a lean-to shack at the back of it. Stortus was with his animals, as usual, giving them fresh water and grooming down their coats, although he stank like a manure-heap himself.

He listened to my question carefully. "It is a long time ago," he said. "But let's have a look. Calvus the butcher – let me see. I gave him old Fatty, I'm sure of it." He went over to the wall, close to a stout little mule with baleful eyes, and looked at a series of scratches he had made. "Here we are. Just before the Ides of Augustus. Just as I thought, he brought it back on time. That's before the shadow reaches the eleventh hour, on the sundial on old Gauss's tomb out there."

He gestured, through the open door, towards the monument. The dead town-councillor had ordered the dial to be built so that every time men looked at the time, they would recall his name.

"That's the time I close the stable door, and settle my beasts for the night. If anyone brings in an animal after that, I charge them for an extra day. That makes them prompt, of course. Naturally, it's more difficult when it's cloudy, like today. Then I just have to guess. All in the contract that is. Here you are, that's my mark for him. Two days – he had it overnight. So he was back in time. That's definite. And it was sunny weather then, as well."

I thanked the old man, slipped him an *as* or two and hurried off, almost as glad to be away from him as I had been to leave the prison earlier. I hoped my tunic hadn't absorbed the smell, as I hastened to the centre of the town, where my patron still maintained a suite of rooms over a wine-shop near the square. I thought of going home to put my toga on, but decided that there was no need for it. I had been visiting the prison, and was already late.

Marcus had me shown into his presence instantly. He was dressed for banqueting, in a toga of dazzling whiteness, set off by the glow of rubies at the clasp and his most glittering rings on either hand. In my smelly tunic, I felt peculiarly ill at ease.

"Well, Libertus, my old friend," he said. The voice was not unkind, but the greeting troubled me. When I am "his old friend", I'm alarmed. "This is about Calvus, I presume. Have you succeeded in releasing him?"

"Not yet, Excellence," I confessed. "But I think I may have evidence which helps. Who will be presiding in the Calvus case?"

Marcus frowned. "Probably the ambassador from Rome, since he is here. This is a capital offence, so it will fall to a senior magistrate."

I thought of my unfinished pavement piece. "He has arrived then?"

"I am entertaining him to a feast tonight. He is at this moment in the guest room here, preparing for the banquet with his slaves."

I was thinking rapidly. "He has come straight from Rome?"

"Via Londinium and Corinium, of course. He wished to see a little of Britannia. He has never ventured to the northern provinces before. He is quite favourably impressed. You know what rumours circulate in Rome."

I did. Marcus himself had come from Rome originally, and he never tired of telling me about the wonders of the Imperial capital, and how things were different there. However,

I had now learned what I'd been hoping for. "In that case, Excellence, there is hope. I believe he will dismiss it out of hand. And if the ambassador presides at the case, the populace cannot accuse you of favouring your own clientes, which they might otherwise have done. Calvus is not a very well-liked man."

His face cleared. "You may have a point. I imagine the Ambassador won't mind – and here he is, in fact. Perhaps you would like to speak to him yourself."

The man who was entering the room looked what he was, a man of power. Not only was he elaborately dressed, he had that well-oiled, sleek, self-satisfied air that the rich and favoured always seem to have. He looked at me with something like disgust. I feared a whiff of Stortus hung about me still.

Marcus caught the look and hastened to explain. This was his apartment, after all. "This is one of my clientes, Ambassador," he said. "He is a citizen, despite appearances. He has been engaged in an errand on my behalf – and would like to have a word with you." I was not an "old friend" now, I noted with a smile, but Marcus was doing his best for me.

The Ambassador gave me a frosty smile. "About . . .?"

I had not meant to be catapulted into this, but suddenly there seemed no escape. I took the plunge. "About a case, your Mightiness, that you are scheduled to try tomorrow at the courts."

"That cutler who was set upon and robbed," Marcus put in. "I think I mentioned it to you earlier."

"You did!" the Ambassador said loftily. "It seems to be a cut and dried affair. The man identified his assailant, I believe, in front of witnesses."

Marcus looked at me.

"Ah!" I said. "That is just the point. He identified the voice, but not the face. He didn't *see* the man who tied him up and took his purse. Calvus seems a likely suspect, I agree. He had a grievance, and he had a knife. But did he have the opportunity? We know there was a trial in Corinium – which began just before the seventh hour. They got there just before the noonday trumpet-call, and no doubt the court officials can confirm the fact."

"Well?" the Ambassador demanded testily.

"And then, by the knife-seller's own account, he went off to the baths. It was only afterwards that he was robbed, when he had set off later from the town."

"Well?" again.

"But I have witnesses to prove that Calvus was back in Glevum before the end of the tenth hour. There is no doubt. He hired a mule, and the owner is prepared to swear to it." I sent up a mental prayer to all the gods that no one sent for Stortus to enquire. I did not know that he was "prepared to swear" at all, and he would not make an impressive witness if he did. "And Calvus was back at his market-stall at dawn," I hurried on, pleased to have thought of it. "Anyone in the town will tell you that – which proves that he was back before they shut the gates."

The Ambassador was looking at me with interest.

"Ambassador," I said, "You came that way today. You know how long it takes to travel between Corinium and here. And you were in a swift imperial gig. This man was on a mule. How could he be outside Corinium at – what? – the ninth hour at least, and be back here in time to manage that?"

"By Hermes," the Ambassador exclaimed. "I do believe you're right. It took me three hours at least to make the trip. It would have taken a man on mule-back more." He scowled. "If this is true, I shall have this Nicodemus flogged and fined for wasting the court's time."

Marcus stepped forwards as if to intervene, but caught my eye. "And Calvus the butcher? What of him?"

"We'd better hold him, since he is arraigned. But see that he has fairer lodging, overnight – on my authority. Tomorrow we'll hear what Nicodemus has to say. It is preposterous. Attempting to identify a robber by his voice."

"As you say, Excellence," I murmured.

Marcus said, "I'll send a messenger to the jail at once – if you would seal the order, Mightiness." He nodded to one of his attendant slaves. "Fetch me some bark and writing ink at once. Best octopus, none of your watered soot." The boy scuttled off to do as he was told, and Marcus turned to me. "Well done, Libertus. Wait here for the letter and you can deliver it."

I did more. Once Calvus was released into the jailer's house I found the inn where Nicodemus was. That wasn't difficult. The whole town was abuzz with news of this colourful visitor. Nicodemus eyed me doubtfully.

"I have a warning for you, knife-seller," I said. "The Ambassador from Rome is here, and he has heard about your case. He has unchained Calvus, on new evidence, and plans to have you flogged and fined when you appear."

Nicodemus laughed. "Don't be foolish, townsman. I have proof. The man threatened me in court, and robbed me afterwards."

"You will find it hard to prove," I declared. "Of course, you know the law – it's clear you understand it very well, that's why you make your contract as you do. But if this comes to court, I promise you, I will be a witness in the case. And I will tell them, if Calvus does not, how you have two sections to your box. You put the good knife into one, get some simple bystander to sit on it, then sell the poor knife from the other side. Isn't that the case?"

His smile faded, but he still said, "What if there are two sections? Both are empty. Anyone may look."

"No doubt they are, at present. That knife is too precious

to leave there, in case someone works out your trick. But I know . . ." I leaned forward and whispered in his ear.

It was a guess, but he confirmed it by the way that he turned pale.

I pressed my advantage remorselessly. "I shall tell them about that, if you appear. It will be the gossip of the town – and rumour spreads like fire before the wind. Before you have reached the next town your reputation will be ahead of you."

His voice was almost a whisper. "And if I don't appear?"

"Then I say nothing. Although, of course, some of the story's out. Calvus accused you of cheating him – that will have spread for miles by this time. If I were you, knife-vendor, I wouldn't try to sell my knives round here again. Now, it is getting dark. If you – for any reason – wish to leave, it would be wise to do it very soon."

I am not good at threats, but that one worked. The next morning there was no Nicodemus at the court, and without him, of course, there was no case to bring. Calvus was released without a charge.

I had turned up at the court to see, and Marcus came across. "Well done, Libertus. You did well. I confess I was surprised myself. I didn't think you'd prove him innocent. I was convinced he did it all the time."

I looked at him. "Of course he did it, Excellence. I didn't prove him innocent at all. I simply persuaded the Ambassador of that, which isn't the same thing. Surely you realised the trick I played? The Ambassador has spent his life in Rome – he doesn't realise that in Britannia, when you divide the daylight into twelve, it varies so much with the time of year. You told me how surprised you were yourself. An hour three months ago, when the attack took place, was naturally far longer than an hour yesterday."

Marcus stared. "That's why Nicodemus spent time in the

baths after the trial in Corninium, before he set off for the *oppidum*? I wondered about that."

I nodded. "There was obviously still a lot of daylight left. But Calvus was furious at the legal trick. He waited till Nicodemus left the town, and then crept up and jumped him from the rear – threatening him with that useless knife he'd bought. Ironic really. He wanted to find the other knife, but though he broke the cutler's box in two and discovered how it worked, there was no knife. He betrayed himself there, incidentally. He knew there was a secret. He might have deduced that, possibly. I did myself. But he also told me that the thief hadn't found the knife and that the soldiers laughed when they found Nicodemus by the tree. So he must have been nearby. How could he have known that otherwise? I'm quite sure Nicodemus didn't report it to the *aediles*."

"So Calvus stole the money?"

"He was really looking for the knife. I'm sure of it. That's why he stripped Nicodemus to the skin – why else would a robber strip his victim bare, but leave the clothes, and break up that lovely box as well? Much more sensible to steal it all. Anyway, most of the money in that purse was his – Nicodemus tricked him out of it."

Marcus looked doubtful. "So what happened to the knife? Nicodemus had it yesterday."

I smiled. "That was the interesting part. It was Calvus who gave me the clue. He pulled down Nicodemus's turban to blindfold him. 'The outer folds,' he said. So obviously, he left the turban on. I believe the knife was under it, wrapped in the inner folds. Probably Nicodemus always carried it that way when travelling. I imagine Calvus was not the first to waylay Nicodemus on the road and try to get the knife he'd bargained for – but Nicodemus would just show the box and demonstrate that it was empty. He virtually admitted that to me last night."

Marcus said, "I see," again, and turned to go. Then all at once he turned back to me. "So – why did you save Calvus from his fate? I didn't think you even liked the man."

I didn't rise to that. "You asked me to, Excellence," I said. "Besides, though he was legally at fault, I am not sure that he merited that fate. I had a certain sympathy with him."

I didn't add, although I might have done, that I bought a knife from a pedlar once. A credulous fool in a tunic, eager to be parted from his coin. I think I may have mentioned it before.

A knife that would scarcely cut a piece of cheese.

Sunshine and Shadow

R. H. Stewart

*This story is also set in Britain just a decade or two after
the previous story, but here we find a Britain which is far
less enamoured by the Roman army. Britain was, at this
time, going through a turbulent period of administration.
Little is known about its Governors, and the weaker ones
were always prey to any discontent amongst the native
British. No matter how Romanized the British became,
deep down they remained British, especially the rebellious
Brigantes, in what is now Yorkshire, whom the Romans
were frequently having to quash.*

Rain sheeted endlessly across heath and hill in drenching
curtains, rendering visibility virtually nil. It brimmed
potholes faster than anyone could fill them in and turned
every gutter and conduit into miniature torrents. Well, that's
what you got in northern Britain.

Lucius Valerianus, known as Apricus – Etruscan born;
army engineer by training and achievement – had no choice
but to call a Stand-easy and allow his men back to their neat,
palisaded camp to coax up sulky fires and try steaming
themselves at least half dry. All the same, he set sentries.
He was optio-in-charge on this job, on his own for the very

first time. The northernmost territories of this Province – subtly seething with disaffection – were not the place just now to be caught on your back foot.

He was road-mending: himself and four craftsmen from Legio VI Victrix, and a draft of twenty troopers of the auxiliary Cohors II Nerviorum. He'd claimed use of the draft because he and the craftsmen had already seen to refurbishing doors, shutters, tiling and drains for the Nervians, who were the incoming garrison of a fort overseeing and guarding a lead mining enterprise in high Brigantian land well to the north and west of Eboracum. They were mending a back road which connected the fort to main routes either side: Stanegate, behind them, which serviced Hadrian's boundary, and the road somewhere south in front of them which ran obliquely south-east to north-west over desolate moorland from Cataractonium to Brocauum, and eventually down to Luguvalium. So far, in these parts, they had not set eyes on one single Brigantian – which wasn't to say there weren't any.

They had already reinstated the back road on the fort's northern side from the Stanegate junction on. Now they faced the remaining two thirds of it, due south to where it met the cross-route at Bravoniacum.

Apricus had decided early that this was the wildest, loneliest terrain he had ever experienced. Now even the weather had gone against him. He sat astride his standard-issue folding stool staring out from under his spattering tent-flap, contemplating a problem.

This problem was one very large, very deep rectangular pit which had been cut across rather more than the entire width of the road, then cleverly obscured with light branches and heaps of leafage from what purported to be a naturally fallen tree. Wrong. Roman roads – even relatively neglected back roads – did not have trees next to them. Trees and scrub were routinely cut back in broad corridors on either side at the time of making, and in general people were responsible for keeping them that way.

Once the tree's bole had been cleared of dirt, it was found to possess no root structure, and had been artfully positioned. While the whole thing wasn't that new – it shouted ambush. As such, it required reporting. Plus: to fill in the trap and make it good meant: i) extra materials; ii) trouble in securing same; iii) considerable delay to the work schedule. Messages would have to be sent to Bravoniacum for relay to Supplies (Catarac.), and to Centurion Ursus – overseer of Works – wherever he might be.

Apricus sighed, sorting out his stylus case and wax tablets from inside a leather bag. Better sooner than later.

To the optio's amazed relief – one day on and with the rain at last thinning to drizzle – Ursus came riding up from the south like a gale of wind.

"Jupiter! You've been quick!" he exclaimed, catching his centurion's bridle.

"You struck lucky!" Ursus grinned down. "I was going out of Bravo just as your man came lolloping in . . . on your mare, I noticed, so I've fetched her back. I sent him on to Supplies, post, and with priority requisitions. What's to do?"

Apricus gestured, "Well . . . as you see . . ."

He had had protective barriers set out along the pit's sides, lowered ladders into it, seen to rigging a hoist and removed some debris from the bottom.

Ursus peered in.

"Anything interesting?" he grunted.

"Not really. No nasty stakes. Animal bones – we've piled them for you to see. Otherwise just a mess of leaves, twigs and little earth slips. I've located the spoil, which whoevertheywere dumped out of sight. Most of it'll fill. Gutters'll need recutting and we want hardcore and gravel for the new topping, as I wrote. Whoever this was meant for never seems to have got to use it, thank the gods!"

"Right. Good. Well done, Sunshine!"

Ursus looked at his most junior, least experienced optio and decided to stay on a day. He'd organized a Quintana wagon with extra rations including a beer allowance – which drew him a cheer.

By dusk time the road squad had doggedly replaced about half the pit spoil. Once the rations cart came bundling in, they knocked off for the night, leaving lanterns on the barrier. They shut themselves inside their tidy camp behind berm and sharpened fence.

Mist came in place of the rain. White and eery, it altered sounds and blotted out the surrounding wastes.

Everyone was relishing fresh bread and the best hot supper in days when a sentry shouted he could hear something. Ursus and Apricus were with him at the double.

"What kind of something?" Ursus wanted to know.

"Hoofbeats, Cent. Very fast. Then I lost them."

Which made sense because the road behind them switchbacked.

Apricus ordered them to arm; then yelled for silence. They waited – straining ears into the night. The mist drifted, muffling them in, increasing unease.

Ursus selected ten troopers with more lanterns, told the rest to keep alert and marched out to the road in front of the pit. He dropped on the nearest grass, his ear to the ground.

"One horse, galloping," he called, "Use the barrier. Five either side in line. Raise your lights."

"From the fort?" Apricus queried.

"Maybe. We'll soon see."

Someone set up flamed torches at the camp entrance. The remaining soldiers closed together. Ursus and Apricus stood aloof, one each side of the road, in the limited, milky pool of light.

A now perceptible distant drumming changed to the staccato clatter of hooves, nearer and nearer, until at last a horse and rider emerged abruptly through shrouds of whiteness.

"Whoa . . .!" bellowed Ursus.

As the rider reined up sharply, Apricus grabbed at his bit ring and hauled the horse to a slithering halt.

If the traveller looked British – long-haired, moustached, swathed in chequer-patterned wool clothing – he certainly didn't sound it. Summing up both legionaries at a glance, he announced in impeccable Latin with a bleak patrician drawl: "What in Hades d'you think you are about? Paws off!"

Ursus wasn't about to be fazed.

"Setting speed records, are we?" he asked roughly and, pointing to the hazard, added, "You wouldn't want to go dropping into that, now, would you? Sir! May I enquire as to your travel warrant?"

There was a hostile silence.

The horse, lathered, began to snort and shake its head.

Neither centurion nor optio budged an inch.

"Don't have any . . . actually," the rider admitted; then, emphatically, "Don't need any!"

Ursus raised sardonic eyebrows.

"Look here," the traveller went on, "I must reach the Governor urgently. Intelligence, right? And I'm being followed in order to be stopped – permanently. Is that good enough? Now, damn you, let me through!"

Ursus remained unimpressed. The two of them argued furiously until, swearing, the man pulled from inside his clothing a small seal on a strong chain.

"See this?" He was exasperated. "Take a good look and leave off impeding me! Jupiter, man – have you no sense?"

Apricus saw Ursus stare and blink. Then, ordering the troopers to the left of the pit aside and to light the way, he piloted the rider past.

"Your nag's near blown," Ursus conceded. "We could swap it."

"I do know! I've ridden all my life, you clod! No time. I'll nurse him to Bravo and change there. If I can reach Ebor, I'm safe. There are two of them out there . . . your genuine Britons. It would be singularly useful if they fell in the hole! Failing which: obstruct them even more officiously than you have me – or, Centurion, you may forget all idea of further promotion. Understood?"

"Perfectly, sir. Dea Fortuna go with you."

The traveller kicked his horse back into activity and vanished in the mist.

"Phew!" uttered Apricus in the aftermath. "So what was the seal?"

"Imperial. The kind only Consulars and the occasional personally appointed high-ups ever get. I've only seen one other."

Already there was a faint approach of fresh hoofbeats.

Just in time, Ursus got the men hidden, with lanterns shut, as two characters much like the first to look at arrived. These spotted the road trap only at the last moment, shouting to one another and milling their horses round hard.

An armed circle materialized from nowhere, shining lights.

At least these sounded like tribesmen ought – with accented, stilted Latin.

One of them was dark; one had hair and moustaches which showed up bright ginger when catching the lamplight.

Ursus made them dismount and had them thoroughly searched, confiscating their spears and daggers for the while. Grumbling, the newcomers brought out apparently valid travel permits. Ursus began nit-picking through them syllable by syllable. Apricus made a business of taking names and notes.

The Britons' story hinged on them joining a cousin-chieftain's household and being in trouble with him, if delayed. But they varied as to where this cousin might be – one saying vaguely "near Eboracum", the other suggesting in rasping tones some obscure Celtic placename. Significantly, neither of them mentioned anything about anyone up ahead of them.

Though the army was at this time under strict orders not to risk provocation, Ursus dawdled, letting their horses chill and stiffen. When he could no longer reasonably hold them, he insisted they be escorted a full mile at walking pace "due to the dangerous state of the road", before finally letting them go.

"Now then – here's a mystery!" he brooded, afterwards, sharing Apricus' tent for reheated stew, a welcome flask of wine, and the use of a camp bed.

"What d'you reckon we ought to do, Cent?"

"Report the whole shebang to HQ. You do it, Sunshine – best writing, eh? Don't worry," he added easily, "I'll back you."

They filled in the pit and finished the road without further incident.

The draft from II Nerviorum piled tents and equipment into its big baggage cart, slapped backs all round in farewell, and turned for home.

Optio Apricus sat his craftsmen in theirs, hopped on his mare and led them gladly down the main road to Eboracum.

In fort he submitted a comprehensive set of tablets to Principia and hoped, fervently, he wasn't about to go making waves.

★　　★　　★

Legio VI Victrix, whose Headquarters the fortress at Eboracum was, had it on good authority a new Governor was in
Londinium – bent, very shortly, on undertaking a full dress
tour of inspection throughout Britannia.

The buzz in the township which clung round the outside
of the fortress walls was of sprucing the place to receive him:
new build; new clothes; new trade. It was true the wine
business direct from Gaul to the riverside quays – despite
difficulties – was flourishing once more – and local merchants from among the Parisi were filling a demand for
quality hides and leather goods in return.

Even the weather, as Spring advanced, and now that Optio
L Valerianus Apricus was back in fort, showed signs of tardy
optimism. He took advantage of a short interval between
work schedules, to write home. He used an ink pen and some
second quality Egyptian papyrus sheets, one of the advan-
tages of being on the technical staff. After the usual pre-
amble, addressing his father, he went on:

> . . . I'm sorry if I upset you, leaving home like that
> but I really couldn't stick the idea of being glued to a
> desk shuffling records all day long! It isn't as though I
> were your one and only, is it? But now I'm trained
> and posted, I thought you and Mother might not be
> too unhappy to see where I've got to and know I'm all
> right.
>
> Briefly, after Basic Training, I did well enough to be
> recommended for army engineering. They sent me to
> Castra Peregrina for a year – we only shared a bit of that
> place because it is huge! Some of the rest of it is given
> over to the Frumentarili – maybe you know this? –
> whom one steers well clear of if one has any sense at all!
> Secret agents and all that stuff. Well, I ended the course
> second top and won the runner-up prize from the

Commandant, so I haven't disgraced you or the family. The prize was a laugh – a very handsome travelling sundial in a case with the provincial latitudes marked out – which of course is necessary and extremely useful, if one has sunshine – but (typical army thinking) they then posted me to VI Victrix in Britain, where it rains nine days out of ten in my experience so far! When we read the posting lists, everyone fell about laughing, and because of the sundial I've acquired my cognomen – "Sunshine". Some twerp who was going out to Egypt smirked could he buy the thing off me, then? I told him where to put himself! We had a big party to celebrate qualifying, and because we're technical were all promoted optio (acting) before leaving. Not having done anything dire, I'm now almost due confirmation in the status, which means the pay rise to match the "paint brush" on my helmet.

The last thing we had before leaving was a crash course in equitation, which was sheer Hell! The instructor was the Frumentarii's senior one – a Gallic Decurion who didn't half fancy himself and tongue-lashed us day after day through what he called "Getting to Know Your Horse"! Naturally, the snoops came crowding out to applaud every time one of us fell off, since they pride themselves rotten on their riding skills. Anyway, I survived, and just as well since we had to travel the roads at speed all the way to Gesiacorum on the north coast of Gaul; hop a mail galley; then post from Dubris to Londinium and from there to here (Eboracum), which is a fair way north in Britannia. I can't think that I could be much further away from you all! I didn't get here alone, mind you, but in company with a centurion called Ursus – yes, he is rather bear-like: burly, hairy and dark of colouring – but a good superior to have. He is overseer of works – a kind of roving boss in the field – reporting direct to the legion's Architectus. There was also this character called Blandus who was far from smooth – a joke, you see, like me being "Sunshine" – who possessed the most vile grating voice I've ever had to listen to and, guess what, turned out to be a snoop into the bargain! At least he peeled off at Londinium. He was a dead show-off about working for the Procurator double-checking taxation rolls. Ursus and I took that with a pinch of salt but he was met by a pony cart labelled "OFFICIUM PROC. BRIT." in very large letters. Ursus and I agreed after he'd gone that we'd rather not find ourselves on the wrong side of his tally-sticks and abacus.

The chaps I mess with are a decent bunch, and our Legate (very swish) knows his soldiering. The centurion Architectus tries out the new boys like myself but once he sees you can do the stuff, he very much lets you get on with it, which is good. So far, I have helped refurbish buildings in two forts, done a drainage system – well half of one – measured out an exercise school for some cavalry – and have just completed making good an entire road, which has been my first job where I was in charge. Your little lad is thus proving useful! There is a lot needing done, actually – either because of depredations from a few years back when that idiot Clodius Albinus tried fighting the Emperor – or from sheer age and weathering of infrastructure. Since anything here worth mentioning came in with the Divine Hadrian, eighty-something years ago, it has all grown old together, so it's mend-and-make-do as fast as we can.

There's a funny atmosphere at this end of the province. You need to watch your back. The Parisi round us are all well settled and that, but the Brigantes up-country and nearly all the tribes beyond are fermenting like beer in a tub. Plus: we have a brand new Governor just arrived: C. Valerius Pudens – know anything about him, Pa? Word is: the monies and agreements with which Governor Virius Lupus negotiated a while back, have gone like snow in the desert, and the tribes are looking round for more. Just about every Governor in turn has asked Emperor Severus for heavy military reinforcement, or even an Imperial visit, but so far no dice. The current Procurator, by the way, is none other than M. Oclatinius Adventus who, since he doubles as head of the Corps of Frumentarii, cannot be entirely without significance.

Please tell Mother I am fit and well, and finding my feet legionwise. Yes, Ma, they do feed us properly and I do change my underpants regularly! Give my best to the brothers. I append the proper location below should you now feel you can send me a line in return – which I'd like. A lot of chaps hear from home and it is a good day when the dispatch couriers come belting in. Must stop – I've filled two sheets and the clerks grouse like mad if you cadge too much too quickly!

Farewell, from your errant son, Lucius.

On an afterthought, he scribbled postscriptum up the margin: "You're in Archives, Pa, can you tell me if Albinus was killed for definite in battle at Lugdunum? And would he have rated a Consular seal?"

Having skip-read his letter for errors, Apricus folded the written sheets down to quarter size, covering them with a third, blank one, which he secured with strong twine. The package was addressed to:

M. Valerianus,
Senior Clerks' Offices,
Imperial Archives,
Rome.

Apricus sealed it with wax and the impress of his smart new signet – a design of a tiny shining sun cut intaglio on a lozenge-shaped yellow gemstone.

The dispatch courier he gave it to was not one he'd seen before, but very affable. He took it with one hand while holding out the other for the usual kick-back regarding private post.

"Oh, yeah," he remarked cheerfully, glancing down as he slid the letter into his pouch, "Archives – eh? You'll be well in, likely!"

The Architectus decided on a rapid spring-clean of the fort, due to the impending tour of inspection, so that Apricus, along with several colleagues, spent most of a month on such work. Hardly had they begun to see the end of it, when a Governor's staff officer arrived in haste to see the Legate.

Every available man was summoned urgently to Principia, where mourning streamers in black and purple had been looped on the Legion's Standards in its Headquarters shrine, and it was announced with great regret the Governor would not be visiting Eboracum after all. Indeed, His Excellency wouldn't be going anywhere: C. Valerius Pudens was dead.

In response to a stir among the ranks and several queries, the Legate, looking grim, was unable to give any cause of death – best to reckon on some unforeseen sickness. Yes, he understood messengers were already halfway to Rome; the Emperor would nominate a replacement, surely, the moment he knew. Meanwhile, the Procurator in Londinium would act as Governor and everyone must carry on. He need not stress that any loose speculation overheard among civilians should be firmly squashed; anyone thought to be "trying one on" out there must be reported for possible interrogation. Keep your ears open and your eyes peeled. The Legate stepped back on his tribunal dais – for the Primus Pilus to dismiss them.

Hard on the heels of the staff officer came a caucus of Frumentarii. They took over an entire barrack. They had the window shutters replaced with narrow iron bars and added security locks to every door – using their own workmen. Then they ruffled feathers among all Principia's clerks by initiating a trawl through tablets and paperwork right back to the year dot.

In the circumstances, Apricus was not too sorry to find himself redeployed.

Riding out upcountry with Ursus at the head of a bunch of skilled men, they had been told the job was to mend some Hispanic Cohort's Bath-house.

"Shouldn't take you long," the Architectus had said. "Ten days or so, I daresay . . . Get cracking or the poor souls'll start attracting flies!"

However, II Asturum Equitata were new to Britain and had been assigned to a fort which lay empty through the post-Albinus troubles, and had then been broken into. When VI Victrix's detachment reached Aesica, high in the craggy terrain of the centre of Hadrian's wall, it was to find the Spaniards gazing disconsolately at considerable despoliation. The only good thing was: there were plenty of them to get down off horseback and lend a hand.

Once Corstopitum sent materials, and they had finally been able to turn from securing and cleaning up the fort to its actual Bath-house system, the tanks and drains were found blocked with unbelievable rubbish – while a great deal of cooking seemed to have gone on at some point, in the middle of the main bath floor, damaging the waterproof concrete.

Ursus had to send a messenger back to Ebor with the news they'd be engaged on this one for some considerable time.

It was almost mid-summer before they got back.

The Frumentarii were still there. An occasional wan face might be glimpsed peering out through window bars in their requisitioned barrack.

"Who are those?" Apricus asked Ursus.

The centurion shrugged.

"Little Brits, presumably . . . 'wanted for questioning' – as that lot always say."

VI Victrix was informed from Londinium that one L. Alfenius Senecio had been appointed replacement Governor – and had actually arrived.

"Hum," said Ursus – the fount of all knowledge, "North African. A tough nut. Like the Emperor. Things're looking up."

Apricus, drawing pay in Principia, was told: "One for you, Sunshine – came with yesterday's courier," and found himself clutching a letter from home.

It appeared his father had forgiven him. Apricus picked open the letter and sprawled on his bunk in contubernia to read it. If the seal came away rather easily – he didn't notice.

. . . Lucius – dear boy. It was a great happiness to receive word of you and to know that you live and thrive. When I took the letter home, your mother alternately wept with relief and sang songs to herself in the kitchen for three days on end! It may be added that though I took what I felt was a correct stand with you about joining up the moment you turned eighteen, I have not been entirely popular with her since the day you and I so differed. However, enough of that. You

have brothers – as you remark – and indeed I am pleased
to relate that young Marcus has finished his schooling
well enough to to be taken on among the juniors here.
So all is well.

By calculation – knowing the time-span for basic
training, and allowing for what you tell us was a year
at Castra P., then estimating a few months more for
your equitation and travel, you must have reached
Britain last autumn. Your mother wonders how you
managed through the winter, and badgers me for money
to send you a clothing parcel in advance of this winter
coming: tunics, underwear and socks. She will not rest
until this is organized, so look out for it in another few
months!

We are very proud to hear that you have begun so
well – prizewinner and everything – and do hope that by
now you have had your status confirmed and receive the
extra pay. The army certainly seems to be *the* great
career nowadays, and surely, the Emperor had a huge
task these several years reorganizing it all. Since you
were so set on joining, it is well if you make the best
possible fist of all you do.

With regard to your queries: I knew very little of
Valerius Pudens, and now we have news here of his
death – which makes your question redundant. I did
ascertain he was regarded as a safe pair of hands for
Britain, and that in the past he was a staunch opponent
of Albinus. As regards the latter, I had difficulty in
gaining permission to view the relevant scrolls. It was
always assumed that he died at Lugdunum but there
does not seem to be any record of a body or actual
remains identified. That does not signify: the massacre
was terrible and it is most unlikely he survived – or
would have wished to. Nor, I am sure, has the Emperor

ever ceased to be vigilant! Albinus would probably have
had a Consular seal – was he not designated Caesar until
even that lofty height grew insufficient for him? I do
wonder why you ask.

I have written this in my noon break but now my
colleagues come trooping back, so must close. Marcus,
Tertius and Aemilius all send greetings to their best of
brothers, and your mother, of course, her love. The
gods be with you. Write when you can.

This from your no longer displeased father . . . M.
Valerianus.

VI Victrix's domestic refurbishment was back on again,
amidst renewed talk of high-powered visitors. Apricus was
kept in fort supervising painting jobs – anything from clean
white walls in barracks to smartening a suite of guest rooms
attached to the Legate's house. He played safe on this – not
trusting himself to be aesthetically original – getting the
painters simply to go over existing decor. Once, the Legate
looked in, grunted, "Same again, eh?", grinned and went
away.

He had more time off-duty to explore the town and found
his way to a taverna called "The Full Amphora" where the
wine was decent and there was food as well. The place was
popular among the optionate and more junior centurions.
Apricus stood his rounds; diced without incurring heavy
debt, and eyed a pretty girl who worked there called Candida.

"Aw . . . you'll never get her, Sunshine," his friends
joshed, "she's the stepdaughter. The old man keeps a tight
rein . . ."

He had written home again – family gossip – remarking
only in passing that there had been a strange incident early in
the year with a traveller using a Consular seal, that was all.

He couldn't see anything would come of it. He went on to mention, obliquely, the girl at the "Amphora", whose late father he had discovered, had been a VI Victrix legionary from Etruria called Candidus. ". . . as everyone knows, serving soldiers cannot marry, so Mother needn't have the hab-dabs about her. There is quite a movement growing in the army to petition for removal of this regulation, though I don't suppose for one moment Emperor Septimius Severus sees it that way . . ."

Returning to barracks one rose-and-gold summer evening just as the fortress prepared to close for the night, he had to jump aside until persons Senatorial were swept through the great gates in a blare of curled copper trumpets, jingle and glitter spilling off the escorting cavalry.

A night or two later, turned in on his bunk and thinking of Candida, Apricus became aware of the gritty tramp of marching boots advancing steadily his way along the barrack pavement outside. When they stopped, his door crashed open. A black figure loomed in silhouette against the moon-hung sky, throwing dark shadow in over the threshold and across various protesting mess-mates.

"L. Valerianus Apricus – Optio?" demanded a Frumentarius heading a small section of night guard.

"Yes . . ?"

"Under arrest! Surrender your weapons and follow me!"

They took him to their security block and shoved him in a holding cell, answering none of his questions. Ursus was already inside. At least they weren't fettered.

"Jupiter Optimus Maximus!" Apricus exploded. "Now what?"

Ursus looked at him wearily.

"Best guess is: it's to do with the nighthawks we stopped that time."

"But we have no real idea who any of them were!"

"Nor have they, I reckon. It's called thrashing about, Sunshine!"

There was nothing to rest on.

They sat side by side on the floor, backs to a wall, unsleeping, growing stiff and cold. Daylight took an age returning.

They were kept two days, without explanation and on minimal rations.

During the third evening, not given any chance to clean themselves up, they got marched through the late dusk into Headquarters.

The tribunal dais in the cross-hall was full of people in white tunics – some displaying the broad Senatorial stripe. The Legate was there – and the Architectus, fiddling worriedly with scrolls and papers on a table. Ursus nudged Apricus. Behind one shoulder of the person who appeared to be the most prestigious visitor stood Frumentarius Blandus.

A staff officer they didn't know, asking formal permission of the Legate, established their identities, duties, and what he called, snuffily, "your authorship of this report". He held up what Apricus recognized as his set of tablets from the Spring. Apricus almost nodded acceptance before Ursus elbowed him hard in the ribs. The Architectus, clearing his throat, insisted they be allowed to look over the tablets before agreeing. Once this was done, the staff officer ended haughtily: "His Excellency has decided to cross-examine you in person."

The prestigious visitor, who was altogether bony, with a skull-like visage, hooded eyes and yellowed skin, regarded them keenly.

"I am Procurator of this Province," he said, in a voice

reminiscent of the dry rustle of dead leaves. "You may know of me: M. Oclatinius Adventus."

Apricus thought, dismayed, "Dea Fortuna . . . lend me strength!"

In the background, Blandus smiled mirthlessly.

"Which of you was responsible for this report?" Adventus began.

Ursus and Apricus answered simultaneously: "I am . . . sir."

"Come now . . ."

Ursus said: "To be exact – the optio wrote it out. He was in charge on the job at the time. But I was present. In view of the strangeness of the incident, and because I was his senior in the field, he asked my advice as to what was best. I recommended a report."

"Very well. What struck you particularly about the first traveller?"

"In what way?" Apricus queried.

"What did he look like . . . how did he seem?"

"A Briton. To look like, he appeared British," Apricus replied. "I have described him, sir . . ." He nodded at the tablets returned to the table. "But as soon as he opened his mouth, you could tell he wasn't – far from it."

"How so?"

"His Latin, Excellency . . . very patrician. Drawled down the nose, just like y . . . just like they do – senators and such."

Ursus added: "No Brit could fake that!"

Adventus' gaze moved from one to the other and back again. He blinked expressionlessly, lizard-like.

"And?" he prompted.

"When we argued, he dragged out this Consular seal. I have seen one once before. It was for this reign."

"He might have faked *that*!"

"He might," conceded Ursus, "but he'd have had to go to great lengths to get it done."

Apricus joined in: "Look, sir – it was night and there was a thick mist. This man came out of nowhere. He insisted he had intelligence for the Governor . . . the Governor-as-was, that is, and that he was being chased because of it. We had nothing else to go on. He said if he reached Ebor, then he'd be all right. And he was followed. It's all in there . . ."

"Ye-es. But he didn't come here, did he? No one has any recollection of him."

"If you say not, sir."

"You handed in your report on return, but you never thought to find that out?"

Centurion and optio exchanged glances.

"Not our bag, sir, really – was it? We are here to mend forts and roads," Ursus offered truculently.

The Legate coughed.

Adventus repeated his lizard impression, allowing a pause.

"But he reached Londinium," his voice creaked like icicles in the wind, "and when he did, Governor Pudens died."

The enormity of this implication settled like dead weight.

"You are telling us, Excellency," stated Ursus flatly, "that we should have stopped this man on no reasonable evidence and in the face of an Imperial seal. And that because we didn't, he murdered the late Governor."

"In a nutshell."

"May we know if you have made your mind up to that?"

"You try my temper, Centurion! But I have not . . . yet."

The Architectus, grey-faced, unexpectedly stuck his neck out.

"Excellency, I protest! These are valuable members of my staff: trained engineers. The Emperor has spent years encouraging such skills, of which we are woefully short. I cannot see how you expect them to have acted other than as they did in such a surprise situation. They know nothing, I am certain, of politics or secret agents – and I for one, though you have never canvassed my opinion, here and now testify to their probity!"

Adventus swung round, looking him up and down.

"Naturally, Martialus, you defend your own!" he uttered bitingly. "I note it. Let me remind you that before the appointment of your present General – ever since it supported Albinus' ridiculous adventure – this entire legion has been under a cloud. Do not forget it!"

The Legate cleared his throat again.

"Excellency," he intervened, "both of these men are very recently posted. They arrived together from Rome only last autumn. Before we all get carried away, may I point out Centurion Ursus' impeccable record of loyalty to the Imperial house, having served in several Provinces, and that Apricus was a mere youngster in . . . where . . . Etruria? . . . at the time Albinus was removing troops to Gaul."

Adventus shot him a cold glare but subsided.

"Neither of you have any idea, then, I suppose, of what that late adventurer looked like?" he persisted.

"No sir," they answered, Apricus adding, "This man we saw – whoever you think he might be – had gone to pains to pass for British: long hair, moustaches; tribal clothing. Might he not have had to try the seal business on with other soldiers?"

"There are no accounts of it."

Adventus, for the first time, seemed defensive. In other words, their unexpected road block apart, this man had melted as resourcefully into invisibility as he had into the northern mist – British in one context; Roman no doubt in another. Nor had they caught him, or none of this would be going on.

Ursus perked up.

But Apricus, at least, was not yet out of the wood.

"Your father is in the Imperial Archives," the Procurator addressed him alone.

"Yes, sir."

"You have had a good education."

"Yes, sir. Inasmuch as he could afford. Me and each of my brothers."

"Why did you enquire about Albinus when you wrote home – and of a Consular seal?" Adventus turned to Blandus, who put a sheet of papyrus in his hand. "I quote . . . 'you're in the right spot, Pa, can you tell me if Albinus was killed for definite in battle at Lugdunum? And would he have rated a Consular seal?' What put that in your mind?"

"Obviously, the traveller, sir. May I see that?"

Adventus passed it to him wordlessly. It was a neat copy of his letter. Presumably intercepted in Londinium. Though he tried not to show it, Apricus had to assume the reply had been copied also.

"Thank you, sir."

He passed it back.

"Are we accurate?" Adventus sneered.

"Sir!"

"Strangely – this traveller made you think of Albinus?"

"Ursus told me Consular seals are rarely given. I couldn't think of anyone else who might have had one – except another Governor, perhaps . . . or yourself. My father, as you surely know, rather agreed."

"Ye . . . es."

The Procurator nibbled a nail.

Ursus shifted impatiently and took a chance on blowing the thing wide open.

"The truth is," he said bluntly, "our report, and a chance remark in a letter, is the only evidence this character exists at all! And you didn't get him!"

Adventus looked bleak. There was a sharp, barking laugh from someone at the rear of the dais.

Borne up on Ursus' optimism, Apricus stated, "If Governor Pudens was killed it could only be either a private enmity or an attempt at destabilizing the Province . . ."

"Correct," Adventus conceded and, like a leech to blood, turned voraciously on the attack. "The two following, that night, were definitely tribesmen?"

Apricus was learning caution.

"We thought so. That is to say, they sounded how they looked."

"Go on."

"There was a dark one and a ginger one. The dark one did the talking – mostly. The red-haired one only spoke up the once. About where they were headed – some place called Cam-something. I hadn't heard of it."

"Cambodunum," grated Blandus self-importantly.

A key clicked over in Apricus' mind.

"That," he said pointing and angry, "was precisely the voice! The bloody ginger one was you! And whoever the killer was – whatever he intended – you lost him!"

Blandus scowled, making quick, scathing remarks about Apricus' stupidity. The optio roared back how was he to know who-was-who – in the mist; in the dark; under hanks of false red hair?

"You know both of us," he shouted. "We rode here together last year. What was so bloody secret that night, that you couldn't make yourself apparent?"

He tried to rush the dais.

"Enough – or you all face charges!" bellowed a new voice.

Alfenius Senecio strode forward to restore order.

"Adventus," he continued evenly, "you've had your turn and I've listened to all I need. I'm satisfied these soldiers acted in good faith – as best they might in very unclear circumstance. If you ask me, your own staff might stand examination – but that is your business!"

Conferring briefly with the Legate, he announced: "Centurion; Optio – case dismissed."

The dais began to empty of people.

The Architectus, mightily relieved, clacked concertinas of tablets back into neat, closed squares.

"Consider yourselves reprimanded," said the Legate to Ursus and Apricus, "that is: for the outburst at the end. For the rest – we live on the edge at the moment, though it isn't policy to say so. Senecio tells me, however, that fresh cohorts are to be drafted in in numbers – and the Emperor does see he may very well be needed in person before too long. If and when that happens, the Brits won't know what hit them!"

"Sir?" queried Apricus.

"Mmm?"

"Did Albinus die at Lugdunum?"

"It was always thought so. Who knows? But the Frumentarii, believe me, are going to have to rake their way through this entire land! Smarten yourselves. Reclaim weapons. Report for duty in the morning."

The Case of His Own Abduction

Wallace Nichols

*For seventeen years Wallace Nichols (1888–1967) wrote
his stories about Sollius, the Slave Detective, for the
London Mystery Magazine. It is still the longest running
series of Roman mystery stories, over sixty of them, none of
which were ever collected into book form. The stories are
set, for the most part, during the reign of another mad
emperor, Caracalla, in the early years of the third century,
just a few years after the previous story. Nichols was at
heart a poet, though he also wrote boys' adventure stories
and for a while served as an editorial assistant on* The
Windsor Magazine *in the thirties. This was one of the last
Sollius stories that Nichols wrote.*

A distraught man knocked heavily and persistently on the
great bronze door of the mansion on the Esquiline
belonging to the old Senator Titius Sabinus. The doorkeeper, in a twittering state, opened and remonstrated.

"Do not add to our troubles," he quavered angrily. "Get
you gone – oh, is it you, Cordus? What would you?"

"I would see the noble Sabinus," panted the other. "I
need help – I need the help of the famous Slave Detective."

The doorkeeper started, and hurriedly let him in.

"Have you news of our Sollius?" he asked, and led him at once into the atrium, where the whole household seemed assembled in a general hum of uncertainty and distress.

Sabinus himself, seated on the rim of the fountain in the centre, appeared dazed, and his great-nephew and adopted son, Sergius Falba, was bending over him, uttering what consolation he could.

"It may all be quite explainable. He may be on a secret mission for the Prefect."

"Licinius always punctiliously asks for his services," replied Sabinus. "No, Sergius, some disaster has befallen him. Who disturbs us so roughly, doorkeeper?"

"Your humble client, lord," said the intruder, falling to his knees. "I am in great trouble . . ."

"So are we here," sighed the old Senator.

"But I, most noble Sabinus, am nigh ruined, and only one man in Rome can solve my puzzle . . ."

Before he had time to explain further, Licinius, the City Prefect, in full military bronze, was ushered in by a slave.

"What news, my friend?" asked Sabinus hopefully.

"I grieve, but none," was the answer. "I have planted informers in every quarter of Rome, but none of them reports anything to the purpose. Sollius is like Curtius, swallowed up by the ground!"

Sabinus sighed deeply – and Cordus stared hopelessly around.

"The Slave Detective missing?" he stammered.

"These three days," said Falba.

"The Gods help us all!" groaned Cordus.

Sollius sat twiddling his thumbs on a stool in a cellar lit only by a small grating high in one wall. He went over his abduction. He had been limping homewards after finishing an errand for his master when, in the narrowest part of a narrow by-street, he had suddenly been attacked by two men who, as he had approached, had been lazily leaning against a high wall. It was of no use to struggle; he had let himself be gagged and blindfolded and led away. Now, freed from bandage and gag, he sat on his stool, deeply ruminating.

Ear and nose alike suggested to him where he might be – buried in the unsavoury intricacies of the Subura, probably underneath one of its evil taverns. He knew that he had many enemies among the criminals of Rome, men whom he had delivered up to the justice of the City Prefect. But why, when they had him at their mercy, had they not ruthlessly killed him? Were his captors holding him to ransom, hoping that his master would pay for the release of his favourite slave? He was certainly not being ill-treated for he was fed regularly, even if the food was rough and the wine harsh. Abruptly he ceased twiddling his thumbs. If it had been a question of ransom his master would by this time have paid. But now the answer had come: he had been temporarily abducted because he was feared. Someone was contemplating a crime, and dreaded his being called in to investigate. When it was safe to release him he would be let loose. His reputation had been his undoing.

He rose, and began pacing about. Surely Lucius had learned enough of his methods to smell out the place where he was. It would be a test for the younger man. Besides, Licinius the Prefect would not desert his old friend but would turn Rome upside down to find him. He smiled. He had only to wait.

Lucius was on his mettle: it was the first time that he had had to prove himself as a detective. However, he was not allowed to give the search for Sollius his sole attention. Sabinus had bidden him attend to the case of Cordus.

"What is your trouble, O Cordus?" asked Lucius, sighing heavily.

"My fine farm – a little off the Appian Way – has been burnt down, not by accident of a fallen lamp, but by a deliberate firing. Some enemy did it – but who, O gods, is my enemy? I live in harmony with all I know, and have no debts in Rome. Find the man, O Lucius, who fired my farm. I want a complete revenge."

Reluctantly Lucius accompanied the farmer to the ruins of his property. Cordus, with his wife and only son, had found refuge in a cottage of his own nearby. The wife was continually weeping; the son, by name Satrius, sullenly angry.

"Have you lately dismissed, or unduly whipped, one of your slaves?" asked Lucius, but they shook their heads.

"Our slaves and other workers are all contented; we have no trouble with them, unlike others that I know," Cordus answered.

"Did your farming pay?" abruptly questioned Lucius.

"Fortune, slave, has befriended me," replied Cordus coldly.

"Then may not some neighbour, less befriended of Fortune, have maliciously vented his spite?"

"I cannot believe it," answered Cordus in a tone of finality, and Satrius nodded agreement.

"Have you seen any roving groups of disbanded legionaries – to whom, perhaps, you refused alms?"

"None," was the curt reply.

Lucius asked all the questions which he would have expected Sollius to ask, but none of the answers illuminated his mind.

"How I praise the gods," suddenly broke in Cordus's wife, "that Delia was away from us. In her delicate state it would have more than troubled her. She loved our farm almost more than any of us did."

"Delia?" inquired Lucius.

"My daughter," answered Cordus. "She is on a visit to her

uncle, a merchant in Rhodes. She . . . had to go . . ." he said
with meaning in his tone.

"She is to marry her cousin," murmured Satrius.

Eager to be gone on what he considered the more important case, Lucius hastened back to his master's house on
the Esquiline.

Sollius was brought his food by an old, haggard woman
slave, broken by her long, harsh lot, and living in a constant
haze of semi-sobriety. She was ugly, slatternly and lachry-
mose, yet he saw in her, had he been a Christian, what he
would have considered to be an angel of light, but, in his
pagan persuasions, seemed an instrument, however unlikely,
ready for the cunning of his brain.

It took him days to penetrate through her tearful mist, but
gradually she would nod her grey head and leer when he
promised her so many sesterces of money or the purchase of
her freedom by favour of his master if she would help him to
escape. But then she would only grin and leer, wave her lamp
drunkenly, and leave him unanswered.

A little later in his captivity she came in with his food,
obviously excited, incoherent, and waving her lamp uncertainly above her head. She mopped and mowed rather than
spoke, and Sollius was hard put to it to distinguish the
pathetic plea for her freedom.

"By Jupiter himself, it shall be yours," he promised
emphatically.

She seemed satisfied, laid down his platter with its rough
contents, and prepared to go. Reeling, she weaved her way to
the door, and there, stumbling, she dropped her lamp. The
clay splintered into fragments, and the blazing oil ran over
the stone slabs and caught the dry wood of the half-rotted
door, which, in a moment was ablaze itself. It caught the
woman's clothes, too. She shrieked and fell.

Sollius seized the instant, and daring the blazing oil, stumbled out through the door. Then he turned to draw the old woman clear, but her shrieks abruptly ceased and he saw that she was dead, killed by the shock. He left her where she had fallen, still with her clothes on fire and the stench of her scorching flesh.

Swathed in the smoke, he limped chokingly up the stone steps ahead of him and along a narrow stone passage which led both into an unsavoury outside alley and, by a low arched entrance, into the still more unsavoury tavern in the cellar under which he had been held. Edging carefully past this entrance, he could see a dozen or so of the worst types in Rome, drinking and quarrelling. He made no pause, but limped on towards the open alley. As he did so he heard a voice speaking above the hubbub in the tavern, into which the smoke had hardly yet begun to drift – a voice that spoke in high-bred, patrician Latin – and it uttered Sollius's name. It was too risky to go back and peer into the tavern; his business was to escape: but he knew that he would remember that voice.

At last he was out into the night. He knew the byways of the Subura well, and made his way to the less evil streets of Rome. Suddenly he paused, stood still for a moment in thought, and then changed his direction, turning away from his master's house.

Cordus, crying for revenge, pestered the Prefect and Lucius alike. The latter, sick with fears for Sollius, haunted the evil life of the Subura where his instinct told him that his friend would eventually be found – alive or dead. He spent more time seeking for Sollius than for Cordus's unknown enemy or seducer of his daughter. The house on the Esquiline was filled with apprehension. Sollius had been loved by all, not least by his master, and Sergius

Falba, the old Senator's adopted son, willingly joined Lucius in his expeditions.

He appeared, in fact, to find amusement in searching Rome's dark places, many of them already known to him during a wild youth. But he was in earnest enough, and more than once brought with him on the excursions a noble friend of his, one Terentius Cremutus. Both young men endeavoured to uphold the young slave in his almost despairing hopes.

"Sollius will be found," said Falba. "He'll come home one day with a perfect explanation."

"So clever a man," echoed Cremutus, "can find his way out of any labyrinth," and he laid a comforting hand on Lucius's shoulder. "I'll bet you a golden aureus, slave, that you see him again, safe and sound."

They were in a thoroughfare, and suddenly a slave approached Cremutus in an agitated manner.

"What is it, Sosius? What news do you bear?"

The slave took his master apart and spoke hurriedly to him. Cremutus beckoned Falba over to him, and they spoke together for some minutes. Then the slave departed at a run, and the two young patricians rejoined Lucius.

"My friend," said Falba with a laugh, "is buying a new and very handsome slave-girl – and she has disappeared! From now onwards," he added with another laugh, "he'll join our searches with even greater eagerness, eh, Terentius?"

Sollius, having begged and received secret quarters in the barracks of the Urban Cohorts, was in conference with Licinius, the City Prefect.

"So the tavern was not burned down?"

"Burrus, the tavern-keeper, and his cronies had a fright because of the smoke, but only the cellar door flamed," affirmed Licinius. "There was little wailing for the old woman, and you yourself wished no one – as yet – to be arrested. But I bet that Burrus's back has felt a few stripes from him who employed him to hold you! But why, my friend, did you not go home? The noble Sabinus is grievously anxious over you."

"I've asked myself," Sollius answered, "why I was abducted – but not killed – and have come to the notion that someone, about to commit a crime, feared that its solution might be referred to my known deftness in such matters, so wished to have me for certain days, or weeks, just out of the way. Can you suggest such a crime, Prefect?"

"There is one, and one for which your aid was sought. As it is, your younger associate Lucius has been trying his hand – to little effect, I know, and my own informers have equally failed," and Licinius outlined the case of Cordus.

"I'll take it up," said Sollius, "and remain missing while I do so. That will at least keep the criminal worried. He'll know by now that I've escaped."

"That fellow Cordus again, sir," said a soldier, entering.

"Let him enter," ordered Licinius. "This is your case now, old friend. Ah, Cordus, come in!"

"Any news for me, O Prefect? Am I to lose my property and no one suffer for it?"

"This," said Licinius, "is one of my sharpest informers. He has your case in hand, he will do everything he can."

"If only," sighed Cordus, "he were the Slave Detective! Is there no news either of the great Sollius?"

Both Licinius and Sollius lugubriously shook their heads.

"My poor, lovely farm!" burst out Cordus, obsessed by his own trouble. "It was so well sited between two woods, and a stream ran through its gardens. It was a site for a villa rather than a farm. I've had offers for the site – but I would never have sold my patrimony. But now it is gone – and no money for it!"

Sollius then proceeded to ask some of the same questions which his pupil Lucius had put to the farmer before, and received the same answers. Finally he asked another which Lucius had not asked.

"Did you recently turn away a beggar unsatisfied and who turned nasty?"

"By the gods, but I did!" exclaimed Cordus. "A great, hulking fellow with a scar across his face – like a retired gladiator. Find that man, Prefect, and we'll have him whipped till he screams. I'm sure that's the man. There is no need for the Slave Detective after all! Find a gladiator who survived the arena, and you've the man!"

He took his leave, grimly satisfied with the new chance of revenge. Immediately afterwards the same soldier came in again.

"The noble Sergius Falba and the noble Terentius Cremutus wish to see you, sir," he announced.

Licinius lifted an eyebrow towards the Slave Detective.

"Do you wish to be 'found'?" he asked.

"I think not yet. Can you hide me – and where, perhaps, I might hear?"

"Step inside my scribe's room yonder. You'll hear there well enough. Show the two noble gentlemen in to me, soldier."

When the two friends entered they found the Prefect alone.

The preliminaries of the interview were curt and blunt.

"We're not satisfied, Prefect, and my father Titius Sabinus is not satisfied, at the progress made towards the finding of our slave Sollius."

"I am sorry," answered Licinius, "that the illustrious Sabinus feels I've been negligent in my duty. I assure you I've had all my men on the hunt for him."

"It is certainly not enough, Prefect," said Cremutus, who

seemed even more angry than his companion though Sollius was no slave of his.

"He may already be dead," added Falba.

"Then where is his body?" drily asked Licinius. "If dead his body would have been flung out to the crows – and so found."

"We're not satisfied!" repeated Cremutus.

"My friend has a plan," said Falba.

"It is this," Cremutus explained. "We suggest enrolling a body of picked slaves from our two households and searching Rome thoroughly ourselves – but it needs your permission: it were a stupid folly, Prefect, for our men to be picked up by the Urban Cohorts as disturbers of the peace."

"You may use your slaves so," replied Licinius stiffly. "It will do no harm, at least, to shake up the Surbura. Our own nets, cast in after you, may draw in a few fish from the disturbed mud."

"You take this very lightly, Prefect," said Falba. "The Emperor himself has expressed his concern in this disappearance to my father."

"Also to me," equably answered Licinius. "His Divinity is continually informed of our progress."

"Your progress!" snorted Cremutus. "Come, Sergius. We have our permission, and the sooner we pick our slaves the better. Good-day, Prefect."

As soon as they had gone Sollius emerged from the scribe's room.

"Did you hear?" smiled Licinius. "I shall be glad when I can produce you!"

"I heard – and something more than I expected," Sollius answered, and he patted one of his ears as though he thoroughly approved of the accuracy of that organ. "Where does Cordus dwell? I must see him again. But lend me a centurion to go with me – and confirm who I am."

*   *   *

Sollius and the centurion found Cordus in his cottage on the edge of his farmlands.

"Have you laid hands on that broken gladiator?" he asked them.

"Do you believe in him – on second thoughts?" retorted Sollius with a smile. "It was but a question I had to ask for the sake of the record. Have you told *everything* to the Prefect?"

"Did I not tell you, Satrius my son, that only the Slave Detective could be trusted? And now he is dead," he said in a great gloom, and suddenly clapped his hands as though in a moment of illumination. "May it not be part of the plot against me: to kill him in order that he of all people should *not* look into our trouble?"

"The Slave Detective," quietly answered Sollius, "is not dead. I am he!"

Father and son stared at him incredulously.

"This *is* Sollius the Slave Detective," confirmed the centurion.

"Now I can believe again in the gods!" cried Cordus. "Why was I told you were missing?" he asked suspiciously.

"I *was* missing; I was abducted – but escaped. No matter for that now!"

"At last, father, we can dare speak out," said Satrius.

"How 'dare' speak out?" asked Sollius, but he was smiling as though he knew very well.

"Who but you," answered Cordus, "could accuse the powerful without a whipping? How I wished I could really have deceived myself over that suggested gladiator! But . . . I fear my enemy is a patrician."

"Give me his name."

"Neither my son nor I know it – or he would be dead. I have a daughter," he added, sighing, "and she has a danger-ous beauty."

"He came to the farm at night," interposed Satrius. "I

nearly caught him once. But it was too dark to see his face, and he got swiftly away in a rich man's chariot with two spirited white horses. My sister will not give his name. Though infatuated, she fears him."

"I would question her," said Sollius.

"I have sent her to her uncle in Rhodes. He has an only son, and is a rich man. She may even come to good in the end. He will have burnt down my farm in revenge for my sending her out of his reach."

"You should have told this to the Prefect," said the Slave Detective severely.

"And had one patrician cover up for another? I know my Rome. The seducer of my daughter may even be in the circle of the new Emperor."

"You should still have told the Prefect – and even I am afraid of Caracalla!"

"You're afraid of no man," said Cordus, "or your fame is false. Get me but the man's name, and I'll kill him even at the Emperor's feet!"

"And I will strike with you," cried Satrius. "I love my sister."

"Come," said Cordus in a milder tone. "Let me show you my burnt-out farm, and you will know my double cause for hate . . ."

He led the way. It was a walk of less than a quarter of a mile. They came to a scene of black destruction, desolate in spite of the Appian sunlight. Cordus suddenly gave an angry exclamation. A man was standing in the midst of the ruins, looking about him.

"Who is this trespasser?" cried Cordus.

"I think I recognize him," said Sollius. "It is Tranquillus, a lawyer."

Cordus bristled, and went forwards.

"What do you here?" he demanded.

"You are the freedman Cordus?" was the polite inquiry.
"What of it?"

"I am a lawyer from Rome, Tranquillus. Ah, Slave Detective, so *you* are here, looking into the fire? Well, freedman, my presence is easy to explain. I have a business proposition for you from a client. He would buy the land on which your farm stood."

"I shall not sell!" answered Cordus.

"He offers a good sum," said Tranquillus, and he named a certain number of sesterces.

"Even that is too cheap," replied Cordus contemptuously.

"You haven't the capital to rebuild," said Tranquillus with a dry smile. "Why waste so fair a country prospect when you can sell it?"

Cordus obstinately shook his head.

"The land as it is now," the lawyer pursued, "is worth little or nothing to you. It might as well have been ploughed with salt. Sell when you can, my friend!"

"At that low price? Never! At any price? Never!"

"I can go a little higher . . ." and Tranquillus advanced the number of sesterces. "But my client will not barter. I can only strongly advise you. No one will give you more. Don't you agree, Sollius, that he will be a fool to refuse my client's offer?"

"Who is that client?" brusquely snapped Cordus.

"I speak for him. I have the money here. There is no need for a name where there is hard money, freedman. Let me pay you now. See, my slave yonder carries a large bag . . . filled with coin, O Cordus."

"Take your slave and his bag away together, lawyer! I will not sell. Who is your client?" he repeated.

"Since you refuse his offer, freedman, there is no need to name him," answered Tranquillus blandly; he saluted them, and turned away towards a waiting chariot.

*   *   *

A puzzled Lucius, summoned peremptorily to the Prefect's quarters, found Sollius with the Prefect himself – and flinging up his hands in his amazed relief, he burst into tears.

"Save your wonder!" smiled Sollius. "I will tell all of my adventures in time. But for now listen." He spoke quickly and concisely, and Lucius listened in growing surprise and excitement.

"But aren't you coming home?" he asked. "Our master is truly in grief over you."

"Leave me my love of cunning," Sollius laughed. "I shall come it may be at this very day's time of dusk, and you must be ready to help me over the wall behind the carp-pool. Now you, Licinius," he went on, turning to the Prefect briskly, "have you chosen your two soldiers?"

"They are already wearing slaves' tunics, and have had your instructions."

"Good," answered the Slave Detective, "let them be off on their missions now. By Apollo, I can lay a plot as well as unravel one!"

At the time of dusk, as promised, Sollius was on the outer side of the wall of his master's house. More than once Lucius, crouching by the carp-pool, thought that he heard him, but now, he was certain.

"Is that you?" he called softly.

"Help me over," bade Sollius. "We can wait amongst these laurels."

The Roman evening was fair and calm, and a star of sapphirine crystal was mirrored in the carp-pool.

"What do you expect?" whispered a deeply puzzled Lucius, but before Sollius answered the figure of Sergius Falba came down a cypress avenue and stood silently, as though also waiting, by the pool.

Presently a quick step was heard approaching down the same avenue, and another figure joined him.

"What is this urgency, Sergius?" asked the voice of Terentius Cremutus. "What has happened that you sent a slave to me, making this secret appointment here?"

"*I* sent a slave to *you*? It was you who sent a slave to *me*!"

Though they could see only each other's outlines in the gathering dark they stared at one another with shocked intensity.

"Someone," muttered Falba, "has done us an evil turn."

"It will be your cunning Sollius," answered Cremutus. "Had we only caught him again after he escaped that fire at Natta's tavern! He must have been slyly watching us. I told you we should have killed him at first," he added fiercely.

"That I would never have done," firmly said Falba. "I owe that to my father Sabinus. I was mad to do so much . . . and for nothing!"

"For nothing, indeed, and for me, too," bitterly burst out Cremutus. "Where has that sly slave been hiding – and what does he know?"

"His cunning is so," replied Falba, "that he may have us both."

"Then why not come out from his hiding-place and accuse us to our faces? Can he be hiding in the house?"

"Do you think I haven't secretly searched?"

"If only," went on Cremutus through his teeth, "he weren't so incorruptible! A good bribe could save us. Gods, where is he?"

"He is here," said Sollius, and stepped with Lucius out of the laurels.

The shadows of Falba and Cremutus started convulsively against the darker shadows in the calm, round mirror of the carp-pool.

"You terrible slave!" burst out Cremutus.

"So you have come home!" said Falba, recovering himself. "My father has been much troubled for you."

"You, lord, could have spared his white head!"

"Do not be insolent!" cried Falba.

"I am always ready to be insolent, lord, in the service of truth – and my master will uphold me. Answer not, lord, but listen. I have knowledge of two facts: the ignoble pursuit of a beautiful girl, and the burning down of a man's farm in the selfish desire to possess its site cheaply for the building there of an idle man's villa. But you are too incompetent for crime! You, Cremutus, should never have visited Natta's tavern while I was held there: I heard your voice – and again in the Prefect's office. And you, lord," he added, turning to Falba, "should not have driven your well-known *white* horses to a seduction. I have opened to the day too many conspiracies to miss such clues."

"You are going to betray us?" asked Falba.

"The girl is beyond your lust, lord, and I shall say nothing to my master – he is old and loves you. Let him think that I was captured by a gang of thieves who hated me. I have but one other price for silence. Let your friend pay Cordus sufficient compensation for his farm."

"By Hecate, this is too much, you rascally slave," cried Cremutus.

"Tranquillus, an honest lawyer, will tell the truth," said Sollius.

Cremutus cursed by all the Nether Gods and stormed out.

"We never intended to harm you . . . in time you would have been set free," murmured Falba awkwardly.

But the Slave Detective made no answer and walked contemptuously away, returning to his own quarters in the house.

The Malice of the Anicii[1]

Gillian Bradshaw

*It isn't often that I find a story works with footnotes, but
the following won't work without them. It is told by
Ammianus Marcellinus (c. 330–395), Rome's last great
historian, though much of his History of Rome, a con-
tinuation of that by Tacitus, is lost. Nevertheless what
survives provides us with a rare glimpse into the last
decades of the Eternal City. A classical scholar, and
recipient of the Phillips Prize for Classical Greek (in
1975 and 1977), Gillian Bradshaw is a noted writer of
both fantasy and historical fiction. Amongst her recent
books,* Cleopatra's Heir *(2002) will be of especial interest
to fans of ancient Rome.*

Concerning the idleness and profligacy of the Romans, I
have amply written elsewhere. However, certain flat-
terers and sycophants have seen fit to rebuke me for it, saying
that I, an Asiatic Greek, should not venture to criticize
illustrious men whose names descend from the pristine

1 This manuscript appears from its references and style to be the work of
the fourth century historian Ammianus Marcellinus. If it is genuine, it
constitutes a fascinating expansion upon many of the hints of the surviving
books of his history (the *Res Gestae*). However, this is probably a modern
forgery.

age of the Roman state – believing, I suppose, that those who
bear great names should be revered for the names' sake, even
if they never by word or deed accomplish anything worthy of
their great ancestors. Since, then, statements I have made in
my history have been considered outrageous, let me here set
out more fully an account of the conduct of some of those
who are held in honour at Rome.

I first came to the Eternal City after the death of Julian
Augustus[2] in order to consult accounts written in Latin, for I
intended to compose a history of the reign of that heroic
emperor. I had a letter of introduction from my friend and
countryman Libanius, that most renowned of orators, to
Aurelius Symmachus, who is generally accounted the most
cultured nobleman in Rome.

Symmachus welcomed me very warmly; indeed, when I
saw how much attention that wealthy and distinguished man
lavished upon me I thought my fame and fortune were
assured, and I regretted that I hadn't come to Rome years
before. My pleasure was much abated the following day
however, when, obedient to his urging, I called upon him
again, only to find that he had completely forgotten who I
was, and stood regarding me in doubt, wondering whether or
not I might be one of his clients. In the end he did recognize
me, and admitted me to his circle and – what was more useful
– to his library, yet, for all that I spent years assiduously
waiting upon that blockhead, I never advanced any further in
his friendship and received only scanty and unhelpful patronage for my history. On the occasion when a famine was
feared and foreigners were compelled to leave the city, he
interceded to secure the residency of his mistress's hair-
dresser, but extended no such assistance to me; and when I
returned to Rome, after an interval of a year, he did not even

2 AD 363; however, Ammianus is generally believed to have spent some
years in his native Antioch after that event.

notice that I had been away, or ask where I had gone. Such is the learned and eloquent Aurelius Symmachus.

However, as a pigeon may appear outstanding for beauty and sweetness of voice if it struts among crows, so Symmachus appears pre-eminent for virtue and wisdom among the nobility of Rome. Many other men of illustrious ancestry care for nothing but gain, and, in the immortal words of Cicero, consider that nothing in human affairs is good unless it is profitable.[3] Some are so overborne by greed and ambition that their arrogance knows no bounds – and chief among them are the clan of the Anicii, whose name is famous throughout the whole world. It will suffice, in place of many examples of their conduct, to set down this one, to which I myself was a witness.

I was in the Library of Trajan in Rome, devotedly handling one of the many books of Latin history, when Symmachus chanced to come in. On seeing me he exclaimed that good fortune must have guided our meeting. "For," he said, "your friend Eutherius has arrived in Rome, and I have invited him to dinner. I need one more guest to fill the lowest couch, and I believe he would be pleased to see you."

I was normally spared attendance at my patron's gluttonous and unwholesome banquets, since his guests, when they were not senators and high officials, tended to be persons whose company senators and high officials find entertaining – that is, horse-breeders and experts at gambling. I was pleased to escape such company, and would have been pleased to escape Eutherius as well. A eunuch, he had been chamberlain to Constans Augustus and afterwards to Julian, and he had recently retired to Rome. Though I had some acquaintance with him – we both served Julian when he held the rank of Caesar in Gaul – I had never been his "friend"

3 *De Amicitia*, 21, 79.

nor ever wished to be. I have seen too many honest men destroyed by the jealousy and greed of imperial chamberlains, and, although Eutherius had always been reported honest, if Socrates himself had given me a good report of a eunuch, I should have accused him of departing from the truth. However, I had by then been long enough in Rome to know that it would be better to kill a nobleman's brother than decline his invitation to dinner, so I had no choice but to thank Symmachus and accept.

When the time of the ill-omened banquet arrived, I went to Symmachus' mansion, where, having failed to bribe the slave who was to announce my name, and having in consequence been kept waiting in an antechamber for some time, I was at length admitted.

The other guests were already reclining at the table, and on seeing them I was dismayed, as though I had walked into an arena full of wild beasts. Eutherius, indeed, reclined on the central couch beside Symmachus, but next to him lay the former praetorian prefect, Petronius Probus, who married an Anicia and was in consequence compelled to seek high office in order that his relatives might perpetrate their crimes with impunity. On the next couch were more of the clan: Anicius Hermogenianus, Probus' brother-in-law, and two cousins, Anicius Auchenius Bassus and Anicius Paulinus, the latter a young man, though already old in lawlessness and greed.

I was unknown to the Anicii at the time, so when the slave grudgingly announced me, my arrival passed unremarked. Indeed, Eutherius was speaking, and the rest of the company were hanging upon his words with open mouths, since each man hoped to gain some advantage from the eunuch's recent knowledge of the situation at court. I went to the lowest couch in silence, and took my place next to two others of Symmachus' clients.

Eutherius, however, when he finished some anecdote of

life in Mediolanum[4], glanced about himself with great affability, and, when he noticed me at once sat up, crying, "Marcellinus! I last saw you in Antioch. What are you doing in Rome?"

I explained my purpose, and he praised it. "Our Lord Julian Augustus," he said, "was a prince well-deserving of some memorial, and I can think of no one better to provide one. I still remember the account of the siege of Amida[5] which you recited to the court, and which was so wonderful for its vividness and power."

At this I was as much flattered as I was taken aback. The Anicii, however, regarded me threateningly, like savage bulls, and Probus proclaimed my purpose to be impious. "Julianus Augustus," he declared, "was an apostate, a madman who turned against the Christian faith in which he was raised and chased instead after the fables of poets. Because of this, God decreed that his reign soon came to an end – though not before he had cost the Roman state dearly! It would be better if he and all his works were buried in oblivion."

I was filled with the passionate indignation, and would have spoken out, had not Symmachus intervened first. "Surely noblemen are not to be judged solely on their faith, illustrious Probus!" he exclaimed. "If that were so, religion alone would be sufficient to distinguish a bad prefect from a good one."

Now Symmachus had at that time achieved the rank of Prefect of the City of Rome[6]; and, as all the world knows, is more firm than prudent in his adherence to the ancient gods of the city, scorning as expedient the conversion to

---

4 Milan. In the fourth century, emperors did not reside at Rome, which was too remote from the frontiers.

5 AD 359 *Res Gestae XIX*.

6 Q. Aurelius Symmachus held that office in 384.

Christianity of such notables as the Anicii. (And indeed, it might well be thought that the Anicii would have little sympathy for the pure and simple Christian religion if it did not enjoy imperial favour, since in all other respects they worship luxury and power.) Probus therefore had no ready reply, for he was unwilling to accuse his host at the table where he himself was a guest; moreover, he did not dare to criticise the emperors, who have all appointed pagans as well as Christians to high office. There indeed the whole matter might have ended – except that Symmachus, elated by the sound of his own voice, and aroused by the opportunity of speaking to so many distinguished men, could not resist pouring out more of his famous eloquence.

He began to speak at length on the virtues of highly placed pagans, and – most unwisely, in that company – he included among his examples some who had been convicted of disloyalty. I noticed that as the Anicii listened to him, their menacing scowls gave way to looks of calculation, and I grew afraid for my patron. As a great river flowing into the sea is swallowed up without raising the level of the salty waters, so all the wealth of the Anicii cannot satisfy their greed – and Symmachus was wealthy.[7]

I consoled myself that the present emperors[8] are less suspicious than some who have worn the purple, and that those who wish to ruin a great house can no longer do so merely by distorting a few incautious words, but are obliged also to provide proofs. Yet I was still troubled, for where proofs are lacking, the ingenuity of wicked men has often contrived them.

And indeed, a mere eight days after that Damoclean feast,

7 An informer who brought a successful prosecution for treason was entitled to a portion of the traitor's estate. Ammianus accuses the Anicii of enriching themselves in this way in XVI.8.19 and and XXVII.11.3 as well.
8 If this dinner took place during the prefecture of Symmachus, the emperors in question would be Theodosius and Valentinian II.

I heard that one of Symmachus' slaves had been found dead in the street, and that the man who found the body belonged to the household of Anicius Paulinus.

I went at once to Symmachus' house, and, so great was my concern, bribed the slave to obtain a meeting swiftly. Symmachus, however, laughed at my anxiety and dismissed it. The slave who had died was known to be a frequenter of wineshops, one whose love of drink had several times before caused him to be late returning to the house after running an errand. That he had delayed in a wineshop once too often, and paid dearly for it was a sorrow to his master, but it was not cause for suspicion, since the city has always been much troubled with thieves and robbers. Neither was it suspicious that a slave of the Anicii should have found the body, for the Anicii have many slaves, and the house of Paulinus stood not far away from that of Symmachus himself.

I was in part reassured by this, but as I was about to take my leave, I thought to ask Symmachus on what errand the dead slave had been sent.

"He was carrying a letter," said Symmachus. When he saw how much this alarmed me, he laughed and added, "There was no harm in it! It was only a note to my friend Claudius, ordering provisions for the prefectural games." And he dismissed me with the air of one who has conferred a great favour just by listening.

I departed in anger and doubt, at one moment ashamed because my groundless alarm had caused me to appear a fool in front of my patron, at the next wondering if I should turn back and beg Symmachus to take steps to protect himself. I was still in this uncertain ardour of mind when I arrived at the house of Eutherius, which stood across the Tiber from that of Symmachus, not too far away.

I had by then visited the former chamberlain privately, according to his own invitation, and we had spoken together of Julian Augustus, and of the wars between Romans and barbarians. Finding him kindly and intelligent and possessed of a prodigious memory, I had asked him about the reign of Constans Augustus, as I was becoming convinced that I needed to expand the scope of my history to include rulers who preceded Julian. Eutherius had replied that Constans and his fate were matters of too much substance to deal with quickly, and had invited me again. When I was admitted to his house on this occasion, however, he at once noticed my agitation, and instead of resuming our historical discussions, asked what had transpired to distress me.

When I had recounted the matter, Eutherius, too, was troubled, perceiving, as I had, the danger inherent in a letter, however innocent its subject. "Do you remember," he asked me, "the letters by which Dynamius destroyed Silvanus?"

I replied that I remembered them very well. Dynamius had removed the original text of some of Silvanus' letters with a sponge, leaving only the signature, and had written instead other words which implied that Silvanus was planning treason. His plot was eventually discovered, but not before many men died.[9] "Yet, surely," I said, "since that matter became so notorious, anyone investigating such letters now would scrutinize them more closely. It is impossible to sponge away writing so completely that it leaves no trace at all upon the parchment."

"Perhaps," replied Eutherius. "Yet if the letter carried by the prefect's slave dealt with provisions for the games, it may well have spoken of supplying weapons and men to fight, or made arrangements for the payment of large amounts of gold. An unscrupulous scribe could, by adding only a few words here and there, make it appear that it concerned more

9 The full story is in *Res Gestae XV*, 5. Ammianus undoubtedly would remember it "very well", since he helped to arrange Silvanus' assassination.

serious contests than those of the arena. Moreover, Symmachus' enemies know that at present he is vulnerable to slander. He is not in favour at court. He has protested excessively about the removal of pagan monuments from Rome, and Valentinian Augustus is not only pious, but also much influenced by the bishop of Mediolanum[10], who considers Symmachus his most formidable opponent. If your patron is wise, he will fear his enemies."

I replied that Symmachus possessed far too lofty an opinion of himself to be cautious, and I became still more agitated than before. Perceiving this, Eutherius urged me to be patient, and declared that we should investigate the matter further to learn whether we had just cause for our alarm.

"And how should we do that?" I asked. "Symmachus dismisses the whole affair, and it is pointless to go to the Anicii. As well Odysseus should go to the Cyclops to inquire whom next he wishes to devour!"

"We must discover how the prefect's slave died," said Eutherius. "If he frequented wineshops, his friends will know which taverns were his favourites. Someone in such a place may well have seen him there on the day he died, and provide us with information about the circumstances of his death. What was his name?"

I replied that I had never heard it, and objected that we were unlikely to learn anything of the dead slave from his friends. Slaves will tell you nothing, except when they are put to the torture, at which they will tell you anything.

Eutherius, however, said, "It is true that slaves would refuse to speak freely to you or to me, since they would fear to be tortured if the matter came to judicial investigation – but to another slave they will be more talkative." And he ordered his steward to summon two of his own people.

Presently the two slaves Eutherius had sent for appeared, a man and a woman unremarkable in appearance, and the eunuch related to them the subject of our enquiries and promised to reward them well for any information they might obtain concerning the dead slave. He sent the man, whose name was Sannio, to Symmachus' house with a gift of spices for the kitchen, and the woman, Aenis, to the house of Anicius Paulinus in the guise of a pedlar. Then, seeing my surprise and perplexity at this proceeding, he turned to me and said, "It is true that we will learn only the gossip of the kitchen – but that should at least include the dead man's name and something more about the circumstances of his death."

I told him that I understood as much, and that my surprise was rather that he should take so much trouble on behalf of Symmachus, a man he barely knew.

"I have been his guest," he told me. "And I loathe these fortune-hunting informers. I have seen far too many of them succeed, to the corruption of justice and to public loss."

This sentiment I entirely agreed with and admired, and I reflected that since I, too, hated informers, and since I was moreover a member of Symmachus' circle and more closely bound to him than was Eutherius, I ought to be more active in my own enquiries. Besides, it struck me that if Symmachus were under an obligation to me he would be compelled to become more generous in his patronage. I therefore took my leave of Eutherius, telling him that I would go and speak to Symmachus' friend Claudius, who was to have received his letter. The eunuch approved this, and asked me to return to his house when I had done so, saying that by that time he should have reports from his two slaves.

Accordingly I set out to visit Symmachus' friend Claudius, by whom I supposed he meant Claudius Adelphius, a man of high rank whose house stood near the Appian way, on the other side of the city. On arriving there after a long walk, however, I found the mansion emptied of people, and almost the sole remaining slave, a feeble old man, informed me that the master with the rest had just then gone out to the baths.

Unwilling to waste the journey, and fatigued by the long walk across the city, I hastened to look for Adelphius in the Baths of Caracalla, which were not far away.

On entering the lofty and resounding bath-house, my ears were assailed by a clamour from the massed ranks of Adelphius' slaves, who were busily crowding the common people back out into the street. In the centre of the changing room stood Adelphius, fanning himself with his left hand so as to show off his many rings, and crying out dolefully, "Oh, such a filthy mob! Where, where are my attendants?"

I made my way over and greeted him. He gazed at me menacingly, unsure whether to recognise me or not. I reminded him that I was a client of Symmachus', and asked him if he had received the prefect's letter.

"What!" he cried, "Symmachus sent me a letter about you?"

I explained that, on the contrary, the letter concerned arrangements for the prefectural games.

"What, another one!" he exclaimed. "Give it to me, then!" And he snapped his fingers to summon a slave to take it.

I denied that I had a letter, and – seeing his look of indignation – explained that I was merely inquiring as to whether he had received one the day before, as the slave who had carried it had been found murdered, and we did not know whether he was killed before or after he delivered the letter.

"It must have been before, because I received no letter yesterday," Adelphius said irritably. "And indeed, I wondered at it, for I've received a letter from the prefect every other day this month. He might well save himself the ink. I have already told your patron that I will inform him as soon as my brother arrives in Rome, and then the two of them can make whatever arrangements they like about the prisoners."

"Prisoners?" I asked, full of misgiving.

Adelphius sighed as though I had unjustly hauled him into court to defend his patrimony. "The Frankish prisoners of war my brother acquired in Gaul, whom your patron wishes to purchase for the arena! And no, I do not know how many of them are left. Your patron must discuss it with my brother. What a tiresome business it is to be the friend of a prefect! Oh, the misery of wealth!" And he informed me, unasked, how much land and how many estates he possessed, and lamented the intolerable burdens placed upon him as the inheritor of such riches.

I thanked Adelphius and – since I saw that he had appropriated the Baths of Caracalla for his private use that afternoon – departed. Tired as I was, I tried to hire a sedan chair outside the baths, but those whom Adelphius had expelled earlier had already taken them all.

When at length I arrived back at Eutherius' house, I was much comforted to be greeted hospitably and seated upon a couch and given wine, though I was ashamed that I, a former soldier, had become so weary merely from walking about Rome. I thanked Eutherius and asked to hear his news.

It seemed that the female slave had been refused admittance to the house of Anicius Paulinus, but the male slave Sannio had accomplished his errand successfully. Symmachus' murdered slave had been given the fanciful name of "Achilles" on account of his swiftness of foot. The household had purchased him when he was still a boy, and Symmachus had frequently employed him as a courier. According to the report current in the kitchens, his body had been found near the house of Anicius Paulinus that morning. Anicius had ordered someone to notify the prefect of the city, who had duly had the body collected, and only then realized that it was his own slave. Achilles' body now lay in Symmachus' house, anointed for the funeral. It had been stabbed four times, and was to be buried that evening.

"The other slaves," said Eutherius, "found nothing unbelievable in the suggestion that Achilles delayed in a tavern after delivering the prefect's letter, and was murdered because of some quarrel there. Several people pointed out that he would not have been in the vicinity of Paulinus' house unless he was returning from one of his favoured taverns, as the house of Claudius Adelphius lies in the other direction."

I objected that he could not have been murdered on the way back from delivering the letter, since Claudius Adelphius denied having ever received it, and I recounted what I had learned in the Baths of Caracalla. I added that it seemed to me that a courier was unlikely to delay in a tavern before delivering his message, though he might well do so afterwards. I found it ominous that the letter was missing, the more so as it concerned a party of Franks who were to fight. Though that bold and warlike nation has more than once plagued the Roman state as enemies, still many Franks serve in the armies of the empire, and they are always eager to join in Roman intrigues. In particular, Arbogast, the most prominent of those commanding in Gaul, was a Frank and suspected of aspiring to a more lofty station – as indeed he later proved by his conduct.[11]

"Then the matter is not yet resolved," concluded Eutherius. And after adopting and then rejecting several measures, we decided at last to pursue inquiries at the taverns the slave Achilles had favoured, and, if that failed, to try again to question the slaves of Anicius Paulinus. Eutherius once more proposed his slave Sannio as a suitable person to make

11 In May 392 Arbogast rebelled, naming a Roman associate Eugenius as emperor.

inquiries, though he suggested that I accompany the man to the taverns, since, as he said, Sannio might otherwise prove forgetful of the questions he was meant to be asking. "A fine and intelligent man," he told me, "but overly fond of wine."

I loathe wineshops and the other amusements of the rabble, yet in the hope of doing a service to Symmachus, I agreed, and accordingly Sannio and I set off. It was by then early in the evening.

Sannio at once displayed intelligence to justify his master's opinion of him, for, after regarding me for a little in silence, he suggested that I should claim that I was seeking to learn what had become of something-or-other I had been sending to Symmachus by means of the dead slave. "For," he said, "unless you claim an errand, the tavern keepers will be suspicious. No one will believe that a learned gentleman like you would go into a cheap slave wineshop just for a drink." I approved the good sense in this suggestion, and we adopted it.

Accordingly, when we reached the first of the taverns Achilles' friends had named – a squalid place, of the sort the Roman mob most love, a haunt of dice-players and street-corner whores – Sannio called out a cheerful greeting to the sullen hostess, and told her that Symmachus' slave Achilles might have lost a book of mine while in the tavern, and that I would pay generously anyone who restored it to me.

At the mention of a book, the barefoot patrons of the establishment regarded me as if I were some barbarian king come into their midst, but the landlady made a disgusting sound by drawing back the breath into her nostrils, as is common among the mob, and told us that Achilles was dead – "Murdered in the street!" she cried loudly, in Latin so vulgar and uncouth that I could barely understand it. "Not four blocks from here; I heard about it this morning!"

Sannio replied that we knew as much, but that we hoped to find the book at one of the places he had visited the day he died. At this the landlady shook her head, and asserted that she had not seen Achilles that month. Sannio thanked her, then, lowering his voice, asked if she knew anything about what had happened, "For," he said, "I wouldn't like to meet the ones that did it."

At this the whole tavern assailed us with gruesome accounts of robberies and murders, until one would think the streets of Rome more deadly than the arena, but it was instantly clear that not one of them knew any details about Achilles' fate. Sannio exclaimed and thanked them all, and we made our way to the next insalubrious den to repeat our inquiries.

In the second tavern we had no better fortune and I despaired of learning anything; however, in the third, which was the last of those named by Sannio's informants, the host indicated in doubtful and obscure terms that he might know something about the subject of our inquiry. At this Sannio advised me to offer money, and with this inducement the host informed us that Achilles had indeed been in the tavern the day before, at about noon, and that he had had two men with him, who had been paying for the wine. He had seen the three of them together before, he said, on several previous days. He claimed not to know the names of Achilles' companions, but said that they were frequent visitors to the wineshop, and that, indeed, he would be surprised if they failed to come that very evening.

I was elated with this success, and at once proposed to the tavern-keeper that he allot us a private booth, so that we had a peaceful place in which to wait for these two men. In fact I hoped to observe them unseen before deciding whether or not to question them. If, after seeing them, I judged that a bold approach would be ill-advised, Sannio and I could still follow them when they left the wineshop and thus learn who they were.

The tavern-keeper readily agreed to my proposal, for a further monetary inducement, and Sannio and I were soon seated in a malodorous booth behind a curtain, the sort which prostitutes use when entertaining their clients. Sannio asked the attendant for wine, a small trespass on my purse which I in my good humour overlooked.

We had been there only a short while, however, when a number of men burst in with drawn knives, glaring with savage eyes. The tavern-keeper at once indicated with his nodding head the curtain behind which we were concealed, and the men turned towards us. I was still gazing at them in stupefaction, wondering how this had come to pass and how I might defend myself, when they tore aside the curtain. At this I set myself to sell my life dearly, but, as the law requires, I was unarmed, and the bandits, assaulting me with barbaric violence, soon overcame me. Then they dragged me from the tavern with many curses, and forced me in haste along the street.

It was by this time perfectly dark, about the second hour of the night, and I was at first unsure in what direction we were hastening, but presently I noted a familiar landmark, and understood that we were approaching the house of Anicius Paulinus – which, as I have said, lay near to that of Symmachus in the area of Rome known as Transtibertina. I was filled with despair, for I deduced that the keeper of the tavern was a client or tenant of the Anicii, and for that reason must have sent to his patron the news that someone was inquiring into the death of the slave Achilles. This lawless response revealed how unwilling the Anicii were to have the circumstances of that murder made public.

My assailants dragged me into the house, and with many blows and curses led me through a spacious courtyard adorned with gilded statues of a multitude of Anician ancestors. Presently we came to the dining room, and there they cast me on the floor and stood about me threateningly. Half-stunned, I gathered myself up as well as I could, and found that I was in the presence of Anicius Paulinus. He frowned at me disdainfully and greeted me with these words, "The Greek historian!"

I became aware only then that Sannio was not with me. I was uncertain whether or not to regard this as fortunate, for the assault had so confused me that I did not know whether Eutherius' slave had escaped or whether he had been killed. I was nonetheless filled with a hope that he had escaped and might summon help – though as to that, I was unsure what help could benefit me, caught as I was in that den of the many-formed Chimaera.

Paulinus began to question me, demanding to know why I had been inquiring into the death of Symmachus' slave. I answered boldly, asking what affair that was of his, but at this one of his people struck me, cursing me as insolent and interfering.

In the hope of preserving my life, I attempted craft, imagining that if Paulinus thought me innocent of any suspicion he might order his people to release me. I protested that I had not been inquiring into the death of Achilles, but had merely been looking for a book which I supposed that the slave had been carrying back to his master when he was killed.

Paulinus, however, ordered his people to strike me again. "You know very well," he declared, "that the slave was not carrying a book or anything else from your hand. He had been sent to Claudius Adelphius with a letter."

At this I saw that he had put aside any pretence, and I understood that he must have already fixed upon my death. I resolved to speak nothing but the truth, for the perfection of truth is always simple, and may be grasped in pain and confusion where the complexity of lies slips away. "I was seeking to learn how the slave died," I told him, "because I suspected he might have been killed for the letter he was carrying, and feared that you might have conceived a plot against my friend Symmachus."

Paulinus smiled and said, "And so indeed we have," as though it were a matter for boasts rather than for shame.

Outraged at his arrogance, I asked Paulinus what the ancient consuls and tribunes whose statues lined the court-yard would have made of his lawless proceeding. At this he was enraged, and he commanded his slaves to beat me. I strove to endure it like a philosopher and a soldier.

When at length they stopped, Paulinus commanded them to give me wine, for I was dazed and incapable of speech. As soon as I had recovered sufficiently, though, he asked me whether Symmachus was aware of what I had been doing. I answered truthfully that I had tried to warn Symmachus of his danger, but that he had dismissed it.

"You were acting on your own, then?" Paulinus asked, elated with the thought that he might protect his plan merely by having me put to death.

"No," I told him, "I have had help from Eutherius. It was his slave who was with me when your people seized me."

At this Paulinus regarded me in consternation, as one who receives news of an overthrow. An imperial chamberlain, even one who has retired from his office, can by no means be treated negligently. Even where some one of the chamber-lains has been guilty of a manifest crime, still his fellows have been able to work upon the emperor and contrive by one shift or another that their friend escapes justice. Anyone who wrongs a chamberlain, however, can be certain that the matter will fly directly to the emperor's ears. Paulinus was well aware that if Eutherius wished to accuse him of con-spiracy, not even Probus could protect him.

Paulinus cried out indignantly that I was lying, and that Eutherius knew nothing of what I was about. I was much encouraged, however, that he did not boast that the slave who had accompanied me was dead. I set my resolve and swore by the divine power that it was true. At this Paulinus ordered his men to beat me again; however, they had barely begun when I became aware that one of Paulinus' slaves had come into the room and was announcing that the most illustrious Eutherius requested admittance.

Paulinus was still hesitating over what order to give regarding the eunuch, when Eutherius himself came in. Sannio was with him. Eutherius showed no surprise at the abject state to which my tormenters had reduced me, but Sannio cried out and hurried to help me up, then led me to one of the dining couches.

"I told your doorkeepers that they would not wish to strike an imperial chamberlain," said Eutherius, smiling mildly at Paulinus, "and they agreed. Do take note, my friend, that all my household know that I am here."

Paulinus was so overcome that he could not speak, and merely stood glaring at Eutherius. Sannio, meanwhile, began cleaning my injuries with a napkin dipped in wine, an attention for which I was deeply grateful.

"I perceive from your reception of my friend Ammianus," Eutherius continued, "that his suspicions were indeed well-founded."

At this Paulinus recovered himself enough to protest that Eutherius should not trespass in a private house in order to interfere in a private quarrel.

"And when did you quarrel with Ammianus?" Eutherius asked him, still in a mild tone. "It cannot have been over some public affront, for then I would have heard of it. If it was a private offence, though, then you must have invited him to be your guest here before, because he has no interests or business commitments which coincide with yours. And if so, is this how you treat your guests?"

Paulinus ground his teeth in rage, but found himself at a loss: to a nobleman of such distinction, the accusation of failing in hospitality to a guest is more shaming than that of murdering a rival. At last he flung up his hands and told Eutherius to take me and to go.

"I shall do so," said Eutherius. "But I ask first that you return the letter which the prefect of the city wrote to his friend Claudius Adelphius, which you intercepted."

Paulinus at first began to protest, but then, realizing that he had been betrayed by his own mouth and conduct, yielded and said sullenly that he had given the letter to his cousin Anicius Bassus, but that he would instruct Bassus to return it the following day.

"So Bassus was involved as well?" asked Eutherius. "Who else?"

Paulinus, however, did not answer except to curse him. "The letter will be returned," he declared. "There has been no crime committed, unless you choose to regard as a crime my quarrel with your Greek friend."

"A slave was murdered," Eutherius reminded him.

This Paulinus dismissed, and said, "A slave of mine lost his temper. They are all worthless scoundrels, so what is one to do with them? If the man does anything similar again, I will have him punished."

Eutherius heard this in contemptuous silence, and did not dignify it with a reply. Instead he ordered Sannio to help me to my feet. As we left, he turned again to Paulinus and said, "I expect to hear that the letter has been returned to the prefect tomorrow."

Paulinus spat, but did not hinder our departure.

It was with great joy that I left that fatal house. Eutherius had a covered litter waiting in the street outside, and to my great relief I was able to rest my aching limbs beside him as the bearers carried us swiftly away. The eunuch kindly invited me to rest the night in his house, but I asked if he would instead take me to my own lodgings, for I longed for the comfort of my own bed and the care of my own household. To this he at once agreed, and gave the necessary orders to his bearers.

As we were borne swiftly across the city, I asked Eutherius if he believed that Paulinus would indeed return the letter.

"I am assured of it," he replied sadly, "for, as he says, once he has returned it, he evades the charge of having conspired against Symmachus. That is the only crime which he has committed which could put him in any danger: the rest he can simply shrug off. My friend, I know that he has behaved towards you like some Isaurian bandit, but, truly, if you try to bring him to account for it I would fear for your life. He would undoubtedly invent some story to discredit you, and enlist clients to perjure themselves on his behalf, and in the end you would be lucky to escape without worse harm than you have suffered already. As for poor Achilles, you know as well as I that Anicius Paulinus would not be punished for a slave's death even if it were to be proved that he committed the murder with his own hand. Most likely, though, he never intended more than the theft of the letter, and spoke the truth when he said that one of his own men lost his temper."

I was surprised at this, and Eutherius explained, "Sannio has told me what you learned in the tavern. Probably the tavernkeeper told you the truth, if only a partial truth, for he would have found it safer to say nothing that another person in the tavern might contradict. I suspect that Achilles agreed to let Paulinus' men read his master's letter in exchange for drink; indeed, probably he had done so several times before. I expect they used some pretext such as wanting information to use in gambling on the outcome of the prefectural games, and he saw no great harm in it. However, when they saw that this letter was one which their master could use, they tried to take it from him. At that he would have become afraid, either because he realized they meant harm to his master, or else merely because he knew he would be punished for losing a letter. Probably he tried to seize the letter back and flee with it, and Paulinus' men grew angry and used violence to stop him. Paulinus could not have intended that: it attracted attention to the matter. If Achilles merely came home saying he had been robbed, not even you would have felt any concern about it – and Achilles would be very unlikely to confess the whole truth to his master when he would escape more lightly by claiming to have been set upon by thieves."

"You understand slaves well," I told him, impressed by this reasoning.

"I have been a slave," he replied simply.

I was startled by this, though on reflection I realized that it was to be expected in a eunuch. I afterwards learned that Eutherius had been freeborn in Armenia, but while he was still a small child he had been captured by a hostile neighbouring tribe, who castrated him and sold him to some Roman merchants, and he had grown up a slave in Constantine's palace. It was a tribute to the nobility of his character that he had nevertheless remained – as I had come to appreciate – a man devoted to virtue, always eager to render kindness to those around him.

We arrived at my apartments, and, since my lodgings were on an upper floor, Eutherius sent Sannio to fetch help for me from my household, since I was weak from my ordeal and unable to face the stairs unaided. He offered to send his own physician to attend me. I thanked him, but told him that I thought I had suffered no lasting harm and indeed had received worse injuries in falls while riding.

"That I believe, for men die from falls while riding,"

Eutherius remarked drily. "My friend, if you wish to bring charges against Paulinus, I will support you as well as I can. I do urge you, however, to remain silent. I would be grieved if your great history remained unwritten."

I was moved by this, and I thanked Eutherius warmly and told him that I would not risk pressing charges against Paulinus, which seemed to reassure him. My own household having come out to assist me, I descended from the litter and went to rest in my own bed.

I remained there for several days, for the ill treatment I had received brought on a fever which made it impossible for me to rise. Eutherius sent Sannio every day to inquire how I was. On the first of these visits I remembered to express my gratitude, not only to Eutherius, but also to Sannio himself, for I was well aware that if the slave had not brought his master so speedily I would have perished in the house of Anicius Paulinus. Sannio confessed himself relieved by my thanks, saying that he had been ashamed at abandoning me to the intruders in the tavern, but that he had seen no other way to secure help. I praised his clear thinking, and made him a gift of money.

Sannio was able to tell me that the Anicii had returned the stolen letter to its author, pretending that it had merely been found by Achilles' body. Eutherius, however, had written a note to Symmachus, advising him of the true state of affairs, and, so Sannio said, informing him of my own part in the matter. At this I was elated, despite my bruises, for I anticipated great benefits from Symmachus' gratitude.

On the second day of my illness, Sannio brought further evidence of Eutherius' noble nature, for he carried a very beautiful edition of the *Annals* of Cornelius Tacitus, which his master had sent to keep me occupied, as he said, in my illness. It did indeed occupy me most fruitfully, for as I admired again the beauty of that lofty prose, I was struck by the thought that no historian since could match him. It was then that I conceived the notion of extending my own history to cover all the events that have transpired since the end of the works of Tacitus, in tribute to that great historian.

When I was at last able to rise from my sickbed, however, my first thought was to call upon Symmachus. Accordingly I hired a sedan chair and went to the house of my patron.

I expected that as soon as I entered the atrium, the slave would rush to announce me to his master, and I was surprised to receive instead yet another solicitation of a bribe. When I declined to pay it, the insolent slave left me to wait in a small and very familiar antechamber. I consoled myself that Symmachus would be angry to hear that I had been kept waiting, and that in future I would be received with far more courtesy.

When I was at last admitted to the dining room where Symmachus received his clients, however, I found the prefect of the city distracted and inattentive. When I advanced to give him a friend's embrace, he turned aside, and offered me instead his hand to kiss. "Ah, Ammianus," he said. "I hope you are feeling better?" His manner proclaimed that he felt he had shown me abundance of courtesy in remembering that I had been ill.

I told him that I was much better, and asked him to assure me that he had indeed recovered the letter that had occasioned me so many pains.

At first he seemed doubtful as to which letter I might mean, but, at length recollecting it, said that, indeed, Anicius Paulinus had returned it, though he did not know why Eutherius and I attached so much importance to it, since it was merely an inquiry about provisions for the games. It was very foolish of me, he said, to have trespassed in Paulinus' house to retrieve it, and it was not surprising the slaves had taken me to be a thief, and beaten me.

I was so entirely at a loss how to respond to this that I was bereft of speech. Symmachus, perceiving this, told me that at least it showed a commendable devotion to himself, and, offering me his hand again, urged me to take myself home and rest, as I was dreadfully pale.

I neglected to kiss his hand and departed in a passion, cursing the injustice of Fate and the vanity of human endeavour. I made my way to the house of Eutherius, where I was at once admitted, and there I unburdened myself to my friend, who listened patiently until I fell silent, and then commanded his slaves to bring us wine.

"I feared that you might meet with such a reception," he told me. "I received a similar response to my own letter, but I did not want to disturb you on the subject while you were ill." Then he spoke very wisely, pointing out that ingratitude and negligence are such common ills that we should rather wonder when we do not meet them than when we do, and that philosophy teaches us to bear them patiently. "Though indeed," he said, "it must be very hard, to be obliged to suffer the malice of the Anicii in silence, and to be cheated of any reward by your patron's complacency. I myself would gladly offer you patronage for your history, but I know I could never equal Symmachus in wealth, let alone in culture and esteem."

I told him that in my esteem he far surpassed the prefect, and that a true friend is far more precious than a patron. "But," I continued, "you are wrong to think that I am obliged to suffer the malice of the Anicii in silence. Though I do not dare to bring charges against them, still I can speak out. I shall tell the truth about them whenever I have occasion to mention them in my history, and thus reveal their disgrace not just to the present age, but to all posterity. As for you, however, I will devote an entire chapter to your praise."[12]

12 It's chapter 7, *Res Gestae XVI*.

At this Eutherius laughed. "And what will you give to Symmachus?"

"Since he has done nothing of note," I replied, "I do not see why I should mention him at all."[13]

The Finger of Aphrodite

Mary Reed and Eric Mayer

These final two stories are set after the traditional fall of the Roman Empire but show the continuing influence and importance of the Roman World. Strictly speaking only the Western Empire collapsed. The Eastern Empire, based at Byzantium (now Istanbul), continued for another thousand years. In fact Rome itself did not fall overnight but went through an episodic, occasionally convulsive decline, through the fifth century. During the sixth century there were attempts by the Eastern, or Byzantine Empire, to restore Rome. The last Latin-speaking Eastern Emperor was Justinian, who reigned from 527 to 565. In 540, Justinian's general, Belisarius, recaptured Italy from the Ostrogoths, though it remained a cat-and-mouse campaign that ran on for another thirteen years. The following story is set during Belisarius's capture of Rome and features Justinian's Lord Chamberlain and envoy John the Eunuch. I published the first story about John, "A Byzantine Mystery", in The Mammoth Book of Historical Whodunnits *in 1993, and I'm delighted to present the latest here.*

J ohn sensed movement above him and jumped aside just before a marble Aphrodite plunged head first into the soft earth at the base of Hadrian's mausoleum. Up on the ramparts of the turret-shaped bastion, guards shouted. A dog barked nearby.

Oblivious to the commotion, John's rotund companion bent over the broken statue. "If this isn't Praxiteles' work, I'm the pope's bastard!"

"Hurry up! Zeus is liable to show up next and he won't care whose bastard you are," John replied. "I thought you said this aqueduct came out on the other side of the Tiber?"

The river blocking their escape was a featureless band of darkness, its presence announced by the choking stench of putrefaction emanating from its waters.

"No wonder this purported map cost so little," Cupitas muttered. "When I find him again, that scoundrel's going to regret bilking me!"

He remained rooted, staring at the sculpture. When he spoke again his breath formed a faint cloud in the chilly air. "Do you know what a genuine Praxiteles is worth, my friend? I've never glimpsed anything but copies. Few have. If there were just some way I could get her out of here –"

John suddenly tugged the man's arm, pulling him aside. A cobblestone toppled out of the twilight to embed itself in the ground an arm's length from where the two conversed. Perhaps the Romans had exhausted their arsenal of statuary in the Goth attack the day before.

Casting looks of longing at the recumbent goddess, Cupitas allowed himself to be led around the side of the massive tomb. John hoped the shadows clustered there would hide them from arrows.

He'd already called up that he and Cupitas were Romans, shouting first in Greek, then Latin and finally Egyptian, since he wasn't certain from which part of the empire

General Belisarius had recruited these particular men. Not surprisingly, the guards paid no attention. Goths seeking to breach Rome's defences weren't likely to announce their real identities.

"At least this expedition hasn't been a total loss," Cupitas grinned.

John saw the man had a delicate marble finger clutched in one pudgy hand. Had it broken off the statue when it hit the ground or been snapped off afterwards?

"An exquisite finger of the love goddess," orated Cupitas, "shaped by Praxiteles himself. Snatched from under the noses of Witiges' hordes as they besieged the army of Belisarius in Rome in the year 537. A truly desirable item!"

Despite his annoyance, John smiled. "Don't forget to add that you were assisted in retrieving it by none other than the Lord Chamberlain to Emperor Justinian."

"An excellent selling point which one might think would doubtless add to its value, but unfortunately who would believe such a ridiculous claim?"

John was about to remark that he himself could hardly believe he was trying to help such a fool as Cupitas out of danger when he heard the jangle of chain mail and a huge figure loped out of the darkness to confront them. The shadowy giant displayed an axe. John's hand went to his blade.

Then the figure let out a bellowing laugh and stepped forward. John recognised the dark features and jet black hair of the Moorish auxiliary, Constantine.

"I see it is my friend from the inn." The man addressed John. "You shouldn't be out here. They say night air is bad for the health."

"Especially when it's filled with falling statuary," remarked Cupitas.

The big Moor directed a scathing glance at the plump

trader, but spoke to John again. "You're fortunate I found you. I'm about to go off duty and none too soon. Patrolling the walls is a lonely job without Achilles for company. Come on, I'll escort you both back to Mount Olympus."

The sprawling mountain of brick and masonry looked across a forum overgrown with weeds. A mosaic cross set in the wall beside the inn's door gave assurance that its pagan name was merely an homage to the city's glorious past. Only when John stepped into its smoky interior did he realize just how cold he was. His fingers had turned almost as white as the precious marble digit Cupitas carried. The warm air of the inn was redolent of the usual simmering porridge and, this evening, something more savoury.

The slightly built, balding innkeeper, Titus, hurried to greet the arrivals as they entered.

"So you haven't left us after all, Lord Chamberlain! Excellent!" He beamed and gave a bob of his head that passed for a bow. "I have obtained a goat for dinner! I found it wandering around the Capitoline Hill. Consider it a gift from the old gods for our illustrious guest from the emperor's court!"

"A gift you'll expect us to pay a good price for," Cupitas grumbled.

Constantine gave the trader an impatient frown. "I hear there's gold to be had for any kind of meat, but then I'm sure you're already aware of that."

"Fronto's almost finished cooking the meal," Titus said. "As soon as he does, I'll be able to offer you a real banquet."

John, who didn't care much for banquets, thanked Titus and went to warm his hands over the brazier. Spring was still weeks away and since many of the besieged city's ancient pines and stately cypresses had already been sacrificed for fuel he was grateful that the innkeeper had managed to find enough to warm his establishment. It had been some weeks since he had travelled from Constantinople to deliver Justinian's congratulations to General Belisarius on the reconquest of the empire's birthplace. Unfortunately the Goth leader Witiges had arrived with his army before John was able to leave.

John looked up at the sound of a grating voice.

"Back so soon, Cupitas? Did you really suppose the Lord would let a black-hearted blasphemer creep away to safety without retribution? I'll have an audience with the pope before you do, you and your vile frauds. Relics? Salted cuts of meat, more like."

The speaker was the Greek pilgrim, Makarios, a withered man who was practically a relic himself. He was perched as always on the three-legged stool in the corner furthest from the brazier.

Cupitas merely sighed. "Those without ambition always envy men of business," he observed to John. "Now, I was wondering, do you have anything I could persuade you to part with? A personal seal perhaps? Something I could show a prospective buyer to prove that Justinian's Lord Chamberlain really did assist me in obtaining this priceless memorial to the siege of Rome?"

John had no time to reply to the outrageous question because Cupitas spotted a burly man entering the room.

"I saw that fellow driving a cart across the forum the other day," the trader remarked. "He has a most sturdy-looking vehicle. I wager it'd hold a statue of Aphrodite, if we could just contrive to hoist her up on it." He hurried away to engage the man in conversation.

"Sir? If I may trouble you." A stooped, elderly man, his sinewy, brown speckled hands clenched together, stood at John's elbow. Fine white hair rose from his pink scalp like a marsh mist. John had the impression he had been waiting, silently, to speak to him for some time.

"Of course, Fronto. What is it?"

"The master wonders if you have a preference as to wine? There are several amphorae of fine vintages in the cellar even yet, if you would care to inspect them and make your choice."

"Wine? Drinking wine as the bodies pile up around us?" Makarios put in loudly from his perch on the stool.

John ignored the pilgrim and indicated to Fronto that whatever wine the innkeeper served would be acceptable.

"If you please, sir, I would be most grateful if you'd make the selection. The master doesn't like to leave anything to Fortuna, or so he always says." Fronto swayed slightly, looking exhausted.

"Very well, I'll see what's there, but you'll have to allow me to carry the amphora upstairs."

Fronto feebly protested as he led John down a steep stairway into a stone-walled cellar that smelled of mildew.

"It isn't your place to help me, sir," the servant said. "It's true my master has run me off my feet, ever since Belisarius ordered all the women and children out of the city. I don't question the decision, you understand. It means less mouths to feed and moves the less hardy out of danger. But Titus employed mostly women as servants and now all their jobs are mine as well as the cooking. The mistress did that, and a fine cook she was too."

A few rats scrabbled away as Fronto chose an ornate if tarnished silver serving dish from a cobwebbed shelf. "I hope this will be acceptable once I've polished it up. The master has always prided himself on having every detail perfect."

John looked around. Sculptures, rolls of fabric and other decorative items formed a heap in one corner. A wall hanging bordered in garish red lay partly unrolled atop the pile, revealing a lusty scene from the Goths' legendary association with the Amazons. Several busts of their king, Theodoric, dead now for a decade, stared out into the vermin-infested room.

"I pray General Belisarius can defend the city," Fronto was saying as he brushed cobwebs from the tarnished dish. "We had to bring all those busts of King Theodoric down here practically before the Goths had run away, just as Belisarius arrived at the gates. As you probably noticed, the master has replaced them with marble Roman emperors who've been languishing down here in the damp for years. I don't have the strength to keep changing allegiances at my age, especially when it involves hauling busts and statues up and downstairs. Damian did most of the heavy work here, and now he's left in a pique."

To Fronto's horror, John picked up an amphora of the inexpensive, raw Egyptian wine he preferred from a dusty crate shoved into a damp corner.

At the top of the cellar stairs they were met by Cupitas, who clapped his fat hand on Fronto's bent back.

"There you are, you old villain," the trader said in a jovial tone. "Hiding in the cellar again when you should be stoking up the brazier in my room." The trader turned to John. "It's as cold as the member on a bronze stallion up there. And talk about draughty! Cracks so big a whole troupe of performing dwarfs could fit through them. Ah, but better times and lodgings are in my future. That cart driver thinks he can help me win the favour of fair Aphrodite. Now if I can just manage to bribe some guards to look the other way when we elope with her. Do you think that hulking Moor might assist with the lifting? Let's not talk business now, though, since I see it's time to eat."

Sunset was fading as John stepped outside. The innkeeper's promised banquet had turned out to be a spare repast consisting of stewed, stringy meat that had not tasted like any goat which had appeared on John's plate.

A chilly wind was rising. It would be another cold night, he thought with a shiver. The innkeeper and Cupitas however were keeping warm by means other than a brazier, for as he strode briskly around the side of the building to escape the wind, John heard the two of them arguing.

"No, the tree we cut down yesterday was the last one left around here!" the innkeeper shouted as John turned the corner of the building. "Everyone got there ahead of us. You'd be lucky to find a twig anywhere by now. Pretty soon we'll have to start burning the furniture! Not to mention when the fuel runs out, we'll all be eating uncooked food, assuming we can even find any."

Cupitas muttered something unintelligible.

"Oh, of course," Titus shot back. "You think you're entitled to take anything you can get your hands on. I know your sort!"

The two men stood near the inn's back door. Beyond lay the desolate space which had been a garden filling the vacant area where a building had stood in more prosperous times. Cupitas turned on his heel as John appeared. With a curt nod at him, he went into the inn and slammed the door.

Titus released a long sigh and rubbed his face wearily. "My apologies, sir. Sometimes my guests are difficult to please. I should not be short-tempered with them, I know, but Cupitas has been complaining about the cold ever since he got here. I'm sick of hearing about it. We're all cold, not just him. Then today I have been forced to cut down my wife's rosebay. It was a hard thing to endure. I'd hoped to preserve it for Tullia's return." His voice faltered.

John glanced at him keenly. The man looked stricken.

Titus bent to pick up a small branch and placed it in the basket he carried. "It was a special tree to us, you see, sir. I planted it for my wife the day we were married. I wish you could have seen it when it flowered. Covered in red blossoms every year, it was." Tears formed in his eyes. "When Tullia was forced to leave with the rest of the women and children and slaves at Belisarius' order, she promised me she would be back before it bloomed again."

"Perhaps she will," John offered awkwardly.

Titus scowled. "She didn't want to leave and I didn't want her to go. What husband or father would? There's no food to be had in Campania. Belisarius took the entire harvest for Rome. What's she going to do without shelter or anything to eat? And now when she gets back she'll be heartbroken about our tree. That miserable bastard Belisarius!" he burst out. "I notice it's all right for his wife to stay in Rome, but not the wives and families of decent citizens!"

John shook his head. It was a not uncommon complaint in the city, he had noticed even in the short time he had been trapped there. Before he could frame a suitably tactful answer, Titus hefted the basket.

"I apologize for burdening you with my troubles, sir," he said, obviously regretting his outburst and particularly that he had spoken hastily to a man who was in Rome to see the general. "I should not criticize Belisarius. No doubt he has the interests of all at heart. Now I have work to do, short-handed as I am." With that, he stepped back into his establishment, leaving John to continue his interrupted walk through fast-encroaching shadows.

Few were abroad that evening. It was not the hour for the watch to change and the Moorish dog patrols had yet to appear. Everyone was apparently sensibly staying indoors. John continued his circuit of the inn, then crossed the deserted forum in front and before long was pacing rapidly alongside the city wall. He could make out the fires of the besieging army twinkling as night drew rapidly on. No doubt the Goths would also be preparing their evening meals. It was a strange thought that the two opposing armies had one thing in common apart from the desire to occupy Rome and that was that on both sides of the river cooking pots were being stirred and whatever food the day's foraging had provided ladled onto waiting plates.

But such philosophical musings were dispersed to be replaced by the gloomy thought that soon rats would be eating better than either Romans or Goths, for John had caught a shadowy glimpse of several bloated corpses in the debris floating downriver.

John slept fitfully during a chilly night. The morning sun brought to the inn scant warmth and an emissary from Belisarius.

"Procopios!" John greeted the lean, elegant man shaking street dust from a deep blue cloak whose colour bordered dangerously near to purple.

The general's aide glanced around and arched an eyebrow. "I am surprised you disdain our hospitality for these rustic surroundings, Lord Chamberlain."

"It suffices. I am a man of simple tastes."

John did not mention his other reasons for preferring to keep his distance from Belisarius. John's friend Anatolius, Justinian's secretary, had helped compose the congratulatory message John had delivered to the general. The indiscreet young secretary had mentioned to John that, although the emperor's letter instructed Belisarius in great detail concerning preparations for the siege that would doubtless follow the occupation of Rome, it offered no immediate reinforcements for the forces defending the city. Given that Justinian had ordered Italy be regained as part of his plan to restore the empire to its former glory, the oversight seemed strange indeed and John was not certain how Belisarius might treat the bearer of such ill tidings. What was more, he had no desire to remain anywhere in the vicinity of the general's wife. Antonina was a confidante of Empress Theodora, whose enmity towards John was no secret.

Procopios might have read John's thoughts. "If only Antonina had such simple tastes," he lamented. "Belisarius has instructed me to find a gift for her. There's nothing suitable left in the city to buy, needless to say. However, I've been advised to ask here for a man named Cupitas. Apparently he has quite a reputation for putting his hand on items others cannot obtain."

"Yes, he has a finger in everything, including the most vile sacrilege." It was Makarios, the pilgrim, perched on the stool where John had seen him the previous evening. Had he even left the room? The man seemed to have a remarkable talent for remaining rooted to the spot. "What is it you want for Antonina, anyhow? Some ingredients for her diabolical potions?" His voice was strident.

"Pay no attention to him," John advised his visitor. "The man's a devout Christian. Not dangerous at all."

Procopios gave the vague smile he often displayed, reminding John of his initial impression that the comments that came out of the man's mouth had little relation to what he was actually thinking.

"I am aware of Antonina's reputation, John, including what the gossips say about her," Procopios said. "She practices magick, they claim. She employs love philtres so the great general crawls around at her feet, snuffling and panting like a dog. She knows every poison, from hellebore and monk's hood to oleander and aconite, and isn't averse to using any of them." He laughed softly. "Ludicrous rumours, all of them, and not worth repeating."

Titus emerged from the kitchen. The innkeeper's face turned white when he spotted the man, so obviously of high rank, speaking to John. Cupitas had not yet descended from his room, he said with a low bow in response to Procopios' inquiry. The innkeeper appeared relieved to learn that the official visitor had arrived on a personal errand and urged the new arrival to take a seat.

"My apologies, good sirs," Titus went on. "The morning meal would be ready if my servant weren't such a sluggard. I suggest you sit by the brazier, well away from our religious friend." He wrinkled his nose. "I swear he hasn't been out of those greasy robes since the days when there was a Roman on the throne. Speaking of which, I am something of a student of history and you might be interested to hear Romulus Augustulus stayed in this very inn whenever he came into Rome from Campania."

After some time Fronto, looking even frailler in the morning light than he had the night before, set boiled eggs and bread out for the guests. John and Procopios ate slowly. The Moor Constantine clattered downstairs and Procopios asked him if he had seen Cupitas.

"No. Doubtless he's still lazing in bed, dreaming up new thefts," was the curt reply.

John guessed their strenuous but ultimately fruitless journey through the underground aqueduct the day before had exhausted the corpulent trader. He was pondering whether he should ask for the return of his contribution to the fee paid for the fraudulent map when the cart driver who had been there the night before arrived. He was in a foul temper.

"He was supposed to meet me by the fountain outside an hour ago," the carter complained to the innkeeper. "We were going to pick up some goddess or other, or so he said."

John suggested it was time Cupitas was roused.

A rap at the trader's locked door elicited no response. John knocked harder and called out his name. Still no reply came.

Constantine, who had followed John and the others upstairs, banged the door planks briskly with the handle of his axe.

Silence.

After years at the imperial court, John could sense something was wrong.

"We'll have to break the door down. Don't worry," he told Titus, who looked horrified at the prospect of his property being destroyed, "I'll compensate you for the damage."

Constantine grinned as he hefted his axe. "Maybe Satan's carried the bastard off in the night!"

The axe smashed the lock. A second blow punched a hole in the door. Shockingly, as if to confirm the big Moor's words, a cloud of acrid smoke billowed out into the hallway.

John kicked the door inwards. It resisted briefly, impeded by a rolled up robe placed along its lower edge. Coughing, covering his mouth and nose with his tunic sleeve, John made his way to the pallet where Cupitas sprawled.

The man was as lifeless as the marble goddess he had so desired.

John turned the marble finger of Aphrodite over in his hand. It had been sitting on the sill of the window beside Cupitas' bed.

Unfortunately, it had not been pointing at a culprit. In war-ravaged Italy scores died every day from disease, deprivation and armed skirmishes. Why then should this particular death be investigated simply because it was unexplained?

But the choice was not John's to make. Procopios had suggested he do so and such a suggestion was tantamount to an order from Belisarius.

"Since the day we entered Rome, there are some who've been quick to blame Belisarius for every woe that has befallen the city," Procopios had said. "If we are to withstand the siege, we need the population on our side. The trader was found dead during my visit to a rather obscure inn. Everyone in the city will have heard the story before nightfall, and too many will draw the wrong conclusions. We must have a satisfactory explanation of this death."

John had reluctantly agreed to look into the matter. In Constantinople, the Lord Chamberlain held a higher position at court than the general's aide but unfortunately this was not Constantinople.

Now John sat in the kitchen of the inn, talking to Titus.

Titus wiped watery eyes as he spoke. "What's the mystery? The man obviously suffocated." A tear plopped into the wine cup clutched in the innkeeper's hand. Even though it had been some time since Procopios had departed and the body had been moved to a small back room. the effects of the harsh smoke lingered.

"Emperor Jovian died in the same manner, suffocated by fumes from a charcoal brazier in his bedchamber," Titus went on. "And Cupitas was fat. He probably suffered from some weakness of the lungs as well, as such men often do."

"Unfortunately, Procopios was adamant that I prepare a report for Belisarius," John observed. "I agree with you, Titus. It was obviously an accident. After all, a brazier isn't a very reliable weapon. As I pointed out to Procopios, if Cupitas hadn't stuffed a robe under the door to keep draughts out once he retired for the night, the smoke wouldn't have been trapped in the room."

"He was always complaining about the cold. I trust the eternal flames of Hell are warm enough for him!"

The innkeeper's vehement tone reminded John he had heard the man arguing with Cupitas the night before. "You disliked Cupitas?"

Titus ran a hand nervously over his sparse hair. "No, of course not. I was just thinking how quickly he made enemies here. The pilgrim's always muttering about his blasphemy, and even Fronto complained about the wretched man."

"What was Fronto's grievance?" John asked.

"I had another servant here, Damian. He had an argument with Cupitas not long before you arrived. I understand the boy thought the trader was ordering him around too much. Young men have hot tempers, as we all know. Anyhow, Damian stormed off and without him to help, Fronto has had a lot more work to do. At least he imagines he has. Every time I ask him to cook a meal or fetch kindling or clean a room, he starts to grumble about Cupitas."

"You have no reason to suspect anyone here of killing Cupitas?"

Titus shook his head. "Although I'd be surprised if there weren't a few he'd robbed who'd be glad to hear he's dead," he added, getting to his feet. "You must excuse me, sir. Even with as few guests as we have, there's much to be done. I have to keep up the inn's reputation, in case – when – Tullia returns."

The innkeeper trudged from the room. He might have been carrying the entire inn on his back.

There seemed nothing suspicious to John about the trader's death. It appeared simple enough. Cupitas had gone to bed at his usual hour, pushed a robe in the gap under the door to keep out draughts, and gone to sleep for eternity.

Even so, John decided it would be wise to look into the man's business affairs if only to be able to include a summary of them in his report. Cupitas had stored his wares in a small outbuilding behind the inn. The crumbling masonry structure had evidently once been used as an annex and the key was easily obtained from Titus, who had immediately taken possession of it upon discovery of the departed Cupitas.

John stepped into the small structure's musty interior.

Enough light came through its cobwebbed windows and arched doorway to reveal a few precariously piled crates lining its walls, along with a heap of sacks amidst what remained of the bales of straw that had apparently been stored there. Any animals that had grazed in the forum in the shadow of Mount Olympus had long been consumed, or perhaps vanished with the retreating Goths.

A quick glance at the crates showed they were secured, but exuded the unmistakable odour of overripe cheese. John pulled a lumpy sack open. It contained a shrivelled human foot, a hand and numerous bones, some with bits of withered flesh still clinging to them. These were doubtless the supposed relics Cupitas had bragged about so often. John, who had seen enough of such scraps of flesh newly scattered on the battlefield, closed the sack quickly. Another held a few copper goblets of poor workmanship and a third a set of codices which proved to be mostly small volumes of Ovid's love poems. They were however even less valuable than the goblets, since most of their innards had been torn out.

John heard footsteps and turned as a strangled gasp of terror announced Fronto's arrival. The old man stood in the doorway but John wasn't certain if Fronto was clutching his chest or had clasped his hands together in prayer.

"Thank the Lord it's only you, Lord Chamberlain." Fronto wheezed in an alarming fashion.

John asked if he had mistaken him for someone else.

"No, sir, not really." Fronto sagged against the door frame. "This is what the master calls the emperor's private apartments, sir. Once it served as the grandest part of the inn. Hard to believe that looking at it now, isn't it? This is where visiting dignitaries stayed. The master often boasts that Romulus Augustulus slept here but what few know is that his shade still frequents the place, for this is the very inn where the emperor was brutally murdered."

"It's generally said that after he was deposed he was given a pension and lived out his days in Campania," John observed mildly.

"Doubtless the Goths would like us all to think so too, sir. But if you had observed the inexplicable things that I have . . ."

"What would those be, Fronto?" John asked patiently.

"Strange happenings, sir, flickering lights, shadows with nothing to cast them. Just last night the shade walked. It must have sensed death nearby."

"You saw this shade?"

"Heard it, sir. A hideous, inhuman whimpering. And scrabbling. Just the noise a clawed demon might make."

Or, John thought, the noise Cupitas might make clawing through his wares, for some unknown reason, in the middle of the night, when everyone had assumed he was in his bed. Normally the inn would have been too crowded for anyone to creep about it unobserved. Now, with so few guests and most of the servants gone, there would have been no one to see the trader. Unless the pilgrim Makarios was as permanently attached to his stool in the corner as he seemed.

"The innkeeper would not think it strange that I choose to sleep on a stool if he had lived on a pillar for fifteen years as I have. When you are accustomed to sleep standing up, it is hard enough to sleep sitting down, let alone in a bed." Makarios spoke too loudly, perhaps because he was accustomed to having to shout down from a high perch.

John decided the pilgrim probably had lived atop a column in Antioch, as he claimed. Makarios had the emaciated appearance of those holy stylites beneath whose wild gaze he often passed in Constantinople, and his skin was weathered, as from endless exposure to the elements.

"So you didn't see Cupitas again after he went up to his room?"

Makarios shook his head stiffly. "No, that was the last time I glimpsed the foul heretic alive. But as I was saying, fifteen years I dwelt on that pillar, mortifying the flesh, glorifying the Lord. Until a dove alighted on the icy railing and spoke to me. 'Throw off your chains,' it said. In perfect Latin, mind you, not Greek. 'Journey to Rome and carry my message to Pope Silverius.' So I did."

With some interest, John asked what message the bird wished conveyed.

"It told me as soon as I obtained an audience with the pope it would return and tell me," Makarios replied. "Yes, it was a miracle. After all those years standing in such a cramped space, my legs still worked. Once I'd pulled my feet free of the platform, that is. My soles remain there although the rest of me is here, as you see. However, I have yet to gain an audience with Silverius and now I begin to wonder if the bird was a demon in disguise."

John asked why the former stylite considered Cupitas a heretic.

"What else would you call a man who seeks to turn faith into coins? And by fraud at that! He came to Rome in hopes of selling holy relics to the pope. He told me he tried to gain an audience with him through various officials in Belisarius' entourage. When that failed, he got the notion that I could arrange a meeting and pestered me endlessly about it. He showed me his prize relic. It's a shrivelled piece of meat he claimed was the hand of Joseph, our Saviour's father. 'Look, you can see the calluses where he held his hammer,' he told me. 'Imagine, these fingers touched the holy child.' More likely the villain chopped the hand off a corpse in a ditch. There's plenty of them around. He'd preserved it in salt, you know."

Unlikely as it seemed, John thought he detected the flicker of a smile cross Makarios' leathery visage. "You find that humorous?"

"Certainly not! Blasphemous, more likely. I was thinking about Achilles, that savage black dog that accompanied the Moor on his patrols. It had a much keener interest in those relics than the pope did. In fact, it got hold of a shinbone one afternoon. Cupitas was furious. Up until then he and Constantine seemed friendly enough."

"Constantine mentioned patrolling alone," John said thoughtfully. "What became of his dog?"

"It disappeared, and the Moor is convinced that the mongrel was boiled in a delicate wine sauce and ended up on someone's plate. Meat of any sort is hard to find these days. Given his nature, I agree it's more than likely Cupitas stole the beast and sold it to a hungry family. The trader had a habit of taking whatever he pleased. A dog, a bit of cutlery, the innkeeper's wife."

John said he found the latter hard to believe.

"That he stole a mongrel and a knife, or that he dallied with the innkeeper's wife? How can that surprise you? Flesh is weak. Cupitas had travelled the world. While righteous men recognize a corpulent fraud, poor Tullia, confined to this pile of bricks, saw him as an exotic figure, a modern day Herodotus. Cupitas read to her. Salacious poetry, that's what it was. To whet their vile appetites. I pray I will soon receive the dove's message and then I can climb up out of this stinking morass of sin and return home to breathe again the sweet air atop my column. I just hope it is as yet unoccupied," he concluded gloomily.

John realized there was no point in questioning Makarios further, since scurrilous rumours were unlikely to advance his investigations. He thanked the pilgrim and prepared to leave.

"I see you doubt me, sir. Well, before you go, why don't you see what Titus has been burning in his braziers?" Makarios suggested.

John took his advice. The brazier on the other side of the room smouldered feebly. Taking a stick from a pile of kindling beside it, he prodded the ashes beneath its embers. A partially blackened scrap surfaced.

It was a page of love poetry.

Constantine laughed. "If Tullia craved excitement there's plenty willing to offer it to her. She didn't need to turn to someone like Cupitas."

John had caught up to the Moor during his solitary patrol. Now the two stood on a parapet overlooking the noisome Tiber, observing the tents of the besieging Goths on the opposite bank.

John asked Constantine what he meant by his remark.

"Belisarius didn't order the women and children out until after you had arrived, so you must have met Tullia. Didn't you notice she is a very attractive woman? And a lot younger than her husband. I'm not surprised Titus has been half-crazed with grief since she departed. Naturally he calls down curses on the heads of those who forced her to leave him. Before that, she was just another set of hands to help around the inn. Strange how one fails to appreciate the value of a thing until he no longer possesses it, isn't it?"

"I didn't have much opportunity to speak with her, although I do have the impression Titus appreciated his wife while she was here. He mentioned having planted a rosebay for her when they married."

"So he says," his companion replied.

"Do you think Makarios was lying about Cupitas reading Ovid to Tullia?"

"She was probably bored. He'd got a good bargain on

those books, he told me. Some fleeing aristocrat had space in his wagon for furniture, clothes, silver, everything but poetry. But it seems no one in this city is in the mood for poetry right now. At least not at the price Cupitas wanted. He said he was so bored he'd actually been reduced to reading the miserable drivel, just to make himself sleepy."

"Do you think he stole Achilles?"

"You have been talking to that fool Makarios!" Constantine's voice had hardened. "The dirty zealot squats there watching everything, and then spouts gossip disguised as helpful remarks. Of course Cupitas stole poor Achilles! He did it as much to aggravate me as to turn a profit. Well, the bastard's cooking now and will be for a lot longer than Achilles did. That's some consolation, I admit, but I sincerely hope someone in this city has a huge bellyache too!"

Across the river a few grey threads of smoke rose into the cool air. John recalled the stringy meat Titus had served in a stew that had not really tasted like goat. His stomach churned. He had felt vaguely unwell all day. It was nothing more than lack of sleep and poor food. Dog meat, he reminded himself, was not poisonous.

John left the Moor sunk in surly silence. Here and there along otherwise deserted streets merchants sat, hunched hopefully beside their scanty stock of wares. In the midst of war people still clung to their routines, it seemed, however futile they might be.

When he arrived back at the inn he found Fronto gathering stray sticks in the garden. Most of it had been swept clear, but a few twigs lying in the dry basin of the fountain which had been the garden's centrepiece had been overlooked. The servant added them to his basket and struggled to lift it, even though it was barely half filled.

"I don't know what we'll burn next," he told John. "This

afternoon the master told me to tear up those codices Cupitas was trying to sell, but even so I fear you will have to pull your pallet closer to the brazier tonight, sir. Unless the master has managed to find some extra wood for you again."

"Extra wood? Again? What do you mean, Fronto? I made do with a few embers last night. I'm not complaining, mark you. Plenty in the city have even less than that and it was a cold night."

"I'm glad someone isn't complaining," Fronto replied. "It makes a change from Cupitas' carping about everything. Nothing was ever acceptable to the man. You might have thought the Goths were camped around Rome to besiege him personally. And of course it was his fault that Damian left so suddenly . . ."

A thought occurred to Fronto and he paused as they turned towards the inn. "But surely, sir, you must have seen the wood I placed in your room? The master called me aside yesterday evening. He had a basket full for you. 'Saved specially for our distinguished guest,' he told me."

Puzzled, the pair entered the building.

"Still wasting your time looking for a culprit?" Makarios called out as soon as he saw him. "It was heaven's work, sir. That's the truth. It's not what Procopios expects to see in his report, though, I'll wager."

The mention of Procopios stirred something in John's memory. "What was it that Procopios mentioned the gossips said about Antonina?"

"Belisarius' wife? The evil magician? He said she knows every poison, from hellebore and monk's hood to oleander and aconite. She concocts love philtres. I believe it too. In fact, I can tell you much more about that slut than he dared to mention. For example –"

John, however, had already heard enough and was on his way up the stairs to examine the brazier in Cupitas' room.

It had already been emptied of ashes.

He strode into his room next door. There had been no reason for him to examine his surroundings when he'd thrown off his covers that morning, or so he'd thought. Cold as he was, he had been in a hurry to get downstairs to the relatively warmer room. Now he took a more careful look around. On the floorboards, near the door, he spotted something.

He picked up a long, pointed leaf.

He frowned, trying to remember all of Procopios' words, not just those concerning Antonina. This time he didn't need Makarios' assistance. The general's counsel had stated that he didn't want Belisarius to be blamed for the trader's death. There were some who blamed the Romans for every woe, he'd said.

John put his hand on the door and pushed it. Like Cupitas' door, it did not fit well, leaving a gap along the bottom. Unlike Cupitas, John had not thought to block the opening. He didn't like cold, but having lived in tents as a young mercenary he took a fatalistic view towards draughts.

He examined the outside of the door. Stuck to a splinter at the lower edge, he found a couple of threads, the brilliant red of freshly spilt blood.

By the time he had paid a quick visit to the inn's cellar, night was creeping into the city like a black fog. John hardly heard Makarios' ramblings as he passed by on his way out of the inn.

He now knew that Cupitas had, indeed, been murdered but the reason rendered his investigation more ironic than he had imagined.

Now, however, he felt it would be wise to make another examination of the trader's wares to make certain he had overlooked nothing in his rather cursory inspection earlier.

He did not wish to give Procopios any opportunity to point out oversights to Belisarius and an inventory of the trader's stock in trade had best be included in his report.

The interior of the shabby outbuilding was dark. Just enough twilight filtered in to show that Cupitas' crates and sacks remained as John had left them. He picked up the sack of supposed relics.

As he straightened, a shadow came flying through the open doorway. Instinctively John ducked, dropping the sack and grabbing for his blade. He glimpsed the axe embedded in a crate and leapt backwards, knocking a precarious pile of crates sideways. Several fell to the straw-covered floor with an echoing crash.

For an instant it sounded as if the whole Goth army was pounding on the city gates. John drew further back and squinted towards the man holding a lantern and standing in the doorway.

"No wonder you rose to hold such a high position at court, Lord Chamberlain," Titus remarked. "You're a very clever man. I've been watching you. You've worked it all out, haven't you?"

John remained silent.

The innkeeper sighed sorrowfully. "If only you had been clever enough not to deliver that letter to General Belisarius! It was certainly no coincidence my poor Tullia was ordered away with all the others practically an hour after you arrived. It was at Justinian's orders, wasn't it? Yes, I know it is unfair you must die," the innkeeper continued. "Your masters should pay the price too, but heaven has placed only you within my reach. Perhaps in due course it will see fit to grant me the general and the emperor."

"So you wanted me dead because I delivered Justinian's message to Belisarius?" John replied softly. "I was not responsible for the orders I carried, Titus. I'm not even certain Justinian ordered Belisarius to send the women away with the slaves and children. Besides, why do you suppose your wife has come to harm?" He shifted his feet, readying himself to leap forward to grapple with the innkeeper. His toe touched something and he glanced swiftly down.

A hand rested against his boot.

The desiccated hand of Joseph.

"I must have been unforgivably careless," Titus rambled on. "Was some remnant of that old wall hanging left on your door? That's why you were in the cellar examining it just now, isn't it? And doubtless you deduced immediately that I'd used it to block the space beneath your door, to ensure smoke stayed in the room. Unfortunately Cupitas stole the wood Fronto delivered to your room."

Again the man sighed. "Cupitas never would respect other people's property. What he wanted, he took. Unless that fool of a servant delivered it to the wrong room . . ."

"Fronto did his duty, Titus. I saw a leaf on the floor of my room."

"Ah. Did you recognize it? It was special wood, Lord Chamberlain, cut from the rosebay Tullia loved. Oleander, some call it. Every part of it is a deadly poison, even its smoke."

John, still gauging the situation, continued talking, noting that doubtless his inhalation of the smoke in Cupitas' room had been the cause of his feeling unwell earlier that day.

"If only you'd breathed more deeply of it!" Titus snapped. "I didn't want to count on getting rid of you by suffocation alone. Besides, it would have been fitting for one involved in destroying Tullia to have been killed by her rosebay, don't you think?"

"If you had succeeded, Tullia would have come back to find you had been executed," John pointed out.

"If I was caught. If she returns." Titus swung the lantern,

sending light swimming across the cluttered room. "How should I handle the task now, do you think? Ah, I have it. A guest might be waylaid, stabbed by thieves and his body tossed into the river. That wouldn't raise an eyebrow, even if anyone saw you floating downriver."

John heard a light scrabbling, accompanied by a strangled whining. Were they manifestations of the shade Fronto had described?

Titus however apparently noticed nothing unusual, since he continued taunting John. "On the other hand, perhaps a fire would be best. No need to haul a body to the river and risk being seen on the way. Especially as I do believe this straw will burn very well if I throw this lantern . . ."

As Titus raised the lantern to suit action to threat, a shadow moved amid the toppled crates. John kicked the hand resting against his boot. It bounced across the floor, like an ungainly spider, landing at the innkeeper's feet.

A snarling demon flew out of the darkness after it.

Titus screamed as massive jaws clamped on his ankle. In a panic, he dropped his lantern and pummelled the attacker as the pair was propelled out into what remained of the inn's garden.

By the time the guests had raced out to help John put out the smouldering straw, Titus' throat had been ripped open.

The black demon leapt at Constantine as soon as he appeared. The auxiliary let out a bellowing laugh. "My prayers have been answered, Lord Chamberlain! I was looking for my axe and instead have found Achilles!"

Two days later John and Constantine stood talking with Procopios in front of Mount Olympus. "Cupitas must have muzzled Achilles, crated him and locked him in there to await the cooking pot," Constantine said. "When John knocked some of the crates over, that freed him. So it was

Achilles that Fronto heard scrabbling and whimpering. He thought it was a shade. Though I suppose his error is not surprising, since he tells me that the last Roman emperor ruling in the west was strangled to death at this very inn!" Constantine reached down to pat his canine friend's massive head affectionately.

Procopios raised an eyebrow and then smiled. "I always thought Romulus Augustulus was pensioned off, but that makes a much livelier tale. In fact, it's almost as entertaining as how John solved this mysterious murder."

John shrugged. "An ironic story, certainly. Consider, Procopios. If I hadn't been sent to Rome there would have been no mystery to solve, because Titus would not have killed Cupitas while trying to murder me."

"Oh, someone would have killed Cupitas eventually," Procopios replied confidently. "But let's be off and leave Fronto to manage the inn. Perhaps when Damian hears what happened he'll come back and give him a hand until Tullia returns. Not a holy hand, of course!"

John took his leave of Constantine.

"So you're going to try to leave Rome the next time the Goths attack?" the auxiliary asked.

"They can't be everywhere at the same time," John pointed out. "I'll slip out through some unchallenged part of the defences while they are fighting elsewhere along the walls."

"I see you are determined to attempt to return to Constantinople, Lord Chamberlain," Procopios put in. "Before you go, then, let me tell you that Belisarius directed me to convey his appreciation to you for the great service you have rendered him."

John observed that given current conditions in Rome it was heartening that the great general concerned himself with the death of an ordinary trader in an obscure inn.

Procopios laughed. "I'm not referring to that! What pleased him mightily was the gift you found for Antonina. She's been wearing it on a gold chain ever since you sent it and now she too can't wait to get back to Constantinople to display it at court. After all, not even Empress Theodora possesses a finger from a genuine Praxiteles Aphrodite!"

The Lost Eagle

Peter Tremayne

Our final story features Sister Fidelma, an Irish princess and a qualified dálaigh, or advocate, of the law courts of Ireland under the ancient Brehon Law system. Fidelma has appeared in a series of novels, starting with Absolution by Murder *(1994), plus a collection of short stories,* Hemlock at Vespers *(2000). We have moved on another century from the previous story, but elements of the Roman world still remain, especially through the growing power of the Papacy. Here we see how the old and new worlds of Rome come together in the city of Canterbury in Saxon Britain.*

"This is Deacon Platonius Lepidus, Sister Fidelma. He is a visitor from Rome and he wishes a word with you."

Fidelma looked up in surprise as the stranger was shown into the *scriptorum* of the abbey. She was a stranger in the abbey herself – the abbey of Augustine. Augustine was the former prior of St Andrews in Rome who had died here scarcely sixty years ago, having been sent as missionary to the King of the Cantware. It was now the focal point of the Jutish Christian community in the centre of the *burg* of

Cantware. Fidelma was waiting for Brother Eadulf to finish some business with the Archbishop Theodore. The religieux who had announced the Deacon's presence had withdrawn from the library shutting the door behind him. As Fidelma rose uncertainly the Deacon came forwards to the table where she had been seated.

Platonius Lepidus looked every inch of what she knew to be a Roman aristocrat; there was arrogance about him in spite of his religious robes. She had been on a pilgrimage to Rome and knew that his aristocratic rank would immediately be recognisable there. He was tall, with dark hair and swarthy of complexion. His greeting and smile was pleasant enough.

"The Venerable Gelasius told me that you had rendered him a singular service when you were in Rome, Sister. When I heard that you were here in Cantwareburg, I felt compelled to make your acquaintance."

"How is the Venerable Gelasius?" she rejoined at once for she had warm memories of the harassed official in the Lateran Palace where the Bishop of Rome resided.

"He is well and would have sent his personal felicitations had he known that I would be meeting with you. The *scriptor* has informed me that you are on a visit with Brother Eadulf, whom the Venerable Gelasius also remembers fondly. I was also informed that you are both soon to leave for a place called Seaxmund's Ham."

"You are correctly informed, Deacon Lepidus," Fidelma replied with gravity.

"Let us sit awhile and talk, Sister Fidelma," the Deacon said, applying action to the word and inviting her to do the same with a gesture of his hand. "I am afraid that I also have a selfish interest in making your acquaintance. I need your help."

Fidelma seated herself with an expression of curiosity.

"I will help if it is a matter that is within my power, Deacon Lepidus."

"Do you know much about the history of this land?"

"Of the kingdom of these Jutes? Only a little. I know that the Jutes drove out the original inhabitants of Kent scarcely two centuries ago."

The Deacon shook his head swiftly.

"I meant knowledge of this land before the Jutes came here. Before they drove the Britons out. The time when it was called Britannia and a province of Rome. You know that in the days of the great Roman Empire our legions occupied and governed this land for several centuries?"

Fidelma bowed her head in amused affirmation at the slight tone of pride in his voice.

"I do know something of that history," she replied softly.

"One of the legions that comprised the garrison here was called the Ninth Hispania. It was an élite legion. You might have heard of it?"

"If my memory serves me right, this élite legion was reduced by a Queen of the Britons called Boudicca," Fidelma smiled with irony. "Something like six thousand foot soldiers and almost an equal number of auxiliaries were killed when she ambushed them. I have read your historian, Tacitus, who wrote about the battle."

"The Britons were lucky," snapped Deacon Lepidus in sudden irritation. Clearly his pride was patriotic even though the incident was an ancient one. It had happened a full six centuries before.

"Or Queen Boudicca was the better general," Fidelma murmured quietly. "As I recall, the legion was cut to pieces and its commander, Petillius Cerialis, barely escaped to the shelter of his fortress with some of his cavalry. I think that there were only five hundred survivors out of the thousands of troops."

For a moment Lepidus looked annoyed and then he shrugged.

"It is clear that you have read Tacitus, Sister. The Venerable Gelasius was fulsome in his praise of your knowledge. The Legion, however, saved its eagle and was then brought back to fighting strength. Cerealis, in fact, went on to become Governor of the province in recognition of his ability. You know what the eagle symbolizes for a Roman legion?"

"The eagle is the standard of each Roman legion, thought to be divinely blessed by being bestowed personally by the hand of the emperor who was then thought to be divine. If the eagle fell into enemy hands, then the disgrace was such that the entire legion had to be disbanded," replied Fidelma.

"Exactly so," agreed the Deacon in satisfaction. "The Ninth Legion survived and served the emperors well. It pacified the northern part of this island, which was peopled by a fierce tribal confederation called the Brigantes . . ."

The man's voice was enthused and Fidelma, who disliked militarism, found herself frowning.

"All this is ancient history, Deacon Lepidus," she interrupted pointedly. "I am not sure why you are recalling it nor what advice you seek from me."

Deacon Lepidus made a quick gesture of apology.

"I shall come to that immediately. Did you know that the Ninth Legion disappeared while on active service among the Britons?"

"I did not know. I have read only Tacitus and some of Suetonius, neither of who mention that."

"They would not have been alive to record the event for it happened some sixty or seventy years later. My ancestor, the Legate Platonius Lepidus, was the officer in command of the Ninth Legion, at this time. He was commanding it when it vanished."

Fidelma began to realize why the Deacon was interested in ancient history but not why he was raising the subject.

"So, your ancestor disappeared with six thousand men or more?"

"He did. He and the eagle of the Ninth Hispania vanished as well as the men. There were rumours that the Legion had disgraced itself and was disbanded. Other stories say that it was sent to fight against the Parthans and eliminated. Yet other stories say that it had lost its eagle and all record of it was then stricken from the books. A few claimed that the legion was marched north across the great wall built by the Emperor Hadrian to protect the northern border of this province from the unconquered country of the Caledonii. You see, all the record books are now destroyed and so we have no knowledge of what happened . . ."

"It happened a long time ago," observed Fidelma patiently. "What is it that you want of me?"

"It happened well over five hundred years ago," Deacon Lepidus agreed. He was silent for a moment or so as if preoccupied with some thoughts. Then he stirred, as if making up his mind. "The fate of my ancestor, the eagle and the legion has become a matter of contention within our family. It is a matter that pride bids us attempt to resolve the mystery."

"After so long?" Fidelma could not help but sound sceptical.

The deacon smiled disarmingly.

"The truth is that I am writing a history of the Ninth Legion and want to insert into that history the facts of what their fate was and also exonerate the name of my ancestor. He has been blamed for the loss and even now the aristocracy of Rome does not readily forget this besmirching of the good name of our family."

"Ah." That Fidelma could understand. "But I cannot see

how I might help you? I am not of this country and the area in which this legion disappeared, the land of the Brigantes, has been occupied for over one hundred years by the Angles, so any local traditions will have vanished when their culture and traditions replaced those of the Britons."

"But you are an adept at solving mysteries," pressed Deacon Lepidus. "The Venerable Gelasius has told me of how you solved the murders at the Lateran Palace."

"What do you expect from me?"

The deacon gave an almost conspiratorial glance around him and leaned forwards.

"The name Lepidus is well known in Rome. We are a princely family. We descend from Marcus Aemilius Lepidus who was a member of the great Julius Caesar's council and formed the triumvirate to govern Rome with Mark Anthony and Octavian Caesar." He halted, perhaps realizing that the history of his family in ancient Rome was of little importance to her. He went on: "Some months ago a merchant arrived seeking our family villa. He had been trading between here and Frankia."

"Trading between here and Frankia? How then did this merchant get to Rome?"

Deacon Lepidus absently placed a hand inside his robe.

"The merchant brought with him a piece of ancient vellum that he had acquired. He thought it valuable enough to come to Rome and seek out our family. He sold it to my father because it bore a name on it."

"The name of Lepidus, undoubtedly," Fidelma smiled trying not to sound sarcastic.

"The name of the Legate Platonius Lepidus," affirmed the other significantly. "The name of my ancestor who commanded the Ninth Hispania Legion at the time of its disappearance." He paused dramatically. "The merchant bargained for a good price for that vellum."

"He obviously expected it, having travelled all the way from these shores to Rome to sell it," murmured Fidelma.

"The vellum was worth much to me and my family," agreed Deacon Lepidus.

"And will you now produce this vellum?" asked Fidelma. When a suspicious frown crossed Lepidus' face, she added: "I presume, because you placed your hand inside your robe when you spoke of it, the vellum reposes there?"

Deacon Lepidus drew forth the piece of fine burnished calves' skin.

"The original is now in my family archive in Rome but I have made a precise copy of what was written on that ancient vellum."

Fidelma reached out a hand.

"I observe that you have also used vellum on which to make your copy."

"I made the copy as exact as I could to the original. The text is as it was written nearly five hundred years ago."

Fidelma spread the copy on the table and looked at it for a moment before asking: "You have copied the exact wording? You have not altered anything at all?"

"I can assure you that the wording is exactly as it was. Shall I translate it for you?" the deacon asked eagerly.

"My knowledge of Latin is adequate, I believe. Although five centuries have intervened, the grammar and its vocabulary seems clear enough to me."

She began to read.

". . . his wounds and weakness having prevented the Legate from falling upon his sword in his despair, I bound his hands to prevent such a disaster occurring in future should consciousness return after he had fainted. Thereupon, we lay hidden in a culvert until darkness descended while our enemies revelled and caroused around us. They had much to celebrate. They had annihilated the greatest

Legion that had marched from Hispania under the burnished eagles of the empire.

"All that remained of the famous band of six thousand fighting men was the wounded Legate and their eagle. History must record how Lepidus, the last survivor of those fighting men, grasped the eagle in that final overwhelming attack and stood, surrounded by the dead and dying, his *gladius* in one hand and the eagle in the other until he, too, was struck down. Thus it was that I found him. I, a mere *mathematicus* whose job was only to keep the Legion's account books. His grasp on the eagle was so tight, even in unconsciousness, that I could not sever his grip and thus I dragged him and the eagle to the culvert which ran not far away from that bloody field. Mars looked down on us for we were not observed by our enemies.

"How we survived was truly the decision of the gods. The Legate had become feverish from his wounds and I dragged and hauled him along the culvert further away from that grim field of slaughter until we reached the safety of a copse. There we lay a further day but, alas, the Legate's condition deteriorated. By morning, a calm had seized him. He knew he was dying. He gripped my hand and recognized me.

"He spoke slowly: 'Cingetorix,' he addressed me by name, 'how came you here?'

"I replied that I had been with the baggage train when the Caledonii attacked it and fled, I knew not whither. Only after being lead blindly by fate did I come upon the remarkable scene of the commander and a few men about the eagle, making their last stand. When they were overcome I saw the Caledonii had neglected to gather up the eagle and, knowing of its value, I had made my way to the now deserted bodies in an endeavour to save it. That was when I saw the Legate was still alive albeit barely.

"The Legate Lepidus was still gripping my arm. 'Cingetorix, you know what the eagle means. I am done for. So I charge you, take the eagle and place it in the hands of the emperor of Rome whence it came that he might raise it once again and declare that the Ninth Hispania is not yet dead even though the men have fallen. Proclaim that Lepidus shed his life's blood in its defence and died with the eagle and his honour intact."

Fidelma paused and looked up from the vellum.

"This text is surely the authority you need to write your history?" she asked. "What now brings you to this country?"

"Read on," the deacon urged.

"The Legate tarried not a moment more in this life. Therefore I removed the eagle from the shattered remains of its wooden pole and wrapped it in cloth to make it easier to carry. I then waited until night fell again and slowly began to place what distance I could from the still celebrating Caledonii. However, they were blocking the roads to the south and so I resolved to move westward into the country of the horse people – the Epidii.

"My story is long and complicated and I will transcribe it as and when I can. However, I must insert at this point that I could not fulfil my promise to the Legate Lepidus, may the gods honour him. It took me years to return to my own town of Darovernum and the gods smiled on me for I brought the eagle with me. But there is much disorder here at this time and age has spread a shadow over me. I cannot take the eagle to Rome and I fear to give it to the Governor Verus lest he take the credit himself. He is a man not to be trusted in such matters. I have therefore determined to hide it with some account in the tiny house I have which lies close to Tower Eight towards the north-east corner of a building some Christians have erected to honour one of their leaders named Martin of Gaul. I have hidden the honour of the Ninth Hispania in the hypocaust. There it will remain until my son

has grown and can, under my instruction, resume the journey to Rome and can fulfil my . . ."

The vellum ended and Fidelma stopped reading. She
looked up at Deacon Lepidus with eyes narrowed slightly.

"Now that I have read this document, what is it you want
of me?"

Deacon Lepidus gave a winning smile.

"I had thought that there were clues in the document,
which might tell you where this man came from and where
the eagle might be hidden. If I could take the eagle and more
details back to Rome, if I could have a trustworthy witness to
its rediscovery, then I could write my history with confidence. My family, the family of Lepidus, would be able to
raise their heads in Rome and aspire to all the great offices
without a cloud hanging over the past. Why, I might aspire
to Bishop or Cardinal . . . there is no limit to the temporal
and spiritual ambitions that . . ."

He paused and smiled quickly as if in embarrassment.

"My concern, however, as an historian, is simply to discover the truth. Perhaps this man, Cingetorix, was writing
lies. Perhaps . . . but if we could discover where he lived and
where he hid the eagle, if it was his to hide, then what a great
historical mystery would be solved."

Fidelma sat back and examined the man carefully.

"There are many Britons who are more qualified than I
am to examine this document and point to the clues."

Lepidus shrugged.

"The Britons? They never venture now beyond the new
borders of the kingdoms into which the Saxons have confined them. They certainly would not venture into the
country of the Saxons. And have they not consistently fought
against we Romans? Not simply in the days when our legions
ruled their lands but even in recent times when they refused
to obey the rule of the Mother Church in Rome. Their kings

refused to bend their necks before Augustine, who was the Bishop of Rome's personal envoy and missionary here. They preferred to stick to their idolatry, to the heretic Pelagius and their own leaders."

Fidelma raised an amused eyebrow.

"Surely, we of Éireann are also condemned by Rome for our churches, too, believe in the theology of Pelagius rather than the attitudes adopted by Augustine of Hippo?"

Lepidus smiled disarmingly.

"But we can always argue with you folk of Éireann whereas the Britons are proud people, inclined to test their belief at sword point."

Fidelma was about to say "just like the Romans" but thought better of it.

"I know a little of the history and language of the Britons, but I am not an expert." She glanced at the vellum again and smiled thinly. "Certainly there are many clues in this account."

Deacon Lepidus leaned forwards eagerly.

"Enough to track down where this man Cingetorix came from?"

Fidelma tapped the manuscript with her forefinger.

"That is simple. See, the man has written down the exact location."

The deacon frowned.

"Certainly he has. But he has written Darovernum. But where is that place? I have asked several people and none seem to know."

Fidelma chuckled.

"It is a name recorded by the geographer Ptolemy about the time when the deeds mentioned in this story are said to have taken place."

"What does it mean?"

"In the tongue of the Britons, *duro* means a fort and *verno* is an alder swamp. Therefore it is the fort by the alder swamp."

Lepidus looked dismayed.

"That is a fine example of linguistics, Sister Fidelma, but where can we find the location of this place?"

Fidelma regarded him steadily.

"The Romans called the place Darovernum Cantiacorum – the Cantiaci fort by the alder swamp."

"I am at a loss still," Deacon Lepidus confessed.

"You are in the very town because the Cantiaci fort by the alder swamp is what the Jutes now call the *burg* of the Canteware."

Deacon Lepidus' features dissolved into an expression of amazement.

"Do you mean that the eagle might be hidden here? Here, in this very town?"

"All I mean, so far, is that the place mentioned in this document is this very town," replied Fidelma solemnly.

"But this is incredible. Are you saying that this man, Cingetorix, the man who took the eagle from my ancestor, brought the eagle to this town? Is there anything else you can tell me?" Deacon Lepidus was clearly excited.

Fidelma pursued her lips thoughtfully.

"Since you have mentioned it, the name Cingetorix is a name that is also associated with the Cantiaci. Any student of Julius Caesar's account of his landing here would recognize it. But it is a strange name for a lowly *mathematicus* in the employ of a legion to have – it means 'king of heroes'. It was one of the names of the four kings of the Cantiaci who attacked Caesar's coastal camp during his landings," affirmed Fidelma.

Deacon Lepidus sat back with a sigh. After his moment of excitement, he suddenly appeared depressed. He thought for a while and then raised his arms in a hopeless gesture before letting them fall again.

"Then all we have to do is find the location of the house of this man, Cingetorix. After five hundred years, that is impossible."

Fidelma shook her head with a sudden smile.

"The vellum gives us a little clue, doesn't it?"

The deacon stared at her.

"A clue? What clue could it give to be able to trace this house? The Romans have gone, departing with the Britons, and the Jutes have come and settled. The town of *burg* of the Canteware has changed immeasurably. Much of the original buildings are old and decaying. When the Jutes broke out of the island of Tanatos and rose up against the Britons it took a generation to drive them out and for Aesc to make himself king of Jutish Kent. In that time much of this city was destroyed."

"You appear to have learned much history in the short time you have been here, Deacon Lepidus," she murmured. Fidelma rose with a whimsical expression crossing her features. She turned to a shelf behind her. "It is by good fortune that the librarian here has some old charts of the town. I was examining them only this morning."

"But they do not date from the time of my ancestor. Of what use are they to us?"

Fidelma was spreading one before her on the table.

"The writing mentions that his house stands near a tower; tower eight. Also that the house is situated at the north east corner of a building which some Christians had erected in honour of one of their leaders, Martin of Gaul."

Deacon Lepidus was perplexed.

"Does that help us? It is so many years ago."

"The ten towers built by the Romans along the ancient walls of the town can still be recognized, although they are crumbling away. The Jutes do not like occupying the old buildings of the Britons or Romans and prefer to build their own. However, there is still the chapel dedicated to Martin of Gaul, who is more popularly known as Martin of Tours. The chapel is still standing. People still go there to worship."

A warm smile spread across the deacon's face.

"By all that is a miracle! What the Venerable Gelasius said about you was an underestimate, Sister Fidelma. You have, in a few moments, cleared away the misty paths and pointed to . . ."

Fidelma held up a hand to silence him.

"Are you truly convinced that if we can locate the precise spot that you will find this eagle?"

"You have demonstrated that the writer of the vellum has provided clues enough that lead us not only to the town but the location of where his house might have stood."

The corners of Fidelma's mouth turned down momentarily. Then she exhaled slowly.

"Let us observe, then, where else the writer of the vellum will lead us."

Deacon Lepidus rose to his feet with a smile that was almost a grin of triumph and clapped his hands together.

"Just so! Just so! Where shall we go?"

Fidelma tapped the map with a slim forefinger.

"First, let us see what these charts of the town tell us. To the east of the township we have the River Stur. Since you are interested in these old names, Deacon Lepidus, you might like to know that it is a name given by the Britons, which means a strong or powerful river. Now these buildings here are the main part of the old town. As you observe they stand beyond the west bank of the river and beyond the alder swamp. The walls were built by the Romans and then later fortified by the Britons, after the Roman withdrawal, to keep out the Angles, Saxons and Jutish raiders."

Deacon Lepidus peered down and his excitement returned.

"I see. Around the walls are ten towers. Each tower is numbered on the chart."

It was true that each tower had a Roman numeral, I, II, III, IV, V and among them was VIII on which Fidelma tapped lightly with her forefinger.

"And to the west, we have the church of Martin and buildings around it. What buildings would be at the north-west corner?"

"North east," corrected the deacon hurriedly.

"Exactly so," agreed Fidelma, unperturbed. "That's what I meant."

"Why," cried the deacon, jabbing at the chart, "this building here is on the north east corner of the church. It is marked as some sort of villa."

"So it is. But is it still standing after all those centuries?"

"Perhaps a building is standing there," Deacon Lepidus replied enthusiastically. "Maybe the original foundations are still intact."

"And would that help us?" queried Fidelma. Her voice was gently probing, like a teacher trying to help a pupil with a lesson.

"Surely," the deacon said confidently. "Cingetorix wrote that he would hide the eagle in the hypocaust. If so, if the building was destroyed, whatever was hidden in the foundations, where the hypocaust is, might have survived. You see, a hypocaust is . . ."

"It is a system for heating rooms with warm air," intervened Fidelma. "I am afraid that you Romans did not exactly invent the idea, although you claim as much. However, I have seen other ancient examples of the basic system. The floors are raised on pillars and the air underneath is heated by a furnace and piped through the flues."

Deacon Lepidus' face was a struggle to control a patriotic

irritation at Fidelma's words. He finally produced a strained smile.

"I will not argue with you on who or what invented the *hypocaustrum*, which is a Latin word."

"*Hypokauston* is a Greek word," pointed out Fidelma calmly. "Clearly, we all borrow from one another and perhaps that is as it should be? Let us return to the problem in hand. We will have to walk to this spot and see what remains of any building. Only once we have surveyed this area will we see what our next step can be."

Fidelma had only been in the town a week but it was so small that she had already explored the location around the abbey. It was sad that during the two centuries since the Britons had been driven from the city by Hengist and his son Aesc, the Jutes and their Frankish and Saxon comrades had let much of it fall into disuse and disrepair, preferring to build their own crude constructions of timber outside the old city walls. A few buildings had been erected in spaces where the older buildings had decayed. Only recently, since the coming of Augustine from Rome and his successors, had a new dynamism seized the city and buildings were being renovated and repaired. Even so, it was a haphazard process.

Fidelma led the way with confidence to the crumbling towers that had once guarded the partially destroyed city walls.

"That is Tower Eight," she said, pointing to what had once been a square tower now standing no more than a single storey high.

"How do you know? Just from the map?" demanded the deacon.

She shook her head irritably.

"It bears the number of the lintel above the door."

She pointed to where "VIII" could clearly be seen before turning to survey the piles of stone and brickwork that lay about. Her eyes widened suddenly.

"That wooden granary and its outbuilding appear to stand in the position that is indicted. See, there is the church dedicated to the Blessed Martin of Tours. Curious. They are the only buildings near here as well."

Deacon Lepidus followed her gaze and nodded.

"God is smiling on us."

Fidelma was already making her way towards the buildings.

"There are two possibilities," she mused. "The granary has been built over the villa so that the hypocaust is under there. Or, that smaller stone building next to the granary may have been part of the original villa and we will find the hypocaust there." She hesitated a moment. "Let us try the stone building first. It is clearly older than the granary."

While they were standing there, a thick-set man, dressed in Saxon workman's clothing, stepped out of the shadow of the granary.

"Good day, reverend sir. Good day, lady. What do you seek here?"

He smiled too easily for Fidelma's taste, giving him the impression of a fox assessing his prey. His accent was hard to understand although he was speaking in a low Latin. It was the deacon who explained their purpose, playing down the value of the eagle but offering a silver coin if the man could help them locate what they were looking for.

"This is my granary. I built it." The man replied. "My name is Wulfred."

"If you built it, did you observe whether it had holes in the ground or tunnels underneath it?" Fidelma inquired.

The man rubbed his jaw thoughtfully.

"There were places we had to fill in with rubble to give us a foundation."

Deacon Lepidus' face fell.

"The hypocaust was filled in?"

Wulfred shrugged. "I can show you the type of holes we filled in, if you are interested. The little stone building has such holes under the floor. Come, I have a lantern. I'll show you."

They were following the man through the doorway when Fidelma suddenly caught sight of something scratched on one of the side pillars supporting the frame of the door. She called Deacon Lepidus' attention to it, simply pointing. It was a scratch mark. It looked like an "IX". There was something before it, which neither of them could make out.

"Nine?" whispered Lepidus, with sudden excitement. "The ninth legion?"

Fidelma made no reply.

It was cold and dirty inside. Dirt covered the floor. Wulfred held his polished horn lantern high. It revealed a room of about four metres square. It was totally empty. In one corner was a hole in the floor.

"Down there is where you can see the tunnels under the floor," volunteered Wulfred.

Fidelma went across and knelt down. The smell of decay was quite prevalent. She asked for the lantern and peered down. A space of about seventy millimetres lay underneath the floor. Little brick piers supported the timbers at intervals of a metre from one another, forming little squares.

"A hypocaust," she said, raising herself and handing the lantern back. "But now what?"

Deacon Lepidus made no reply.

"Perhaps some sign was left . . .?" he ventured.

Fidelma glanced on the floor. What she saw made her frown and begin to scrape at the floor with the point of her shoe. The earth came away to reveal a tiny patch of mosaic. These were the type of floors that she had seen in Rome. She asked Wulfred if he had a broom of twigs. It took half an hour to clear a section of the floor. The mosaic revealed a figure clad in a Roman senatorial toga, one hand was held up with a finger extended. Fidelma frowned. Something made her follow the pointing figure. She suddenly noticed a scratch mark on the wall. There was no doubt about it this time. The figure IX had been scratched into the stone work and a tiny arrow pointed downwards beneath it.

"We'll break into the hypocaust here," she announced. "With the permission of Wulfred, of course," she added.

Wulfred readily agreed when Deacon Lepidus held out another coin.

Lepidus himself took charge of making the hole. It was the work of another half an hour to create a space through which a small person could pass into the hypocaust below. Fidelma volunteered. Her face was screwed into an expression of distaste as she squeezed into the confined darkness, having to lie full length on her stomach. It was not merely damp but the walls below were bathed in water. It was musty and reminded Fidelma of a cemetery vault. She ran her hand in darkness over the wet brickwork.

"Pass me down the lantern," she called up.

It was Lepidus who leaned down and handed her the polished horn lantern, giving its opaque glow in the darkness.

Fidelma breathed out softly.

By its light she could see the brickwork and almost immediately she saw scratch marks on the brickwork: "IX Hispania". She put the lantern down and began to tug at the first brick. It was loose and gave way with surprising ease, swinging a little so that she could remove it. The other long, thin bricks were removed with the same ease. A large aperture was soon opened. She peered into the darkness. Something flickered back in the lantern light. She reached forth a hand. It was metal, cold and wet.

She knew what it was before her exploring hand encompassed the lines of the object. She knew it was a bronze eagle.

"What is it?" called Deacon Lepidus above her sensing her discovery.

"Wait," she instructed sharply.

Her exploring hand felt around the interior of the alcove. Water was seeping in, damp and dark. Obviously the alcove was not waterproof.

Then her exploring hand felt a piece of material. It too was wet from the seepage. She drew it forth. It was a piece of vellum. She could not make out the writing by the limited light of the lantern. So she turned and handed it upwards. It was only about a metre in length for it was lacking its wooden haft. She handed it up, ignoring the gasps and sounds from the Deacon Lepidus. Then she passed up the lantern to Wulfred before she twisted on her back and scrambled back into the room above.

A moment or so later she was able to see the fruits of her sojourn in the dank darkness below. Wulfred was holding the lantern high while Deacon Lepidus was almost dancing as he clutched the bronze eagle.

"The eagle! The eagle!" he cried delightedly.

A dark bronze eagle surrounded by laurel wreaths, its claws apparently clutching a branch. Then below the circle of laurel leaves surrounded a scroll on which the letters "SPQR" were engraved. *Senatus Populusque Romanus*. Lepidus tapped the letters with his forefinger. "The ultimate authority for any Roman legion. The Senate and People of Rome."

"Let us not forget these finds have been made on Wulfred's property," she pointed out, as Lepidus seemed to forget the presence of the granary owner.

"I will come to an accommodation with Wulfred. A third silver coin should suffice for he has no use for these relics. Is that not so?"

The granary owner bowed his head.

"I am sure that the reverend sir is generous in rewarding me for my services," he replied.

"My ancestor's eagle has induced such generosity," Lepidus smiled.

"What of the vellum that was with it?" Fidelma asked.

Lepidus handed it to her.

She took it, carefully unrolling it. She examined the handwriting carefully and then the text.

"At least it is short," Deacon Lepidus smiled.

"Indeed," she agreed. "It simply says – 'I, Cingetorix of the Cantiaci and *mathematicus* of Darovernum, place the eagle of the Ninth Hispania Legion, for safe keeping, in this place. My son is dead without issue. So should a younger hand find it, I entreat whoever you are, take the eagle to Rome and hand it to the emperor and tell him that the Legate Platonius Lepidus gave his life in its defence, having exhorted me to make the journey to Rome so that the legion might be raised again under this divine standard. I failed but I hope the words I have written will be testament to the honour and glory of the Ninth and to its commander, Platonius Lepidus, may the gods give him eternal rest.'"

Fidelma sighed deeply.

"Then there is no more to be said. You have what you wanted, deacon. Let us return to the abbey."

Deacon Lepidus smiled appreciatively.

"I have what I want thanks to you, Sister Fidelma. You are witness to these events, which will ensure no one questions them. I shall go to the Archbishop Theodore and tell him what has transpired and that you may confirm my testimony."

Fidelma grimaced.

"Immediately, I need to bathe after crawling around in that hypocaust. I will join you and the Archbishop later."

★　　★　　★

Archbishop Theodore sat in his chair of office and was smiling.

"Well, Fidelma of Cashel, the Deacon Lepidus has much to say in praise of you."

Fidelma had entered the archbishop's chamber with Eadulf at her side. Deacon Lepidus was standing to one side, nodding happily.

"It seems that you have done a singular service by solving an ancient riddle for him and his family."

"Not so, my lord," replied Fidelma quietly.

"Come, Sister Fidelma, no undue modesty," intervened Deacon Lepidus. "You have discovered the truth of what happened to my ancestor and to the fate of six thousand soldiers of Rome, the fate of the Ninth Hispania."

"The truth?" Fidelma glanced towards him suddenly scornful. Her voice was sharp. "The truth is that Deacon Lepidus wished to perpetuate a hoax, a fraud, an untruth, in order to give himself and his family prestige. He sought to write a fabricated history, which would elevate him in society in Rome where his ambitions might know no bounds."

"I don't understand," frowned Archbishop Theodore.

"Simple to understand once told," replied Fidelma. "Deacon Lepidus faked an eagle which he claimed was the five-hundred-year-old regimental emblem of the Ninth Hispania Legion which disappeared in Britain at a time when his ancestor was supposed to be its legate or commanding officer. He wrote two accounts on vellum which explained what supposedly had happened to the legion and how the eagle could be found."

"This is nonsense!" snapped Lepidus. "I will not stay here to be insulted."

"Wait!" Archbishop Theodore said quietly as Lepidus turned to go. "You will stay until I give you leave to go."

"And you will stay to hear the truth," added Fidelma. "Do

you think I am a simpleton, that you could fool me? Your complicated plot merely needed me, my reputation, to confirm the veracity of your claim. You came with a vellum, pretending that you needed my help to solve the clues given in it. There were enough clues for an idiot to follow. It was to lead me to a house in this town and to the old hypocaust where I would find another vellum and the bronze eagle."

"This is an insult to me, an insult to Rome," spluttered the deacon.

Archbishop Theodore raised a hand.

"I will judge what insults Rome, Deacon Lepidus. Sister Fidelma, have you some evidence behind this accusation?"

Fidelma nodded.

"Firstly, I demand Lepidus produce the two pieces of vellum. The first is a text said to be written five hundred years ago . . ."

"I never said that!" snapped Lepidus triumphantly. "I said it was my copy from the original which resides in my family library in Rome."

"So you did. And I asked you very clearly whether you had altered the text in any way or whether it was a clear copy of the original. True or false?"

He nodded reluctantly.

"What you neglected to take into account is that language changes over the centuries. In my own land we have our modern speech but we have the language that has been used in the inscriptions which we put up in the alphabet we called Ogham, named after Ogma, the old god of literacy. That language is called the Bérla Féine which many of our professional scribes cannot even understand today. I have seen Latin texts of ancient times, having read Tacitus and Caesar and others. This text of five hundred years ago is the Latin that is used today called vulgar or popular Latin.

"Next, I found it strange that Cingetorix, who is supposed

to have written this, is a *mathematicus*, an accountant employed by the legion, yet bearing a kingly name which Romans might have found an objection to in one so lowly in their eyes. Cingetorix is a name well known to those who read Caesar. This same Cingetorix is a Cantii but he calls himself a Cantiaci, which is the Roman form, just as he describes his native town as Darovernum in the form recorded by Ptolemy, as I recall. Had he been a native he would have recorded it as Duroverno. Both these things were strange to me but not conclusive of fraud as Cingetorix is writing in Latin."

"That is exactly what I was about to point out," intervened Deacon Lepidus. "All this is just foolish speculation to show how clever the woman is."

"I was interested when I said that the abbey library had some old charts of the town and turned to get them," went on Fidelma calmly. "You immediately said that the charts did not date to the time of your ancestor. How would you know unless you had first checked out everything? You seem to know much of the history of the town as well. When I was speculating on the destruction of buildings in the town since the coming of the Jutes, you were quick to point out that while buildings might be destroyed the foundations could remain. You emphasized that the text claimed the eagle was hidden in the hypocaust and thus in the foundations. So it proved . . . as if you knew it already. The house had long since vanished and a new granary stood on the site. But a small part of the villa, one room, stood and under it was the hypocaust. Amazing."

"It is still speculation," observed the Archbishop.

"Indeed. I have had some dealings with the people of this country. The owner of the granary did not seem perturbed at our demands to search under his property. Nor surprised by what we found there. Whereas some might have demanded either the property or some high reward, the man Wulfred was quite happy for Lepidus to take eagle and vellum away on payment of a few coins. Not typical merchant's behaviour."

"Not typical but not proof of any wrong doing," Archbishop Theodore pointed out.

"I concede that. When we found the alcove in which the eagle and the second vellum were, I was surprised that the interior was really damp. Not just damp but almost running with water. My hand was covered in water as if I had immersed it."

"What does that prove?"

"While a metal object might have survived longer in those conditions, it would be very rusty. After all, bronze is not gold and is liable to deterioration in such conditions. The other item – the vellum with writing on it – that would hardly have lasted months, let alone centuries." Fidelma turned to the deacon. "You were not that clever, Deacon Lepidus."

The deacon was finally looking less than confident.

Brother Eadulf was smiling broadly.

"My lord Archbishop, if we could persuade Deacon Lepidus to allow us to have his precious eagle for an hour, there are smithies of quality in this town who would, I am sure, be able to estimate whether the bronze was cast over five centuries ago, or whether it was recently cast?"

"That is a good idea," agreed the Archbishop Theodore.

Fidelma intervened with a quiet smile.

"I am sure that Deacon Lepidus would not wish to trouble us to do so. It is too time-consuming and wearisome. I am sure that on reflection that he would prefer to admit the truth. The truth of what he was attempting was plain from the very moment he presented me with the first vellum in the abbey library. The fact that it was a fake leaped from the text immediately that I saw it."

Archbishop Theodore's eyes had widened. Brother Eadulf smiled brightly.

"Do you mean that when you saw that the Latin was so modern, you realized that it could not have been written five centuries ago?"

Fidelma shook her head.

"When I read how Cingetorix talked about the position of his house, the forgery stood out like a sore thumb."

Archbishop Theodore was shaking his head.

"But you found the hypocaust of an ancient Roman building exactly where he said it was. And there was the ruined defensive tower on the old city wall, which is marked number 'eight'. Each tower bears a Roman numeral."

"Surely, and his house was by the north east corner of a church being raised by Christians to Martin of Gaul, who we call the Blessed Martin of Tours," agreed Fidelma.

"So? What is significant about that? There have been Christians and Christian communities in Britain for about a hundred years before the time that the Ninth Legion was said to have disappeared here?" pointed out Brother Eadulf.

"Indeed. But Martin of Tours who had such a profound effect on the Christian communities not only in Britain but in my own land of the five kingdoms of Éireann, was not born until a century and a half after the events supposedly recounted by Cingetorix. Deacon Lepidus had done some research but not well enough. I went along with him to see where he was leading me. In my own language, Archbishop, there is a saying *is fearrde a dhearcas bréug fiadhnuise* – a lie looks the better for having a witness. He wanted me to be witness to his lie, to his fraud. But even a clever man cannot be wise all the time."